Burn the Wild

AVA HUNTER

A RUNAWAY RANCH NOVEL

Also by
AVA HUNTER

Babymoon or Bust
For Better or Hearse

Runaway Ranch Series
Tame the Heart
Rope the Moon
Burn the Wild
Ride the Sky

Nashville Star Series
Sing You Home
Find You Again
Love You Always
Need You Now
Bring You Back
With You Forever

Playlist

Deep End | Gavin Adcock
Out and Down | Randy Houser
I Remember Everything | Zach Bryan, Kacey Musgraves
Pretty Little Poison | Warren Zeiders
I Wrote the Book | Morgan Wallen
Birmingham | Shovels & Rope
Hope That's True | Morgan Wallen
She's Every Woman | Garth Brooks
Paying for It | Levi Hummon, Walker Hayes
Me on You | Muscadine Bloodline
Grease | Lainey Wilson
Worst Way | Riley Green
Take Me | George Jones
Valentine's Day | Pillbox Patti
Nobody's Girl | Bonnie Raitt
I'll Never Get Out of This World Alive | Hank Williams
Lady May | Tyler Childers
White Horse | Chris Stapleton
Delta Dawn | Tanya Tucker

To anyone who has ever been lost in the darkness of this big ol' world, here's to finding the light.
And maybe a broody cowboy who sees it.
You deserve it all.

Psst.
The next page contains trigger warnings.
Please skip if you wish to avoid spoilerish content.

A Note from Ava

Dear Reader,

This story deals with themes of suicide and suicidal ideation as well as depression, alcoholism, and drug abuse. There are mentions of pregnancy, infertility, parental abandonment. There are scenes that feature stabbing, stalking and violence, as well as the death of a horse due to injuries associated with foaling. There are many uses of the word *fuck*.

It does also contain spoilers for *Tame the Heart* and *Rope the Moon*.

If you're sensitive to subjects such as these, please use this warning to make an informed decision about whether to proceed with the story.

As always, take care of yourself. Your mental health matters.

Ava

Burn the Wild

Reese

I HAVE THIS SPOT.

I call it the black hole. The bad voice. It's followed me ever since the loss of my parents. It's not real of course, but it feels like it—hovering just above my head, over my shoulders, up in the sky. Over the years, it's grown. Especially when I'm on stage. In *this* life.

It wants to unhinge its jaws and swallow me alive.

And sometimes I want to let it.

I have this theory that it's all the bad that won't come out of me. Or maybe it's all the good that wants to come in.

I haven't decided yet.

A hand reaches out and squeezes my thigh. "Babe. Babe."

I put my hands to my face to block out the annoying noise.

"*Babe.*"

With a groan, I blink open my eyes. A cracked ceiling greets me. I'm half on, half off the bed, wearing lace boy shorts and a cropped purple and white top that says COWBOY PILLOWS.

The room spins. My body has all the makings of a lawless Friday night. Cotton mouth. Acid tongue. Carousel brain. In other words, a righteous hangover.

The gold bangles on my wrists jingle as I push myself up. Even after all these years, phantom pains still rake over the delicate flesh there. My fingers clasp the bangles, stilling them. Willing those old ghosts not to surface.

"Oh god," I choke out when I see a pile of dried vomit beside me. *My* dried vomit.

I glance at the stocky guy in my bed. He's nude, only a thin sheet covering his crotch. An eagle tattoo across his chest flexes as he leans over. But he doesn't reach for me. Instead, he reaches for the coke on the nightstand.

"You made a mess, babe," he says, staring at me with narrowed, accusatory eyes. "Fucking nasty shit."

"Tell me how you really feel, Ky." I wipe my mouth, swallowing down shame. Anger.

I could have choked to death in my sleep, and no one would have cared.

Strike that—they'd only care because I'm their paycheck.

Kyler pats my back with a clammy palm. "It's all right. We'll get a maid to clean it up," he says, then snorts a line of coke.

Last night's a blur. A show at the Ryman. Drinks on Broadway until two in the morning. I'm sore between the thighs, which means we fucked.

Unfortunately.

Cringing, I swipe a hand over my face, erasing the images. Only I'm not that lucky. Because Kyler's still here. In bed with me.

Phone now in his hands, he scrolls through tonight's social media headlines.

Romance Brewing for Our Country Barbie?

Superstar Reese Austin Steps Out with Rumored Boyfriend Kyler Kitt

Country Crooner Has 'Heart Eyes' for New Beau

"Fuck yeah," he breathes. "We made the *Star*."

I don't need to make the *Star*. I'm in it every damn day without him.

Kyler Bridges is one of Gavin's newest clients. As an up-and-coming country singer who's the second opener for my Denim and Diamonds tour, Kyler and I have been pushed together for optics. The tabloids have dubbed us "Country Ken and Barbie." Which is hilarious because I highly doubt Ken and Barbie ever snorted a line of coke off a limo driver's cap.

When Kyler goes in for a celebratory boob grab, I slap his hand away. "Stop," I grit out. I'm so sick of people touching me.

"What time is it?" I ask, pushing away from him. My gaze shifts, sailing over the plush hotel room suite. An empty minibar. A trashed living area.

"Seven. The show's at nine."

"Shit." I scrape my greasy hair away from my face and look at the bedside clock. "That means—"

The hotel door flies open.

Right on time.

Stylists with racks of clothing and hairdressers with bottles of hairspray burst into the room with wild eyes. Behind them, my publicist, Diana, and my manager, Gavin Cross.

Instantly, Gavin's eyes land on me. I expect him to remark on my appearance, but he gives a nod to me and Kyler. His brow furrows when he spots the vomit. Into the earpiece he wears, he barks, "Clean this up." His beady eyes move to a housekeeper who's materialized with a mop. "And get her a whiskey. A big one."

Darkness rises and I shake my head. "No. I don't want—"

My words are cut off as someone pushes a drink in my hand.

Fuck it.

I swallow it. The alcohol slips down my throat. Warms my insides. Fogs my head.

Someone pulls me to standing and pushes me into a makeup chair. My face is scrubbed and plastered with cover up, while another stylist parts my long blonde locks to make room for more extensions. I sit there half-naked, still drunk, sipping champagne through a straw as a hair-stylist flat irons my waves into stick-straight strands.

They see all of me, but they don't really see me.

My eyes drift to the wall. The hole that hovers there. Ever-changing. It gets worse on show nights. Shrinks when I'm alone, healthy, sober.

I don't know how I sing night after night when I'm half-drunk or stoned. But I do. Since I was seven, it's all I've ever known. Over and over, my voice has saved me. And yet, no matter how big the stage, the audience, the money, I still feel alone. I'm singing songs I don't like be-cause it's all I know how to do.

When I'm finished with hair and makeup, I blink at my reflection. I always blink. Fake lashes. Bleached blonde hair teased to high heaven. The girl in the mirror is never me. Even with eight records under my belt, three Grammy awards and a sold-out stadium tour, I feel like an imposter.

The hairstylist, a woman with a cheek tattoo, purses her lips. "Smile, hon. It's your night. You should be happy."

Happy.

Be happy.

I'm horrified when sharp tears spring to my eyes. *Fuck.*

It all blurs together. The sheet music with all the sad, shitty songs I didn't write. This life that has never once felt like mine.

I'd never tell Gavin that, though.

He made me.

In the mirror, I watch as my manager storms toward me. In his tailored gray suit, with his sallow face and stout physique, he reminds me of a shark out for a kill.

"Who did her makeup?" he barks. The makeup artist flinches. "She looks like a fucking clown. Get this shit off her face and fix it."

I sigh as I'm attacked with makeup brushes once again.

Gavin can never attempt decency. Known as the Magic Man in LA and Nashville for creating successful singers, he's brash, arrogant and gets what he wants. Always.

When my makeup is retouched, I stand.

"Better?" I ask, turning to Gavin.

He scrutinizes me, then pinches my waist. "Have you gained weight?"

I wince. I haven't had a meal in days, and I would kill for a bag of Combos. Eighties junk food is officially my weakness. "No. I haven't."

My pulse kicks up a notch.

Of course, that's his first priority. Because if I gain weight, I don't sell records. Briefly, I wonder if I was twenty pounds heavier if he'd still love me, but I bury the thought. It's easier that way.

"These…" He grabs my pills off the makeup stand, his brows tightening as he reads the label. "I told you not to go back to that shrink." Gavin wags the bottle in the air, rattling the pills, before chucking it into the trash. "These make you fat. And she puts those fucking thoughts into your head."

My skin pricks cold. I glare. "You can't let me have this one thing."

"If I let you have everything you wanted, you'd still be nothing, wouldn't you?"

I bite my lip and stare at the bangles on my wrists.

It's been ten years, and he still uses it against me. Still acts like I don't deserve everything he gave me. I'm the one who made my millions. It's my voice. Even if it hasn't felt like it for so long now.

Gavin pulls an orange bottle from the inside of his jacket pocket. "You go to the therapist I found for you. She knows what you need."

"I don't like her," I say, even as I accept the antidepressants he shakes out into my palm. "She makes me feel—"

"Crazy?" He lifts a brow, staring at me with an expression that makes me feel simultaneously like an idiot and a child. "You are crazy, Reese. But you're also my shiny little shooting star and I need you."

With that, he leans into me. The second he kisses my cheek, I go soft. I hate myself for it.

Gavin whirls to face the people in the room. "She has a show in two hours. I need her cleaned up and presentable."

My stylist, Vix, motions. "Come here."

I wander to the clothing rack, exhausted and carved out. Hollow.

It's over soon. Just one more show.

The refrain in my head reminds me I'm so close to being done with this tour. So close to rest. It's the only thing getting me through it.

Vix gestures and I strip down.

Quickly, I'm dressed in a lace corset, short leather fringe skirt and sky-high cherry red heels. To top it all off, a huge rabbit fur coat settles on top of me. I weigh a thousand pounds.

I am all fur, really, like a wild animal caught in a trap.

When I'm sure Gavin isn't looking, I steal a chocolate-covered strawberry off the minibar and cram it in my mouth. And fuck. It's so good.

That's when I see Diana lean into Gavin.

I shake my head, eyes narrowed. "*Narc*," I mouth, slicing a finger across my throat. She's disliked me ever since I drove a car into a pool last year because I had too much whiskey at the CMAs.

I'm messy enough that people find it amusing. I'm pretty enough that people forgive me.

Heart racing, I swallow the strawberry and watch them confer with a blank face, then sigh as Gavin stomps his way over to me.

It's in this moment that I realize I'm terrifyingly alone with no one to rely on. Even my publicist isn't on my side.

"For god's sake, Reese," Gavin shouts. "Green juice or whiskey, not food." He needles his brow. "I don't want to see that fucking belt buckle on stage."

Gavin's narrowed eyes move to Kyler, who's scratching himself beneath the sheet. "We have to get this thing between you and Ky off the ground. You two can be the king and queen of country music. You need a relationship, Reese. It looks good on you."

I scoff, but my eyes burn. "Playing matchmaker isn't your strong suit, Gavin."

He pinches the bridge of his nose. "Listen, Reese. After the show, you do whatever the fuck you want to do, eat whatever the fuck you want to eat, but tomorrow, I need you on your game. We're going to Vegas."

Dread attacks my heart. "Vegas?"

"I booked you a residency at the Wynn. It starts in three days."

His news nearly sends me into a fit of hysterical sobs. This tour's almost over, and I thought—I had hoped—that I'd have some time off.

"I need a break, Gavin. Please." I lick my dry lips and whisper, "I'll die if I don't have a break."

"Don't be so dramatic, Reese. You take a break in this industry, it breaks you."

Crossing my arms, I try for cool and cavalier. "And I agreed to this?"

He shrugs, adjusting his cuffs. "You don't need to agree to it, remember? I make the rules."

He does. Another thing that's my fault.

As much as I thought Muirwood was a prison, this is worse. Gavin claims he's tried to save me, but all he wants to do is cage me.

The spot presses down on me. It crushes my lungs, my shoulders, until I can't breathe. Because I realize these are my choices. All the ways I have been stupid and powerless and fake to give the world control of my life.

I remember a quote I saw on some bullshit message board in my Pilates class. *You can't heal where you're sick.*

What the fuck am I doing? Going along with my day, singing my shitty songs, surviving the numb fog of drugs and sex and good old rock and roll. What would it be like to be awake, to be alert, to be true, but mostly, to be happy?

The thought is sharp, razors slicing my skin.

Water. I need the water.

And then Gavin's giving Diana orders about the next news story to leak to the press, something about Kyler and I being engaged.

The earth beneath my feet moves. *I'm* moving. Out of the hotel room. Down the stairs, two at a time, in heels. I'm a pro.

All the immediate unknowns are better than staying here to meet this fucking fate.

I hustle through the hotel's lobby, ignoring the stares and the finger-points. It's the bleached hair, the damn fur coat. I'm easily recognized.

A fan shouts, "Can I have a photo, Reese?" and the tidal wave inside of me rises.

I hear my name called in a husky, familiar drawl, but I ignore that too as I shove through the crowd, tears building in my eyes.

Somehow, I escape them. The paparazzi. My manager. The crowds.

And I walk.

Away from everything. Away from the stage, the music, the burn of the neon.

Away, away, away.

I've never walked out on Gavin before. Not on the shoot of *Hell or High Water* or that time he smashed my dinner plate on the ground when I took a brownie for dessert. Disappointing Gavin is like kicking him in the balls, but I don't care. Not anymore.

Before we took the stage, my mama would say that to be truly brave, you have to be afraid first. Well, I am very fucking afraid. Afraid of myself. Of my songs. Of a freedom I'll never get. I don't know how to find myself or be myself anymore. They took it all away from me. I'm just a husk.

Maybe it's a little too late.

Maybe girls like me don't get shiny clean slates.

In ten minutes, I'm on the banks of the Cumberland River.

Water. The only place where the dark spot disappears. Everything quiets. Brain, body, and soul.

I look around to make sure I'm alone—no cameras, no fans—then I wade into the water. The rippling movement is hypnotic, made even more so by the crescent moon above and the distant lights of Broadway.

I hiss a breath as the cool water hits my waist like its soft edge might cut me. Chill bumps dot my arms. The soggy rabbit fur coat is like a heavy chain dragging me down.

Even so, that deep, dark hole constantly hovering above me shrinks. My lungs open up. I can breathe again.

Just be brave, Reese.

I move deeper through the rippling water.

A hand wraps around my arm. "What the fuck? Reese?"

I'm yanked backward and spun around. A tall cowboy frowns down at me.

My anxiety ebbs a little when I see who is in the water with me.

Grady Montgomery. My first opening act. Disheveled brown hair, an endearing grin. I've barely known him for two months, but he's relentlessly cheerful.

He glances at the murky water behind me, and I know what he's thinking. His gaze lands on my face, and his eyes aren't accusatory. They're worried. It's the same expression he's worn for our last six shows. I'm hit with a memory of him, making me sit and drink water before the show in Los Angeles.

Dark brown brows draw together. "You okay?"

I shake my head, a hysterical sob bubbling in my lungs. "No. I'm not."

He studies me for a moment and then his hands clasp my shoulders. "What do you need?"

I tense at his question, then fling myself into his arms.

"I don't know what to do." It's a breathless rasp into Grady's chest. My arms wind around his waist. "I hate this life. Nothing feels right anymore. No one cares what I do. Or where I go. They just care that I make them money."

It's all rambling nonsense, but somehow Grady hears me.

"I care," he says, rubbing my back. He has no scorn or sarcasm in his tone. Only concern. "I care, Reese."

I hug him tighter. Until this moment, we've been strangers, but it feels like he's seen more of me than anyone ever has.

Is it possible that Grady Montgomery is my only friend in the world?

He releases me. "You need to go."

My gaze shoots to Grady. "What?"

He tilts my chin up, his expression gentle. "I want you to go to your place, pack a bag and go. Lie low."

Helplessness crashes over me. "I don't have anywhere to go."

"I have a place."

My throat closes up for a second. "Where?"

"Runaway Ranch."

"Runaway Ranch," I echo.

Grady nods. "It's my brother's ranch in Montana."

Montana. Already, it sounds like heaven. The perfect place for quiet. For secrets.

"Really?" My voice comes out small, distrustful.

"Really." His earnest eyes bring tears to mine. "I won't tell anyone where you are."

A sob climbs up my throat, but I choke it down. Now's not the time to lose it. "Thank you."

"You look tired," Grady says. "It'll give you time to—to rest."

I close my eyes, appreciating him not saying *to get better*, even though we both know I'm this close to having a mental breakdown.

"I'll text you the address. They're good guys. I'll call them and tell them you're coming."

With a careful grip on my elbow, Grady walks me to the bank of the Cumberland. "Take my car." Cool metal presses into my palm. "Parking garage. Third floor, black Mustang." He drops my arm, his voice soft with encouragement. "You got this."

I inhale a breath, clinging to the promise of hope, of quiet, of the wild burn of freedom that awaits me.

Just be brave, Reese.

I run. Away from my life and into another.

Even if a little voice in my head tells me it's hopeless. Gavin will find me. He always does.

1

Ford

I WAKE TO A HARD-ON AND A PHONE CALL.

"Fuck." I rub my brow, fighting my way through the dream of some soft-eyed blonde grinding her ass against me. Blowing out a hard breath, I pat the sheets, adjust myself.

The phone, however, is still buzzing.

Turning over, I glare at my nightstand. My cell phone falls silent.

With a shake of my head, I decide it's time to get back to sleep.

And back to my dream girl.

Only the air rushes out of me as a furry dark ball lands on my stomach.

I groan. "Jesus, Mouse."

The black cat my sister-in-law pawned off on me last year prowls forward. Her big green eyes flicker in the dark. She raises one svelte paw and gives it a lick.

I lift up on my elbows. "Can you not stalk me? I don't need this shit in my life right now."

Mouse settles for kneading my stomach. I give her a scratch on the rump as she settles into my side. As annoying as she is, she's my shadow. A dirty, dumpster-diving garage cat, but I can't help but love her.

My phone erupts. Mouse launches herself off the bed.

"Fuck," I blast.

This time, I'm alert.

If someone's calling at this ungodly hour, something's wrong.

My family.

The thought causes my heart rate to spike. I snatch up my phone.

"Ford?" The voice comes tinny and harried.

"Wy?" I squint into the dark. "Where are you?"

"Vegas."

"How'd you do?" I close my eyes. He and Fallon are in Vegas for the PRCA rodeo. "You win?"

A cocky scoff. "What do you think?" Then, "Ford, I got—Listen…I did—stupid."

"Wy, you're breaking up. Wyatt?"

The line goes dead. I frown.

These days, the more he and Fallon are together, the dumber his decision making gets. Who fucking knows what he got into? Here's hoping he still has both legs and his wallet.

Two seconds later, my phone rings again.

"Wyatt?"

"What? No, it's Grady."

"Grady?" I blink. Hearing from my little brother is rare these days. He's a big-time country singer now, always on the road. "Jesus. It's two in the morning, man."

"Yeah, I know. Sorry about that. Just got done with a show."

Sleep is canceled, effective immediately. On a sigh, I roll out of bed and cross to the window. My apartment above the garage gives a prime vantage point of the ranch.

Even in the dark, the beauty of Runaway Ranch takes a man's breath away.

"You busy writing songs or chasing women?" I ask my little brother.

Grady chuckles. "Both. Listen…"

My ears pick up the reluctance in his tone. It reminds me of when he was a little boy, and how he'd always get nervous asking me to play baseball with him.

"You need something, kid?"

"I'm gonna send someone your way."

"What kind of someone?"

Grady hesitates. "Someone who needs help."

"Great. Just what I need," I grumble, moving back to sit on the edge of the bed. I flex my right hand, the broken index finger that gives me hell on restless nights. "What about me? I need help from dickhead little brothers who call at two in the fucking morning."

He laughs, happy. That's Grady, even getting yelled at.

"I think you'll survive, Ford." Grady lowers his voice. "So, will you help her?"

"Yeah, yeah." I scrub a hand over my face. As much as I moan and grump, my little brother has a heart of gold. If he's telling me something's wrong, I listen to him.

"Her name's Reese Austin. She needs a place to lie low."

That gets me to cock an eyebrow. "Lie low? Like hide out?"

"Maybe. I don't know."

Mouse nudges her way under my hand. Absentmindedly, I stroke her fur. "You don't know much do you, kid?"

I can practically hear him rolling his eyes. "Just give her a place to stay, you asshole. Put her in a chalet."

That gives me pause. "You're tellin' me she's famous?"

"I'm tellin' you to just do it."

I rub my brow, not liking where this is going. Trouble stays in those chalets. Rich, spoiled, pampered celebrities who've never been told no in their life.

High-maintenance drama is not up my alley. Never again.

"That's what I'm getting? Some rich bitch?"

Grady sighs. "You can't tell anyone she's there."

"I ain't the one, kid." I don't need more bullshit in my life. I've barely been able to keep myself on a straight line as it is.

"It's a favor, man. I'll owe you."

I consider it. "You'll owe me double."

"You got it. She should be there any day now."

"Anything else I should know?"

"Yeah. Don't let her have any whiskey."

I chuckle. Someone shouts in the background.

"The bus is here," Grady drawls. "I gotta go. Thanks for your help with Reese."

I yawn. "Yeah. Right. Reese."

"Go back to sleep."

I snort. The good lord knows I need it.

After I hang up, I sit in the dark. Worry eats at me. What did Grady get himself into? He's got a good head on his shoulders, sure, but he's also the baby of the family. Davis and I were long gone before we had a chance to pummel useful common sense into him.

Shaking off my worry, I reach over to my nightstand, unearth a bottle of pills in the drawer and take my med. Might as well. Dawn's on the horizon.

Flopping into bed, I will my mind to sleep, but it has

other ideas. It returns to the dream. That blonde bombshell bouncing on my lap. The pouty part of her pink lips. Fuck. My cock thickens. I give it a quick stroke, then groan.

Christ. I gotta get laid. It's been two damn years.

Not like it's ever been a problem. I could have my pick of any woman in town, but I worked my way through them when I first landed here seven years ago. Resurrection girls are bad news. Old hat. These days, it's all about out-of-town trysts. Getting laid when I'm away at auctions or rodeos. I never worry about the morning-after because I give them a number I don't plan to answer. It's easier that way. No strings. No commitments.

Because you're fucked if you're not free.

Warmth presses by my side, and sharp claws dig into my bicep.

"Cat," I growl, but I pet Mouse's glossy dark fur. "I'm rooting for the dogs, you know," I tell her. "You lick your own ass. That's disgusting. You need to be put out of your misery."

Still, I don't fight it when Mouse curls up next to me. Her purr is a soothing rumble, and soon I fall back into a restless sleep, cursing little brothers and black cats.

⁓

Opening day smells like sunshine and bullshit.

Sunshine because May's going out with a bang—the best way to kick off the season.

Bullshit because I'm damn tired. After the phone call with Grady, I barely got two hours of sleep before the blast of my alarm hit me.

Coffee cup in hand, I snag my climbing bag from the garage, then head to the UTV parked outside. Mouse leaps onto my seat. She's got our routine down pat. I fire it up, and as we roar across the field, I take it all in.

Crystal clear views. Snow-dusted mountain tops. Emerald-green pastures. A field of bright yellow sunflowers. Runaway Ranch vans shuttling loads of guests.

I fucking love the morning. I love opening day. Work is busier, chaotic. Our focus isn't the tedious fixer-upper work we tackle in the winter. It's putting together activities for tourists who make Runaway Ranch their home for a few weeks during the summer. I stay busy, sunup to sundown.

The ranch is like working for the mob. It kicks your ass until you pay your dues.

The gravel-covered road stretches out in front of me. I set a course for the woods.

As I pass the lodge, I lift a hand to Tina, who opens the lodge doors for a new group of guests.

Runaway Ranch is fully booked. And pretty fucking fancy these days.

We hired new staff, better security. Opened a small general store in honor of the now shuttered Corner Store run by none other than Stede McGraw. Even had uniforms designed, which I refuse to wear. Davis and Charlie can wear their logoed shirts all they want, but I already played a team sport.

A full guest book is a fucking nice problem to have when three years ago we were pissing in the wind trying anything and everything to fill a cabin. My fault with that damn video that made the rounds, effectively ruining our reputation and bringing trouble we didn't need. But hell, if it weren't for my mistake, Charlie would never have found Ruby, and we wouldn't be where we are. She brought our brother back.

But it still stings. Just another tick on the Ford Fucks Up scale.

Look forward, don't dwell on the past, is what my therapist says. I try to do that.

Especially these days. It's best to focus on my work and let all the what-ifs go.

Because, man, I love this fucking life of mine.

I slow the UTV as I break through the forest and roll onto the gravel drive leading to Davis and Dakota's place in the Edens—a mammoth white farmhouse with a wraparound porch, black shutters, and a gabled metal roof.

The lodge and Charlie's place were always the spot for get-togethers, but once my brother and his wife finished their farmhouse, it became the go-to spot for family shit. Judging from the trucks parked haphazardly in the driveway, everyone's already gathered. I blame Duke. That kid is baby bait. Too damn cute for his own good.

After throwing the UTV into park, I pat my shoulder and Mouse hops onto it. Then I head for the house.

I duck through the long foyer and enter the kitchen, where I immediately crush a set of blocks and two toy tractors.

"Shit." I look down and kick at the clutter.

Davis and Dakota's house is eternally littered with random objects, like they live inside a claw machine. Between raising a baby, running a ranch, and getting Dakota's bakery ready to open, it's the frazzled state they've lived in for the last year.

Dakota's behind the island, cracking eggs one-handed into a bowl. On her hip, Duke. He's cherub-cheeked, with jet-black hair and chubby fists. "Perfect timing," she says, bouncing her son. "Uncle Ford's here."

I place Mouse on a stool and take him as Dakota passes him off to me. "What's up, you little monster?"

Even at a year old, the kid's the tiny terror of Runaway Ranch. He chases horses. Sneaks up on Mouse. Bosses my brother's Belgian Malinois, Keena. I keep telling Davis he takes after Wyatt, but my twin refuses to hear it. It scares the shit out of him.

I kiss his cheek and set him on his wobbly feet. He just turned one last week and has mastered the art of walking. "Hey, kid, show me what you got."

Duke squeals and makes grabby hands for a banana on the island.

"Okay, okay." I peel it and break the banana in half.

Ruby sweeps through the back door, a basket of flowers in her hands. Her long, rose-gold hair drapes over one slender shoulder. "Hi, Ford," she breathes, her blue eyes lighting up.

"Hey, Fairy Tale." After passing the banana down to Duke, I lean over and kiss Ruby's cheek. Charlie's wife is made of literal golden sunshine. She can make the saddest person in the world happy.

Giggling, Ruby ruffles Duke's hair, before moving on to Mouse, giving her a butt scratch for the ages.

For one long second, Duke stares at the banana in his hands, then he does a dramatic deadweight fall. An unholy wail pops out of his mouth.

I stick my hands in my pockets and watch the madness. "Why are you like this, kid?" I say, unfazed.

"What'd you do to him?" Ruby asks, amused.

I pull back slightly and laugh. "I didn't know I could ruin somebody's day by serving the banana in half instead of whole."

Dakota sets a quiche on the island next to a platter of honeybuns and nudges it toward me. With her bakery set to open at the end of the season, we're all her personal taste testers. "It's Squish's world and we're just living in it."

"Sad," a deep voice booms. Davis rushes into the kitchen, his face set with the intense focus only a dad can muster. Keena, at his heels, beelines for Mouse.

My twin flashes me a dry smile. "Bullied by a one-year-old."

I grin back. "Learns from his father."

Davis swears as he trips over a monster truck. I smirk. A Marine, Davis runs a tight ship, but Duke's blown up his neat and orderly world. He loves it.

Davis scoops up his wriggling son. Instantly, the kid quiets and proceeds to squish my brother's cheeks, babbling away. Davis does his best to look dignified.

"What's on your schedule today?" he asks.

I fight the urge to roll my eyes. My twin's bossy as hell. In return, I take great enjoyment in pissing him off. We don't look alike and we're complete opposites, but he's my best friend, the fucking thorn in my side and the never-ending conscience in my ear.

"I'm taking a group horseback riding." I lean over to inspect the tray of biscuits Dakota's pulled from the oven. "Then tending bar before the welcome toast at the lodge."

I've used the last seven years on the ranch to teach myself odd jobs. I can change a carburetor, mix a perfect martini, and cast the best line ever seen. There's a reason I live above the garage. I can tinker whenever I want, live my solitary, no-strings life, and when the day is done, kick back with a cold one and a ballgame.

"Fuck. I forgot about that." Davis looks frazzled. "Can you take a group fishing? We're short-staffed."

"On opening day?"

Davis swears as Duke does a free fall in his arms. Before the kid can defy death a second time, Davis tucks him tight against his muscled chest. "Son," he drawls. "Hold your britches." To me, he says, "Yeah, well, shit happened."

"Yeah, well, I can't," I say. "I'm headed to the dome." Nothing comes between me and the mountain.

"What about Charlie?" Davis turns, clocks the room with his sharp gaze, then looks at Ruby. "Where is he?"

Ruby bites her lip. "Someone yelled at me in the parking lot of the market last week and he finally found the truck."

"Jesus," Davis mutters, hustling around the island. With one hand, he crams a protein bar in his mouth, with the other, he lifts Duke by his diaper and places him in Ruby's arms. She smiles and nuzzles his hair.

Davis rolls out his neck and shoulders. "It's opening day. I'm not getting into this."

I cross my arms. "So don't. Not your problem."

"Yeah, don't." Dakota comes up behind my brother. Her hand slides over his shoulder and all the tension in his frame melts away. Not a surprise. Dakota's the best thing that's ever happened to my uptight twin.

My brothers drew the rarest of hands when they married their wives. Lucky bastards the both of them.

The door swings open. Charlie strides in with a squirrelly-looking smile and a crazed glint in his eye.

Davis pivots from Dakota. Frowns. "Let me see your knuckles," he orders.

Charlie rolls his eyes but sticks both fists out.

Davis scrutinizes Charlie's knuckles. I do too, but mostly to know how proud of him I should be.

When it comes to our younger siblings, my twin and I play good cop, bad cop. He's the hands-on type. Me? I only pull the big brother card when there's imminent danger of death.

Satisfied, Davis nods and turns back to his wife.

While Davis isn't looking, Charlie, proud as hell, takes a busted windshield wiper out of the back pocket of his jeans and sets it on the kitchen table.

Ruby squeaks and covers Duke's eyes.

"Fucker had it coming," Charlie says to me in a low voice.

I snicker. "Who was it?" I feel for the poor bastard on the other end of Charlie's wrath.

"Clyde Krenshaw."

"Charlie," Ruby gasps.

"What're you two bellyaching over?" Davis asks, eyes narrowing.

"Nothing," we reply in unison, earning us a glare. Irritating Davis is always gratifying.

"Well, while you two are having the time of your lives laughing over whoever's ass Charlie beat…" Davis glances at Charlie. "We're short-staffed."

Charlie's face turns professional. "Wyatt gets back tonight. We'll put him to work."

That reminds me.

"Speaking of little brothers," I say, and all eyes land on me. "Heard from Grady last night. Two in the damn morning."

Dakota snaps off the oven. "He okay?"

"He's sending someone to the ranch." I shrug carelessly.

"Some big-shot country singer. Wants her to stay in a chalet."

Both Davis and Charlie look unhappy.

We all know what that means. More work. Ridiculous demands.

For a second, I'm half tempted to tell my twin it's his problem, but the dark circles under his eyes tell me Duke's kept him up again. I don't have the heart to be an asshole.

"I'll handle it," I say. "Whatever it is."

Mouse hisses and swipes a paw at Keena, who launches into a series of frenzied barks. Like Fallon and Wyatt, their peace is tentative and wary.

Eyes on the animals, Davis sighs and holds up a big hand. "For one summer, I'd like to steer clear of fucking messes."

"Okay, you grumps," Dakota says, pulling a bottle of champagne from the fridge. Her brown eyes glow with amusement. "No more negative vibes."

As Ruby pours and hands out glasses of champagne, I slap Charlie on the back. "C'mon, give us a pep talk no one asked for."

Charlie grumbles, but he grins as he takes Ruby's hand and pulls her forward for his speech.

A tightness fills my chest as I lift my glass and look around the kitchen.

I love this ranch. I love my brothers. My sisters-in-law. My family.

And last year I almost fucked it all up.

All because I was an angry asshole.

I put down Charlie and Ruby's relationship. I fucked with Wyatt and his feelings for Fallon. I said bullshit words about Dakota. Fucking with my twin's relationship was my rock bottom. I could have lost it all. I should have.

Ford, if you ain't happy with your life, fix it, Davis had said.

So I did.

I put my ass back in therapy. Being a jackass might have worked twenty years ago in the major leagues, but alienating my family was a long overdue wake-up call.

Since then, I've tried to do less. Less drinking, less women, less fighting.

Because when I do more, it reminds me of everything I lost. Everything I want. And don't have.

"Ford?" Davis meets my eyes and grins. "You good, brother?"

Shaking myself from my daze, I grin back. "Damn good."

Everyone clinks their glasses together, and I choke down the bubbly liquid with a grimace. The only one who doesn't *cheers* is Ruby. Instead, she stares longingly at Duke, now cradled in Dakota's arms.

I nudge her shoulder. "You okay, Fairy Tale?"

"I'm okay." A thick sheen coats her bright blue eyes. She swallows, then blurts, "I have to go to the garden."

She's out the door before anyone can say anything else.

Charlie runs a hand through his thick brown hair. "Fuck," he swears, and then his boots are stomping out of the house after his wife.

A pang lights along my sternum. Davis clears his throat before turning back to Dakota and Duke.

This is the kind of situation that has me looking for an early exit.

Plucking Mouse from the floor, I flip a wave to Davis and Dakota.

As soon as I step outside, I breathe easier.

Dogs and cats and wives and kids. Everyone's world is loud except mine.

2

Ford

THE APEX OF CRYBABY FALLS OFFERS A HIGH-RISE view that no city can beat.

I check my stopwatch when I get to the top, grinning when I see I've beaten my best time. It's not the biggest or most dangerous spot to climb in Montana, but it's close to the ranch and gives me the daily dose of adrenaline I crave. Nothing beats the rush of dangling into space with only a thin fucking thread to catch you.

I'm three hundred feet in the air, and I hang there in the stillness. No people. No responsibilities. Only me and the wild blue yonder.

The ranch stretches out below me in stunning, pristine views. Woods to the right, glimpses of bright green pasture interspersed by cabins and chalets.

Home. Even if sometimes it feels the furthest thing from it.

My fingers search for a crack in the limestone rock, the mid-morning sun hot against my bare arms. With a grunt, muscles stretching, I hook myself into the side of the mountain. I follow the route laid before me, unhooking from a bolt and lowering myself down a notch.

I move with agility and speed, breathing easily in the crisp mountain air. I could do this route blindfolded. Without a rope. That cocky confidence—that fuck-it attitude—got me far in baseball, but the start of the season makes me take precautions. Dying on my brothers isn't an option. Even in the grave, they'd never let me hear the end of it.

I hook into an anchor, and right as my feet find good footing to descend, the tinny buzz of my phone sounds through my pack.

I snort. I can't believe I have a signal up here.

I pull it out and check the ID.

UNAVAILABLE. It could be spam, but I think of Grady last night and answer it.

"Hello?"

"Ford? Ford 'Flamethrower' Montgomery?"

I wince at my old nickname. *Fucking A.* This is why I hate answering the phone. It's always bad news.

Like Jim Donovan. Nearly ten years later, and I can place that perfunctory bleat like it was yesterday.

I lower my brow to the rockface. "The one and only."

"Have you ever been told you're a hard man to track down?"

"What can I do for you, Jim?" I'm not in the mood for small talk. Especially not with Jim Donovan, owner of the Phoenix Renegades, and my ex's father.

"Listen, son, I'll admit it. It's no secret we've had our... issues." I snort. *Issues* is putting it lightly. "Trust me, this phone call is purely business. We're looking for someone to take over as the Renegades' new television play-by-play broadcaster. Big leagues. Big time."

"And you thought of me," I say dryly.

"We did." I hear the flick of a lighter. Jim inhales— most likely a Cuban cigar. "You're the type of voice we need, Ford. Hell, you're the voice of the team. One of the greatest pitchers of all time. A former star player with a massive ego, but that's what America wants. America wants to watch you strut your stuff from the broadcast booth. Our team always loved your straightforwardness and Southern drawl."

I laugh roughly. He's determined, I'll give him that. "Compliments, Jim? Don't seem to remember getting much of those back in the day."

A long silence. I've pissed him off. Perfect.

"It's a new day, son."

I close my eyes and clench a fist. I wish he'd stop calling me that.

"A new chance. That's why we want you. It'd be a two-year contract. You'd work out of New York. A nice salary. Not as much as when you were in the major leagues, but you can't go back, can you?"

I grit my teeth and stare down at the dizzying drop.

No, you sure fucking can't.

"No one wants me." Frowning, I attach a hook to the side of the rock. "Not after that video."

A smug smile in his voice. "Which video?"

Which video is fucking right.

Jim's voice shifts from carefree to alert. "We buried the one of you and Savannah. It wasn't good optics for either of you." He clears his throat. "And no one remembers that other video anymore, Ford."

I swallow. Maybe he's right. But I fucking remember it.

"It was an accident. In baseball, collateral damage comes with the territory. Hell, yesterday, Nico Dolan's bat struck the catcher. You can't escape accidents."

Except what I did wasn't a fucking accident.

An image of that day pops into my mind. The whip of my arm, the roar of the crowd, the chaos that followed.

"What do you say?" Jim asks, pulling me from my memories. "Come back to your brothers."

"Can't commit," I say, watching a red tail hawk soar through the sky. "Not yet."

"You're on a ranch, son." Disdain stains his voice. "In Montana."

Annoyance prickles my spine. That's the bastard he's always been. A smug, rich asshole who thinks the entire world is a cement city.

"I'll take the ranch any day of the week."

"That's your brother's place," he argues. "*You* gotta make a place for yourself. You did it once. You can do it again."

Restlessness rattles beneath my skin. A grudging admittance that he's right. "You think pissin' me off is really the way to my heart, Jim?"

He chuckles. "You saying no?"

I grit my teeth. As much as I dislike the guy, the offer's tempting.

But I don't know. Leaving my brothers doesn't sit right.

"Give me the summer," I say. "You're not gonna put anyone new in a booth, especially with it bein' mid-season."

He blows out a rush of air. "I'll wait. Just make it worth my while."

I roll my eyes. "Right."

"Ford."

"Yeah?"

"Who's going to win the World Series?"

I grin. "White Sox," I tell him. "They'll come back after being shut out for five innings. Then, Colm Meeney will get a solo homer in the tenth and end it."

"See?" Jim laughs. "Gotta get you in the booth."

I hang up and pocket my phone.

Instead of continuing my descent, I remain suspended.

I swore I'd never get back into baseball after what happened. What I did.

But Jim Donovan's out-of-the-blue offer has struck a nerve. Thrown me a curveball I never saw coming. Or maybe I never wanted to see it.

The one thing I knew since I was eight years old was I wanted to play baseball and I wanted a family. Clear natural law.

And do I have either of those? I sure fucking don't.

He's right. What am I doing with my life? Bumming around while everyone gets married and has babies? Living my life like tomorrow's ten years away? I'm thirty-seven years old. Except for a little infamy, a few titles, and some money in the bank, what do I have to show for the last ten years? Everything on this ranch is Charlie's. Davis has the Warrior Heart Home. Hell, even Wyatt's entertaining offers to open his own rodeo school.

And me?

What do I have? I'm not sure I want to answer that.

It's something I talked about in therapy.

I pretend like I don't care when I do.

I act like I don't want what my brothers have when I do.

Hell, I had it for a time.

I swung and missed at love.

And I'm not trying again.

My emotions ramp up as I stare down at the three-hundred-foot drop.

I take a breath to relieve the pressure building in my chest. Shake my head to clear it before I start my descent. It's dangerous climbing when your mind is long gone.

In the past.

Bad memories.

Savannah.

A lawyer, blonde, bright, beautiful. We were opposites. She was a good girl who had her shit together. I was a southern boy bumming around on a baseball field. But I loved her. I loved taking her out and showing her off. Our song was George Jones' "He Stopped Loving Her Today" and on late nights she'd lean over to me in bed and whisper, *"It can't get better than this, Ford."*

We dated for three years before I popped the question. Planned it out to a fucking tee. Even asked Jim for his permission. During our warm-up, I brought her onto the field, because Savannah loved spectacle. Drama. Anything she wanted, I wanted to give it to her. I got down on one knee. With my heart hammering in my chest, I pulled out a ring.

Only…

She said no.

She left me kneeling on the mound, feeling like a used-up fool. As a chorus of boos filled the stadium, I put the ring back in my pocket. I rallied and pitched the best game I ever had in my life.

All the while, it felt like she had walked off and left me to die on that field.

Later, she found me in the locker room.

"I can't, Ford."

"You need time, I get it."

I tried to touch her, but she stopped me. "I don't need time." *Her pretty face screwed up.* "I need someone else. Someone better. You're—you're white trash, Ford. You're not here." *She held her hand to a spot below her heart.* "It was supposed to be fun. Not forever."

Fuck. That hurt.

It all fucking hurt.

It hit at once like a lightning strike. Everything clicked, though it was about three years too late. She wasn't the one. Never once did she go home with me to Georgia. The way she'd micromanage every little thing I wore, especially when we went to one of her fucking parties. How she hated when I wasn't with her but wasn't happy when I was. The way we never had good days. They were either amazing or awful—so high or so fucking low. It was never good enough.

I was never good enough.

It was all a waste of time. A waste of my heart.

Love can't be trusted because it's never real. It's all a bomb waiting to blow up.

After Savannah ended things, I was in a new stage of grief. The woman I loved left me. I felt everything closing in on me. The life I had worked so hard for—gone. I said *cheers* to all my troubles. Too much alcohol. Too many pills. All I wanted was a warm body and a cold beer.

It was the end of the season, and we were in the World Series. I showed up to practice drunk and stoned but I was still pitching strikeouts.

But in the last game, I was off. In the second inning, I wound up, stumbled ten feet from the mound, and let that ball fly. In the wrong direction. Horrified, I watched it soar into the stands and—

"Fuck," I yell.

Groaning, I scrape a hand down my face. My heart won't quit slamming against my ribcage. I shake my head, clearing the memory. There's no use going back.

I can't change a damn thing.

That's the fucking truth.

With that, I unhook my line and drop into oblivion.

⌒

Un-fucking-believable.

Gritting my teeth, I stare at the flat tire on my glittering blue '67 Chevy pickup.

I pull out my phone and pace while I try to get a signal. Fucking figures, I get goddamn reception on the mountain, but in town, I'm shit out of luck.

When I see the time, I groan.

It was meant to be a quick two-hour climb, but without a doubt, I'll be late.

Davis and Charlie are going to have my ass. Opening week is stressful as hell and we're already short-staffed as it is. Which means I fucked up.

I take my job seriously. I let down the ranch, I let down the guests, I let down my brothers.

My phone chirps.

NO SIGNAL.

"Shit."

I gotta get back. Now. If it means hitching a ride—so fucking be it.

I blow out a breath and search the road.

A black Mustang is coming toward me. Fast.

A tan arm hangs out the window.

I stick out my thumb, step into the road.

But the Mustang doesn't slow down. It accelerates at an alarming rate, and blows right past, leaving me in a cloud of dust and exhaust.

"Slow down, asshole," I mutter, catching a glimpse of the out-of-town license plate. Great. Just what the

Resurrection locals need. Some dickhead out-of-towner plowing them down.

And then, the hand lifts and flips me off with expert precision.

An armful of gold bangles dangle from a slender wrist as the driver careens down the freeway like they're an outlaw on the run for their life.

3

Reese

WHISKEY. IT'S THE FIRST THING ON MY MIND and the last thing I need.

Grady's Mustang rattles down every bump and divot in the winding drive. I gape as I pass under a massive iron sign that proclaims Runaway Ranch. Montana has stunned me. With its indigo skies and emerald forests, I envy every creature that gets to live out here. That gets to be free.

Sleeping at a gas station in Kansas City was *my* first act of freedom.

So far, so good. So long Gavin.

Yeah, right.

I've only been gone—missing, I suppose—for fifty-two hours and already Gavin has a story in the *Nashville Star*.

Rehab for Country Singer Reese Austin. All Projects Suspended Indefinitely.

Rehab. Gavin's deep dark secret. Our cover story. It always works. Because to the world, I'm just one more washed-up singer.

Not to mention, Gavin needs to cover his ass. Probably because I'm fully in breach of my contract. What's in it— God knows. I've always signed whatever my manager set in front of me. He was constantly reminding me that I owed him. That I was his investment.

Well, no more. As soon as I'm settled, I plan to review

my contract and figure out what the fuck I signed back when I was sixteen.

I hope it's not too late.

I haven't turned on my phone yet. I'm too afraid of Gavin's wrath. When I think about what I'm skipping out on—the album I'm supposed to write, awards shows—the black tide of responsibility threatens to sweep me up. But I had to run. One more show, one more fake smile, and I'd lose it. Maybe I already have. I feel so detached from the world that created me.

A shiver snakes its way over my spine as I wonder if I'm doing the right thing. Despite how he's treated me, Gavin's the only family I have. He cares about me. He has to. Doesn't that mean something?

Guiltily, I reach across the seat and stick my hand into a bag of red licorice. I enjoy every bite of the overly sweet sugar while I let a plan rise in my thoughts.

I need this. It's safe here. As long as no one in my other life can find me. *Lie low*, Grady had said. And that's what I plan to do. Rest my brain, review my contract, and figure out a way to make my life mine.

Heal.

If that black hole wants to follow me around this ranch. Let it.

The Mustang gurgles. I wince and pound the dash. It hasn't let up with the noise since my last gas station stop. Hours of that sound has fried my nerves, but all I could do was drive on.

The road goes on for another quarter mile, passing a line of cabins, until I round the corner. And there, rising like the mountains surrounding it, is a stunning lodge.

Three stories tall, its showpiece is a massive front-facing

vaulted window that overlooks the ranch. A large outdoor
deck surrounds it. Guests file in and out of the massive
double doors, cold beers in their hands.

I made it.

I did it.

Myself.

Gratefulness and hope make my heart flutter as I stare
at my surroundings. The green fields. A barn the size of a
mansion. Horses roaming in an emerald pasture. It's beautiful. It's breathtaking. It's—

"Shit!" I slam the breaks, narrowly avoiding colliding
with a horse the size of a tank.

"Lady." Atop the horse, a cowboy glares down at me
through my open window. "Watch where you're going."

I exhale and feel my stomach drop. "Sorry."

Quickly, I park in the gravel driveway, haphazardly
taking up two parking spots. On numb legs, I hop out,
leaving my bags in the car. I stopped by my penthouse to
grab only the necessities: my guitar, my laptop, and whatever clothes were within arm's reach.

I'm sleep-deprived and exhausted. I want a bed. A bed
for *one*, just me. I want clean, cool sheets. A fully stocked
fridge. Not like I would know what to buy though. Or eat,
for that matter. For the first time in a long time, I don't have
anyone telling me what to do or where to go. It's heaven.

But really, it's Runaway Ranch. My temporary home.

Caught up in a wave of guests, I step inside the lodge
and finally allow myself to breathe.

With its high ceilings and natural light, the lodge is
alive and breathing. A line of people patiently waits to
check in and boisterous laughter fills the air. Balloons,
streamers, and a sign proclaiming OPENING DAY hang

from the high ceilings. Music plays over the speakers—
country. Phenomenal country. The kind of country that
got me into singing just like my daddy.

Old-school Randy Travis. My lips move with the tune
as I glance around the space.

In one corner, there's a rustic-looking bar with three
cowhide stools waiting at the counter. A neon sign on the
wall glows BAR M. The sight of it makes my mouth water.
I shouldn't drink, but it'll help take the edge off of all this
newness.

On the drive here, I promised myself I'd be New Reese.
No drinking. No dancing. No dark mind. Clean slate.

But God. Old Reese really wants a drink right now.

My heart hammers as I head for the bar, aware of stares
on me. It's right around this time I'm realizing if I wanted
to lie low, the outfit isn't helping. At my penthouse, I just
threw on whatever was closest. Mini skirt, mini shirt—the
only things Gavin lets me wear. *You have a style, Reese,* he'd
always remind me. *It doesn't include cozy.* Thigh-high boots
covered in crystals cast rainbows across the wood wall.

I look like a train wreck. But that's me, right? Reese
Austin, messy as fuck.

I rummage through my bag and slip on a pair of oversized sunglasses.

After five minutes of waiting in line, it's my turn.

I belly up to the bar.

"Hi, one second, please." A pretty girl with long strawberry blonde hair dives for a beer glass. She looks flus-
tered as she pulls the draft and spills half of it on her
shaky hands.

A door slams open. I turn, expecting more guests, but
it's another cowboy. His loud boot stomps echo throughout

the lodge. He looks pissed. The front of his T-shirt is covered in grease.

From somewhere to the left, there's a loud shout. "You're late."

I glance over and see a huge guy with muscles like bowling balls pointing a finger at the cowboy.

"No fucking shit," the cowboy snaps, glaring. After a string of curses, he takes his place behind the bar, rushing to help the blonde girl.

I bite my lip.

I may be exhausted, and he may be filthy, but I'm not blind.

Dusty and muddy, he looks like he just galloped out of the lyrics of a country song. His plain gray T-shirt stretches tight across his broad expanse of chest. Tan, sinewy forearms wrapped with veins show he's worked in the fields, if not the gym. He's the word *country boy* come to life, and I can't stop staring. A *real* cowboy. Not like those pretty posers I've worked with.

My eyes trail lower. Huge, calloused hands. Long, nimble fingers. A tapered waist hugged by blue jeans.

"Here, Fairy Tale." His lazy drawl interrupts my wandering gaze, and I watch as he takes the tray of glasses from the girl. The softness of his tone does something strange to my heart.

My eyes shoot back up to his face. A mistake. That sharp, square jaw. Full, lush lips. A mouth that would feel good on a dark starry night.

Mind off the cowboy. Focus on the drink.

That's when I realize he's frowning at me.

"Help you?"

Finally, some service.

Pushing my sunglasses on top of my head, I give him my most charming smile. "Hi."

He wears a backward baseball cap that covers a shaggy head of golden hair. It reminds me of a lion's mane. His narrowed eyes are deep brown streaked with gold, almost honeyed. Like the whiskey I want.

He crosses his arms, jerks up his chin. "What?" The question is brisk, annoyed.

"Whiskey. Top shelf."

He says nothing, just gives me a lazy once-over and an eyebrow raise.

While he pulls the whiskey, I set my arms on the bar top, adjusting the bangles on both of my wrists. The familiar jingling sound settles over me like a lullaby.

I glance up and the cowboy stands there, frozen, whiskey bottle gripped in his fist. His eyes land on my bangles. Something like recognition filters into his gaze. "Not from here, are you?" he asks, sounding surly.

I rack my brain to think if I've seen him before. No. He's just a dusty, crabby cowboy who should be pouring me a drink. "How'd you guess?"

His nostrils flare. "Because when people are stuck on the side of the road in a small town, you typically stop to help." He pours whiskey into a crystal glass.

I scoff. "Strange men, hitchhikers? I don't think so."

His frown deepens to a scowl. "Let me guess, that's your car out there takin' up three parkin' spots."

Whatever's put this bad-tempered cowboy in an even worse mood, I want no part of. My sigh is weary as I drum my nails on the lacquered countertop. "Look, give me the drink and I'll go."

His gaze returns to me like a magnet. "Let me break

it down for you, honey. You won't get far givin' the orders 'round here."

I bristle at the term *honey*. I've been called it every day of my life. It's just a throwaway word for a throwaway girl.

"Don't call me honey." I swallow, push aside the pang of hurt. "Seriously. Give me my goddamn drink."

He lays a long, cocky look on me, instantly annoying me. "The whiskey's for paying customers. Guests." His lip quirks up. "You have a room here? You lost? Because I have a map with directions to the best way out of town."

For a moment, I tense, unable to shake off that unwanted feeling. Then I slam my purse on the bar and rip out my wallet. "Here," I snap, throwing my credit card at him. It bounces off his broad chest, and I watch those long, calloused fingers snatch it up.

"Fuck me." He stares at my credit card as if it's a bomb. A muscle jerks in that chiseled jaw as his amber eyes lift to mine. "You're Reese?" he demands.

"I am." I toss my hair. "And I suppose you are the unfortunate grouchy cowboy welcome wagon."

He scowls.

My jaw tightens. I hold out my hand. "The drink."

The glass bobs in his hand like he's considering something. Then he drawls, "Sorry, honey. Don't think you need this today."

I watch in horror as he downs my drink in one long shot. Smirks.

A squeak comes from the blonde girl behind him. Her blue-eyed gaze pinballs from me to the cowboy.

Fists clenched, I stomp my heel. "You—you asshole."

"Tell it to the judge. Here." With a cocky grin that

lights a fire in my chest, he slides a glass of water toward me. "Cool off."

I narrow my eyes, trying to fight off the Old Reese. I picture the cowboy pinned beneath a tractor, or better yet, his throat in my hands. The image is only semi-satisfying, and I can only fight my impulses for so long. So, I give in.

I grab the glass of water and splash it in his face.

There's a collective gasp from the guests in the lodge, then…silence.

I stare at him, and he stares at me. His gaze sharpens, as if he's deciding whether to choose violence, then he drags a hand down his water-soaked face.

Satisfied with my recklessness, I turn on my heel and storm out of the lodge.

I stand in the late afternoon sun, chest heaving. Worry rising.

Grady was wrong. I don't need this ranch. I don't need anyone. Let alone a cowboy with anger management issues. I'll get back in my car, find a map, and head somewhere else. Figure out what to do next.

There's only one problem.

My car.

There's smoke rising from the hood. Karma, I suppose for taking up multiple parking spots.

Panic swarms me, that tight familiar feeling of suffocation.

"Oh shit." I fan my hands over the hood, heat seeping into my fingertips. "Shit, shit, shit." My high-heeled boots wobble across the gravel as I hover around the car, pushing at the smoke like I can make it all go away.

Like that black spot isn't hanging over my shoulder laughing at me.

It can't get any worse.

"That ain't gonna help you, honey." The sharp southern drawl sinks into my stomach and pools there like warm butter.

I grit my teeth and close my eyes. "Leave me alone."

The crunch of gravel tells me he's circling me. Like a vulture. "I'd love to. But I promised my little brother I'd give you a place to stay and since big brotherly duty frowns on reneging on promises…looks like you're stuck with me."

Ugh. Of course, this broody cowboy is Grady's brother.

I cock an eye to find the man staring at me with a furrowed brow. My breath hitches. In the sunlight, those serious amber eyes are accompanied by faint crinkles at the corners. It's unfairly sexy.

"Not you," I say, horrified. "You're the last person I want to be stuck with."

He heaves an annoyed sigh, looming over me as he places a disarmingly big hand on the engine hood. "Believe me, I feel the same way about you."

I draw back at the way he says it—at the look on his face. It's an expression I know all too well. Loathing combined with a tinge of amusement.

Fantastic.

The cowboy slaps greasy hands on the thighs of his jeans. "Whether or not you wanna get away, you won't get far with this car. You got a leaky radiator."

I blink. "Since when?"

A vein pulses in his temple. "Since I looked at it."

The hope I had mere moments ago disintegrates.

"It started making a noise back in Illinois." My tongue prods at the inside of my cheek. "I just kept going."

"Yeah, you would do that, wouldn't you?"

Heat darkens my cheeks. "How long will it take to fix?"

"Don't know," he clips.

I roll my eyes. "Aren't you a cowboy? You're supposed to be charming. Helpful."

He snorts so hard it's a wonder he doesn't pop a vein.

"So what do I do?" I ask, tilting my head back to keep eye contact. His tallness is startling. They must grow them like weeds on Runaway Ranch.

"You stay here." A shrug of his broad shoulder. "Unfortunately."

"Absolutely not." With a huff, I stalk away from him. But the boots I'm wearing have no grip and I slip and slide over the gravel drive.

My knees are buckling when a big, calloused hand wraps around my wrist. "Please tell me you ain't planning to wear these boots around the ranch." His voice is stern, but the way he grips my wrist is almost tender.

I glance up to find his eyes dragging their way up my bare thigh. I have to fight the low swoop in my stomach. "So what if I am?"

He grunts. "Bangles need work, too. You're loud as hell."

"Good thing I'll be out of here before you can work yourself into a froth," I say with my sweetest smile. I've already decided there is no way in hell I'm staying. I'll tell Grady *thank you, but hard pass,* and tomorrow morning, I'll hit the road.

Even if I have no idea where I'm going.

He stares at me, his gaze a dark storm brewing on the horizon. His hand stays wrapped around my wrist, the sensitive skin there tingling with a memory I try to push away. *Burning. Falling into dark.*

He must read something in my face because he drops my wrist.

Without another word, he strides toward a monstrous camo-colored UTV, muttering uncomplimentary phrases about women raising his blood pressure. He stops, turns and stares at me for a long beat, then waves a hand. "Well, get over here."

It's stern. Disapproving. Country and cavalier. It shouldn't make my pulse race.

"Where are we going?" I ask, cupping my bangles in my hand and jogging after him. God forbid I jingle on the way.

"I'm taking you to your lodging." He looks like he hates the idea.

I halt. "Not in that." For a long second, I miss limos. Private drivers.

He grunts and keeps going, his long lope casting lazy shadows across the gravel drive. "Suit yourself. But trust me, it's a long hike to where you're staying."

I remain rooted in place, arms crossed, unwilling to budge until he tells me where exactly he's taking me.

"By the way," he tosses over his shoulder. "Your card's been declined."

4

Ford

REESE TOTTERS ON HER HEELS LIKE SHE'S planning to fall over again. "Wait, what?"

"Your card," I state. "Declined." Not like I was planning to charge her for the room. But the water she splashed in my face was going to be an expensive as hell charge.

Her face falls.

Fuck. My day's already gone to shit. First, the call from Jim, then the flat tire, and now I'm stuck playing babysitter to a girl I've never met. This strange girl who looks like she's about to burst into tears.

"Shit," she whispers as her eyes go glassy.

Fuck no.

I keep walking, resisting the hard tug of my heart. A woman crying is my goddamn kryptonite. "Come on, it can't be that bad, can it? Just call up someone and get a new one. Easy."

The pissed-off expression on her face suggests she wants me to shut the hell up.

"Let's go," I say through gritted teeth. "I don't have all day."

"Hold on. My bags."

I climb in behind the wheel of the UTV and fire up the engine.

Reese heads to her car and leans all the way across the driver's side to reach the passenger seat. It's hard not to do a double take when her skirt rides up, revealing tan, toned thighs, and a gorgeous round ass.

When Grady said he was sending some starlet to the ranch, I had my doubts. But Reese looks every bit the part of a dolled-up country singer. A sheer low-cut blouse tied high at the midriff. A tight black skirt. Boots covered in diamonds or crystals or whatever shit that makes her glow. Platinum blonde hair that's as stick-straight and as skinny as she is.

Then there's her face. Heart-shaped, high as hell cheekbones, long lashes, and pouty pink lips. Eyes that remind me of the pasture on the first day of spring.

Although, I've never seen eyes that young look so damn old.

I'd say she's just my type if I didn't know exactly what type she is. Spoiled. Drama. High maintenance. Everything Savannah was. Entirely too beautiful—and no doubt she knows it.

I already hate the way my cock sprung to attention the second I grabbed her wrist to keep her from face planting. Last thing I need is to take care of her.

But since I already promised my little brother I'd get her settled, the least I can do is play chauffeur. The sooner she's at her chalet, the quicker she's out of my life.

Louis Vuitton duffel and guitar case in hand, Reese trudges those long legs toward me. Taking her damn sweet time. Christ. She's like a horse. Stubborn mule I'll have to wrangle.

"Your chariot," I say when she meets me at the UTV.

With a dirty look, she dusts off the seat with her long nails, then settles beside me.

I throw the UTV in drive. Reese squeaks and grabs

the handhold bar, looking like she wants to throw herself from the UTV the second we start moving. On a roar, we head off in the direction of the chalets. I want Reese as far away from the ranch as possible. Out of sight, out of mind. Whatever she's here for, she can handle it herself.

"Well?" she begins.

"Well, what?"

"Which brother are you?" Her lips quirk. "Dopey?"

I clench my jaw. "Ford."

Intrigued, her eyebrow arches. "And you're a mechanic?"

"Bartender. Outdoor activities. Ranch hand. Pick your poison."

"Oh," she sniffs.

That's right, honey. I'm too low class for you. Not your type and you know it.

For some reason, it makes me feel like shit.

She's a city girl. Even the fake country accent she puts on riles my nerves.

Reese opens the bag cradled on her lap and pulls out a licorice rope. I slow for a group of guests out on a horseback ride, using the opportunity to peek into her bag. A bottle of Coca-Cola. A bag of Funyuns. A jumbo bag of Sour Patch Kids.

Got it. She eats like shit. She's a gorgeous girl, but she's dead-eyed, dead tired. The best thing I can do is get her to her place and leave her there.

"So, you're what?" I ask. "On the lam?"

She gives me a scathing look. "None of your business."

"When you're on the ranch, it is my business." I don't care, don't want to know, but because Davis will ask, I better get it out of her while I can.

"It's a long story." She tucks her chin into her shoulder. "Just…pretend I'm not here."

"Already on it."

"And you're already a pain in my ass," she snaps back.

I take a sharp right onto a thin dirt road. "Good. One thing we agree on, honey."

Her eyes flash with annoyance. "Don't call me honey."

Honey. Princess. Sweetheart. Lukewarm terms of endearment that let me keep women at a distance.

We drive the rest of the way in silence. The jingle of her bangles set my teeth on edge, but I keep my mouth shut. I've already argued to my limit today.

I slow when we reach the West Chalets. The large, storybook-looking homes sit at the edge of the forest, pressed up against the mountains and surrounded by untouched wilderness. Across the shimmering lake, the East Chalets mirror their charm. Both groups of chalets are a good fifteen-minute walk from the Lodge, far enough to feel secluded but close enough to remain connected.

I park in a clearing and cut the engine.

Reese faces me, wide-eyed. "All the way out here?"

"Privacy, princess. Thought you'd like it."

As Reese gets out of the UTV, she freezes. Closing her eyes, her head inclines to the south. "There's water around?"

"Good ear." I nod at a pale buttercream two-story chalet to my right. "There's a lake about ten yards past that chalet."

Her gaze drifts to the forest. "Can I have that one?"

I shrug. "Suit yourself."

She reaches for her bags, but I beat her to it. As I grab them, my hand brushes her arm, and a sizzling scorch dances over my skin. Warm, sweet, electric. I don't move away as fast as I should, probably because some fucked-up part of me wants to hang onto that feeling as long as I can.

"This all you got?" I ask, clearing my throat. "A duffel bag and a guitar?"

The smile she gives me is dim. "Sounds like a country song."

I almost chuckle.

Hefting her bags, I trudge across rock and grass. At the door, I fish through the ring of keys I grabbed earlier. Inside, I flip the lights. Behind me, Reese's boots make sharp clicks on the wide-plank pine floors, the sound echoing up into the cathedral ceiling above.

I drop her bags on the kitchen table. "Here you go, honey. Home sweet fucking home."

She stares at me for a long minute before her eyes move around the space.

Mine follow. Downstairs is one large living space. There's a mini kitchen next to a plush bed. Upstairs, an alcove with a sitting room and a rock wall fireplace.

I cross the floor and head into the kitchen. A lace-curtained window over the sink looks out onto the small back porch. The yard's a tangled, snarled mess. Shit.

Annoyed that I care, I turn, ready to tell her goodbye, tell her she's on her own. But the words catch in my throat when I see her unpacking her duffel bag. A box of hair coloring. A laptop. Some files. A small stack of bright clothing and high heels. A tube of Pringles.

My stomach turns. I flinch at the meager contents. That's it? Everything she needs, everything important to her, crammed into one fancy fucking duffel bag.

That's when I spy a bottle of pills.

Fuck.

I think of Ruby. I think of myself. I think this is getting way more complicated than I need.

"Look," I say, wiping a layer of dust from the countertop. "We don't want trouble here."

This time, those big green eyes lock onto mine, her lips quirking as if I amuse her. "You think I'm on the run from bad guys? Don't worry. I can take care of myself."

I highly doubt that. The strain on her face, the hunch of her shoulders, tell a different story. She looks ill at ease. Exhausted. Almost fragile. Like she's barely keeping it together.

I don't know what her health plan is, but damn if she's getting enough sleep.

With a sigh, Reese sinks onto the bed. I watch as she unzips her boot from thigh to ankle. Another sigh of relief pops from those pretty pink lips. The tall sides of the boots fall open, exposing slender, tan thighs. Heat licks its way over my spine.

Fuck.

I jerk away and squeeze my eyes shut to fight the image. Fight the erection that's popped up in my jeans. But it's too late.

It's attraction. A dangerous one. Especially with a woman like this. One with secrets. One who makes me want to wring her pretty little neck every time I look at her. Maybe it's because she's a mess. Maybe it's that sad look in her eyes. Either way, I want her out of my head.

"So…" She crosses her arms over her chest. "What do I do now?"

Christ. She wants me to entertain her?

Hell, I could think of several ways. A few nights between the sheets, a bottle of wine. But that breaks my rules. No more locals. Even if she's not staying.

I focus on getting the key off the ring. "There's a general store back at the lodge. Dinner's from five to eight in the cantina."

She tilts her head. "And how do I get back to the lodge?"

"You walk, honey. It's called roughing it. You don't like it, you can leave."

"I plan to," she snaps. "You know, for a cowboy, you surprisingly do not have a way with words, or women, for that matter."

I grunt.

"See," she replies, smug. "My point proven."

With that, she digs frantically through her purse until she finds her phone. She stares at it for a long second, but doesn't turn it on.

I frown, crossing my arms. "If I had good common sense, I'd say you're hiding out."

Her chin lifts, a haughty motion that has my cock, once again, springing to life. "So, what if I am? It doesn't affect you."

"If it affects the ranch, it affects me."

"It won't."

Again, there's no elaboration. I tell myself it's better this way. I don't need to know, but it eats at me.

I give a nod to her pill bottle. "You ain't out here to off yourself, are you?" It comes out gruffer than I intend. "Because I don't want to walk in here tomorrow morning and find you face down on that bed."

Explosives detonate in her eyes. "Then all your problems would be over, right?"

I meet her hard stare with one of my own. "Sure you're not running away?"

"I'm sure."

"Nobody likes a liar."

"Good thing you don't have to like me."

A muscle jerks in my jaw as questions spin through my mind. Normally, I'd press her for more, but she's not staying. Whatever this girl's got herself into isn't my business. The last thing I want to do is worry about her. Get attached.

She's not my fucking problem.

But before I can say anything, Reese shakes her blonde head.

"Listen, Country Boy, I'll save you the trouble," she says with a sad little smile. "I'm just going to take what's going on in your head and say it out loud. Fuck off, okay?"

Her cutting words have an ache building dead center in my chest.

Because I think they're directed more for her than for me.

I clench my jaw, leaning over to drop the keys on the kitchen table.

Reese doesn't reply, and sits there, her phone clutched in her hands as I turn and walk out of the chalet.

Trouble.

And none of my damn business.

‿

Adrenaline. Chaos. That's where I thrive. But promising Grady I'd let Reese stay at the ranch? I must be a damn idiot. I tried calling my little brother to ask him what the hell he saddled me with, but all I got was his voicemail.

At least she's not my problem anymore.

I head to the Bullshit Box—a tiny, corrugated metal house we use as a business headquarters to debrief and decompress. And maybe do some paperwork.

Davis and Charlie barely look up from their desks,

lifting their hands in greeting. Keena bounds out of her bed when I stomp inside.

I give her a hearty pet, then settle behind my desk. I open my guidebook, the reservation schedule that lets me see what groups to lead the next day. My eyes scan the words, quick and deft. Even though I no longer struggle with reading and spelling, to this day, damn if I don't still feel some panic whenever I have to read in a public setting.

"How was today?" I ask.

A grunt from Charlie. "Good."

"How good?"

Charlie gestures. "Time-to-have-a-beer good."

I lean forward to fish a beer out of the cooler. The clock on the wall shows it's 6 p.m. Three years ago the ranch was a twenty-four-seven job. But now, with more staff, we're able to have lives instead of working ourselves to the bone. I'm proud of my little brother. He got his head on straight after the death of his fiancée. He makes a decent living. He has a good wife. All that matters in a cowboy's world.

Charlie, a grin on his face, says, "I'm more interested in your day."

I shoot him a dirty look. After the day I had, I'm not in the mood. "I know I was fuckin' late, okay? I couldn't help it."

"You get her settled?" Davis asks, glancing up from his security monitor.

I crack the beer, lean back in my chair. "I did. West chalets."

Davis gives me a smug look, like he already knows how attractive I find her. "How is she?"

I roll out my neck. "She's a brat with an attitude to match."

"You think she'll be okay out there?"

"Why wouldn't she be?"

Davis turns back to the security monitors. "Those chalets are in the middle of nowhere. Girls get scared of the dark."

Tongue probing the inside of my cheek, I slide my gaze to the window. Maybe it was a bad idea to leave her up there alone. It's obvious she's incapable of handling anything herself.

"You assholes miss me?"

Our heads snap up to find Wyatt standing just outside the door.

Grinning, I shove out of my chair and welcome him with a hard hug and a slap to the back. "I see you survived Vegas in one piece, kid." I frown when I see the sling on his arm. "Almost."

"What happened?" Davis asks, eagle-eyed.

Wyatt gives a devil-may-care shrug. "Snagged rope yanked it out of place. It'll be healed end of the week."

Davis looks doubtful. "Seems like a good time to think about that offer, doesn't it?"

Wyatt's retirement has been up for debate ever since the West Coast Saddle Bronc Riding Association approached him last winter. They made him an offer to establish his own rodeo clinic.

Wyatt sighs, long and annoyed. "No. It doesn't."

Mine and Charlie's eyes slice to Wyatt. Davis is bossy as hell and we all give him shit for it, but he does the work at keeping our younger brother on course. Wrangling Wyatt is a thankless job and almost physically impossible.

"Why not?" Davis argues. "Working with Rand Younger could be a good thing. You did it before."

Wyatt's face clouds at the mention of his old coach. "Yeah. Maybe."

"You ain't no spring chicken, Wy," I tell him.

Wyatt took some hard falls last summer. Recovery was tough, even for the guy who let a horse's hoof stomp open his bicep.

"You're thirty-four," Charlie says, kicking a boot up on his knee.

Wyatt helps himself to a beer and sits on the arm of the couch. "I'm still pretty spry, man."

"In rodeo, that's fuckin' ancient," Charlie points out. "You can't do it forever."

But he could. And he would.

We all know why he's staying in it, even if he won't say it—to look out for Fallon. If she's on the circuit, so is he.

Charlie clears his throat. "Ruby and I are going to put an offer in on the old ice cream parlor." A strange grin creases his rugged face, and I bite back a laugh. If anyone can get him to smile, it's Ruby. "Time to give Ruby her flower shop."

"Fuck yeah, man," Wyatt says, relieved the attention's off him.

"When you thinking?" Davis asks.

"As soon as we can. Ruby needs it," Charlie says, his voice weary.

I feel for my brother. Ruby's aching to be a mama, but it's not in her cards. Not with her heart condition.

"Get in line, brother," Davis says, a proud grin on his face. "We open Dakota's bakery at the end of the season." Last year, Dakota bought her father's old general store. Late summer is when she plans to open her very own bakery called The Huckleberry.

Davis sighs, shuffles through the papers on his desk. "We need to start working up a list of changes for next year."

"We just opened," I complain.

"Yeah, well, shit's changing fast," Charlie agrees. "Gotta get ready."

My head hurts from the news. The ranch is really changing, and what am I doing? Absolutely fucking nothing.

"Jim Donovan called me today," I announce, and my brothers go quiet.

Davis's face storms. "What'd he want?"

"Pricks got some nerve," Charlie mutters.

"To offer me a job." I tug a hand through my hair. "Wants me to be a commentator for the Renegades."

"You'd leave?" Charlie asks.

Davis dips his chin.

"If I took it, yeah." I take a sip of my beer, ignoring the way it settles heavily in my stomach. "Y'all drive me batshit crazy, anyway."

Maybe it's time to move the fuck on. I never thought I'd want any other life except Runaway Ranch. It saved me after Savannah. But what if I'm stuck? What if all I am is a washed-up pitcher with a bad rep and a video to haunt me?

I could lie and say I don't want what my brothers have, but I do. I did. Once upon a time. A Georgia mansion in the country, and a damn good woman by my side. But that's a fairytale. My ragged heart doesn't dare touch anything resembling love.

"You boys bitching?"

Blinking out of my daze, I grin at the sight of Dakota and Ruby in the doorway. The Bullshit Box is now a full-on family affair.

Charlie chuckles and reaches for Ruby. "Bullshitting, baby. Bullshitting."

"I have treats for you." Dakota unpacks a mountain of pastries from the basket looped around her arm. "Homemade

pop-tarts. Lemon pie with Fruity Pebbles. I'm thinking of serving these on opening day."

A chair rips back and Wyatt's already at the table.

"Did you find out what Reese's story is, Ford?" Ruby asks, settling on Charlie's lap.

Annoyed, I cross my arms. There are too many people bringing up Reese and making her my problem. "It's none of my business."

"The girl's on my ranch," Charlie reminds me, adjusting Ruby in his arms.

"We need to know who's on the property." Davis accentuates his point with a punch to his keyboard. "I don't want trouble this year."

I'd roll my eyes, but Davis is right. The last two years have been a shitshow. We've dealt with the Wolfingtons, actual fucking wolves, fires, slimy developers, and kidnappings. If we can get through the summer in one piece, it'll be a miracle.

"Grady said something about her needing a break," I mutter.

"Rehab?" Davis's frown deepens.

I groan.

"She's not just a girl, you know," Wyatt says, opening his big fat mouth. How he heard the news through the grapevine, I have no goddamn idea. "She's Reese Austin. A superstar country singer." He shoves the last bite of pop-tart in his mouth. "She was in that movie ten years ago about a teenage horse trainer. The hot one who broke her neck."

"Goddamn, Wyatt," Charlie says, half-chuckling, half-wincing.

"She's a big fuckin' deal." Wyatt stands and leans in to use my laptop. "I'll show you."

"Christ," I complain, but stand to give him room. Wyatt hasn't known about personal space since he started walking. "And how do you know all this?" I couldn't give two shits about pop culture. I've never been one for trends or social media—I like to live in the moment—but right now, I realize I don't know fuck all about Reese Austin.

Wyatt wiggles his brows. "Cause y'all are old and boring," he says, and the three of us scoff. With a flourish, he spins the laptop to the group.

Everyone crowds around the desk. I hang back, arms crossed, refusing to watch. But it doesn't last long. As soon as the song starts, I'm captivated by Reese Austin clad in nothing but a sheer slip dress. The crowd roars their approval as she rolls her hips and belts into the mic. The husky edge of her voice has a surge of blood racing to my dick.

Fuck.

"Look her up," Davis orders when the video is over.

The news headlines aren't any better.

> Reese Austin, 26, Scores 1M-Per-Show Deal
>
> Missing Country Singer in Rehab (Again) or in Hiding?
>
> Where is Reese Austin? Troubled Star MIA

"So she is in hiding," Ruby murmurs.

I scrape a hand through my hair, keep it there. "Shit."

Davis looks exasperated. Even Charlie looks annoyed. All signs point to this being something bigger than her just taking a vacation. Just what we need. A big-name celebrity on our ranch, distracting the guests. Hiding out.

I lift my arms. "Look, I warned her—"

"You warned her?" Dakota cuts in. "Like, what, you're going to break her legs?" she teases, brow arched.

Ruby's wide blue eyes find me. "She's out there all alone. What if she's in trouble?"

"The only trouble that girl has is herself." I cross my arms, hoping to ward off Ruby's charm. Her big heart is the sweetest goddamn thing I've ever seen, but saying no to it is an exercise in will.

"You should have asked her to dinner," Ruby admonishes.

I snort. "And get another drink splashed in my face? No thanks."

My brothers snicker, and Ruby giggles as she says, "She got you good, Ford."

Dakota smirks. "Can't be the first time you've had a drink tossed in your face."

Fifth time, but I don't offer that fun fact.

The scream of an engine backfiring has Dakota and Ruby jumping.

"Fallon's home," Dakota breathes.

I keep my eyes on my little brother, whose entire body has gone rigid.

"She still staying at your place, or is she sleeping in her car?" I ask Dakota. Ever since her kidnapping, Fallon has avoided her cottage in town.

Fuck. It's the wrong thing to say. Dakota's eyes fill with tears.

Davis whips his head to me and glares before cupping his wife's shoulder. "Make sure she comes to the house."

Wyatt shoves out of his chair, his face suddenly soft and bordering on desperate. "I'll go with you."

Together, he and Dakota disappear out the door.

"Ask Reese to dinner," Ruby sing-songs. She gives Charlie a little wave and exits.

"It's sundress season," Charlie mutters, his gaze glued to Ruby's departing ass. Groaning, he scrapes a hand down his beard. "And my wife's out to fucking kill me."

"Reese," Davis's deep voice booms, bringing us back to the problem at hand. "If she's in trouble, she's your problem. However long she's here, I want you on her."

I pry my brain away from the image of me literally on top of Reese. Fucking her slow. Dragging my cock through the slit of her pretty pink pussy.

Jesus.

I glare at my twin. "What the fuck are you talking about, man?"

"She's your responsibility." He's silent for a moment. "We'll get Otis to take over the trail rides and the rest of the excursions."

"Bullshit," I blast. Everyone suddenly wanting to bust my balls is pissing me off.

"You can't do it all, Ford."

"It's the start of the season," Charlie says, agreeing with Davis. He's becoming as responsible as my twin.

"How come I get saddled with this bullshit?" I grumble, hating my life. Already this girl's a pain in my ass. Messing up my daily routine. Making me sweat.

"We're married," Charlie says with a cocky shrug.

I roll my eyes. "Your choice."

Davis stands, roughing Keena's fur. "I got a kid."

"Fuck you," I say to him. "What about Wyatt?"

"Wyatt's got enough problems," Charlie says softly. He glances out the window, his blue eyes following the slow lope of Wyatt to the pasture. To Fallon.

"Shit," I mutter.

Davis and Charlie grin in unison. "Good luck."

I flip them off.

When my brothers clear out, I spin the laptop back my way and hit play on the next video.

Reese stands on the end of a catwalk, dolled up beyond recognition in a tiny sequined dress, fake eyelashes, too much makeup, and heels as high as skyscrapers.

Fans scream the lyrics as she sings something about having heart-eyes for a cowboy on a white horse. The song's stupid, but her voice… Jesus. A blast of a falsetto with a faint country twang.

I squint at the screen as if I can see right through the façade of her sky-high boots and bleach-blonde hair. How much of her is an act? How much of her is the real deal?

She wiggles around the stage, shaking that perky ass of hers. Fucking gorgeous. I can't lie.

The camera zooms in.

My stomach bottoms out.

Fuck.

She's crying.

And no one even fucking notices.

5

Reese

BEESTING *HONEY.* I SLIDE MY NAIL UNDER THE BOX of hair color I nabbed at a gas station in Red Lodge and pop the top. A quick glance at my reflection in the bathroom mirror tells me my platinum locks need help. They're fried and lifeless. Exactly how I feel.

In less than twenty minutes, my hair's wrapped and processing. My hairstylist—not to mention Gavin—will have a fit, but I don't care.

Even with my scalp on fire, I feel better than I did forty-eight hours ago.

Wrapped in a fluffy white towel, I cross the wooden floorboards. Each groan and creak beneath my bare feet reminds me I'm far from LA. There's something peaceful—almost safe—about the chalet. And for a small amount of time, I get to call it mine.

I open the back door and stare out into the night, at the forest, swaying in the whipping wind. It would be heaven to find that lake. To go to the water. But the darkness frightens me. Mostly because I already have too much of it inside me as it is.

On a sigh, I shut the door. How long will it take for me to feel like myself again? For this dark hole to go away?

Maybe running was a mistake. Maybe I should have stuck it out. Sucked it up.

But I couldn't. Absentmindedly, I sweep my hand over my bangles. I don't want to go back there.

Only where am I now?

No money. No car. No friends.

I think of what I missed today. A private jet to LA. Drinks at Serpentine. Whatever boring meeting Gavin had set up. I laugh to myself. Old Reese would want that. Would be in heaven.

I yawn, dragging in a long breath, and head to the kitchen table. I sit down and fire up my laptop. Gaze on the screen, I type a few keywords into the search engine and instantly get hit with:

Superstar Reese Austin's Downward Spiral

"Asshole," I hiss as I scan the article.

Not a surprise. It paints me in a sad, pathetic light and keeps the label off Gavin's back. It's also Gavin's way of punishing me. Just like turning off my credit cards and freezing my bank account. I can't access any of my funds. I'm essentially on an island. Adrift. Alone.

I cover my face and groan.

How did I get here?

What I'd give to go back in time. Dive bars. Intimate acoustic sets. Stadiums that weren't sold out. Wearing my old Levi's and singing songs *I* wrote. Not dolled up the way Gavin likes, singing the songs he picked.

You don't need to write your own songs, Reese, Gavin explained. *No one cares. Just get on stage and wiggle.*

It was a mistake to listen to him, but I didn't have a choice. I was a poor kid, abandoned by my parents, and scared as hell. He took me in, mentored me and made me a star.

He's the only one who's ever wanted me in this world.

Glancing back at the article, something stirs inside of me. A tiny tendril of fear. Guilt.

The last two months, as the tour wound down, Gavin's behavior changed. He became excessively paranoid about money, my whereabouts.

Sometimes, with Gavin, I feel like a computer chip controls my brain.

Tomorrow—tomorrow I figure out a plan.

But first, I need to face the music.

With shaky fingers, I finally turn on my phone. Instantly, I'm hit by a barrage of texts. My chest seizes up.

> **I don't care where you are or who you're doing. I need your perfect ass back here, Reese.**
>
> **Babe. What the fuck? I'm never going to get this gig without you.**
>
> **Don't make me put you back in Muirwood.**

The threat burns into my retinas, and I drop the phone on the table.

I squeeze my eyes shut, breathing through the panic.

I absolutely cannot go back there.

It's what got me into this mess. Signing that contract and giving Gavin power over me, over my finances, my entire fucking life.

"It's your fault, Reese. And this is your punishment. Now just sign the damn contract and I'll take care of you."

Hot tears spill from my eyes. He's right. It was my fault.

All my fault.

"Fuck," I mutter, sucking in a deep breath.

I need to pull it together. Get my contract. Find out what rights I've signed away to Gavin. One thing about him, I already know he's planning to use everything he can against me.

Which is why I have to lie low. Stay here, at least until my car's fixed. Until Ford Montgomery kicks me out on my ass. It's clear he wants nothing to do with me. He only sees me as a mess.

The tightness in my chest burns, and my gaze drifts to my pills. Dutifully, like Gavin's hovering over my shoulder, I swallow one down. The weak rattle of the bottle tells me I need a refill.

I'll go back to my life. I will. As soon as I get better. And this time, I'll do things on my own terms.

Think for myself. Live for myself.

Be free.

A hammering shakes the door, cutting through the buzz of my dark thoughts.

I jolt and glance over to see a broad form standing at the door, illuminated by the porch light. Inhaling a breath, I wipe at my face, then hurry to the door, yanking it open.

Ford. Scowling.

His dark blond hair is a wild mess, swooping low across his forehead. Gone is the dusty cowboy get-up from earlier. Now he wears soft gray sweatpants, and a white T-shirt stretched tight over his chest and biceps. In his hands: a round Tupperware container.

His eyes widen the moment he sees me, and that's when I realize that not only am I still wrapped in a towel—there's also one on my head.

A month ago, I would've been mortified if anyone saw me without lashes and lipstick and a tiny dress. Old Reese would've flirted with this rude cowboy, teased him into a frenzy, and then left him begging for more.

Kyler's face flashes in my mind. His hand gripping my thigh while he asked me over and over again until I gave in. Just like my entire fucking life.

I don't want a man. Least of all this one.

And it's clear from the stormy look on Ford's face that he doesn't want me either.

"To what do I owe this pleasant intrusion?" I ask. "Kicking me out already?"

A muscle jumps in his jaw. "We save the evictions for morning."

"Great. I'll be packed."

He wiggles the knob, and I didn't think it was possible, but that frown on his face gets even deeper. "In the habit of not locking your doors?"

"Are you the door inspector? Did you come to inspect me?" I drawl it out in a tease.

His gaze roams over me, heating the space between us. It lingers too long on my face, like those deep amber eyes can see my secrets. For one long second, I wish he could.

Ford sighs heavily. Tension pulses in his sharp, stubbled jaw. "This far out here, no one can hear you scream."

"That's...comforting." The man needs to work on his cowboy skills. "Unless that's what you want. Knock me off, so I'm not your problem."

His lips twitch. "Believe me, I've thought about it."

I roll my eyes and lean against the doorframe. "What do you want, Ford?"

The porch light catches on the angles of his sculpted face. "I didn't see you in the lodge, so I brought you dinner."

"Oh," I say, as he shoves the Tupperware into my hands. My mouth waters as I'm hit with wonderful aromas.

Freshly baked bread. Mac and cheese. I sniff. Shredded chicken.

"I can't eat all this," I say before cursing myself. Why did I say that? I could eat it all if I wanted to. I'm no longer concerned with what Gavin thinks or wants. Or demands.

His face reverts to its former hardness. "Yeah, well, try." His eyes scan my frame and I shiver. "My sister-in-law went to a lot of work for you."

I have the sudden inclination to smack this bossy cowboy's arrogant head right off those broad shoulders.

That's when a furry sensation wraps itself around my legs. I yelp and jump back. As I glance down, I catch sight of a black cat weaving in between my legs.

The cat meows, sounding like the tiniest tea kettle.

I smile and dip down to pet her under the chin. "Hey there." She flops on her back and lets me tickle her belly. Her green eyes match mine. "Are you the unofficial welcome wagon? You're much better than the current situation."

A grunt or a chuckle comes from Ford and he crouches beside me. "Mouse."

I glance at him. He's so close I can smell his soapy post-shower scent. "Hate to break it to you, Country Boy, but that's a cat."

His lips pull into something resembling a smile. "No. *This* is Mouse." He reaches down and flips the cat into his arms. She curls up without protest. "And she's a menace. Just like you."

Together, we stand.

"Lock your door," Ford orders. "Eat your food."

Then, with Mouse in his arms, he crosses the space between the chalet and the wild woods before climbing onto the UTV and taking off.

I leave the door unlocked. Just to spite him.

~~~

The next morning, I blink away the fog of sleep. Relishing the silence, I stretch cat-like in the cool sheets. Just me. No hangover. No strange man in my bed. No Gavin barking orders.

I smile at the ceiling.

I can do this.

As I slip into a sparkly dress, I realize how poorly I packed. But shimmery showgirl attire is all I owned—all I grabbed in my haste to get out of Nashville. After dabbing my cheeks and lips with dusky-rose blush, and adding mascara to my lashes, I stare at myself in the mirror. My hair, now the color of honey and ash, tumbles in unruly waves.

I chance a smile. I love it.

Ready for the day, I retrieve the slender gold bangles I bought myself after Muirwood from the nightstand and slip them on my wrist. With that, I step onto the front porch, instantly enveloped by the sticky morning heat. No eviction notice in sight, but Ford was right. There is nothing around me, and seeing as they don't have Uber out here, I'll have to walk.

I look down.

In heels.

As if to solidify my terrible fashion choices, when I step off the porch, my heels sink into the soft earth.

My heart thuds and I close my eyes.

I can do this.

But first, I need every ounce of coffee in the entire world. I need to go into town. I need to call Gavin too, but that is a problem for a caffeine-medicated Reese.

With a grunt, I rip my heels from the earth and start moving, breathing deeply until the noise in my head quiets.

For a second, I forget about the trek ahead of me, and lose myself in the moment. The birdsong in the trees. The sunlight on my bare skin. Emerald fields filled with horses. It feels like summer, and a sunrise builds in my chest. The ranch is stunning. There's something about seeing it on a new day that bolsters my hope.

How long has it been since I looked at the world with fresh eyes? Breathed clean air?

It's like taking my first step into a life I've never met.

It's the wild burn of freedom.

A cowboy on a black horse thunders past me. A group of people, fishing poles held in their hands, trek toward the forest with a guide. A white van stenciled with Runaway Ranch on the side putters up the gravel drive to the wrought iron sign in the distance.

I stick on dark sunglasses so no one recognizes me. The last thing I want to do is give away my cover, though most people wouldn't expect Reese Austin to be at some Podunk ranch in Montana.

By the time the fifteen-minute trek is over, I'm at the Lodge. After grabbing a town map, I wander the building. Today is less busy, and I'm not preoccupied with a search for whiskey, so I'm able to pay more attention. The common area is a western sanctuary with plush leather armchairs, a rock wall fireplace, and spectacular views in every direction. There's a cantina and a gift shop next to the front desk. Across the way, a small alcove with a sign above that reads THE CORNER STORE.

I duck inside.

It's adorable. Like a cowboy bodega. While I explore

the tiny store, I scan the shelves. Cans of soup. Boxes of cereal. Bottles of soda. Tampons and blue boxes of macaroni and cheese. A sign posted in the window says HELP WANTED. My mouth waters over the iced coffee machine, surprisingly fancy for the ranch. I need a strong pick-me-up for what's ahead of me.

I open my wallet, and my stomach drops when I see the lone twenty-dollar bill. The only money I have until I can replace my credit cards and access my banking account. I worry my lower lip between my teeth. How long will it last? How long can I?

I cringe at the thought of how much I've wasted on stilettos and designer clothing. How foolish I've been to give Gavin control of my accounts, my money.

I need a job. And a lawyer.

But first, I need my contract.

And I don't even know how to get that.

Before I can slip into a full-blown panic spiral, a voice behind me says, "I love your hair."

I whirl around. It's the girl from the bar, the one who worked with Ford yesterday. She has an entire garden in her tousled strawberry blonde strands. In her violet sundress patterned with honeybees, she looks like summer come to life.

I touch my hair, suddenly self-conscious. "Thank you."

"Don't worry," she says. Her blue eyes sparkle. "We won't tell anyone you're here."

I attempt to smile.

"I'm Ruby." With a bounce in her step, she crosses to me and sticks her hand out.

I lift my sunglasses and shake her hand tentatively. "Reese."

She tosses me a curious look. "Do you need something?" she asks.

My gaze lights on the iced coffee machine. I'd kill for an iced coffee, heavy on the cream and sugar, but I think of the meager twenty in my wallet. "Oh, I…I don't know."

"Give me a list, and I'll have it delivered to your room." Her smile brightens. "With the biggest iced coffee you've ever seen."

I shake my head. "You don't have to do that."

"Of course I do."

Sudden tears prick the backs of my eyes. It's been a long time since I've had kindness.

"Are you okay?" Ruby asks, looking concerned.

I shake my head, tamp down the dampness in my eyes. "I just think you're my new favorite human."

Ruby blushes and grins.

"Don't worry about it," she says when I reach for my wallet. "We'll charge the groceries to your room. No rush."

After scrawling a small list on the back of a receipt—mostly junk food and pasta—I hand it over.

Ruby pockets it, then tilts her head. "Do you need Ford?"

Ugh. No.

"Yes," I say.

"He's in the garage." Ruby laughs. "He's not so bad. Don't let him scare you. He's all bark."

I flash her a grin. "Good thing I can bite."

Within minutes, I'm at a building situated about fifty feet from the lodge.

As soon as I step inside, a strong gasoline odor hits my nostrils. A glittering blue Chevy pickup sits in the center of the garage. Along one wall, a low work bench overflows with a jumble of tools and cinnamon candies. Above it, a pegboard wall pinned with baseball cards. Music drifts from an old-school radio, and a baseball game plays on the wall-mounted TV. A cup of black coffee sits forgotten on a bright red toolbox.

Curious, I approach the baseball cards. Mickey Mantle. Babe Ruth. Joe DiMaggio. And—

I blink.

It's Ford.

The text reads *Ford "Flamethrower" Montgomery*. He's wound up in a typical pitching stance, a resolute expression on his face. Phoenix Renegades is emblazoned across his jersey in bright colors of royal blue and orange, and his baseball cap has a pair of fiery wings.

Damn. The audacity of that uniform. Tantalizingly tight and accentuating all the right angles.

Against the better judgment of my brain cells, my mind rewinds to last night—Ford shoving food into my hands before abruptly bolting to get away from me. And the way he looked in those gray sweatpants… My stomach flip-flops.

No. It doesn't matter what he did.

Sworn enemies until the day we die.

Movement across the floor catches my eye.

I smile. The black cat from last night is on the hunt. Mouse has her nose pressed close to the cement floor as she stealthily stalks her prey. I follow her deeper into the garage, where she climbs a stack of tires and curls up inside, sunbathing in the light streaming from an open window.

I run a hand over her glossy black fur, and a purr vibrates from her slender frame. "Pretty kitty," I croon. I'm mid-pet when the squeak of wheels hits my eardrums.

Ford slides out from beneath the truck on some type of bench with wheels on it. It takes a full ten seconds for me to realize he's been there the entire time.

He sits up slowly, peeling his long, lanky body off the bench. He's shirtless, in nothing but a pair of greasy blue jeans. His lionlike mane of dark gold hair curls around the sides of his baseball cap.

When he sees me, his eyes dart to my hair before settling on my face. His frown deepens to a scowl.

I eye the ridges in his abs, the streaks of grease across his chest. Heat creeps into my stomach and takes up residence. It's only intensified when he stands and prowls toward me. A solid wall of muscle. Of man.

I back up, but I slam into the workbench. A wrench drops from the backboard, mocking me.

"Goin' somewhere?" he asks.

His languid drawl sweeps over me, and I force my gaze to his.

A mistake. The deep amber color hitches my breath. *Beautiful.*

Shaking my head to chase away my traitorous thoughts, I stand tall. "Yes." I sniff. "I'll take my car. To go, please."

"You mean my little brother's car?" He looks amused, lazily rolling a candy around in his mouth. I'm hit with the scent of cinnamon as he says, "It's not ready yet." His lip curls. "Had to order the part. Could be awhile."

I flap a hand. "Look, I know you tell time by the passing of the seasons, Country Boy, but how long is a while?"

He gives his cat a scratch. "One to two weeks."

"Great," I mutter.

Ford saying it out loud makes my situation seem so

hopeless. I am stuck out here in bumfuck Montana without a car. Without money.

I think of that little girl busking on street corners, singing in dive bars with my parents. We made it work. We survived. I can do that too. I'll make my own money again. That way, Gavin has nothing to offer me.

"I need money," I say.

He shrugs a broad shoulder, cleaning his stained hands on a rag. "Can't help you there."

"Listen, Ford." I step up to him, conjuring my flirtiest smile. "I can work for it."

"Christ." He draws back, face creased in shock.

On instinct, I slam a hand against his rock-hard chest. Heat shoots through my fingers. Ford stiffens, his eyes never once leaving my face.

"Not like that, pervert." Needing a better place for my hand, I prop it on my hip. My heart thuds at the loss of contact. "Look, you have a Help Wanted sign in The Corner Store. I can clean bathrooms or pour coffee. Anything. I just really need to make some money."

I'm too desperate to be angry. To do anything other than beg.

He stares at me for a long, hard beat.

"You got any other clothes?" he asks.

I cross my arms. "Does it look like I have any other clothes?" I let out a weary sigh. "I grabbed what I could."

The cinnamon candy cracks between his teeth. "Should have planned better."

"I don't plan."

He grabs a T-shirt and shrugs it on, effectively ruining my prime view of his body. "That much is apparent."

Cheeks flaming, I stare at him for a stomach-sinkingly

long time. He won't help me. I should have expected that. But here I am, arguing with a man who's given me shit since I arrived. He thinks he knows me. Well, he's wrong. I don't need him.

"You know, whoever taught you to be a cowboy failed miserably." With a flip of my hair, I turn on my heel and stalk toward the exit.

"Hold up a sec," he orders, sounding weary.

I pause at the garage door. "What?"

His nostrils flare. "If you want work, you can work." The second he says it, it looks like he regrets his decision. With a grunt, he grabs a two-way radio from a shelf and hooks it to his waistband. Two big stomps and he's moving past me to disappear out of the garage.

His lope is long, and I have to scurry after him.

"Wait, where are we going?" I ask when I finally reach his side. I stumble on my heels and press my palm against his corded arm to steady myself.

He tenses at my touch. Keeps trudging ahead. "You want a job. You can work on the ranch."

My stomach drops. I stop in the middle of the gravel road. "The ranch?"

For my first real-world job, I was thinking of something less harrowing. Inside. Comfortable. I've never worked outdoors, let alone squatted behind the backend of a cow.

"Funny enough, I've been assigned the job of being your babysitter," he says as if it's the most painful thing in the world. "So, what you're going to do, honey, is work alongside me this summer."

I flinch.

Ford's upper lip curls. "What's wrong? Can't hack it?" He says it like it's a dare.

I glance down at my thousand-dollar cherry red Louboutins, bidding farewell to good heels and common sense. Then I blow out a determined breath, steel my shoulders and meet those stunning amber eyes.

"No. I can."

Ford simply grunts and heads for the barn.

Money, I remind myself. *Freedom. No black hole.*

It's all a gamble, but I have to take it. Even if I don't know what the hell I'm doing.

6

Ford.

HER HAIR'S DIFFERENT. IT PISSES ME OFF.

That platinum mess from yesterday is now a soft honey and ash color that makes her bright green eyes pop. Worse, it's a wild snarl of waves and curls that fall to the small of her back. With her heart-shaped face and long lashes, Reese is the very worst kind of distraction.

My baseball hat shields the late morning sun's rays as we trudge across the ranch. I glance at Reese. Every few seconds she stops, muttering to herself, and tears her heels from the grass, then continues to lurch along. Her heels chew up the green earth better than any rototiller can. Christ, at this rate, it'll be sundown before any of the chores are done.

The whole thing's ridiculous. I know a recipe for disaster when I see it. I can't think of someone more ill-equipped for ranch work than Reese.

In that sparkly silver dress, she's like a walking disco ball, and her stiletto heels probably cost thousands. She's got three gold bangles stacked on each arm, clinking with each move. In every video or photo I saw last night, she wore them. It must be her schtick. The constant jingle grates on my nerves. Almost has me forgetting how fucking beautiful she is.

Almost.

"You need more bracelets," I tell her dryly. "Don't think the whole ranch knows you're coming."

Her nostrils flare. "I like my bracelets."

"Yeah, well, they'll spook the horses."

She squeaks, jumping onto the grass as we approach a rooster pecking his way down the gravel path.

I chuckle. The panic on her face could almost be adorable. "Your ancestors hunted mammoths with a spear, honey. You can walk past a rooster."

She gives me a nasty look. Then, chewing on her lower lip, she gingerly tiptoes around the bird. "I've never seen a rooster before," she breathes. The sweet awe in her voice tugs at my chest.

"How was the spaghetti last night?" I ask, testing her.

"Delicious," she says, absentmindedly.

I side-eye her. Just as I thought—she didn't touch a goddamn bite. I grit my teeth but hold my tongue. She's twenty-six years old. A fully functioning adult. She can survive on her own. Why do I fucking care?

I don't. But she is my responsibility, whether or not I like it.

Besides, I didn't imagine the flicker of panic that flashed over her face when she said she needed a job. Hard times are what she's fallen on, and damn if it doesn't pique my interest.

"You ready to tell me what brings you to Runaway Ranch?" I glance at her beside me, keeping perfect sync with my long strides, even in those stilettos. "It can't be the cows."

"On the run from the mob," she says without missing a beat. "Witness protection."

I eye her. She's fucking with me.

As we pass a tour headed for the falls, I watch her pull her dark sunglasses down.

"You know, if I had good common sense, I'd say you're hiding out." Now that I know she's some superstar starlet who straight-up bolted from her life, curiosity has me pressing for more. In the interest of the ranch.

Her lips quirk with amusement. "Who says you have sense?"

"New hair, sunglasses, it ain't hard to put two and two together."

Reese lets out a long sigh. "Do you have anything else to do other than interrogate me?"

"Nope. You're a hot topic on the news."

"It's not rehab," she says quietly. "If you're wondering."

"I wasn't." She doesn't look like the type to need rehab. There's something soft, something sad about her. But just as I'm about to say that Reese steps into the road.

In front of a van.

"Look out." I grab her arm, hauling her back to my side. "Jesus, you trying to kill yourself?" The girl's a danger to herself, oblivious to whatever's going on around her.

"No," she snaps. "I'm not."

We glare at each other for a few seconds, and then resume our trek.

"I needed a break," she says, picking up the conversation. Her soft voice is clipped, like she's choosing how much to tell me.

I glance over at her. "Is that why my little brother's helping you?"

The dazzling smile on her face drops my insides.

My breath catches. Sharp, painful.

"You and Grady?" I love my little brother, but goddamn if for one second, I don't hate him.

She laughs. The first light and twinkly sound I've heard from her.

"No, he's a friend." Her smile fades, and her shoulders slump. "I wish I had more of those."

The video of Reese crying on stage flashes in front of my eyes. And I'm pretty sure she was crying last night when I brought her dinner, too.

I harden my heart. It's not the time to get sentimental.

"I think it was a bad idea to run," she goes on, pausing as I dip to grab a piece of trash from the grass and toss it in a trash can.

I arch a brow, hearing the unsaid. "But?"

She gives me a sad smile. "But I had to." She walks faster, shaking off whatever's in her head. "Now I'm fucked. I need money. My manager cut off my credit cards. I don't know how to access any of my accounts. I feel like an idiot."

I should tease her for being a spoiled princess, but the soft resignation, the desperation in her voice, fills me with unease.

She has to have money, right? She's a fucking superstar. For a second, I want to hunt down her manager and have words.

"Maybe you're not an idiot and he's an asshole," I grunt.

"He is." She tucks a lock of hair behind her ear. "He thinks I owe him because he made me."

I think of Jim Donovan. "A lot of people like that in the world."

"Yeah," she says quietly. "Unfortunately."

"Gotta be honest, honey. I've never heard of you before."

Reese gasps, but she doesn't look insulted, she looks pleased. "Good. My songs suck." A half-smile crosses her face. "They're all as fake as my hair."

That pulls a chuckle out of me.

Curious green eyes flick to mine. "I've never heard of you either, Ford 'Flamethrower' Montgomery." The way she drags it out, soft and teasing, has my cock twitching.

I give a dry laugh and shrug. "Once upon a time, I played ball."

"Why'd you stop?"

"Bad knees. Bad shoulders." *Bad life.*

She arches a brow. "And you retired to Montana?"

"Something like that," I rasp and leave it at that. I don't want to get into Savannah. The kid.

I slow my stride when we reach the barn. Newly built after the fire that hurt Ruby, it's even better and bigger than our last one.

"In here," I say with a flick of my chin.

We step inside to ice-cold air-conditioning. My tennis shoes sink into the hay and grit covering the floor. The smell of horse and manure waft from the stalls. I glance at Reese and find her standing in the doorway, arms crossed tight over her body.

I toss her a grin. "They don't bite."

Slowly, she struts inside and wrinkles her nose at the smell, lifting her sunglasses.

"These are the horses," I tell her, slapping Big Red's rump. "Spoiled as hell. We use them for trail rides, ranch work…" I pause, waiting for her to approach a stall. Most guests freak the fuck out when they see a horse. Instead, Reese hangs back, nerves all over her beautiful face.

A visible shudder wracks her thin frame. "I have a thing about horses."

"A thing?" I ask. Okay, call me curious.

She shies away, closer into a corner. Her shoulders hike up toward her ears. "I don't like them."

Of course she doesn't.

"How do you not like a horse?" I move to the next stall. Inside, my Appaloosa chuffs. "This little fucker is Eephus. He's tried to kill me numerous times. He's the most incompetent, useless gelding I've ever had the displeasure of meeting. And I still love the bastard."

Eephus whinnies, a demand for affection.

Reese makes a face at me. "What kind of name is Eephus?"

I mime tossing a ball. "Means a slow pitch with a high as fuck arc." Pride heats inside of me. "I used one on Phil Brenna and got the strikeout of the century."

A smile quirks her lips. "Is that your superpower? No shame?"

I arch a brow. "No fear."

Though her eyes are still wary, Reese takes a small step forward. The movement makes her bangles jingle, and Eephus stomps his feet, flaring his nostrils.

"Shit," I swear, holding out a firm hand to stop her. "Stay there."

Her face falls. "I'm sorry."

"Don't be sorry, just listen. Ground rules, okay?" I pet Eephus, calming him. "You don't go near the horses with those things on. You got me?" Frightened horses are a liability. Not to mention, I don't want her getting hurt. Another problem I don't need.

"Sure." Her golden hair catches the sunlight as she looks around the barn. "So, what do I do?"

"Take that hay there and move it up into that loft." I shake my head when she reaches for the pile. "Not with your hands."

"So helpful." She glares at me. "What should I use then?"

"This." I step toward her, pinning her against the wall to reach above her. She's at least five foot four, but I've got almost a foot on her. I stretch up, my libido roaring as my body sweeps against hers. Soft. Hot. Sexy as hell.

Fuck.

"Ford," she whispers, and damn if it's not like the snap of a rein.

I snatch the pitchfork off the wall and blow out a tense breath as I move back. I need to get out of her way, give us both space, before I do something I regret. Like kiss the fuck out of her.

Clearing my throat, I carefully hand Reese the pitchfork. My gaze trails over the pretty pink flush on her cheeks that matches her lips. "Use this to shovel the hay."

Our eyes remain locked until she turns away from me. "I'll get right to it."

I busy myself with the horses, adding fresh food to the stalls and checking on a pregnant mare due any day now.

When the pitchfork slices dangerously close to my shoulder, I whip around. "Christ, woman, you tryin' to impale me?" She's as reckless as she is beautiful.

Reese laughs, white teeth flashing. Even her smile is dazzling. "Would end all my problems, wouldn't it?"

"Get used to it, honey," I say, a wave of irritation washing over me. I don't like the effect she has on my chest.

A tight, dangerous feeling I ache to be rid of. "You're not gonna prance around the ranch all day. You want to stay, you have to earn your keep."

She flips me an exaggerated salute with a flick of her delicate wrist. "Whatever you say, *boss man*."

I set my jaw. "And when you're done with that—see that bucket. Go slop the pigs."

She recoils. Laughs right in my face. "I'm not doing that."

I lean in and give her a grin. "We'll see about that."

Crossing my arms, I watch as she gets to work. Her moves are awkward and reluctant. She's all legs and attitude as she scoops hay from the pile and moves it to the loft.

A darkness settles over me. I swallow hard, tamping down the anger, the ache. She reminds me of Savannah. Spoiled. Bright. Trouble.

Dangerous, beautiful trouble.

I need Reese off this ranch and out of my mind.

Because this is a bad fucking idea. She's too close, poking at something sharp inside of me. Something hungry. Something so pure it hurts to acknowledge.

Reese looks up, hopeful. "How am I doing?"

"Fine," I grumble, already heading for the exit. Trying to pretend I don't see the crestfallen look on her face.

If I have anything to say about it, she won't be here long.

～

Satisfied Reese and her high heels have it under control, I stroll toward the pasture. There, inside the training ring, are Wyatt and the grim reaper of cowgirls, Fallon McGraw.

My brother hangs back near the fence on his horse as she runs hers into a froth.

I hop the fence and sit as Wyatt trots my way. With light blue eyes and hair as shaggy as mine, he looks like a younger, leaner version of me.

He takes one look at my face and asks, "Problems?"

"Yeah, I got a problem. A five-foot-four blonde in need of an attitude adjustment."

"Adds spice to the working day," Wyatt drawls.

"I put Reese to work," I tell him. "She's in the barn cleaning up the hayloft. Think it'll be good for her."

Wyatt chuckles. "Spoken like Dad."

I clock his bandaged elbow. "You seen a doctor for that?"

"Don't need one," he murmurs, absentmindedly.

I follow his gaze. Locked on Fallon.

"How she'd ride in Vegas?" I ask.

Wyatt shrugs. "Reckless. Bruised her ribs all to hell." He doesn't sound happy about it.

"You need anything?"

Wyatt looks at me briefly. "What?"

"You got cut off the night you called me." I squint at him. "Said you did something stupid."

He hesitates before a crooked grin tips his lips. "Lost all my money at blackjack. Planned to ask you for a loan."

I bark a laugh. "Keep dreaming, little brother."

Davis may be my twin, my better, more noble half, but Wyatt and I are cut from the same cloth. Adrenaline junkies. Smart mouths. I'm damn proud of the kid even if all I've done half my life is torment him.

Fallon speeds by us on her horse, Lawless. Dust and grit cloud the air.

"How's that dirt taste?" I ask Wyatt.

"Girl rides like she's immune to gravity," he mutters. The brim of his Stetson casts shadows across his face, his eyes.

Even without it, the kid's got shadows.

Ever since Fallon was kidnapped and attacked last year, she's been jumpy as fuck. Wild as hell.

If anything could have brought her and Wyatt back together, it was the mess with Aiden King. Only Fallon took about ten steps back from Wyatt and anyone who cared about her. Started sleeping in her truck, or at Davis and Dakota's. Taking risks with her riding. Surrounding herself with Pappy Starr and her entourage of managers, who are all ready to bet on the next big thing. And that's her.

It's taken a toll on the entire family, including my little brother. Wyatt misses her.

The only time he can get close to her is on the rodeo circuit. Which is why he's hesitant to retire. He thinks if he's there, he can protect her.

"Fuck." I whistle as Fallon flies by us in a blast of dust. "That horse is running like he pays the vet bills."

"Shit," Wyatt hisses.

Fallon, her horse stationary, is standing on top of its saddle. She has her arms out, her face to the sun.

"She's takin' too many risks," Wyatt hisses. Blowing out a breath of air, he tears a hand through his hair. Only when Fallon slides off Lawless's backside does Wyatt relax.

Fallon McGraw's guardian angel is exhausted.

And so is my little brother.

"Listen, kid." I lean in, drop my voice. Gentler than I was last year. "You're overcompensating for what happened last year, and you can't do it."

Wyatt wishes he had been there to save Fallon. Hell, we all do. But living in the past won't change a damn thing.

If only I could take my own advice.

"You don't know shit," Wyatt says, but his words don't hold any real heat.

"I know that girl is the wind," I tell him. "You can't catch her or babysit her when you gotta worry about your own damn self."

Wyatt stares into the sun, looking pained, but he's listening.

Fuck. I'm not good at this. I can talk to my therapist about my feelings, but talking to my brothers… it's complicated. It fucks me up every damn time.

Still, I have to do my best for my little brother. I put him on the edge of that cliff last year by goading him about Fallon. If I can make up for it, be there for him and listen to whatever comes out of his stupid mouth, I'll do it. I owe him. Because that goofy kid pranking the Wolfington's two years ago is gone, and I can't be sure he's ever coming back. Not unless he and Fallon fix their shit.

I nod at his elbow. "This why you keep busting your stupid ass up? Watching out for Fallon?"

Wyatt opens his mouth, but then quickly shuts it as Fallon and Lawless approach.

"Hey, Ford."

"Hey, honey." I take off my ball cap, set it back on. "That was an insanely risky move, cowgirl." Fallon and I have always had an honest friendship. She's like a feral little sister of mine. I respect her for her risk and her heart.

"Lawless had it." Fallon pats her horse's flank. "Isn't that right?"

Wyatt scowls. "Horse has it until he doesn't."

"If I have to fuck around and find out, so be it," she says with a stone-cold expression, staring right at Wyatt.

I roll my eyes. Fallon will do anything possible not to get help from a man.

A kind of manic energy radiates between Fallon and Wyatt. As they bicker, I check my phone.

One missed text. Unknown number.

Do you have an answer for my daddy?

Fuck.

It feels like a bullet has torn through my chest.

I can hear her voice. See the tap of those impatient nails. Seven damn years now and Savannah still has the power to piss me off.

If this is Jim Donovan's tactic to get me to take that job, fuck that guy.

"Hey, uh, man."

My head snaps up, and I shove my phone back in my pocket.

Wyatt jabs a finger, and I glance over to where he's pointing.

Reese stands near the barn, pitchfork stabbed into the earth, an iced coffee in her hand. Sam, our ranch hand, chats her up. Un-fucking-believable. One bat of her lashes and Sam's already bringing her a gallon of Starbucks.

My hands curl into fists.

Like a flip switched, anger bubbles up inside of me. Maybe it's the text, maybe it's the way she's laughing, tossing her hair and batting those lashes.

Women like Savannah think the world should be handed to them on a silver platter. That they get it for free. That the world owes them. If Reese wants some life lessons, she's come to the right fucking place.

Iced coffee in hand, Reese storms by me and it pisses me off that I take a real long second to admire that perky ass of hers.

Wyatt laughs. "I got Tylenol in my pack because that woman's gonna give you a headache."

I hop off the fence. "Give me your rope."

My brother arches an amused brow. "You sure?"

I grit my teeth. "Give it to me."

Wyatt passes it over and I coil the rope up tightly, grabbing the smaller circle and threading it until I have a loop. Holding the coil in my left hand, I lift it overhead and swing it around and around until I find a smooth rhythm.

Then, with Reese in my sights, I release the loop.

Bullseye.

A good clean catch.

Wyatt cackles.

I grin. Then, I cinch the rope looped around her torso.

Reese screams.

"Ford, you're a fuckface," Fallon says.

Reese teeters in her heels, and one quick tug of the rope has her on her ass in the middle of the field. She's barefoot now, her high heels plunged deep into the earth, and her iced coffee a milky puddle in the grass.

"You lassoed me!" Reese shrieks. Her chest heaves. "Like livestock."

I stride toward her. She's a filthy mess. Blonde hair sticks to her sweaty brow, and the dress she wears slides high over her tan thighs.

I look down at her. "Moo moo, baby."

Her pillowy lower lip juts out.

"This is a ranch. We don't cry."

"I'm not."

"Strutting those long legs up on stage ain't a job, honey. Neither is bossing around the help or getting special treatment."

She delivers a look forged in ice. "Are you always such an asshole?"

Impatience and anger get the best of me. "No, Reese, I'm not. Do you want to know why I'm an asshole? Because you're a brat. Because I don't want to be babysitting your spoiled ass the entire summer. I don't want to miss out on fishing and baseball because guess what? Those are two things I really fucking love. I sure as hell don't want you to stress out my brothers because they have enough on their fucking plates at the moment. In fact, the last thing I want to do is spend time with a spoiled, pampered, pain-in-the-ass princess."

She stares at me, her lower lip trembling.

I cross my arms. "C'mon, scream and shout, blondie."

But she doesn't. Instead, she picks herself up, dusts her hands on the stomach of her glittery dress, and in the smallest voice I've ever heard says, "I hate you."

She grabs her empty coffee cup like she's fully prepared to lob it in my face and then stares into the dregs. A tear slips down her face.

Without another word, Reese turns, and walks toward the chalet, shoeless.

A muscle jerks in my jaw.

Fallon socks me in the arm. "*You* are an asshole, Ford." Another punch so hard I rock back on my boots. "Seriously, go fuck yourself and your high horse." With venom in her eyes, she flips me off and storms for the ring.

The disappointed look Wyatt gives me scalds. "I don't know, Ford. This ain't you, man."

It's not. I think of the text burning a hole in my back pocket.

I glance toward the barn.

The concrete floor is bare and clean, every blade of hay stacked perfectly in the loft.

I couldn't even do it better.

An ache twists in my gut. I tear a hand through my hair. "Fuck."

I am an asshole.

7

Reese

MY COWBOY BABYSITTER HATES ME.
Ford Montgomery thinks I'm an immature, spoiled brat.

Not even the shower has rejuvenated me. I can still feel the iced coffee all over my lap. The sharp scratch of hay. Hear the whinny of those damn horses. Even though I was scared to death being around them, I stuck it out. I didn't run.

I slip on a robe, tousle my wet hair, and slam back a sugar-free energy drink. My measly purchases from The Corner Store all sit on the kitchen counter. The carbonated liquid settles heavy in my belly. I need something electric in my system, otherwise, I'll just crash-land somewhere sad.

I hate it here. Hate Ford Montgomery and his sharp stinging words.

The last thing I want to do is spend time with a spoiled, pampered, pain-in-the-ass princess.

Most of all, I hate that he's right. I don't even want to spend my day with me. I tried hard today. I shoveled that fucking hay. But it wasn't good enough. I never am.

To everyone who knows me, all I am is some shallow pop princess with a fake twang.

Every awful emotion crashes into me. How did I think I could do this? Heal? Be a better person? Because I can't.

I stare at my face in the mirror. My hair is curled

beyond reason and for a second, I'm six years old, singing "Delta Dawn." My mother is clapping along, my father handing me sheet music to my favorite song. Back when I felt like I could do anything. Especially survive.

I pace the chalet, stopping at a window to open the blinds. Though it's 9 p.m., the sun has barely set. It's like it wants to stay up as long as it can. Briefly, my mind lights on the lake I haven't yet seen, but it's not what I want.

Two sides to every coin. And that's how I feel. Halved. A walking contradiction. Old Reese wants to go out and disobey. Dance on bars and drink whiskey. Do anything I want, anytime I want. Room service at 3 a.m. An impromptu flight to Paris.

This Reese, Ranch Reese, New Leaf Reese, should stay here. I'm in hiding, right? I should be a good girl. Sober up. Stay sane. Recharge. Re-live.

Maybe there are two of me. The Reese I created to survive in the real world, and the Reese I get to keep for myself. The hidden Reese that no one knows.

It doesn't matter. No one wants to know the real me.

I don't even know the real me.

Panic builds on top of my lungs, my heart, my chest. I can't breathe. I need to breathe.

Out. I need to go out.

I dress fast. Stilettos. The sexiest dress I brought with me. Makeup. Glitter all over my body. Gold eye shadow.

When I step outside the chalet, my lungs release. I can breathe again.

I scan the dusk-lit field. The chalet is set so far out, it's desolate. A pang hits me that I'm not on the ranch. That another person doesn't want me around. I shake the grim thought out of my head.

I spot a ranch hand headed toward a busted truck and rush up to him. "Hey, hi," I say. "I'm Jane."

It's the same ranch hand who brought me my coffee. It was Ruby's idea. A sweet gesture, even if it pissed off Ford. Good. Whatever his problem is, I want no part of it.

"Can you take me into town?" I gulp air. "A bar. With whiskey."

His eyes graze over my hips before landing on my face. "Whiskey, huh?"

"Yes."

His grizzled features appear amused, but he nods. "Get in the truck."

Hitching rides with strangers. It's quick, impulsive, and feels so much like the old Reese I want to cry.

⌒

Nowhere is a dive bar about thirty minutes from Runaway Ranch in a small town called Resurrection. Sam dropped me off with the prophetic words of warning, "Two o'clock means you run."

I weave through the high-top tables littered with beer cans and ashtrays, headed toward the bar. A jukebox plays outlaw country. Willie and Waylon and Johnny Cash. The scent of whiskey and stale peanuts lingers in the air.

It's not a Vegas nightclub, but it'll do.

"Whiskey and beer," I tell the bartender as I settle onto a stool. I have no idea how I'm paying for it, but that's a problem for Drunk Reese.

"You look familiar," a man next to me says, giving me an approving nod. He wears flannel and a trucker cap.

"Instagram influencer," I lie. "Knitting."

"I don't have Instagram."

I bat my lashes at him. "Lucky you." I lift my beer. "Cheers."

We knock the lips of our cans and chug at the same time.

I finish first.

"Damn, girl, you can put those away," he says, closing the distance between us. I bristle. He smells like tobacco and sour body odor. On his face is a leering grin. He gestures at the bartender, who slides another beer and a shot of whiskey in front of me.

I take a deep breath and debate. I know what the guy's trying to do. But I want that distraction, don't I?

My body is begging my mind to stop thinking, so I silence it with a shot. I down the beer in three quick gulps. The sharp smell of yeast suddenly has me flashing back to Gavin. My first record deal when I turned twelve. His sharp, impatient gaze as I signed the contract. A Vegas nightclub on my eighteenth birthday, and the never-ending flow of liquor. Kyler handing me a whiskey the minute I woke up from a hangover. Sex I don't remember. My stomach curdles at the vile nostalgia.

I don't want to be that person, do I? But I don't know how to stop.

I want to be free. But all today showed me is I don't know how.

The guy's hand slides up my leg.

My heart beats crazily, but I don't stop him.

"Everything okay here?"

I glance up at the disgruntled, growling voice. A surly, bald-headed man wearing a leather-vest and sporting a long white beard stands behind the bar. He gives an icy stare to the guy next to me before shifting his attention to me with a look of concern.

"You from around here?"

"No." I think fast. "I'm a…a guest at Runaway Ranch. Jane."

"Jane." He sets a glass of water in front of me. "You need anything, you holler."

From the corner comes the faint strains of a guitar. I swivel on my stool, wobbling a bit thanks to the whiskey. An older woman with feather earrings tunes her acoustic guitar. A mellow country song from the '70s. Goose bumps run up my arms.

She's who I want to be.

Resolve fills me.

I have to call Gavin. There's no time like the present. No time like liquid courage.

Squaring my shoulders, I pull out my phone and dial.

"Hi, Gavin."

"It's about fucking time," he seethes.

When I hear that sharp snap of anger in his voice, my heart beats so fast that my lungs seize up. Any hope I had that he was worried about me is effectively dashed.

"Where are you?"

"It doesn't matter where I am."

"I need you to think clearly right now, Reese. I'm willing to forgive you if you come back. You got your tantrum out of your fucking system. Now come home."

"You fixed it. You told the world I'm in rehab just like last time. No one cares."

"Everyone cares," he retorts. "The winter tour. The album. You're supposed to host the ACMs, for Christ's sake."

"They'll find a replacement."

"There are consequences, Reese. Big, important consequences." He sighs. "Think of the fans."

"I've thought about the fans since I was seven, Gavin. It's my turn to be selfish."

A small part of me feels like a failure. Because I should want this. Fame. Fortune. But I don't. I never did.

"We have contracts to sign. Meetings to attend. Money to make. We need to capitalize on everything you can do. Not play vacation."

"The meetings can wait, Gavin. I need this." My voice tremors. I can feel the thin thread of exhaustion inside of me stretching tighter. "I need a break. I can't be locked up this way."

"Locked up." He snorts. "Please. You have everything. You've got the voice, Reese. Those fucking legs. That body. Money. What else do you want?"

My eyes flutter shut as his words all jumble together. *Not true. Not freedom. Not my life.*

"I don't want this, Gavin." I grip the phone tight. "Please. I don't want to go back to—to before Muirwood."

"Unbelievable. After everything I've given you, everything I've done for you, and this is how you act? You should be fucking grateful."

I squeeze my eyes shut. My body hurts. *Be grateful.* I should be, but I can't. The sadness pours into me and I can't shake it off, no matter how hard I try.

My eyes snap open. Anger flares through me. "Be grateful? You turned my cards off," I hiss.

"And it got you to call."

"I'm not calling for money," I lie. "I got a job."

"A job? Where?" Now Gavin sounds suspicious.

I smirk. "Face it. I don't need you."

"I should fucking sue your ass for breach of contract."

"Am I in breach, Gavin?" I go for a cool tone and glance at the man next to me. "Threaten me all you want. I currently have a lawyer looking over my contract right now."

Over the line, Gavin sucks in a breath.

"Say hi, Joe." I stick my phone in the man's face.

"Hi—"

I rip back the phone. "See?" I say. "Don't fuck with me."

Gavin's quiet. Too long.

Memory pulls at me. Ten years ago. The day I signed our contract is blurry, but I picked up that pen and gave Gavin control over everything. I never asked questions. But Gavin's uneasy silence, and the pit in my stomach, tells me I should have.

A cold sweat breaks out over my palms. I really need to get that fucking contract.

"How long?" His voice is calm and even. "How long do you need?"

I exhale. My heart trembles, like it can barely believe my win. "The summer?"

"The summer. I understand."

My eyes grow big. "You do?"

"Listen, I'm just worried, Reese."

"You are?"

"Of course, I am. You're so special to me. My shiny little shooting star."

At his words, hot tears fill my eyes.

It's the exhausting fight of loving Gavin and hating him at the same time. Being suspicious and trusting him. Because who else do I have to trust, to love? It's like trying to see beyond the universe. You can't.

"Don't worry, Reese. I just want to help you. I understand how hard it must be, but I will help you. You can trust me, okay?"

"Okay," I whisper.

"I'll do this for you, but you do something for me," he says, his voice low and strained. "Take your fucking pills, you hear me? Check in every few days. The summer will go by before you know it, and you'll be home. And we'll work everything out." Gavin sounds like he's trying to convince himself. "Including the contract."

I hang up the phone. Even though I should feel thrilled by this small victory, all I feel is deflated. Because eventually, I have to go back.

Chest heaving, I stare at the drink set in front of me. Over my head, the black hole shimmers.

A hand slides up my back, and I scrunch my eyes shut at the foreign groping sensation.

You're okay. Be brave, Reese. Be brave.

Tottering on my stool, I shoot back my shot, spin around, and grab the man's collar. "Let's dance."

8

Ford

"**S**HE MADE IT?"

"Oh, she made it all right." Grunting, I tighten the battery cables on the tractor. "She's a piece of work."

"She is." Over the line, Grady chuckles, but he doesn't sound annoyed. He sounds affectionate.

A screw twists in my chest. I slam the hood of the tractor down. I'm pissed at myself. Pissed at the way I treated Reese. I've never acted like more of an asshole. Savannah's text triggered emotions I thought I worked through.

But it's no excuse. I fucked up today.

Ever since she stormed away this afternoon, I've had a head full of steam. I can't get the sight of her tears out of my damn mind. I'm working my way up to an apology, working my way up to telling her she did a great job today.

Bar fights. Little brothers. I thought I knew trouble until Reese landed on the ranch.

"How's she doin' on the ranch?" Grady asks.

"I, uh, might have taught her a lesson."

"What kind of lesson?" He sounds suspicious.

I tug a hand through my hair. "A ranch lesson."

Grady swears when I finish telling him about today. "Ford, you dickhead. I told you she needs help. Not some asshole screaming at her. She already gets that from her manager."

My gut twists. I remember the dark circles beneath her eyes the day she first got here. The relief that blanketed her when she saw her chalet.

I should have given that girl some grace, and I didn't.

There's a long pause before I ask, "Is that why she's running?"

Fuck me. I want to know.

"I think so," Grady admits. "I think she needs a lot of rest. I don't think she'd be okay if she came back. I think she'd do something…unhealthy."

I go cold all over. I had pegged Reese Austin as a spoiled brat, but now I'm not so sure.

"She needs a safe place to stay. Maybe a hug."

"A hug, huh?" My eyes drift to the open garage doors, then beyond them, to the ranch.

Reese.

Grady chuckles. "Just be nice to her. I think she needs it."

Before I know it, my boots are carrying me across the ranch. "Just say you're sorry, you asshole," I grumble to myself. "It ain't hard. You're a cowboy. Own it when you're fucking wrong."

It's what my dad told me. What I strived to be. A cowboy. Honest. Loyal. Courageous. Someone who never takes advantage of others or goes back on their word. Something I've forgotten these last few years. Losing Savannah, then losing myself, watching my brothers fall in love, it all wore me down.

Mid-internal-pep talk, I see Sam headed toward the staff cabins. He slows his truck to a crawl, and I come to a stop beside his driver's side window.

"You headed to the chalets?" he asks, one denim-clad arm hanging out the window.

Impatience rattles beneath my skin. "Yeah. I am."

"Girl's not there," he grunts.

"Where the fuck is she?" I growl, my chest rising with each word.

Sam grins. "Took her to Nowhere."

Less than twenty minutes later, I slam into Nowhere, cursing the atom bomb that is my night. Cursing the blonde bombshell that is Reese Austin. I could be in my garage with my cat, but I'm playing babysitter. Twenty-four hours on the ranch and this girl's already blown up my world.

Beef cranes his bald head, suspicion furrowing his brow. "Wyatt here?"

"Relax," I say, and he breathes a sigh of relief. "Coast is clear."

No fighting for me. Not since I put my hand through the jukebox last year.

Beef polishes a glass. "Drink?"

"No." I sidestep a couple dancing and belly up to the bar. "I'm here for—for someone."

Beef tosses a waitress a can of Bud, while saying, "You here for Jane?"

"Jane?" I follow his eyeline and see bangles, sharp cheekbones, green eyes.

Reese.

She's in a booth next to Lionel Wolfington. With a cheesy smile on his face, the asshole looks like he struck gold. Reese looks it, too. Her shimmery gold dress rides so high on her toned thighs I can see her panties.

Nude lace. Fuck me.

I turn to Beef. "How many drinks has she had?"

"Five," Beef grunts, lifting a wary brow. "Not sure how she's still standing."

"I need an order of fries," I tell Beef. "Now."

When I glance back over, Lionel's hand is sliding up, stroking over those long, tan legs.

A territorial rage consumes me.

I am going to fucking kill him.

"Goddamnit," Beef mutters as I tear away from the bar.

"Ain't gotta stay out all night," Lionel's saying as I approach them. "Take the party back to my place."

My fists clench. I doubt he cares that she's three sheets to the wind.

"Not happening," I say.

Reese brazenly meets my eyes. Her cheeks are bright pink from alcohol. "Ugh, you."

"Yeah, *ugh*, me." I stare at her. "Stop acting like a brat and get up."

"Rude." A smile tilts her lips, and she extends a hand. "This is—"

"I know who he is," I snap.

Batting her long lashes, Reese curls closer to him. Lionel squeezes her shoulder. She's fucking with me, but she doesn't fool me. I catch the flash of panic on her face when Lionel's hand grips her leg even tighter.

Lionel laughs, the barbed wire tattoo around his neck flexing. "What bug crawled up your ass, Montgomery?"

I glare at him. "Wrong answer, asshole."

"You're both boring." She lifts a hand, causing her bangles to rattle. "I'm going to dance." With that, she stands and heads to the dance floor.

Lionel looks pissy. "Thanks a lot, Montgomery."

I jab a finger his way. "You don't fucking touch that girl."

His lips curl and he rises to stand.

I turn to go, but before I can walk away, he says, "I know who she is."

I whip my head to him and slam him back against the wall. "Keep your mouth shut about her."

If people pull out their phones, it'll be over. She doesn't want to be found even if she is doing a piss-poor job at covering her tracks.

"What's in it for me?"

A muscle clenches in my jaw. I want to hit him, but I can't. We have a tentative truce with the Wolfingtons. If I fuck that up, I have to deal with Davis.

"Here." I reach into my pocket, then shove a wad of bills against his chest. "A hundred bucks a day until that girl leaves."

"Deal." Lionel's mouth parts in a sneer. "Although you might want to make sure she doesn't blow her own cover."

Letting go of his collar, I follow his gaze and groan. Reese is at the jukebox, swinging her hips to an old Townes Van Zandt song.

"Goddamn it."

I storm over to her.

"You got a quarter?" she breathes, eyes on the jukebox. I shelled out a pretty penny last year to replace it.

"One song." I drop it in the slot. "Then we go."

Ignoring me, Reese selects a number. The bar fills with Loretta Lynn's melancholy twang.

I lean into her. "Newsflash, honey. Hanna Montana could do a better job at keeping her identity a secret."

"I don't care anymore." She straightens up and stares

at me, emerald eyes flashing. "Go," she says. "No one asked you to come. I have plans to drink, dance, and get drunk."

"You're already drunk," I growl.

Hands on the side of the jukebox, Reese closes her eyes and dances. My cock flexes as she sways her body. Unfortunately, every eye in the bar is on her as well. They can smell fresh blood from miles away.

"Get over here." Hand on her elbow, I guide her to the bar, forcing my breath to steady. After I settle her on a bar stool, I ask, "How many beers have you had?"

"Nunya."

"Nunya?"

She laughs. "Nunya business."

I roll my eyes. "Real mature." I sit beside her. "You've had five beers because Beef over there has been counting."

"*Traitor,*" she mouths to Beef, who looks offended. The pout of her pillowy lips makes her look simultaneously haughty and innocent.

"Anyone ever told you that you drink too much?"

"Hmmm. Several people and they're all dead right now."

I cut her a look. "How were you planning on getting back to the ranch?"

Her lips curve, feline. "I wasn't."

If she's saying it to bait me, it's working. A primal caveman possessiveness overtakes me. Not to mention my cock's a tire iron. This girl's playing a dangerous game of chicken.

"You ain't gonna be a good-old boys' girl," I warn, rubbing my jaw when all I really want to do is punch a hole in the wall. "Not tonight, honey." I sigh and lean in. "Listen, Reese. These guys aren't for you."

Her beautiful face tilts back to look at me. "Oh, and I suppose you know someone who is?"

Yeah. Me.

But I stop myself short of saying it. That would be a big mistake.

Beef sets a beer down, and I level a finger. "You give her one more goddamn drink…"

"Bye," Reese chirps suddenly. She hops off the bar stool and shoves past me.

I curse and attempt to follow, but Floyd Gunderson blocks my path.

"Selling my ranch, Ford. Sure am."

"Well, hell, remind me to put in an offer on that." I put my hands on his shoulders, push him backward. "But right now, I gotta go."

Craning my neck, I scan the bar for Reese. Thank Christ my brothers aren't here to witness the shitshow. Lord knows I'd get an earful about how a grown woman is handing me my ass.

My pulse roars in my ears as I spot her clumsily two-stepping with Travis Wheaton, a local rancher. He drives a Cybertruck, so he's automatically our town's biggest dipshit. I watch as he leans in close to her, his hand sliding low on her back before gripping her ass.

I don't fucking think so.

"Fuck this," I mutter as I stalk across the bar. Reese either came here to try my patience or give me a goddamn heart attack.

I wedge myself between them, breaking Travis's hold on her ass. I don't miss the way Reese takes an immediate step back.

"Time to go," I say, curling my hand around her arm.

Travis lets out a short laugh. "Fuck off, Montgomery. I'm having a conversation with—"

"Jane." I step closer. "And it doesn't look like a conversation. It looks like you're copping a feel. And if you know what's fucking good for you, you'll leave her alone."

Travis holds up his hands. "Whatever, man."

I glance to my right.

Reese is gone.

I whip around. Christ, where is she now? It's like trying to chase a cyclone. Wrangling my brothers is a pain in the ass, but this girl makes them look easy.

Travis's eyes lift, and a laugh erupts from his belly. He elbows one of his cronies. "Get a load of this."

I follow his gaze and understand why that vein in Davis's temple always looks like it's on its last nerve.

Reese is strutting her stuff across the bar top like it's her own personal stage.

Beef stares up at her, his eyes grazing over her long, long legs.

In any other scenario, I'd probably fight back a smile over the fact this girl doesn't give a shit. She's star power incarnate and has my small town slack-jawed and gaping. But she's in hiding, she's in trouble, and most importantly, she's drunk as a goddamn skunk.

I know unhealthy coping mechanisms when I see them. And Reese is a walking red flag.

"Want a drink, Country Boy?" she asks when I reach the bar.

"Get off the bar, Reese," I order. My gaze travels up her toned thighs to those nude panties. If I can see them, everyone else can. I hate that idea.

She looks down and bats her dark lashes. "Have you ever danced on top of a bar? It's actually quite fulfilling."

I grit my teeth, hating my life right now. I'm the fun one, so why does this girl bring out the Davis side of me? Protective. Bossy as fuck.

My fingers dig into the bar top. "One more chance."

"Or you'll what?"

"Either I burn the bar down or you come with me."

She grins. That coy little smile that revs me up. "Burn it down then."

I open my mouth, ready to tell her she's a brat, when some random fucker slides his grubby hand up her calf. And then he leans in and licks it.

He licks her fucking leg.

Reese gasps and stumbles backward, her pretty face twisted in disgust.

Motherfucker.

I've been good the last goddamn year, and now this guy's gonna make me start over.

I turn to Beef, rolling up my shirtsleeves. "Who are these assholes?"

"Townies." Beef shakes his head, even though he and I both know it's pointless. "Ford. You're not Wyatt," he warns. "I just got a new sign."

I roll my neck out. Flex a fist. "Give me a shot."

"Ford."

"Give me a goddamn shot, Beef."

He does it, and I shoot it back.

Then I glance over at the man. He's staring up at Reese like he's already got her in his bed. "Hey, buddy, you like that girl?"

His ugly face grins at me. "Yeah, man, she's got a real nice p—"

I fucking punch him. My knuckles shatter his jaw, and I grin at the satisfying crunch of bone. He stumbles back and hits the ground.

Reese gasps. "Ford, what—"

Screams pierce the air. The music from the jukebox has kicked into some frenetic country song. I glance behind me and realize a new fight has broken out.

I'm shoved forward into the bar. Reese screams and drops to her knees, blonde hair tumbling wildly around her face. Her knuckles turn white as she grips the bar top.

"Don't move," I tell her. She's safe where she is. I don't want anyone trampling her.

My heart beats hard. I love a goddamn fight as much as Saturday night.

Beef has the fire extinguisher out. He catches a townie in the face with a harsh spray of foam. A taller guy nearly catches me in the jaw when I turn my head, but I grab him by his shirt and shove him into the wall. I spin around and take in the chaos.

My heart ratchets up its beat.

There are too many people crowding our space, throwing things.

I have to get Reese out of here. That lone thought takes over my brain.

I don't think twice. I grab Reese around the waist and pull her off the bar. Toss her over my shoulder.

She shoves at my back, making huffy little sounds of protests. "What are you doing?"

"Protecting you, princess." I hate the way she feels against me. Soft, warm skin. The curve of her hip on my shoulder. Her sharp nails digging into my arm. It's sensory overload on my libido.

Reese squirms. "Put me down." Then she screams. "Oh my god! Watch out!"

When I see a leather jacket-clad biker incoming, I greet him with an arm bar. He lands flat on his back, groaning. Reese yelps, jerking in my arms as I whip around. I slide my hand over her ass to keep her steady as I maneuver us through the crowd.

"You want me to put you down or get you out of here in one piece?" I grin because she can't see me. Feisty little thing. "What do you want me to do?"

"Go," she yells. "Go!"

I take a trained breath and muscle my way through the chaos. By the time we make it outside, she's quiet. Or passed out. I can't tell.

Dick aching, I slide her down my body until her heels touch the pavement. My hands stay on her hips. I hate to let her go. Hate to have her anywhere except my arms.

For one long second, we stare at each other, our faces inches apart. Too close, not close enough. The air is so taut, so electric, I can feel it buzzing from her to me. A live wire of want.

Normally, I'd chase this girl. But I'm not a prince and I don't have a white horse. I'm a cowboy with baggage. I'm born to run. There's no sunset in this future.

With a sharp gasp, Reese pushes away from me. She teeters on her heels, and then her eyes roll back as her legs buckle.

I catch her around the waist. "Whoa. Easy, easy."

Face pressed against my chest, she moans and grips my shirt, trying to pull herself up. "I drank too much."

I choke down a quiet laugh. "Honey, you drank a saloon."

I lift her in my arms and carry her through the parking lot. When we reach the truck, I gently settle her in the passenger seat. After buckling her seatbelt, I climb in beside her and lower the windows. She sits there, emotionless, blonde hair like a halo around her head.

I dig under the seat and find a bottle of Gatorade. I hold it out. "Drink this."

She sniffs.

Fuck. If she cries…

When her focus returns to me, silver lines her eyes. "You didn't have to come and get me," she whispers, accepting the Gatorade. "I would have found my way back."

I turn out of the parking lot, leaving the bright neon of Nowhere in my rearview mirror. "I wouldn't be so sure about that. Do you ever think about what someone could do to you when you drink?"

Reese chugs the Gatorade and wipes her lips with an exaggerated gusto that makes me smile. She leans her head back against the seat. "I just wanted to dance. No one likes me here. Especially after today."

"Nothing wrong with dancing. What's wrong is those guys with their hands all over you." I shake my head, back to irritated. "You threw a glass of water in my face for calling you *honey*, but you let Lionel Wolfington put his fucking paws all over you."

Her lower lip trembles. "It doesn't matter what they do to me. Everyone's already done their worst."

A chill goes through me. The way this girl talks.

"You shouldn't let people touch you without your

permission." I still want to kill that creep who licked her leg. Disinfect it the second I get her back to the ranch.

I think of the way she acted tonight. The way she accepted their hands all over her body. Something tells me it's part of her job. And it bothers me. A fucking lot.

"You did." She sits up, turning to laser me with a look of devastation. "You lassoed me."

I flex my fingers on the steering wheel. "You're right. I did."

Tonight is on me. All of it. I miscalculated how much of an asshole I was to her. If I had known she was on the precipice of something this dark, I never would have pushed her. Goddamn it.

Her expression twists, caught somewhere between hope, pain, and suspicion. "Is that an apology?"

"Yeah." I look her straight in the eyes. "It is. I'm sorry, Reese. I never should have done that to you."

She doesn't reply, just turns her head toward the passenger window. Cool night air fills the truck and neither of us speaks. Soon I'm turning onto the old county road.

I reach over and flip the radio to my favorite station. A warbling voice croons through the speakers.

"Conway Twitty."

I glance over at her, surprised she's still awake. I expected her to pass out the second her head hit the seat.

Eyes closed, she says, "I love old country songs. My parents and I used to sing 'em at the bars when I was a kid." A soft, hollow nostalgia fills her voice.

"That's what you did before you were famous?"

"Travelin' band." She smiles. "We played in dive bars across the south. That's how we made our money. When we needed more, my daddy made guitars. We made something out of nothing."

I pass the ranch, not wanting to slow the conversation. She's drunk, but she's finally opening up.

"What about school?"

"Mmm, homeschooled." She cracks an eye. "That explains me, right?"

I chuckle. "An encyclopedia couldn't explain you."

Wistfulness clouds her voice. "The peach trees were my only friends. I'd sing to them, and we'd talk for hours."

"Where'd you grow up, honey?"

"Georgia."

I almost steer the truck off the goddamn road. Another tick on the asshole meter. All this time, I assumed she was faking her accent.

That fucking faint drawl. Blonde. Southern. Beautiful. A lethal combination for me.

"A small town outside of Atlanta. We had a peach farm."

"I'm from Wildheart."

"I've heard of it."

"How'd you end up in LA? In…"

"The bowels of hell?" She doesn't look at me, just wraps her arms around her waist. "My parents gave me to Gavin."

I shake my head like I've heard her wrong. "You wanna say that again?"

She shrugs like it's obvious. "He saw me singing in a dive bar and offered my parents the chance to make a star out of me. We needed the money and they…they turned me over. Like I didn't matter."

My head spins. They gave away their own fucking kid?

I swallow the boulder in my throat. "Shit—Reese…"

"It doesn't matter, Ford. No one wanted me then, no wants me now."

It's a throwaway comment, but something about it twists my gut.

"It's good with Gavin. At least it was." Her shoulders sag as if defeated. "Back when I liked my life."

"Is that what you're doing here? New life?"

"Something like that. Maybe I'll be plain Jane, and I'll matter to someone out there in the wilds of Montana."

I soften when I glance over at her. She stares out the window, her wild curls fanned out over the passenger seat. "Nothin' plain about you, honey."

"I wish there was," she murmurs. "Sometimes I feel so far from the little girl on that Georgia farm singing country songs with her mama and daddy just to earn a buck. Sometimes I feel so…so…"

"Lonely?"

"Lost," she says.

My stomach bottoms out. Instinct bellows at me to ask more, to comfort her, but she's quiet, her eyes closed, so I leave it at that.

I turn toward the ranch at last, my truck rattling down the long gravel road. Despite telling myself she should go back to her chalet, I head for my place.

I park and exit the truck. The night settles around me as I cross to the passenger door, leaning over to unbuckle her seat belt.

She opens her huge green eyes and looks up at me. We're close. Inches apart. Her long lashes bat, and her gaze lowers to my lips.

"Hi, Country Boy," she whispers.

I should hate the nickname—hate what it does to me.

How it carves me into fucking pieces, making my heart still and sped up at the same time.

"Hi." I stroke the sweaty hair off her brow.

My chest hitches. Up close, guard down, she's stunning.

"I'll carry you," I say, snapping out of the hungry trance. She giggles and lifts her arms. "Carry away." I move closer, an arm wrapping around her slender waist. She smells like petrichor and peaches. Sadness and light. The juxtaposition has me off kilter for a minute.

Then her velvety arms slip around my neck.

I cradle her featherlight form in my arms. The full moon illuminates our trek to the garage. Carefully, I climb the steps up to my apartment. Inside, I set her down gently on my bed. A black shadow scurries across the bedroom. Mouse.

Reese blinks, tilts her head. "Why are we at your place?"

I feel slightly sick to my stomach that it was this easy to get her up here. That anyone could have taken advantage of her.

"I don't want you alone." I set a bottle of water and a bottle of ibuprofen on the nightstand. "See? We got the good stuff."

With curious eyes, she sniffs the air. "Your place is a garage."

"I live above it. Makes the working day easier."

Kneeling, I slip off her heels and do my best to ignore her silky skin, her pink-painted toes. I eye her sequined dress doubtfully. "You want to sleep in something that's not scratchy as fuck?" I ask, hating myself.

When she arches a suspicious brow, I lift a hand. "Ain't

tryin' to get you naked, honey, just gettin' you comfortable."
I grab a clean T-shirt from a drawer. "I won't look."

She nods.

"Arms up, baby."

I reach for the hem of her dress, lifting it off. I avert my
eyes, but not before catching a glimpse of her lace panties.
The gentle curve of her creamy, full breasts.

Fuck.

Still, hands-to-myself isn't hard. She's drunk. There's
no other option. I'd cut my dick off before I ever took advantage of a woman like that.

I shove the T-shirt over her blonde head. A soft, sexy
moan pulls from her lips as my fingertips sweep over her
thighs, and I grit my teeth.

"There," I say thickly.

Mouse sits there, silently judging me and my fat fucking erection. I'm so hard it hurts to move.

"No. Not the bracelets," she murmurs when I reach
for her bangles. "They're solid gold. Stolen from pirates."

I sink onto the edge of the bed beside her. "Whatever
you say."

Reese groans, her green eyes swimming.

"Room spinning?"

"Yes."

"Feel like you're going to puke?"

She gulps. "Yes."

I grab the trash can. "Here."

"No," she whines, shoving it away. "I don't want to puke
in a trash can."

That gets a chuckle out of me. "You can do it, princess.
I'll hold your hair, and you let it rip."

She pouts. "I can't."

I grin. "Have faith in me, honey. I got you."

Her eyes fly open, and she lurches forward. I catch her around the waist, bring the can up to her mouth. She leans over and wretches.

I hold her up, feeling the wrack of her slender frame as she gets it all out of her. "Good girl," I soothe, rubbing her back. "Keep going."

She does, and when she's finished, Reese flops on the bed with an exaggerated sigh. "I like your bed. It's fluffy. Like a cloud from the sky." Then her eyelids flutter shut, and she passes out cold.

Christ.

Mouse hops on the bed. Her paws find Reese's flat stomach and knead.

Grady's words fill my mind.

Just be nice to her. I think she needs it.

Seems like no one has been nice to this girl her entire life.

Frowning, I battle a rush of unease as I cover her bare legs with a blanket. Even in sleep, sadness stains her stunning face. I don't like tonight—Reese, raw and on edge. The hollow vault of her voice. The pain in her eyes. It reminds me of…

I stare down at her, and a thousand memories I want to forget well up inside of me.

Curled up on my bed, bawling my fucking eyes out because I had lost Savannah.

The stifling silence that fell over the crowd as paramedics carried that kid out of the stadium.

Contemplating a bottle of pills before Davis called and told me to get to the ranch.

The past makes my pulse race as I sit in the chair

beside the bed. Exhaling hard, I shove a hand through my hair and grip the back of my neck.

And then a sight worse than my memories hits me.

The most beautiful woman I've ever seen in my life is in my bed.

Wearing my goddamn jersey.

9

Reese

I'M IN A COCOON OF COZY, WARM SAFETY, SUNLIGHT cascading over my skin. A tinny clattering noise, bare feet on floorboards, a tiny mewl—perfect, homey sounds.

It doesn't feel the same as when I'm on tour or on a set.

Except *I* feel the same. Cottonmouth. A pounding headache.

The rich scent of coffee drifts through the air. I crack an eye and sit up in bed. Where the fuck am I? Waking up in a strange bed isn't anything new, but this place feels different. My gaze roams around the masculine room. High ceiling beams. Slate-gray walls. Sleek oak furniture.

What happened last night?

Ford.

Bar.

Dancing.

Word vomiting.

Actual vomiting.

"Oh no."

I bared too much. Drank too much. Like always.

So much for New Reese.

As I shove the mound of blankets off me, I see a chair next to the bed. A bag of cinnamon candies and a bottle of water on the nightstand. His boots. A quilt.

A memory sweeps over me. Waking in the middle of

the night and finding myself in Ford's arms as he lifted me up and made me take tiny sips of water.

Ford stayed with me. When I was sick.

Tears prick my eyes. I don't know whether to feel embarrassed or so very grateful.

Bladder screaming at me, I get up and pad to the bathroom. Finding a bottle of mouthwash and an unopened toothbrush next to the sink makes my eyes grow big. A gooey feeling takes root in my stomach, and I shake it off. He probably has women stay over all the time.

I wash my face, scrubbing it like I can erase the wreckage of last night, then head out of the bedroom in nothing but Ford's jersey and my underwear.

I step into a small living room-kitchen combo, my gaze locking on Ford at the counter, wearing gray sweatpants and a backward baseball cap. The sight of him speeds my heart. There's something mysterious about the man. That hard jawline. Those amber eyes. Forearms that should be in a hall of fame.

He hasn't noticed me yet, and I drift forward, drawn to him.

Hunched over the stove, Ford stirs something in a pan. Coffee gurgles in a pot beside him. I smile when I see the black cat on the counter. Every few seconds, Ford stops and feeds her a piece of bacon.

Guess the cat distribution system works its way through even the hardest hearts.

"How are you feeling?" he asks without looking up.

I freeze. Clear my throat. "Currently dying from dehydration, but I'll survive."

"Coffee?" His lazy drawl makes my stomach turn over.

I shake myself out of my admiring gaze. "Oh, uh, yes. Please." My voice is rough.

"Black?"

"Almond milk?"

He sighs wearily. "Really need to stop milking things."

I hide a wan smile and move closer.

Ford returns from the fridge. "All I have is cream."

"That works." I reach for the coffee he sets in front of me and add a dollop of cream. "Honey?" I ask.

He squints at me. "In coffee?"

"It soothes the throat."

While he searches in a cabinet, I scan his apartment. "Is this where you live?" I'm impressed. He has plants that are alive. Photos of his family. Baseball memorabilia. A leather couch. Sparse, but it's clean. Lived in. Just like those gray sweatpants.

"Above the garage," he grunts, running a hand through his thick lionlike hair. "It's not much. All my brothers are on the ranch. This is just as good."

"I like the smell."

He jerks up his chin. "You do?"

"I do. It's better than my penthouse. It's homey."

He returns to me, his eyes meeting mine. "Here, honey. Honey." He holds out the honey bear and I take it, our fingers sweeping against each other. The briefest touch shouldn't make me ache, but it does.

As I add a drizzle of honey to my coffee, my gaze shifts to Ford. His body reminds me of a mountain cat—long, sleek, and athletic, with golden skin.

I should hate Ford. But after last night, I can't. It's been a long time since someone genuinely cared about my actions without using it against me or asking for something.

Moving back to the burner, he lifts the pan, dumping eggs onto a plate. After adding two strips of bacon, he points at the chair. "Sit."

Cupping my hands around the coffee mug, I take it to a small, round table.

My eyes widen in surprise when he sets the food in front of me. "I want you to eat," he says, handing me a fork. "It'll take the edge off your hangover."

I give him a smile, fighting the sting in my eyes. God, the last person to make me breakfast was probably…my mom.

That triggers more snippets of last night to fill my mind. Telling Ford about my parents and our band. Being given up and then, taken in by Gavin. My long ramble about feeling unwanted. All memories I hate talking about when I'm sober, let alone drunk.

I bite my lip. "Listen…about last night. I probably said more than I should have about my parents. My manager. Let's just forget about it, okay?"

There's a quick flash of worry in his eye. "Why?"

Because it's my past, I want to say. *And I hate my past. It's a blur. It's painful. It's just too much me.*

I pick at the eggs, unable to meet his gaze. "It's shit that I don't want in the papers."

"You don't have to worry." A mischievous gleam fills his eyes. "Runaway Ranch has a way of keeping your secrets."

Then I'm at the perfect place. Except for Gavin, no one knows about what happened to me. He said it would be bad for my image, that it would make me look crazier than I already am. How can I trust anyone with my past when they'd only use it against me?

"Reese?" I jerk out of my thoughts as Ford nudges the plate toward me. "I want you to eat."

I flinch when I see his busted knuckles.

"I'm sorry about your hand," I say softly, tucking a lock of hair behind my hair.

"Comes with the territory." His heated gaze rakes over me and I shiver. "Dancin' on bar tops isn't something I see every day."

A smile tips my lips. "Free show. Don't get used to it."

He chuckles. After a second, his eyes drop, and I follow where they've landed. "This you?" I read the jersey upside down. "The Phoenix Renegades?"

He nods.

"You were a pitcher?" I ask. The extent of my baseball knowledge includes singing the national anthem at Chase Field early in my career. I bet Ford's the real deal. He has charisma, an aura about him that screams *star*.

"Yeah." A proud smile blooms on his face. "I fell in love with it when I was eight years old. I wasn't a first-round draft pick, but I proved them wrong when I was named best pitcher in the league in my first year."

I smile. "So humble."

A bright grin tips his lips. "Fucking love of my life." He looks at Mouse, perched on an empty chair between us, and reaches out to ruffle her fur. "Next is this damn cat."

I prop my chin in my palm. "What was your favorite part?"

"Just being on the mound. Tuning everything out, like it was made for me."

That's how I feel about singing. Not performing, not the crowds—the music. The way it lives in me, through me.

I swallow a bite of egg. "When did you stop playing?"

"Damn near eight years ago." Bitterness and regret taint his previously easygoing voice. "Came out with a bad shoulder and a whole lot of headaches."

The happiness on his handsome face dims. There's something grim in his amber eyes, something he's holding back.

Ford chuckles. "Now I'm shoveling cowshit on a ranch and that's what life's all about."

"You make it sound so easy to have a simple life," I muse.

"It is easy, honey." He leans in, his hand almost brushing mine. "Is that what you want?"

"I don't know." Shaking my head, I peer down at the eggs. "This is delicious," I say. The eggs have cheese on them, a little spice, and the bacon is crisp and garlicky.

He gives me a strange look, like he's realizing something. "One thing I can cook is breakfast."

I take my time eating when what I really want to do is shovel it all into my mouth. Gavin would kill me. At the thought, I set my fork down.

Ford sips his coffee. Gives me a long look, like he's slowly piecing things together. "What's with this? You drink too much, and you eat too little."

I've already blabbed my life story, so I might as well be honest. "I can't gain weight."

His expression turns fierce. "Who the fuck told you that?"

"My manager."

Ford appears bothered by the statement. "This is the same guy who turned off your cards?"

I flinch. When someone else says it, it seems so simple. So obvious. So awful.

Flexing a fist, Ford asks, "What did you say your manager's name was?"

"I didn't. Gavin Cross." I sigh. "He manages everything." Embarrassment pushes down my shoulders. "Where I go. What I wear. Who I date."

Now Ford looks annoyed. Interested. "Who do you date?"

"No one," I mumble. Warmth spreads inside of me.

No one like Ford, that's for sure. He's handsome, and older than most men I typically date. Masculine and rugged. Unpolished, yet sexy as hell with his cocky attitude and those amber eyes that crinkle at the corners.

Jaw locked tight, Ford asks, "Why do you stay with this guy?"

Because I'm afraid. Because I don't know anything else.

Instead of that, I say, "I don't have a choice. I have a contract." I let out a shaky breath. "I need to go over it. Which means I need to get it."

Muscles ripple in his cheek. "Let me guess, he has it."

"He does." Frustration slams inside of me. I wish I had never told Ford. I feel stupid enough as it is. "I called him last night, and he gave me until the end of the summer to…" I trail off.

"To?" Questions swim in Ford's eyes.

What do I tell him? To not have a mental breakdown? To reclaim my life? To just fucking be?

"To live," I say, my gaze drifting longingly toward the window. To a ranch I haven't even explored. "I need it. I just…really need it, is all."

I set my fork down and push my plate away. Ford doesn't look happy. "But I can go somewhere else." A teasing smile tilts my lips. "I know you have better things to do than babysit a spoiled, pampered, pain-in-the-ass princess."

Regret widens his eyes. "Listen. I wasn't nice to you, and we're gonna start over, okay?"

I shake my head, because I don't want pity. It's bad enough he swooped in to save me last night. "Ford, you don't—"

"Nah." He folds his muscular arms across his chest and leans back in his chair. "What would my little brother say if I turned you out? Wouldn't be very cowboy of me."

I let out a soft laugh. "Cowboy, huh?"

"Tell you what." His teeth sink into his lush lower lip as he considers something. A low pulse blooms in my core. I hate that it turns me on. "Why don't you come with me to town this morning?"

"I don't want to keep you from your job," I say.

"You are my job, honey," he drawls. But instead of feeling irritation, all I feel is heat. In my stomach, between my thighs.

He flashes a bright white grin. Those broad shoulders, that swagger—Ford Montgomery's a charmer. It just won't work on me.

"I need to head into town to fix a saddle, anyway," he says, standing and collecting my plate. He takes it to the sink. "Since you're staying, you need things, don't you? Can't feed the chickens in sequins."

I laugh. "I bet I could."

He approaches the table, his amber eyes searching my face. "Talked to my brother last night. He said one of the things you need is a hug."

I bristle. "A hug?"

He takes a step forward. "What do you think?"

I open my mouth to laugh, then stop short at the half-smile on his face.

"You're serious?"

His Adam's apple bobs and then bobs again. "One hug never killed anybody."

"Oh."

One hug. I can do one hug.

I rise, feeling a bit shaky, and shuffle toward him.

Gaze locked on mine, he steps into me. My palms land on his bare chest and every nerve ending in my body sparks. Ford's breath hitches.

"This is a bad idea," I breathe.

"Too late."

I yelp when he suddenly wraps me in his strong arms, sweeping me up. Holding me close.

"Oh," I sigh. My body feels deflated in the best possible way. Resting my head on his chest, I close my eyes and breathe him in. Ford smells like hickory and midnight air. Man. Earth. I can hear his heartbeat through his warm skin, and for one long second, I wish we shared it.

We linger there, without ulterior motives. Just a simple, easy moment. Ford hugs me with such tenderness that hot tears prick the backs of my eyes. So many times in my life, I've been offered alcohol when all I needed was a hug.

And then I laugh. I laugh because Ford Montgomery is one of the best things I've ever felt.

"What?" he says gruffly.

"You smell amazing."

His lazy chuckle rumbles through my body. "Don't get any ideas."

I smile into his chest. "Wouldn't dream of it."

10

Ford

I'M A FUCKING IDIOT.

Keeping my distance from Reese is non-negotiable. And yet…thanks to me, here she is. Sitting too close in the cab of my truck. Walking too close beside me down the sidewalk. Wearing my baseball cap and black sweatsuit like they belong to her.

Not to mention, I made her breakfast. I haven't made breakfast for a woman since Savannah.

She didn't eat much of it, but we're going to work on that.

And then I had to go and hug her—the best damn hug I've had in a long time.

Fucking Grady and his idiot words of wisdom.

Bells jingle as I open the door to Zeke's Hardware. Reese struts inside, and instantly, heads swivel.

Including my own.

She's dressed in high heels and one of my grungy sweatsuits, but she looks like a million dollars. Even dressed down and incognito, Reese Austin is breathtaking. And that terrifies me the most. Because the need to keep her close clouds my logic. The rules of the ranch.

Her story from last night weighs on me. Deep down, I know I've only scraped the surface of what this girl's running from. Something tells me she doesn't even know herself.

I already hate her fucking manager for telling her she can't gain weight. A gust of wind could blow her over.

A couple of customers turn as Reese slams into a rack of batteries, knocking a few packs to the ground.

"Oops," she says, lifting her sunglasses on top of her head as she dips to pick them up.

"Keep the sunglasses on, will you?" I growl when she stands.

If Resurrection knew they had a world-famous superstar in their town…they probably wouldn't give a shit. All they'd care about is city folk staying on their side of the grass. But it's not a risk I'm willing to take. I'm familiar with the tabloids. With bad press. Getting mobbed is the last thing she needs. What happened at Nowhere was bad enough.

Reese sends me a scathing look over her shoulder. "What is your problem, Country Boy?"

You. You're my problem. My incredibly beautiful, bratty little problem.

I shake my head, wishing I hadn't brought her along. "While you're busy trashing the place, grab me a pack of flathead screws, will you?"

Reese stares at me like I've just called a baseball play.

Sighing, I step around her and pluck a package off the rack.

"Have you ever been in a hardware store?" I ask wryly.

She tucks a wild curl behind one ear and huffs. "No. Have you ever worn high heels?"

"You got me there, princess."

Rolling her eyes, she follows me to the cash register.

"New hired hand?" Jonas Farrabee's squinty eyes focus

on Reese as he scans the items. Fucker's tongue is hanging so far out of his mouth it could be on the floor.

"Hi." Reese wiggles her fingers at him. And suddenly I have the very strong urge to punch something.

I tuck the small plastic sack into my back pocket before taking Reese's arm and moving her toward the door. I give Jonas a *fuck off* glare over my shoulder.

We exit the shop and turn onto Main Street. At the end of the block, we pass Dakota's new bakery, the Huckleberry. It's boarded off, still needing the sign and finishing exterior touches.

Reese stares at the mountains rising from the base of Resurrection. "It's so beautiful here. Like a dream."

Dream girl.

I shove the thought out of my head.

"What's that?" Reese asks, pointing across the street at a red, white, and blue building.

"That's the Legion."

"And that is?"

I sigh. "Honey, I've barely had coffee."

She bats her lashes. "You brought me along."

I needle my brow. "Goddamnit."

Ten minutes later, when I'm certain I've met my talking quota for the day, Reese stops and stares at the sole boutique in Resurrection—Luxe Loft. Its bright pink door has me and my brothers sidestepping it every damn time.

Her eyes are wide and filled with want.

Fuck. She wants to shop.

Against my better judgment, I lean in. Her hair tickles my nose, and I breathe in her scent. Christ, she smells like peaches and cream. I want to lap her up like a damn cat.

"Go inside."

Planting her hands on her hips, she scoffs. "I think you're forgetting something, Country Boy. I don't have any money."

I scrub a hand through my hair. "You need new clothes, don't you?" I should take her to the Walmart in Billings, but there's longing in her eyes, and I just can't say no to it. "We'll figure that out."

Her lower lip sticks out in a stubborn pout.

I nudge her forward. "Just go look. Pick out what you would buy if you were Jane. If you didn't have that prick of a manager bossing you around."

Her eyes flash like she likes the idea.

I arch a brow. "Either get your ass in there or you're coming with me to strip a saddle."

Terror seeps into her green eyes. "Okay, okay."

I chuckle as she struts those high heels across Main Street.

Twenty minutes later, when I'm finished with most of my errands, and a few extra stops that weren't on my list, I slip inside the boutique.

Rita Foster, our resident town gossip, smirks. "You look lost, Ford."

I feel lost, like I've wandered into the middle of a pink cotton candy world. Silk roses cover one wall, and a neon sign proclaims STOP THINKING, START SHOPPING. I wander aimlessly up and down the aisles, sniffing candles and touching things I'll never buy.

"Reese?" I say, when I don't see her.

"Over here." Her blonde head pops up from a rack of brightly colored tops.

The puzzled look on her face brings a smile to my lips. "You look like you don't know where to start."

"I don't."

I take a step backward. "Well, don't look at me."

She wrinkles her nose. "I've never done this before. Well, for *me* before. Usually, I just go with what my stylist selects. Or what Gavin likes."

I dab a finger against her bangles. "Did he pick those out?"

She jerks her arm back so fast you'd think I burned her. "No." Her words are soft. Sad. "These are mine. I did that."

Concern urges me to ask more, but I stay silent. This isn't the place. Not when Rita's watching us like a hawk. Not when we need to get back to the ranch.

Slowly, Reese explores the store, and I follow. She pauses at a case of shimmery necklaces.

"You like jewelry, honey?"

She flushes, looks back at the case. "Yes," she says. "I like pretty things. I know that makes me shallow, but I do."

"Nah," I say. "It makes you, you. Hell, I've spent an entire paycheck on fishing lures."

Resolve flashes in her eyes, and she grabs up her stack of clothes from a nearby chair. "I'll be right back." With a toss of her hair, she enters the dressing room.

Minutes pass.

The whip of the curtain has me turning. I almost lose consciousness. Reese stands there in a blue jean shirt tied at the midriff and tiny cut-off shorts.

"What do you think of this?"

God, where the fuck is this in my job description? Blood floods straight to my cock.

I shake my head, trying not to look at her. "They're clothes," I say, my voice hoarse.

Reese rolls her eyes. "You're infuriating."

Dragging a hand through my hair, I step closer. "Look. It doesn't matter what I think. If you like it, get it."

I don't know if I've said the right thing or the wrong thing, because she stares at me, then shuts the curtain.

I busy myself by looking down at the tray of necklaces Reese was inspecting. They're all cowboy-themed—tiny charms shaped like horseshoes, boots, and hats dangle from delicate gold chains. My mind drifts, imagining Reese wearing them around her slender throat. My pulse spikes.

"I'm going to get this," she says, emerging from the dressing room.

I look up. Frown. "Just that?"

In her hands is a thin piece of fabric. Behind her, piled on the dressing room floor, a mountain of clothes as big as the Rockies.

She makes a face. "It's all I have in my account. I checked."

I reach into my back pocket and pull out my wallet.

Her big green eyes get even bigger when I hold out my card. "What is this?"

"My credit card. Go buy yourself whatever you want."

She scoffs. "You're a cowboy. You don't have money."

My gaze remains glued to Reese. "I was number one in the national league. You think I don't have money? Think again." Yeah, I'm fucking cocky. Though I'm the furthest thing from a broke farm boy, my brothers and I were hardly born with silver spoons in our mouths. Our parents made us work for everything. All my money from baseball is still sitting in the bank. Beer, outdoor gear—that stuff won't drain my account.

My eyes land on Reese. Now that I think about it, I could use better things to do with my money.

Reese props her hands on her hips. "You don't have enough money for me."

I grin. "Try me, princess."

"I could break your bank account," she insists.

My cock flexes. That haughty fucking mouth. I hate how much it turns me on. All I want to do is shut her up with my lips.

Sick of arguing, I stride into the dressing room and scoop up the pile of clothes.

"What are you doing?"

I grunt. "Buying you clothes."

She grabs my bicep. "No, Ford—"

"Woman, what do you want from me? You're not happy when I yell, you're not happy when I help. Are you ever goddamn happy?"

Reese deflates, and I'm horrified when tears spring to her pretty emerald eyes.

Covering her mouth, she turns and rushes out of the store.

"Shit." I look at Rita and toss the clothes on the counter, along with my card. On second thought, I add a gold horseshoe necklace to the pile. "Ring it up. All of it. We'll be right back."

I find Reese on the street corner and hustle up to her. "You want to tell me why you're out here pouting so I don't have to guess?"

I expect fire and brimstone in her green eyes, but I don't get that. Reese crosses her arms, hugging her waist. "I don't want to owe you anything, Ford." Her voice is so soft, so sad, it momentarily stalls my heart. "I have money of my own and it pisses me off that I can't get it."

"You will get it," I say sharply. Suddenly, it's all I want to do for her. She'll get her money. I'll make sure of it.

I place my hand on her shoulder, and she looks up at me. "But until then, there's no shame in accepting help, Reese. Especially when you have nowhere to turn. God knows I've taken more than my fair share." She tilts her head at me curiously, and I plow ahead, not wanting to get into that story. "We're cowboys. We help our own. Help our neighbors. You're on Runaway Ranch now, and we got you."

"But I worry about it. You accept help, you owe people. They cash in. They hold it against you." She shivers. "Until it hurts."

I battle a rush of unease. What the fuck does that mean?

I slide a finger beneath her chin, tilting her stubborn gaze up to mine. "I ain't plannin' to cash in. Besides, you're working at the ranch, right? This will just go on your tab. You'll pay it off yourself. In the meantime, I stopped by the bank earlier and got you this." I pull a folded account application from my back pocket. "Fill it out and we can stop back by the bank to open your own account."

"Really?" Her voice trembles as she stares down at the slip of paper like it's a bar of solid gold.

"Really," I husk.

She looks up at me, and…fuck. The gratitude shining in her eyes. Something this little shouldn't mean this much.

I tug at the brim of her baseball cap. "Besides, if I'm going to hold anything against you, it's me saving your ass the other night at the bar."

That earns me a smile. A small one, but I'll take it.

"Ford?"

Our heads swivel at the deep voice.

Charlie and Ruby stand on the street corner, staring at us.

I clear my throat. "Hey, C. Long time."

A grin quirks Charlie's bearded lips. "Surprised to see you out and about after the way you tore up Nowhere last night."

I suppress a groan. Fantastic. The gossip mill is already in full swing.

"This is Reese. I'm, uh, showing her around."

"We haven't met," he says, offering a big hand. "I'm Charlie."

Reese takes it. "Nice to meet you."

"How'd the flower shop hunt go?" I ask Ruby.

Ruby shakes her head. "It already sold."

"Damn," I say. With the burgeoning small-town boom, Resurrection's real estate gets snapped up quickly.

"Ford Montgomery, you forgot some things." Rita steps onto the sidewalk, smirking. "You're all set." Before I can say anything, I have six bright pink shopping bags in my hands.

Charlie and Ruby trade amused looks.

Reese's mouth bounces with an almost-smile.

"We'll let you get back to your shopping," Charlie says, a sly look in his eye.

Ruby claps her hands together. "You should come to dinner tonight," she says, her hopeful gaze pinned to Reese. "At the house."

"Oh, uh…" Reese's eyes flick to mine. So do Charlie's.

"Please," Ruby presses. "Everyone's coming."

"Sure," Reese agrees.

Ruby beams. "Great. Six o'clock supper."

After they walk off, Reese turns to me. "I don't have to go," she says quietly.

It feels like a warning, a way out so I don't have to spend more time with her.

And yet, what do I fucking do?

I give an easy shrug. "Gotta eat, don't you?"

"I ate already. Breakfast, remember."

"More than once a day, honey," I say, softening the scold with a smile.

My chest tenses when she hesitates. I nudge her shoulder with mine. "You're from Georgia. You like peaches, don't you?"

Reese tips her head, her cheeks turning a sweet shade of pink. "Yeah, I do."

"Okay. I got a peach pie with your name on it."

Clearly, I've gone insane.

But right now, all I can think about is seeing her again. Tonight.

11

Reese

I SLOW MY STRIDE WHEN I REACH THE EDENS. THE
farmhouse is massive and modern. With a sprawling
front porch, gravel drive, and deer antlers over the front
door, it screams cowboy chic. What seems like a hundred
acres of emerald grass stretch in every direction, framed
by dense woods behind the property. In the distance, the
lake glitters.

My skin itches and I debate on turning right back
around. The black hole hovers. The urge to let it consume
me is overwhelming.

As I climb the porch steps, my attention's drawn to
the four men in the front yard. I realize it's Ford and his
brothers. They're using a bow and arrow to shoot an apple
off each other's heads. Shouts of laughter fill the air.

"Shit show, isn't it?"

A girl with long caramel hair stands at the front
door. Dressed in jeans and a scarlet-colored tank top that
matches her lipstick, she's both beautiful and terrifying.
Muscles like whipped ropes. Tattoos over her entire body.
A bruise on her cheekbone. She looks built like a brick
wall and just as tough.

"What are they doing?" I ask.

She rolls her eyes. "Shortening their life span." She
takes a drag of her cigarette. "We can only hope."

I can't help but stare at the men. They're all tall,

beautiful, and rugged. Like they were raised on muscles and dirt. Two of them remind me of grizzly bears, while Ford and another brother remind me of wildcats. True cowboys, from the Stetsons on their heads to the mud on their boots.

"What do they feed the men in Montana?" I muse.

"Idiot pills," she drawls. "I'm Fallon."

"Reese."

Fallon's hazel eyes skim over me. The corner of her mouth turns up. "So, whose idea was this? Ruby's or my sister's?"

"Ruby's."

Her laugh is dagger sharp. "You'll learn, once you meet her, you can't shake her loose." An affectionate smile stains her face. "But you won't want to either. Come in."

I follow the clomp of her cowboy boots down a hall covered in family photos.

The kitchen is bright and airy, with a lifted deck extending off it that overlooks the backyard. The sliding door is open, offering picture-perfect views of the forest and jagged mountain peaks. Muted country music plays from a speaker.

The scrabble of paws and shuffle of feet catch my attention, and then a dog and a baby are standing in front of me. I can't decide which one is more adorable.

"This little hellion is Duke," Fallon says, snagging the baby and tossing him into the air. A scream of laughter erupts from Duke's mouth. "And that's Keena."

I bend down to rub the dog's ears. "Hi, there."

The dog tilts her head, listening intently.

A woman pops up from the oven, purple potholders

on her hands. "Hi," she says, flashing a smile that makes her dark eyes sparkle. "Please come in."

"Thanks for having me. I'm Reese."

"I'm Dakota."

"Can I help with anything?" I ask.

She shakes her head. "Nope. Just relax."

Fallon groans. "Ugh, figures while the boys play, the women cook like it's 1950."

Dakota laughs and reaches for a bottle of wine. "Trust me, they're not exempt. They get clean-up duty."

"Hey, assholes," Fallon shouts from the porch as Dakota fills a wine glass for me. "It's dinnertime."

Seconds later, the thunder of boots rattle the porch stairs.

And so begins the meet-and-greets and the familial connect-the-dots. Davis is Ford's fraternal twin. Fallon and Dakota are sisters. I meet another brother Wyatt and an older man named Stede, who is Dakota and Fallon's father. Ruby throws her arms around me like we've been best friends for years.

"Let's eat," Dakota orders after we've made introductions.

Chaos ensues as everyone takes food, drink, baby, and dog out onto the patio.

I'm grabbing a bottle of wine when a voice says, "New clothes?"

I smother a smile at the husk of a drawl and glance over at Ford. My gaze tracks over his jeans and charcoal gray T-shirt dusted with dirt. I ignore the smug look on his face despite my overheating heart. "Sure looks like it, Country Boy."

I wave my hand down my outfit—cut-off shorts,

a crochet tank top, and high heels. Reese Austin Lite. Glamorous, but relaxed. I love my heels and jewelry, but it's so freeing to wear something I picked out.

Thanks to Ford.

He's given me my first real speck of hope. I have my own checking account. One tiny step toward freedom. But I'm not about to let a man control me. I won't owe Ford Montgomery anything like I owe Gavin. I'll pay him back for everything. Even if the way he casually handed me his AMEX today had me swooning.

I finger the gold necklace around my neck. "Although, I don't know how the necklace got in there."

He shrugs. "I don't either."

I roll my eyes. I'll never admit how much I love it. It's the first nice thing someone's done for me in a long time.

With that, we head to the deck, where Dakota has spread a feast across the long pine table. The view is mesmerizing, unlike anything I've ever seen. All woods and lake, with fireflies winking in the air. The sun is a bold orange fireball that makes the world look like it's burning.

Davis and Dakota sit at each end of the long table, with Duke in a highchair beside his mother. I take my seat, trying to ignore that I'm next to Ford, but his lean body crammed into my space has my senses on overload. His bare arm grazes mine and my skin catches fire. As if he felt it too, Ford clears his throat and adjusts his sitting position.

I can't help but take him in. His rugged beauty and southern drawl are almost too much. He's like a cowboy hero plucked from the old country songs I used to sing. Riding the plains, dusty and grizzled. Calloused fingertips. Chiseled jaw.

As we dish our plates, Charlie and Wyatt reach for

the same steak. Charlie wins it by throwing an elbow that has Wyatt swearing.

"Only child?" Ford's voice rumbles.

I flush at being caught gawking. "Yes."

Wyatt grins. "Yeah, you never had to learn how to curb-stomp someone for the last burger."

Ford snorts, reaching over the table with those long arms of his to swat his brother across the head. Fallon lifts a brow like *obviously that's my job*.

Davis holds up his hands. "Let's go a night without killing someone."

"When are you gonna shave this?" Ford asks, gesturing at Wyatt's mustache.

"Shut up, man," Wyatt grumbles, shoving at Ford's arm.

I smile at their boisterous bullshitting.

Ford jerks his chin at Fallon. "What do you think of the new 'stache, cowgirl?"

Wyatt doesn't look up from his plate, but his coiled shoulders tell me he's listening.

She tilts her head, contemplating, before saying, "I think he looks like a prepubescent man-child."

Charlie and Davis snicker.

"Fallon, when are you riding next?" Ruby asks, intercepting the argument before it can bloom.

"August. The Rough Rider Rodeo," Fallon says, shoveling potatoes onto her fork. Then she shakes her head. "I need to get in shape. I spent months away from riding. I'm soft on form."

"And hard on everything else," Wyatt mutters.

The wine glass freezes inches from my lips. The tension between Fallon and Wyatt hangs in the air like a smoke ring. Judging from the averted eyes and clattering utensils, everyone else feels it, too.

Stede puffs his chest up in pride. "My girl's been training hard." He pats his daughter's hand.

"Fallon rides bulls," Dakota tells me since I must look lost.

"Bulls?" I stare at Fallon. "Wait. I'm confused. I thought that was—"

"Dangerous as fuck?" Wyatt says, sounding smug.

Fallon scoffs, sending him a look sharp enough to cut. "Never let a man who prefers mares tell you anything about your attitude."

I shake my head, not wanting to come off as rude. "I just didn't know women could ride bulls."

Her red lips curve wickedly. "I'm going to be the best."

"You have to get those migraines under control before you get on the back of a bull," Davis orders, angling a fork down the table at Fallon. "You can't ride until then."

She glares at him. "Watch me."

"What do you think of the ranch, Reese?" Dakota asks, quickly changing the subject. She lifts a spoonful of peas to Duke's babbling lips.

I take a sip of my wine, then set down the glass. "I haven't seen too much of it yet. That'll change since I'm working here."

All eyes land on Ford.

He shifts, looking uncomfortable. "I hired her to help this summer."

Davis glances at Charlie. His stern expression says he hasn't heard the news. His brown eyes return to Ford. "That a good idea?"

"I think it's a great idea," Ruby pipes up, smiling in triumph.

Ford leans back and crosses his arms. "I second that, Fairy Tale."

"I'll lie low," I tell Davis, not wanting to cause trouble or be a burden. "All I want to do is work, make some money."

As I saw through a hunk of steak, I realize everyone is staring at me. My damn bangles. They keep clanging against the edge of the plate. Even Ford is wincing.

"Sorry," I say, but I don't take them off.

Wyatt, scraping up the last of his cornbread, leans in and asks, "Is it true your vocal cords are insured for 1.3 million dollars?"

"Wyatt," Ford snaps, annoyance clouding his features. "Leave her alone."

I laugh. "No." I arch a brow, meet his curious gaze. "They're worth 3.2."

Laughs float around the table.

I smile, but nerves have my shoulders up near my ears. Family dynamics like this—loud, casual, happy—are foreign to me. Even though Gavin raised me, we never did this. Birthdays were held in clubs or spent in hotel rooms, alone. I've always wondered what it'd be like to have this. A family. Love. Fitting in.

Something I'm definitely not doing. I'm an outsider looking in on a perfect circle of friends.

"Heard you had some trouble at Nowhere last night," Davis booms, and Ford and I lock eyes.

"News sure got around fast," I murmur.

Ford grins like we're in cahoots. I pretend I hate the

feeling. "That's a small town for you, honey. Big ears, bigger mouths."

Beside me, Ford stretches out in his seat. Fire licks my body as his elbow sweeps mine. "No trouble," he tells his brother. "Solved it."

Davis watches Ford with an indecipherable expression. "I can see that." He sounds skeptical.

Ford flexes his hand, pride in his voice. "It's been a while since I busted some knuckles."

"Could have let me come along," Wyatt grumps.

Davis crosses his arm, causing his muscles to bulge. "This summer isn't about trouble. It's about staying the course."

Trouble. He's looking at me.

Fallon flaps her napkin at Davis. "Boo. Boring."

My gaze falls to Ford's busted knuckles.

My fault.

Guilt crests over me. I refill my glass again, blinking when I realize the wine's almost gone. I look up to find Charlie studying me over his beer bottle.

Something hot and molten courses through my veins.

I'm nothing but trouble. I'm not worth it. I never have been.

Part of the problem is Ford Montgomery. He's a nice guy. Too nice. I barely know him, and I feel closer to him than any member of my glam squad or even Gavin.

It's dangerous being around him. I came to the ranch to rest and be alone, not hang out with this mechanic-slash-cowboy. Getting close is not an option. He doesn't need to know anything about me other than Reese Austin, a country superstar.

The real me is too real. Too many secrets.

As if hearing my inside thoughts and deciding to throw a wrench into the mix, Stede glances at me. "You were in the western, right, sweetheart? *Hell or High Water?*"

Oh no.

My stomach sinks. The last thing I want to do is talk about that movie. But politeness wins out, so I say, "I was."

Stede grins. He's a handsome old man with hazel eyes that mirror Fallon's. "I knew the trainer who worked with her on it," he tells the table. "We rode together back in Deadwood."

Fallon perks up. "You know how to ride, Reese?"

"No," I reply softly. "It was a long time ago."

"Sure, you do," Charlie says, a grin on his bearded face. "That rooftop horse scene?" He whistles. "You jumped into that pool like a pro."

My heart races. Too many bad memories.

That ice-cold pool.

Being so exhausted that I could barely stand up, let alone act.

Gavin taking my wrists and a length of leather. Saying, *"Let me help you."*

"Hell yeah," Wyatt says. "If you want to ride on the ranch, you say the word. I'll saddle up—"

"No," I suddenly snap. "I fucking hate horses."

Silence.

Shit.

The look on Ford's face tells me I should have kept it to myself.

This nice family and all I've done is offended them.

"Well." Stede gives a good-natured chuckle. "I appreciate old-fashioned honesty."

Honesty. Right. More like foot in my mouth.

"Does anyone want pie?" Dakota asks, sounding nervous.

All I want is to get out of there. The wine and the medication I took earlier sit heavy in my stomach. I feel drowsy and off, the way I feel before I go on stage. Numb, inside and out.

I feel judged, inside and out. Even if they don't know what they see—I do.

That sixteen-year-old girl who went to Muirwood.

The spoiled country singer who drinks too much.

The lost cause who can't get her life together, let alone her own money.

My heart pounds, tears at the back of my eyes.

"Peach. Reese?"

Blinking, I shake my head. "Sorry. What?"

Standing, Dakota gives me a kind smile. "Peach pie. Ford called me up, said you like it, so I made one especially for you."

My face flushes.

Ruby giggles.

Again, all eyes, including mine, land on Ford.

He slumps so far down in his chair, the floor could swallow him. "You know," he drawls with a hint of pink on his cheeks, "I told you that in confidence, Koty."

Dakota scoffs. "Not in my kitchen."

A chirping sound fills the air, and Charlie tenses, glancing down at the watch on his wrist.

"Shit," Wyatt swears.

Eyes wide, Ruby turns to her husband, a silent conversation happening between them. Suddenly, she goes limp. But Charlie's there, quickly catching her up in his arms as she sags against his chest.

"What—" I look at Ford. Around the table. Though they wear worried faces, they sit still and watchful.

"It's okay," he says, his eyes tracking Charlie's movement as he carries Ruby into the house.

"She has a heart condition," Ford explains. I tilt my head back to meet his fathomless amber eyes. "She faints sometimes. Once or twice a year. My brother's got it handled." He stares after Charlie for a long moment, a muscle working in his sharp jaw, then he tosses his napkin on his plate, his expression considerably darkened.

Quietly, quickly, pie forgotten, everyone stands and begins clearing the table. Keena dives for the leftovers as Davis takes Duke inside for bed.

"No, please," Dakota says, waving me off when I reach for a bowl. "You're a guest."

I nod, not wanting to cause more trouble, and hang back. When I'm alone on the deck, I turn to face the Montana wilderness. Playing with my necklace, I watch the hole above me shimmer. A sort of melancholia overcomes me. Why am I here? Does it matter? At the end of the summer, I'll go back to Gavin. Sing my shit songs and shake my ass. Watch everyone pretend they're glad I exist.

Sometimes it feels overwhelming to be alive.

Fallon appears and hands me a glass of whiskey. "He's grumpy because you're pretty."

"Who?"

"Ford."

I gulp my drink. Great. Just what I need, an angry mechanic with a grudge.

Fallon follows my gaze out into the backyard. She sips her whiskey, looking thoughtful. "What's it like to leave everything behind and just go?"

I snort. "I'll let you know when I find out."

"God," she says with a faux shudder. "If one more fucked up thing happens around this godforsaken place, I'm going to fucking lose it."

I cut her a quick look. Her hard mask slips for a brief second, and I see the panic on her face. It's breathtaking. It's sadness and despair.

It's exactly how I felt all those years ago.

12

Ford

I FIND REESE ON THE FRONT LAWN, STARING UP AT the sunset. She's so fucking breathtaking my chest hurts. I shove the thought away before it can take root.

"Way to kill it," I say, coming up beside her. Smirking, I lower my mouth to her ear. "Minus the whole hating-horses bit."

Reese clutches her necklace. "I didn't know dinner would come with a side of interrogation." A sigh furrows her mouth. "I should have lied, but I really hate that fucking movie."

No shit. It wouldn't take a detective to see that Reese was jumpy as hell after Stede brought it up.

"We love hard, but we're also nosy as hell. They'll get over it."

Relief floats into her emerald eyes and she nods.

I've been in her shoes more times than I can count. I know the feeling of putting my foot in my mouth all too well. Meeting my family isn't for the faint-hearted. I don't want her to beat herself up over it.

The wind blows softly through the woods, rustling the trees. A truck door slams and together we watch Fallon, duffel bag in her hands, take it inside the house.

Reese looks up at me. "What happened to her?"

The question catches me off guard. "Fallon?"

Reese nods.

"Let's see…she dated a fucking sociopath who happened to be her sister's ex. She was kidnapped and stabbed." Reese flinches. "Instead of dealing with it, Fallon doubled down on, well…Fallon."

"Are you sure that's all it is?" Her voice is wary.

"What else is there?"

Reese shudders, wrapping her arms around her waist. "She makes me feel like I'm standing next to a bomb."

I look back toward the house, worry simmering in my gut.

Before I can say anything, Reese takes a step forward, our shoulders brushing. "See you, Country Boy," she husks.

With a little wave, a jingle of her bangles, she heads out, taking her honeyed perfume and her scowls with her.

The soft sway of her ass as she crosses the field has my cock flexing in my jeans. It's clear Reese is intent on torturing me with those shorts. That shape, that hair, that smile? God was generous with that girl.

Because I'm a glutton for punishment, I take a second to admire the view of Reese disappearing down the bend. The clothes she bought are still her style, sexy as hell, but they're different somehow.

Softer. Happier.

I head back inside the house, and everyone has gathered in the kitchen. Fallon sits on the counter, and Dakota is at the kitchen table, a glass of wine in her hand, while my brothers clean up. An upbeat country song plays on the Bose speaker. Beside it, a baby monitor shows Duke sleeping.

"You hired her?" Davis asks, scraping leftovers into the trash. Keena hovers, hoping for a stray crumb.

Annoyance rises in my throat. "Look, y'all told me to

keep her close. Keep her out of trouble. That's what I'm doing."

He passes the plate to Charlie. "That include shopping?"

I glare at my mouthy little brother, who's suddenly interested in the bubbles in the kitchen sink.

"You spent the day with her," Davis presses.

To be a contrary fuck, I drawl, "I did, *Dad.*"

"Okay, no dad-speak," Dakota interjects, holding up her wine glass like she's ready to splash the next instigator. "We all know where that gets you two."

Fallon cackles in delight. "Shopping, Ford? That's like third base already."

I tear a hand through my hair, squeeze the back of my neck. Reese was right about the family interrogation. Since when has everything become a family affair?

"There is no first, second, or third base," I snap, my temper waking up. I'm already annoyed Reese barely touched her dinner. "She's too young for me, anyway."

Fallon and Dakota exchange smirks.

Not my type, I remind myself. Too high maintenance. We come from different worlds.

"Ain't she some big-shot country singer?" Wyatt says, dunking a wad of napkins in the garbage. "Where's her money?"

"For some reason, she's broke," Charlie says. "From what Ruby told me, she was in The Corner Store picking out change just to buy an energy drink."

Fallon shoots me a withering glare and mutters, "Bet it was a man. It's always a man."

All three of my brothers stare at me. I clench my fist, grit my teeth.

Only your siblings can make you mad in seconds. And it's a specific kind of mad, too. No one else can make you rage so suddenly.

I swing a finger around the kitchen. "I seem to remember y'all laying this trouble on me. She's my problem, so I'm going to make her my fucking problem."

"I don't want her to give *you* problems." Brotherly concern and annoyance war in Davis's voice.

"What's that supposed to mean?"

He crosses his arms. "You know what it means."

They think I'm combustible since last year, but they don't know I've been working on it.

"I don't know what it means," Fallon says slyly.

Davis turns to her. "Ford doesn't attract what's good for him."

"Again," I say through clenched teeth. "I'm right fucking here."

"She's a train wreck," Davis argues. "I heard about her dancing on the bar at Nowhere, seen those videos. She went to rehab when she was sixteen."

I suck in a breath. Rehab or not, Reese doesn't deserve to have her past thrown in her face. "Hell, who hasn't fucked up when they were sixteen?"

Davis leans in, lowering his voice. "What I'm saying is, you don't need that shit in your life, Ford. You have it together. After Savannah—"

"Savannah almost killed him," Wyatt snarls in a rare show of sibling loyalty. When it comes to my ex, all my brothers have my back.

"She's Savannah." Anger clouds Davis's features. "Times two."

A primal, protective urge to defend Reese surges

through me. I understand Davis is worried, but that doesn't mean he can rag on the girl relentlessly.

Before I can knock Davis into next week, Charlie dries his hands on a towel and says, "We don't need tabloids and press sniffing around the ranch. She doesn't know a lick about ranch work. What if she gets hurt? Hell, what if she decides to sue us?"

"She won't." Ruby's soft voice floats into the kitchen. Finished resting, she straightens out her dress and crosses the room.

The minute he sees her, Charlie's face pulls into a rare smile.

"She needs someplace to go," Ruby says, leaning back against the counter. Charlie keeps a hand on the small of her back. "Whatever she did in the past, we shouldn't judge."

"That's the sweetheart inside of you, Fairy Tale." I give her a soft smile. "You always look for that second chance."

Ruby narrows her eyes. "And you all should, too."

Quiet falls on the room.

I take a breath. The conversation is now at a simmer and I'd like to fucking keep it that way.

"Reese is a little wild, I get it," I say to the room. Everyone wants a fucking speech, so here we go. "She eats like shit, and I doubt she can work a fucking day on the ranch without killing herself. She's a pain in my ass, but I don't think we can turn her out. I think she's in trouble. Or scared or both."

"Ford's right," Dakota says, standing. She lays a hand on her husband's arm, and he instantly softens.

My hard-ass military brother doesn't trust easily. Especially after the events of last year. He's guard-dog protective of Dakota, Fallon, and the rest of his family. And he should be.

But instinct has my own red flags up—an unsettling feeling that if Reese leaves, something bad will happen to her.

Later, when Davis walks me to the front door, I say, "So, listen…" I glance toward the kitchen, making sure my family's out of eavesdropping distance. "I didn't want to do this in front of everyone, but I need a favor."

Davis scrapes a hand over his close-cropped hair. "I don't like the sound of this."

"You still talk to anyone on your team who's a PI?" If anyone has contacts, it's my brother with his military ties. The idea came to me earlier, during my trek down Main Street. The sooner I help Reese Austin, the sooner she can leave—and I can get my life back. Back to the mountain. Back to the ranch.

"I have a few names." He frowns. "Is this for Reese?"

"I think she's in something she doesn't know how to get out of."

"She tell you that?"

"Not exactly."

"Woo-woo shit?"

I grin. "Woo-woo shit."

Baseball players are the most superstitious players in all sports. I once knew a guy who wore a diaper when he needed to right his game. Cinnamon candies were my go-to for getting out of a slump. But when it comes to family, I tend to get a gut feeling when things go wrong. It's unexplainable, but after all these years, and especially after last year when I found Dakota and Davis in the middle of the woods, I trust it.

"You know what you're doing?" Davis asks. "Getting involved?"

"I'm not involved," I grunt, wondering how long I can lie to myself. "Just do this for me."

"I'll put in a call," Davis says in his scary Marine voice. "They call him the Poacher."

"Jesus, man." I laugh. "I don't want to know who you hang out with in your spare time."

This time, Davis cracks a shit-eating grin. "Tell me, is this the kindness of your heart talking, or are you still a cowboy?"

"Fuck you," I say, but there's no real malice there. We fight fast, but we also end it fast. I clap him on the shoulder. "Thanks, brother."

The night air's cool against my skin as I set out for the garage. But I don't get far. I stop on the path that would normally take me to the ranch proper, edginess skittering beneath my skin. Reese's expression at dinner lingers in my mind. Her parting words.

She's not my responsibility.

Yet, here I am, turning and heading in the opposite direction.

My fucking fault. I put her in that damn chalet at the edge of the forest. If I was smart, I would've kept her close. Next to me.

Another bad idea.

But there's something about Reese…something wild. Dangerous.

And all I want to do is rope and ride her.

"I don't fucking believe this," I mutter when I get to Reese's chalet.

Her door's wide open.

"Reese?" I poke my head inside. Makeup on the kitchen table. The clothes she wore to dinner lay in a pile in the middle of the floor. Christ. She can't clean worth a lick.

I step back, scouring the area. In the dirt, I spot footprints.

High heels, to be exact. Long heel marks in the soil.

I move toward the forest, unease spreading through me.

She must have put down half a bottle of wine tonight. Not to mention, traipsing through the forest in those death traps she calls shoes is only asking for trouble.

Those two thoughts push me through the forest with laser-focused speed.

"Goddamn it," I mutter, crunching twigs and brush beneath my boots. I pay more attention to this woman than anything else in my life. Fuck, but it's embarrassing.

Just as I round the grove of trees that shield the lake, I slam into a body.

Reese.

On instinct, I reach out, grabbing her by the waist before she can fall.

"I thought you were going home," I snap.

"Well, I didn't," she huffs, high heels in her hand. "Get your eyes checked."

My gaze travels down. That's when I realize she's wet. Even in the dark, I can see she's wearing nothing but a T-shirt that grazes her thighs, the thin material exposing dark, peaked nipples. Her bare feet are covered by red sand from the lake. Bangles on her wrists. High heels in her hands. Water sluices down her face, and her long hair drips over one slender shoulder like melted honey.

My hands shift on her hips. Still holding tight. I'm

not sure if it's for her benefit or for mine. "Hey, what happened? What's wrong?"

"Always so nosy." She juts her chin. "If you have to know, I was abducted by aliens and probed out in the big, bad woods."

Another lie.

"Don't wander," I tell her roughly, staring down at her beautiful, heart-shaped face, the necklace around her slender throat.

"Don't wander," she says in a spooky voice, brows lifting. Her body moves in a mock shudder and her breasts sweep against my chest. My heart picks up a dangerous beat. "Are you the Grumpy Cowboy Ghost of Midnight Past?"

"It's not safe in the forest." I peer behind her, take in the lake and its gentle current. Did she go for a fucking swim? "We had a wolf 'round these parts last year." If I have to scare her to knock some sense into her, so be it.

Her laugh is sad, and she forces a small smile. "Pity the wolf who meets me. I'm a menace. Isn't that what you said, Ford?"

Angry at myself, I shake my head. "I shouldn't have said that. I shouldn't have said a lot of things."

Apologizing has never been my strong suit, but for this girl, I have the strong urge to get on my knees and do just that.

"Hold up." I catch her arm before she can turn away. "Stop that mouth for a minute."

Her eyes flash. Pissed off. Good. How I like her.

"You sure you're okay?" I ask. Need has me pulling her closer. Has my thumb sweeping over that pouty bottom lip.

Her lips twist in amusement. "If I didn't know better, I'd think you were worried."

My voice is raspy as hell as I admit, "Yeah. I was."

"Oh." Her eyes go wide with surprise.

I quickly cup her cheek and force her gaze to mine. "Tell me you're okay."

"I'm okay," she breathes. Eyes fluttering, her body curves toward me like some magnetic pull. She's warm. Soft. Sweet.

Fuck. I want to kiss her.

I run my hands down her chilled arms. If it was up to me, I'd put her over my shoulder like I did last night and carry her back to her chalet. Spank that spoiled ass until it throbs. Put her in the bed. Fuck her.

And then I'd fuck her again in the shower.

My muscles tighten when she presses a palm against my chest. Only, instead of pulling me in, she pushes herself away from me. "Bye, Ford." The way she says my name—real, gentle—has my cock pulsing. "See you tomorrow."

"Bright and early. Six o'clock," I say as she walks away.

She glances over her shoulder. Playful fire dances in her eyes. "Oh, you're gonna love me at six in the a.m."

There's a bounce in her step as her presence, her soft heat, disappears into the darkness.

With that, I stand there in the dark, hating myself.

Don't care. You absolutely cannot fucking care.

13

Reese

A T SIX, I MEET FORD IN FRONT OF THE LODGE. He's already waiting for me, wearing his usual uniform of torn blue jeans, a tight T-shirt, baseball cap, and boots. In his hand, an iced coffee and a white paper sack.

His heated gaze meets mine as I approach, and for a second, there's a deep tug in my stomach. Like my body has nothing better to do than be attached to him.

"Coffee, breakfast," he says, handing me the bag.

"Which one is poisoned?" I ask.

He ignores me in favor of checking the two-way radio attached to his hip.

I peek in the bag, and my mouth waters. A pastry the size of a small island is inside, along with two hard-boiled eggs and a bottled water.

"Thank you." I laugh lightly. "I didn't know Runaway Ranch had delivery."

"New foot." He grins at me. No contempt or anger in his smile, just a simple honestness. It shouldn't be so sexy, but it is. "If you're workin' on the ranch, you need fuel. Breakfast every morning."

Gavin would be furious. About a lot of things. Like the fact that I skipped my medication this morning. It makes me sleepy, and I want to have my wits about me today.

"Besides…" He grins wider. "If I wanted you out of the

way, we're on a ranch. Hell of a lot more creative options than just poisoning a pastry."

I arch a brow. "So you admit you've thought about it?"

That lazy half-smile appears on his face, causing all my insides to tumble. "Just eat."

I savor the deliciousness of the iced coffee, then take a huge bite of pastry.

He chuckles. "Easy. Finish your breakfast, then we'll get started. No rush."

We sit on the front step of the lodge, watching Runaway Ranch wake up. The slow putter of a tractor in the distance. The first cowboy loping across the pasture, reins in hand. The golden sun lifting above the horizon. It feels magical. Maybe it is.

Ford lifts his coffee cup. A toast to the sunrise. "This is my favorite part."

"Mornings?"

He nods.

"Why?"

"Because the world wakes up, and it's a fresh start. Clean slate."

"Clean slate," I echo. "I like that."

We sit in a peaceful, easy silence. In my periphery, I take in his features. Tan, chiseled hands. A crooked index finger that piques my curiosity. And those long, lean legs. The way his thighs fill out those Wranglers should be criminal.

Ford breaks the quiet. "Sleep good last night?"

I pop a piece of hard-boiled egg into my mouth and roll up the bag to keep until I find a trash can. "It was amazing, if you must know."

"So amazing you still have those dark circles under your eyes?"

"Nothing a little makeup can't handle."

"Still look tired," he says smugly. "Maybe you should stay out of the forest."

"Maybe you should mind your own business."

I can feel him studying my face with those intense amber eyes, and I try to control the blush creeping over my cheeks. It was close last night—Ford catching me in the forest. After dinner, I was burning alive. I needed the water to wash away my night at Nowhere, the awkwardness of the family dinner, the dark hole hovering.

But moving forward, maybe I won't need it.

Because Ford's right. This morning does feel like a new start.

Old Reese would be forced to take a selfie and post it on my Instagram with some cheesy caption, but I don't have to do any of that here. No one's monitoring my social media, my dating life, my clothes.

The thought hits me suddenly—I can do this. I can find myself in the shitshow that is my life. I have three months of freedom. Better enjoy it while it lasts.

I turn to Ford. "Can I see the ranch before it wakes up?"

He almost smiles, which tells me I've said something right.

Ford slaps his hands on the thighs of his jeans and stands. He holds out a hand. "Hell, let's get to work, princess."

⌒⌒

Collect chicken eggs? Check.

Clean out stalls at the Warrior Heart Home? Check.

Pick up trash in the pens and on the sidewalk? Check. And it's only noon.

I've done most of the work. Through it all, Ford stands tall over me, supervising, maybe. Helping? Hovering?

He's shown me all the nooks and crannies that make Runaway Ranch tick.

There's something nice about working with Ford. He's calm. Easy. So different from Gavin's chaotic energy. Ford takes his time to explain the steps until I understand. He's also funny. It's unfair and I hate it.

As we haul bags of feed to the barn, people wave when they spot Ford. He returns the greeting but keeps a steady pace. I keep my face down, not wanting to be recognized. I don't want to cause trouble for Ford or his brothers, so I've been using the name Jane I gave at Nowhere. With my hair in braids and light makeup, so far, no one's been the wiser.

"You have to up the water intake," Ford orders, reaching back to hand me a bottle of water. "Not energy drinks, not iced coffee, not that purple shit all over TikTok. Water."

"If you couldn't guess," I huff, hurrying after him. "I wasn't a girl scout."

"No shit." He sets the bag of feed down and smiles as a sudden barrage of kids from a nearby cabin approach us. They chat for a minute or two, then one boy passes Ford a baseball. Nodding, he winds up and lets it rip.

The ball arcs high in the air and lands somewhere in the pasture.

"Go get it, you little gremlins," he yells, then laughs.

The kids scatter, their excitement filling the air.

He's good with kids. The sudden thought has me blinking. Heating. Has me shaking my head. I'm beyond delirious, even if my ovaries are swooning right now.

"They know who you are," I say, approaching him.

He shrugs. "Some do. Sometimes I play catch with them in the evenings if I'm not tied up."

"That's sweet." I bite my lip, considering something. "Have you ever taught a class?"

He looks baffled, then shakes his head. "Hell, I never thought about that."

I glance back at the kids in time to hear the boy yell, "Incoming," and then whip the ball our way.

The baseball lands back near my boots, then rolls into the gravel drive.

"I'll get it," I say, darting into the road.

Behind me, Ford swears.

Before I can reach the baseball, two black legs come down in front of me. The horse snorts, and I yelp, scrambling backward, right before I'm pulled away by a pair of strong arms.

"Fuck." Ford breathes heavily, securing me against him with a hand over my stomach. I dare a glance at his face. Dark, worried. "Sorry, man," he says, looking up at the rider. "She's still getting her ranch legs. Go ahead."

With a tilt of his Stetson, the rider takes off.

Ford spins me in his arms. I wait for his ire, but he doesn't yell at me. "That horse ain't a Pontiac, honey. No seatbelts." He shoves his fingers through his hair, softens his voice. "You or someone else on the ranch could get hurt. You gotta be careful."

"Okay, I will." I hitch the bag of feed he hands me against my hip. "I'm sorry. Clearly, I'm just meant to shimmy on stage."

The tight tension in his face clears. "Nah, you'll learn."

We resume our walk to the barn.

"It's busy," I remark. Vans of guests are pulling in. The start of a new week.

"It wasn't always like this."

"It wasn't?"

"Nah. I fucked up a few years back. Put the ranch in trouble." Ford looks tense, as though the memory is painful. "Ruby got hurt. It all went wrong." Turmoil laces his drawl.

"Is everything okay now?" I ask.

There's something about a wounded Ford Montgomery that tugs at my heartstrings. Makes me want to help him. The man definitely has demons.

When he doesn't reply, I reach over and touch his arm. "Ford?"

Jolting out of whatever daze held him, he shifts the bag in his big hands. "Yeah. We're back on track."

"Do you own the ranch?"

"Nah. Charlie does," Ford says with a hint of pride. "Bought it during some sort of life crisis. But he got his shit together."

I look down at my boots as they crunch gravel. Life crisis. Is that what I'm having?

"Is that why you came?" I've been trying to figure out why Ford retired from baseball. "To help your brother?"

His eyes collide with mine. There's so much pain in them that I physically feel it.

"I had a mid-life crisis too," he says.

He doesn't offer anything more and I don't pry. This country boy has stories he doesn't want to share. I can relate.

At the barn, Ford slides the door open for me, and a wave of cool air hits us as we march inside. We drop the bags of feed in the tack room, and I can't help but smile as I straighten up. It's funny. For all the dusty cowboys, worn-out jeans, and pickup trucks, this barn is about one level down from the Ritz.

"Stay away from the horses when you can," Ford warns, nodding at my bangles. "Those noisemakers you wear scare 'em."

Feeling's mutual.

I eye the horses warily. Just like they eye me. I can be around them, but riding them is another story entirely. "I'm sorry."

He arches a brow. "Could take them off."

"Can't. They're welded to my flesh."

He snorts. "No more sorries either."

"So many rules on the ranch," I tease.

"No rules," he says easily. "I just don't like you apologizing for yourself when you've done nothing wrong."

Oh.

I don't know what to make of it, only that my heart pounds double time.

I sweep the floor, every so often sneaking glances at Ford.

He is everything rugged and untamed—the Rocky Mountains, rawhide, whiskey—wrapped up in one lean package of man.

Ford moves through the barn with a long stride. The horses lean into his touch, his dexterous hands moving with a surprising gentleness as he pets them. He greets each one with a carrot and a soft murmur. Muscles ripple in his back, the veins in his forearms flexing as he coils the rope and loops it over a peg on the wall.

I've never had a fetish for cowboys. Gavin fixed me up with musicians or pretty-boy actors. But watching Ford work in those tight blue jeans does something infernal to my heart. Causes a soft pulse between my legs.

I'm beginning to think a muscled, hardworking blue-collar man is more attractive than any LA rockstar I've laid eyes on.

The sweep of the broom over the hay-strewn ground has a calming effect, and before long, Ford fades from mind as I lose myself in the work.

At the ping of my phone, my heart leaps. Earlier, I emailed my lawyer to get a copy of my contract. I retrieve my phone from my back pocket and open my email.

> Reese,
>
> Apologies for the delay.
>
> Unfortunately, I'm unable to send you a copy of your requested contract.
>
> I've emailed and copied Gavin on this correspondence. If you need anything further, feel free to reach out to him.
>
> Respectfully,
> H.M. Cline

A hard lump forms in my throat. It's all so unfair. Gavin's behind this. Somehow.

A text pops up, obscuring my email.

I freeze when I see the preview: **You fucking whore.**

Perfect. It's like the cherry on the shit sundae that is my life.

Movement at my side makes me jump, and I scramble to hide the phone. But I'm too late and Ford sees.

"Who the fuck is that?" he says gruffly.

"No one."

"I'm serious, Reese." Before I know it, my phone is in his large hand. He stares at the screen, his knuckles so white I'm afraid he'll crack the screen.

I tug on his arm. "If you break it, I can't afford a new phone, Country Boy."

There's a long moment of silence, then, with fire in his eyes, he hands it back to me. "Open it."

I shove a finger in his face. "It's none of your business."

When he continues to stare at me, I cave first. Sighing, I open my text thread.

> **You fucking ruined everything, Reese. You stupid little bitch. I'm walking away like you want. I'm off the tour. It's all your fucking fault.**

Ford stiffens, moving a little closer to me.

I sigh. "It's okay."

His face is stone. "It's not okay. No one should talk to you like that."

"I get these three times a day. Luckily, I have terrible cell service at the chalet, so they only make an appearance when I'm here." I roll my eyes. "He's a real wordsmith, this one."

"Wait." Now he looks like he wants to punch something. "You've been getting these the entire time you've been here?"

As if to goad Ford further, another text pops up.

> **I'm done with you, bitch. Biiitch.**

His eyebrows gather. "Okay, who the hell is this clown?"

"Kyler."

"Kyler? What kind of name is that?"

I roll my eyes. "Says the guy who's named after a car."

"And you dated this asshole?" Contempt fills his voice.

"I told you that we dated for optics."

"Let me guess. He takes you out downtown to do some lines before passing out."

I arch a challenging brow, curious now. "And you could do better?"

He steps closer, firing all my senses. "Yeah, I could. I'd take you out driving, down to my favorite lake. Catch us a catfish dinner, then I'd bring you back to my place and—"

A smile tug at my lips. "And?"

"And—" I watch as he struggles to keep his breathing even, his jaw tight. Then he clears his throat and says in a gravelly voice, "Treat you better than that, that's for damn sure."

My knees go weak at Ford's sweet words, and hot tears spring to my eyes.

"Now he's making you cry." His shoulders tense. "That means I kill him."

"It's not Kyler," I say, stowing my phone in my back pocket. "He's an idiot." I let out a slow, measured breath. "I emailed my lawyer about my contract, and she won't send it."

"That ain't right. She works for you."

"I thought so." I feel like I've been sleepwalking through my entire career, and only now, on Runaway Ranch with its fresh air and this cowboy talking common sense, am I waking up. "I don't understand any of this."

"So listen." Ford drags a hand down his dusty face. "I did something you might not like."

I narrow my eyes. "What kind of something?"

"I hired someone to help you."

Wordlessly, I stare at him. A horse chuffs in its stall.

"He's a PI," Ford explains. "I thought he could look into your contract. Make it make sense."

"A PI?" My head swims. "If I can't get it, what makes you think he can?"

Ford's eyes light with amusement. "It's my brother's contact. He was a Marine. He knows people in high—or low—places. Dark web shit."

My heart thunders in my chest, and I force my gaze away from him. Ford helping me is sweet, but someone looking into my past, my secrets…the thought of what could come out has me feeling lightheaded.

All the bad parts of my life uncovered.

Panic crashes through me.

Twisting a bangle on my wrist, I move away from him. "I don't understand. Why are you doing this?" I turn, eyeing him warily. "You treated me like shit when I first got here. But then you rescued me from a bar fight, bought me a wardrobe of clothes, let me eat dinner with your family, and now you've hired a PI?"

He says nothing, his face stony.

I cover my face. "Ugh, why couldn't you just keep your brooding personality and make me hate you for the entire summer? Why did you have to go and be nice?"

"Jesus, Reese." There's exasperation in his voice. Slowly, he closes the distance between us and reaches down to take my shoulders, forcing me to look at him. "Someone needs to be nice to you."

I stare at his touch as if in a daze. "I just—" I lick my lips. Questions and suspicions weave through Ford's handsome features. He wants my story. But he's not getting it. "My past isn't great."

"The PI goes through you, okay? Not me. I don't need

to know what you don't want me to know. All I'm doin'
is—"

"Paying for it." The words come out bitterly.

He swears under his breath. "Look, honey, take the
goddamn help. Something tells me you don't have a lot of
people you can trust."

A tear slips down my cheek. He's right. I don't.

Ford's face, his voice, softens. "No one will rat you out,
Reese. You're safe here, okay?"

My breath trips in my throat. "Safe with you?"

He doesn't move a muscle.

"Yeah," he finally rasps. "You are."

My eyes widen as his hand finds my chin, tilts my gaze
to his. The same gentle gesture as last night. Heat rushes
to my stomach. He steps closer, a wall of hard chest moving into my space.

I try to pull back, but he holds me where I stand.
Relentless, the man.

His hand cups my cheek, then tucks a loose curl behind my ear. It feels like a flamethrower ignites my body
as he leans forward. My lips part—

"*We got a code Freedom Fucker,*" crackles from the two-
way radio on Ford's hip, jolting us apart.

Swearing, he grabs the radio and silences it.

"What's a code Freedom Fucker?" I ask, still feeling
Ford's breath against my lips.

"It's Wyatt-speak for the cows got out." Into the receiver, he snarls, "Your turn, asshole."

Then he snaps off the dial. When his gaze returns to
my face, he says, "You, uh, said you don't have service at
the chalet."

"It's okay," I tell him. "I like the quiet."

He holds out the two-way radio. "You should take this."

I blink. "It's yours."

"I don't want you out there without a phone." Gaze tracking my face, he clears his throat. "Besides, I have another. Use it when you need me."

The corner of my mouth turns up. "That's assuming I'll need you." I lean in, fingers grazing his as I inspect the radio. "How does it work?"

"Here." He fiddles with the buttons and shows me the ropes. A random burst of static from the speaker has me wincing. "It turns off and on randomly," he says, banging it against his thigh. "Glitchy wiring."

I laugh lightly. "Sounds like me."

"Channel twelve is the ranch," he gruffs out. "And nine is mine."

"Got it."

He hitches his thumb as he walks backward to the barn door. "I need to help my brothers. Cow shit."

"Duly noted. Cow shit."

Ford shoots me a charming smile. "Same time tomorrow?"

"Same time tomorrow," I breathe.

⌒

The ache in my muscles is bliss. It feels like I've moved two ten-ton boulders after the grueling work today, but I've never felt more accomplished.

A cricket chirps outside the kitchen window. The sun set an hour ago, and the buzz on my phone is non-existent.

Like I said, bliss.

I take the small cheeseboard I made for myself and pad across the kitchen floor to my bed. With a satisfied sigh, I sink onto the mattress and kick my legs up, taking in my freshly painted toes. On top of the quilt is a copy of *French Vogue* and my notepad, scrawled with a what-could-be song.

I could be at the Chateau Marmont drinking bubbly rosé, but this is better. This is real.

For the first time in years, I'm alone. And I'm enjoying it. No pressure. No paparazzi. No social media. Just me writing at long fucking last.

I stare at the bottle of pills on my nightstand. Then, with a nudge of my finger, I flick them into the trash. After today, taking orders from Gavin isn't on my agenda. They don't help with the black hole, anyway. All they do is make me tired. Numb.

From the nightstand comes the crackle of the two-way radio. I left it on to give myself a bit of company. Not to mention eavesdropping on ranch conversations is interesting. Who knew there was such a thing as a barn manager?

Plus, it's like a channel to the outside world. To Ford.

I think of that near-miss kiss today in the barn. His hand in my hair. That look in his eyes. Like? Lust? Loathing? Loathing, I decide. It has to be.

Despite my undeniable attraction to this broody country boy, I refuse to fall for Ford Montgomery. My life is a mess, and a man complicates everything. Besides, I'm leaving soon. He has his choice of any woman he wants. A man like Ford doesn't want a girl like me. He has his life together. He's a bright light, and I'm just that black hole. Existing. Hovering somewhere in the ether.

Even if he doesn't make me feel like that.

For once in my life, he makes me feel like I could have hope.

My fingers itch, and I give in, picking up the two-way radio. I switch the channel to Ford's, telling myself it's a distraction. Simply a way to entertain my runaway brain.

It's not because I miss him. And it's not because he feels like the only friend I've had in a long time.

"Moo," I say into the receiver. "Calling all cows."

For a few seconds, silence. My heartbeat hammers as I wait. Then a rolling rumble of a chuckle comes through the radio.

"Cows have been secured."

I recline into a pillow. "What're you doing?"

"Watching a ballgame." I picture him in those gray sweatpants, Mouse on his lap, and suddenly, wish I were there. Beside him.

"Who's winning?"

"The Braves. What are you up to?"

I look at my notepad and flinch. "I wrote a song. A bad one."

"I doubt that." The sound of the baseball game gets lower. "Play it for me one day?"

I smile. "Maybe."

"It's late," he says almost sternly.

"I know." Honesty makes my heart speed up. "I didn't want to be alone."

A long pause. Then, "I'll keep the radio on."

"Really?"

"Really." I hear him sigh. "Good night, Reese."

I settle back against the pillows and close my eyes. "Good night, Ford."

14

Ford

THERE'S A BLUEBIRD IN MY EAR, AND A DREAM GIRL on my mind.

The fog of the dream clears, although the face in my mind looks suspiciously like Reese.

"Fuck," I groan, giving my dick a quick stroke. It could punch through drywall.

I lie in bed with my arm over my eyes, willing my morning wood to die a slow death.

Thirteen days of sunshine. Thirteen days of Reese.

She's become part of my daily routine. Every morning, I greet her the same way—with coffee and a bagel. The rest of the day, we do chores and Reese keeps me company. I should hate it, but I don't.

The two-way radio crackles, and a melancholy warble fills the air. I lift my arm from my face and blink.

Reese.

It's Reese.

I latch onto the familiar tune—Hank Williams, 1952. One of my favorites. The mournful melody fills my bedroom.

That's when I realize the button must be stuck from our conversation last night. Our MO for the last two weeks. We've talked about everything under the sun and then some. Her favorite color is pink, her middle name is Elisabeth, and Paris is her favorite city in the world, but I still don't know why she's really here or much about her past. Which is fair. I haven't given her anything about Savannah or the shit I've done. Some things are better left in the dust.

That's not to say I'm not damn curious.

My hand comes to my chest, rubbing at the sting. But it soon eases when I focus on Reese.

Shifting on the mattress, I close my eyes and listen.

My heart pumps hard, and I can't catch my breath. For a moment, I'm paralyzed by a desire I don't know what to do with.

Fuck. That voice.

It's clear in her videos and on the radio that she can sing. But I've never heard her voice like this before. Like some old-time yodeling cowgirl. Husky and sweet. Goddamn beautiful.

Bluebird.

She's a fucking bluebird.

Soon Reese's voice mixes with the sound of running water.

I blink myself awake.

The shower. Reese naked. My dick perks up. I picture her wet, soaping those perfect breasts of hers. Blonde hair stuck to her cheek. That pink mouth—

"Hey, y'all hear that?" Wyatt's drawl cuts in, breaking me out of my reverie. "Someone's singing."

Charlie grunts. "Ain't me, that's for goddamn sure."

"Ford?" Davis says. "You there?"

Gritting my teeth, I jerk up in bed.

"Get off her fucking channel," I snarl. It feels like an invasion of her privacy. No one hears my bluebird but me.

I wait until I'm sure the line's clear, then I disconnect.

Fuck me.

I get out of the bed so fast it's embarrassing.

Time to start my day. Time to see Reese.

~

The arched brow Davis gives me the moment I step foot in the Bullshit Box already has me pissed off.

"What?" I grunt.

"You gave her a radio?" Davis asks. His own two-way radio sits on his desk next to a cup of coffee.

"Yeah, I did. You got a problem with it, take it up with HR."

"We don't have HR," Charlie says dryly.

I settle at my desk and shuffle through files and paperwork. The bane of our existence. Any of us would rather be out in the fields.

And I'd rather be out there with Reese.

Through the open door of the Bullshit Box, my gaze latches onto her. Reese struts across the ranch, curls blowing in the breeze, a basket of eggs in her hands. Like the mighty Mississippi, those legs run on for miles. She's put on weight since she's been here and looks healthy as hell. Sexy. A fucking bombshell. A star.

My cock flexes as I watch her bend over. I don't know what's worse. What she wore when she first came to the ranch or what she's wearing now.

She's all leather and lace. Sex and sweetness. Tiny shorts, tinier tank tops, gold jewelry, cowboy boots. And those fucking braids she wears has her looking like a downhome country girl.

Goddamn torture is what it is.

She's running the ranch wild.

Running me wild.

I haven't tried to touch her since our almost-kiss. Hands off is a version of Ford Montgomery I don't even recognize.

But that doesn't mean I don't want to touch her.

I want to fuck that girl raw.

She's so goddamn beautiful. I feel unhinged when she just breathes near me. I haven't felt this way in a long time. Damn if that girl isn't drilled into my skull.

A sigh has me looking over.

"What?" I demand.

Davis needles that vein in his temple and holds up a package Reese was in charge of delivering. "This was supposed to go to Koty's bakery, not here. Now I have to get someone to cart it back to town."

I pick up a letter opener, slice through a piece of mail. "Go easy on her, will you? She's trying."

I've given her easy farm chores, but she's been an absolute disaster on the ranch. Last week, she lost control of a wheelbarrow, and it smashed through a fence. Yesterday, she drove the UTV over Ruby's flowerbed.

I thought for sure she'd give up after the first week, but she's hung in there. Pride swells in my chest. She's not the least bit intimidated, and she's always ready to learn. I was wrong about her. She's a damn hard worker.

"You can always take it out of her paycheck," Charlie says.

My head snaps up, and I open my mouth, ready to rip my brother a new one when I see him grin.

I glare at him. Bastard's trying to bait me. It's working.

"She's a beautiful girl." I shrug, channeling all the nonchalance I can. "Ain't for me."

"Since when?" Charlie lifts a smug brow. "She's—"

"Don't say it," I warn.

"Your type," Davis finishes, his eyes narrowing.

"Yeah, she's really fucking cute, and she's an absolute nightmare." I lift the guestbook. "How's the rest of the season look?" I ask, hoping to distract them away from pointed questions about Reese.

But they don't bite.

"Have you kissed her yet?" Davis demands.

Almost.

"Fuck off," I snap, feeling combative.

Charlie laughs. "Holy shit, you haven't."

"Have you tried?" Davis asks.

I give my brothers another frosty glare. "We're friends."

A snort from Davis.

Charlie's eyebrows shoot to the sky. "Friends? When was the last time you've been friends with a woman?"

Never. I've never been friends with a single woman. It's downright torturous staying away from Reese.

"Girl's got secrets," Charlie says. "I'm not sayin' it's a bad thing, but it's her thing. And maybe you ought to know, Ford."

I blow out a breath, hating the reminder that she's hiding something. Hating the fact that I want to know. "Since when did you get so smart?"

"Since you shut the fuck up," he retorts, lifting his coffee cup to his bearded lips.

"Yeah, well, we're gonna figure that out soon." I drum a hand on the desk and look at Davis. "Your contact came through. He's going to get the information to us soon."

I got the email this morning after I showered, jerking off so vigorously to Reese that I saw stars.

Davis looks unimpressed. "Hope it helps."

Me too.

"Got something I want to talk to y'all about." Charlie rotates his chair to face both me and Davis. "Floyd Gunderson's farm is up for sale."

Currently, Floyd lets us use the land known as Old Mill's Farm to graze our cattle. The farm is a thirty-acre spread right next door to Runaway Ranch.

Charlie arches a dark brow. "Could be good for us. Let us expand."

"I have enough expansion." Chuckling, Davis swivels his head to me. "What about you?"

With Reese here, I haven't given Jim Donovan's offer much thought.

The two-way radio crackles, and Sam's voice floats through the speaker. "*Can we get a medic on-site?*"

"Shit," Charlie swears, head jerking up.

"*Pasture two. Jane took a spill.*"

Panic twists in my throat like a blade, and the rational part of my brain shuts off.

Without waiting for a word from my brothers, I drop everything and run.

It feels like an eternity before I spot Reese. She's sitting on the grass near the training pen, her basket of eggs overturned and her sunglasses lying beside her hand. Sam and a few ranch hands and guests circle her.

"What happened?" I shove my way through them before dropping to my knees beside Reese.

"I was leaving the pen, and the gate dropped too soon." Her face is pale.

I look up at Sam, ready to strangle him. "Those gates were supposed to be fixed weeks ago."

Reese hisses as I extend her right arm. Above her wrist, on her forearm, is a bloody slash.

"You're okay," I murmur, mostly to reassure myself.

She nods. Squeezes her eyes shut. "I hate the sight of blood."

I lift my baseball cap so I can see her better. "We need to get you bandaged up, Birdie."

Her eyes widen. "Birdie?" Her full mouth parts in a smile. "Whatever happened to princess? Honey? Brat?"

Dry-mouthed, I scrape a hand through my hair. The slip-up is damn embarrassing.

"Birdie suits you better." I tug on her braid. "You came here to give me a heart attack, didn't you?"

Her smile is soft. "I'm keeping you on your toes, Country Boy."

Voices sound above us.

"Is she okay?"

"You look familiar? Do I know you?"

Reese flinches as several guests crowd around us.

"No," I snap. "You don't know her." I move closer to Reese, tucking her protectively against my chest.

"I have a kit in the garage. I'll take care of it," I tell Sam, wanting Reese away from prying eyes.

"Ford," she whispers. Worry in her beautiful green eyes.

"I got you, baby."

She doesn't argue as I pick her up in my arms and make the trek to the garage.

As soon as we're inside, I gently place her on the workbench. She waits there while I hunt for a first aid kit.

My heart beats heavily in my ears as waves of pent-up anger sweep over me.

My head is fucked up. I never should have turned her

loose on the ranch. I'm responsible for her. Those gates could have crushed her.

Finding nothing, I swear. Slam a drawer.

"You're acting awful angry, Country Boy." She sounds amused.

"I'm pissed," I say, strain evident in my voice as I try to keep my cool.

"At me?"

I blow out a slow breath. "No, Reese, not at you."

"Well, I'm pissed." She wrinkles her nose. "I broke my eggs."

I want to laugh at the grumpy expression on her face. I also want to grab her by the shoulders and shake her. Hell, she gives me butterflies, but she's also guaranteed to give me high blood pressure.

"Eggs are the least of your worries." My eyes land on her bloody arm. "You almost got crushed to death by a fucking gate."

Finally, I find a first aid kit in a toolbox.

"Let me see." Gripping her wrist, I extend her arm. The cut isn't deep, thank Christ. As I reach out to clean it, I run a thumb across her bangles. The thin skin on the inside of her wrist.

Paling, she jerks away. "It's fine. I'll do it myself."

Frustrated, I drop the kit onto the workbench. "Goddamn it, woman, you never let anyone help you, do you?"

With her back to me, she digs into the kit, then haphazardly slaps a bandage on her arm. Shitty work. Just like her attitude.

She sucks in an impatient breath and juts her chin. "I don't need your help."

My jaw tightens at the haughty tone of her voice.

This is why she turns me on. One minute we're friends. The next, she's pushing my buttons every chance she gets.

"I've had people helping me my entire life," she says with a toss of her braids. "That's why I'm here to help myself. The last thing I need is you."

My chest feels like a bullet just tore through it. That fucking emerald gaze of fire burns into me as she stands and pushes past me for the door, but I'm on her heels.

"Drop the attitude." I catch her by the hips and pull her against me. She gasps and wiggles in my firm hold.

"Rude," she snaps.

I spin her around. "You need a little rude in your life. You also need a goddamn spanking." For a moment, only the sound of our ragged breaths. "Cut the tantrum shit out right now," I growl. "And sit your ass down."

With a defiant huff of breath, she stares at me. "No."

There's something in my ribcage. A taut string. And the minute she steps into me, it snaps.

The fire between us finally combusts.

This maddening woman.

Fuck it.

I grip the back of her neck and slam her mouth to mine.

Reese clutches me tightly in her arms, and her lips return the kiss with startling urgency.

I melt into the kiss, my hand clasping the back of her neck to keep her against my lips. She tastes like I expected. Dangerous.

Deadly.

Goddamn exciting.

Kissing Reese is like soaking my soul in gas and setting my heart on fire.

Before I'm ready for it to end, Reese pulls away from
me, her plump lips a pink pout. "We can't do this," she
murmurs. Her lower body shifts against me.

Torturously.

"We can," I rasp. The arch of her body into mine. The
flare of her nostrils. I read her signals loud and clear. "We
can, Birdie Girl."

I drop my face into her throat and walk her backward
until she reaches the side of the Chevy. I don't need to
hear the reasons we shouldn't do this. I already fucking
know them.

She's twenty-six, I'm thirty-seven. She's a rock star,
I'm a fucking mechanic. She's my employee, I'm her boss.

So many things are wrong between us, but it feels so
right.

I've wanted this girl since she walked onto the ranch.

One taste of her and this obsession will be out of my
system.

I press her against the Chevy and lean in, dragging
my mouth across her throat. "You want it as bad as I do?"

With a whimper, she rakes her nails through my hair.
"Yes," she gasps, her words music to my ears. "Yes, God,
yes. I want you."

"That's not my name, honey, so let's try it again."

Her long lashes flutter. "Ford," she whispers.

Without taking my gaze off her, my hands run along
her creamy skin. Thighs. Hips. Throat. "I'm gonna break
you, baby. But in the best kind of way."

She arches her back as my palms slide beneath her
tank top. Her mouth parts in a perfect O. I yank her tank

top down, exposing full, beautiful breasts and perky, pink nipples.

I edge back, taking her in, and stop breathing. She's always stunning, but she's absolutely breathtaking in my garage, half-naked, with nothing between us.

Perfect in every fucking way.

"Christ," I mutter, my eyes drinking in every soft curve. "Baby, your tits look so fucking good."

She writhes against me. Her hand goes to my jeans, cupping my erection, eager and anxious.

It makes me chuckle. Makes me hard as hell.

I dip my head and close my mouth over one pink nipple. Reese goes limp in my arms, her nails digging into the meat of my shoulder. She presses herself closer, plumping her breast in my mouth. Gently, I bite her nipple, and she releases a half-cry, half-moan.

I slide off her shorts and panties, her flawless body glowing in the soft lights of the garage. Blood surges to my cock. She's all golden curves and wild, unraveled hair. She's never looked more beautiful. I'm ruined. Absolutely ruined.

"Turn around," I order.

Reese nods, her eyes glued to my face, then complies with my demand.

I grin, about to deliver on what I promised her.

I pin her bangled wrists in one hand and let my other hand fly, smacking her ass. Reese gasps and arches up on her toes. Eyes fluttering shut, she dips forward against the Chevy, releasing a small moan.

Ass still up.

Goddamn.

The realization sends a hot rush of blood to my cock. She likes it.

I spank her again, reddening that silky ass of hers and drawing another cry from her lips. "Be a good girl and take it."

Her chest rises and falls. A feline smile curves her lips as she glances over her shoulder and husks, "Who says I'm good?"

Fuck me.

My cock punches against the zipper of my jeans.

One more bite of my palm against her bare ass, and I turn her to face me.

"I'm going to fuck you like a cowboy, honey. Treat you like a princess." Her eyes are green orbs in the hazy light of the garage. "But first, let me touch you."

Panting, she spreads her trembling legs.

I drop my hand and fit two fingers inside of her, watching the way her stomach sucks in, the little shivers that run through her.

So goddamn wet. Drenched.

"Birdie Girl," I hum. "You feel as good as you look."

She sucks me in deeper, vise-like. My fingers worship her. The scent of her arousal whips through the air, driving me insane. Feral.

"Ford." A sob falls from her mouth.

She's a wild little thing in my arms, writhing like she's never had a good fuck. Which I intend to rectify. When she leaves this ranch, there will be no doubt in her pretty little head about who fucked her the best. She'll never forget this cowboy.

"I know, baby. I know." I settle my hips against hers, driving my hard-on against her bare pussy. I graze my mouth against hers. "It aches, doesn't it?"

In response, she lets out a soft whine. A sexy sound that has all my control deserting me.

"You want more?" We're both fucking famished for each other.

She whimpers and knots my shirt in her hands. "I need you. *In* me. Now, Ford."

Grinning, my hands go to my back pockets.

"Fuck." I freeze. "I don't have a condom."

"I'm clean," she gasps. "I can't have kids."

That stops me for a minute. "We're gonna come back to that," I growl. Not sure why I say it. Not sure why I care.

"Kids *right now*. I have an IUD," she murmurs, tugging on my lower lip with her teeth. "That's one thing I know is in my contract. Gavin's orders."

What the fuck?

Before my mind can spin out of control, before anger can rise up, Reese grabs me and kisses her way down my throat. She's everywhere. A flash of gold, trembling breath, and warm skin.

Groaning, my head falls back as she attacks my belt buckle, then my zipper. Her hands feel like flames as they stroke over my rock-hard cock.

The way she works me over, the perfect friction, drives me fucking wild. I attack her pouty mouth, kissing her like she's my last breath. It's like the moment before a big pitch—complete tunnel vision. Reese is all I see.

I'm fucking shaking. I want to take her in every way possible.

The old Chevy groans as I lift her and pin her against the side of the car, one arm beneath her hips to keep her steady. I fist my cock and guide it between her trembling thighs. Right into her tight little pussy.

"Fuck," I growl, beginning to pump. "Fuck me." I practically gasp for air as she squeezes me so perfectly. Reese is even better than I imagined. Better than my dream girl. Better than any woman I've had in the last seven years.

Reese cries out, her hair a golden halo as her head falls back, exposing the column of her delicate throat.

"Every inch of me fits you perfectly." I bear down harder, pumping away. "Perfection, baby. So fucking tight. So fucking drenched."

Her glazed eyes find mine, and her slender arms loop lightly around my neck. "More, Ford. *Faster.*" She lets out a husky growl that spurs me on.

I drive myself harder, thrusting into her heat. She's so fucking slippery, her pussy sucking me in, my balls pounding off her supple ass. It's a dream. It has to be.

"Fuck," I grit out in between frantic kisses. "Look at me slip-sliding in the gorgeous mess all over your thighs."

Together, we look down at where we're joined. My heart buckles at the sight. Too perfect for words. Pulling out slightly, I drag a finger through her soaked pussy.

Reese's pleased whimpers are music to my ears. So sexy it's criminal.

My gaze settles on the necklace I gave her, and I gently wrap my hand around her throat. I squeeze lightly, relishing the arch of her slender body. Relishing the fact she still wears my necklace.

"Come inside of me," she whispers, digging her nails into my back. "Like a good country boy." Her smile is teasing, torturous.

I ignite, and a roar thunders from my lungs. I'm ravenous for this girl. Don't know how I've stayed away this long.

I slam back into her, thrusting frantically, holding her

tight, bearing down, like I can absorb every perfect part of this girl.

She gasps, shudders, and then she's coming.

She screams my name. *My* name. It's the voice of an angel. And it fucking terrifies me.

I like it too goddamn much.

My orgasm isn't far behind. I roar my release, shaking violently as it flows through me. Starbursts plume behind my eyes.

Dream girl. My fucking dream girl.

Breathing hard, I kiss her temple before slowly slipping out and lowering her back onto her feet. She sways once, then smiles.

Need has me gathering her against me. I cup her cheek and stroke a thumb over her pouty lips. Searching her eyes, I take in every inch of her gorgeous face. "You good, Birdie?"

"I'm good." A rosy flush stains her cheeks. "You?"

"Better than." I yank up my jeans and grab a clean paper towel off the workbench. After wiping the mess from her thighs, I help her get dressed, then settle her onto a stool.

"Let's get you cleaned up," I say, nodding at the first aid kit. "And that includes the arm."

With her lips pursed, she listens instead of argues.

As I clean and bandage her arm, Reese looks up at me. "So…what does this mean?" She bites her lip, seeming reluctant. "One time, right?"

My heart rate kicks up, the idea like a detonation in my chest.

It's then that I realize I'm a fucking fool if I think I can stay away from her.

I shrug. "Could keep it casual."

Her face lights up. "Sure," she agrees. "No strings."

Thank Christ. The relief I feel at keeping this going is borderline embarrassing.

Hell, it looks like red flags and beautiful girls are destined to run in my DNA.

Satisfied her arm is properly bandaged, I snip the end of the gauze. "Just friends for the summer," I say, taping the bandage.

She giggles. "Friends. Do we shake on it?"

I laugh, lean down, and kiss her lips. "Bluebird, I think we just did."

15

Reese

WHO KNEW THAT SUNLIGHT COULD CLEAR the mind of its troubles? Or that a shortage of whiskey and midnight dips in the lake could work wonders. That watching a bare-chested, broody cowboy hauling hay would bring its own sort of peace. Oh, and the sex.

All the sex.

The summer heat makes people do all kinds of crazy things. Like me, for example. Doing Ford Montgomery.

A month ago, I was surviving. And now? Now I feel relaxed for the first time in my life. My credit card came through. I have my first paycheck. Money *I* made. A PI is on the hunt for my contract. Thanks to Ford.

Ford.

I bite my lip, watching Ford and Wyatt toss hay bales with pitch-perfect precision. As I pass by on my way to the chicken coop, I catch Ford's eye, and he tilts his cowboy hat, giving me that charming smile.

I flush.

Birdie.

He calls me Birdie.

A crank turns on in my heart, like it's pumping extra blood, winding up emotions I thought I'd buried. Emotions—no chance of shutting those off.

Because Ford is a winning combination. Funny and

sexy, confident without the cockiness. He doesn't take himself too seriously. I always laugh when I'm with him, and I haven't done that in a long time.

Still, we're not anything serious. We're doing casual naked things for the summer. For the feral horniness that comes over me whenever I'm around him. For the plot.

I can live with that. I need that. When I'm with Ford, he makes me forget. He's a steady, reliable, handsome distraction in my life. When I'm with him, I don't think about my music, my contract, or my hovering black hole. I think about myself.

We'll fool around for the summer, and when it's over, I'll go back to the city and leave this country boy alone. Because even though he's a cowboy, my life isn't a country song. There's no hero. I have to save myself.

Every step on the ranch is me moving forward. Every heartbeat means I am alive.

Chicken squawks greet me when I reach the coop.

I smile. This is one of my favorite chores. The chickens are smelly and loud, but they're free and curious, which I find fascinating. They squabble and cluck without a care in the world. We should all be so lucky to be chickens.

Humming, I step inside the coop, the two-way radio bouncing on the side of my hip. Instantly, a barrage of chickens peep and purr in my presence. I say hi to my favorites, giving them extra-long pets.

"I'm so sorry for stealing your babies," I say as I collect their eggs. "I truly would not blame you if you pecked my eyes out." With that, I loop the basket around my wrist and step outside.

I freeze.

Standing outside the chicken coop is a tall, broad-shouldered man with jet-black hair and a scar slicing down one cheek. He looks like a brutish Clark Kent.

The man steps into my space.

"Employees only, sir."

He moves, blocking my path. "Reese Austin, right?"

"Sorry." Anxiety bubbles in my stomach. Press or fan, I can't tell. I keep my head down in case he tries to snap a photo. "You must have me confused with someone else."

"No, I don't," he says simply. "I've been looking for you."

Panic flares to life inside of me. I've had stalkers before, but they've never gotten this close. "I'm working. I can't give autographs."

"I don't want an autograph. I want you."

My heart races as I take a step back, boxed in by the chicken coop and the man. Thinking quickly, I drop a hand to my hip and bring the two-way radio to my mouth. "Help," I say into the receiver. "Ford, help."

There's a crackle of static. Silence. Then, Ford.

Across the pasture, I watch him drop the hay bale and whip around, finding me instantly. He must see it all over my face because he leaps off the baler, and races toward me at a dead run.

A flash of gold tooth. "You don't need help, Reese. What you need is me."

His raspy voice makes me shiver.

When Ford reaches me, he grabs my arm and pushes me behind him.

"Ford…" My breath hitches.

He remains rigid, his hands fisting at his sides. "Who the fuck are you?"

The man chuckles. "I'm your fairy fucking godfather."

It's eerily quiet in the lodge. Mid-afternoon, most guests have already checked in and out on tours for the day.

At the dining table in the cantina, Bo Bosko, the private investigator Ford hired, sets up a makeshift office. Files and laptops spread out over the long surface. With his crisp three-piece suit, slicked back black hair, and gold tooth, he's professional, if not slightly terrifying.

Now that I know he's not a stalker or here to kill me, I've relaxed. The same can't be said for Ford. His face is mutinous. He's all clenched fists and gnashing jaw, prowling and protective, pacing behind me like an anxious wildcat.

"He's here to help," I remind him. "You hired him."

Ford crosses his arms. "He should have called."

"It ruins my entrance," Bosko says blandly. He sets aside a stack of papers and closes his briefcase.

I lean in. "Why do they call you The Poacher?"

Bosko grins. "Because I steal things."

I'm deciding if that's a good thing or a bad thing when Bosko slides a copy of my contract across the table to me.

"Here it is," he proclaims. His Marine Corps pinky ring catches the light from a nearby window.

I stare down at the contract like it's a mirage. When I glance up at Ford, his scowl has melted away and now he looks worried.

"You can stay," I tell him.

"You sure?" he asks, thumbs hooked through his belt loops.

I nod. For some reason, I want him here.

Pulling out a chair, he sits beside me.

I flip through the pages. There're are some clauses I

remember, but the majority of the document is redacted. Long passages have been blacked out. When I get to the end, I frown.

This contract is hereby effective immediately and expires ████████████

I tap the signature line. "It looks like it's missing a part."

"It is." Bosko shuffles the papers around. "A lot of parts. This contract was marked *Reese*. Which makes me think this marked-up version is the one your manager's been showing you."

Ford, reading over my shoulder, says, "Hell, even our MLB contracts weren't this fucking confusing."

"It's essentially a conservatorship," Bosko explains. "You signed over a majority of your rights. Guardianship. Control over your career."

Shame sweeps over me. "I know."

"You were sixteen?" Bosko asks.

I nod and look back down at the contract. "It's my fault. I shouldn't have signed it—"

"Not your fault, Birdie." Ford gives me a gentle look. "You were a kid."

Bosko gestures my way. "And you were at Muirwood—"

"I was," I say sharply, cutting him off. Every muscle in my body tightens. "I signed it when I was there. After— after everything that happened."

"Wait." Now Bosko looks interested. "You signed the contract at Muirwood?"

"Yes."

I can feel Ford watching, curious, but he says nothing.

God, I'm beginning to wish I hadn't asked him to stay.

I don't want him to think I'm crazy like Gavin does.

What if I show too much of myself to him, and he runs? I'll lose him like I've lost everyone else in my life.

Even though he's temporary, he's still my friend, and I don't have many of those.

As if he can read my hesitation, Bosko nods. "We'll come back to that."

I nod, sick to my stomach.

"Everyone who's seemingly employed by you is paid by Gavin. Everyone answers to him. Lawyers, doctors, publicists, your record label. Not you, Reese. You have no power. You have no say."

"Fuck me," Ford mutters under his breath.

It's like a bucket of icy water splashed in my face. I sit there and absorb the blow.

Bosko's right. I have never had control. I lost myself so long ago, I've forgotten who I am. All because I handed my life over to Gavin on a silver platter.

"I also found a strong possibility Gavin's been mismanaging your financials."

"What are you talking about?" Over and over, I twist my bangles on my wrist. When I see Bosko's shrewd eyes on me, I drop my hand and reach for Ford's. I need him like I need air.

"Reese, you're a superstar. According to *Variety*, you're worth two hundred million. Yet you have no money?"

I blow out a breath, my frustration rising. "Well, Gavin cut off my cards and access to my bank account."

Bosko gives me a long, squirm-inducing stare. Finally, he speaks. "No. I mean you have *no* money. Zero. It's mostly gone."

My stomach sinks, and I'm mortified to feel tears pricking my eyelids. It just keeps getting worse.

Gavin always allotted money to me, like an allowance. Which is bullshit because it's mine. I earned every cent. He always said it was part of the process, that it was coming, but he had to have the accountants divvy it up first to those who needed their cut. Tours, merch, album sales—where has it all been going?

"Gavin." The words drip from my mouth. "It's been going to Gavin."

"Exactly. I think he's stealing from you."

My jaw drops. "Based on what?"

"It's a hunch. But I'm working to pull some statements," he says calmly. "You followed your hunch and left. Why?"

I grip the edge of the table, thinking of the black hole that's shrunk since I've been at the ranch. "I don't—I don't know. It felt bad. Dark."

"You trusted your gut," Bosko says, and I immediately feel vindicated. "Have you spoken to him?"

"I called him—"

"You called him?" Bosko sighs like I've royally fucked up.

"Once. Just to check in."

"How did he act?"

"He wanted me to come back." I bite my lip. "We're supposed to sign a contract…he wouldn't tell me what."

"Does he know where you are?"

"No."

"Keep it that way." Bosko's craggy brow furrows. "He said he's going to help you?"

"Yes."

"He ever said that before?"

A shiver of paranoia runs through me. "All the time."

Bosko nods and taps my contract. "The key's in this. The end date."

I stare at my loopy sixteen-year-old signature. The Old Reese who didn't know what she was doing. But I know now. I can fix it. I can be the woman she needed back then.

"My advice." Bosko's clipped voice has me looking up. "Sign nothing the man puts in front of you without your own lawyer. This contract is something you need out of, Reese. At first glance, it's fraudulent, not to mention abusive."

Ford squeezes my hand. "She's here for the summer."

The gesture of solidarity is so sweet my eyes flood. He's on my side one hundred percent. It feels incredible.

"Excellent. That gives us some time. I'll dig around." Bosko's blue-eyed gaze lands on me. "Meanwhile, Reese, you start hiring your own team. Lawyers, publicists. I have a list of people you can trust. I'll send them over."

Ford stands from the chair and hustles over to the front desk to help a late arrival.

Bosko opens his briefcase. "You get to decide how you live your life, Reese. What you did in the past doesn't make the future."

"Can you really do all this by the end of the summer?" I ask, feeling overwhelmed. This was supposed to be a break, but now it feels like an escape.

"I move fast," he says, his voice low and dangerous.

"Muirwood." My eyes flick to Ford, handing over a key to a family of three. "You know."

"I do. But it's your secret, and I'm in the business of keeping those close."

I smile. Bosko is creepy, but he's also charming. He

gives me hope, while also making me feel like he'll break someone's legs.

"You don't deserve what happened to you, and you don't deserve someone taking advantage of it." Bosko stacks his papers and laptop in his glossy black briefcase. "If you signed under duress, it should be easy to get you out of your contract. Just hang tight. Try not to give Gavin any indication of what you've been up to. It's safer that way."

"She ain't safe?"

Ford stands there, his eyes on us. His voice has dropped into sub-zero temperatures.

Locks click on Bosko's briefcase, and he stands. "Just keep her here," he tells Ford. To me, he says, "Whatever you do, don't go back with Gavin. Delay. Lie if you need to buy yourself time. And remember that you make the calls now, Reese. You have the power. Stay here. Stay out of trouble."

Goose bumps prickle on my arm.

I hope it's that easy.

16

Ford

"**T**HIS IS IT. THE HONEY HOLE."

Reese arches a brow. "I knew it. That's what you call all the girls."

I laugh. Give her ass a squeeze. "Nah, baby, just you."

Self-control deserting me, I lean in and kiss her pouty lips. Reese clings to me as her tongue tangles with mine.

I waited too damn long to kiss this girl, and now I'm taking every chance I get to have her mouth on mine. But kissing isn't all we've been doing. Sex. In the barn. The lodge. My apartment. Her chalet. We've fucked all over this goddamn ranch.

I can't keep my hands off her.

I need a neon sign above my head that flashes the reminder We're Just Friends. Because at night when I'm buried in her sweet pussy, I forget about all the reasons it won't work. I forget to be careful. My brain only has space for Reese. I'm obsessed.

But I'm not an idiot.

This is for the summer. I'm helping her out—for Grady.

And then she'll go.

"What exactly is a honey hole?" Reese asks when we break apart and continue our trek to the river.

"It's a fish mecca." The fishing poles bounce over my shoulder. "A secret spot no one knows about."

She laces her fingers with mine. Wrinkles her nose. "Should we be sneaking off in the middle of a workday?"

Hell yes. She needs a distraction. After the visit from the private investigator last week, the pretty wrinkle in her brow hasn't budged. Not that I blame her.

My stomach's been in a knot since I heard the news.

I said I'd respect her privacy, that I wouldn't dig into whatever she's running from. One thing is obvious, though. She's a vault of fucking secrets.

I shouldn't get involved. I should step back and let her deal with them herself.

But a little voice inside of me says it's impossible.

Reese spreads out a blanket and settles on the riverbank while I bait and cast the lines.

"Is it true the fish can hear you?" she asks, pulling out snacks from the basket she brought along.

I laugh. "Nah, Birdie. My dad just wanted me to shut the fuck up."

Above us, the hot June sun shines. Birdsong sounds in the trees.

I smile as I settle beside Reese. Instead of sandwiches or water—actual nourishment—she's brought along bags of chips, gummy bears, and Sprite. It's like her body exists on sugar alone. As long as Reese is eating, that's all that matters.

Leaning in, I spin my baseball cap backward so I can kiss her properly. "What's with the junk food?"

A flush spreads over her cheeks. "It's my way of rebelling. Gavin never let me have sweets. Not even on birthdays."

"Hell, you never had a birthday cake?"

Her teeth tug at her lower lip. "No. We never had

parties. Or at least real parties with balloons and candles. It was either in a club or I was alone in a hotel room." She thinks about it. "I think the last party I had was when I was seven. My mom made me a unicorn cake."

My stomach tightens.

"Gavin always checked us in under the most ridiculous names," she says, stretching out on the blanket. "For hotels or tours, we were the von Trapps or the Waltons or even"—she laughs—"the Bradys. But we weren't happy. Not like those perfect families on TV. I think maybe he thought of us like that."

There's so much sadness in her voice. All I want to do is take it away.

I drag a hand through my hair. "You ever think about tracking down your folks?"

"Sometimes." She exhales and stretches in the sunshine. "Sometimes I wish I could see my parents. For one day. Just get answers. Sometimes I don't understand why they gave me up." She shrugs. "Sometimes I do."

I give a nod, not wanting her to be sad any longer. "Go on, Birdie girl, put those pretty toes down in the water."

She does, giggling as her pink-painted toes meet the ice-cold water.

"Doing things different, that's what you're doing."

She smiles, a certain fragileness in her expression. "Yeah. I like that." She rests her head on my shoulder. Her blonde locks tickle my arm. "I like the way you make me feel, Ford. Like I can do anything."

Damn if that doesn't steal the breath from my lungs.

"You can, you know." When she doesn't answer, I ask, "What would you do if you could do anything?"

"I don't know. I think that's what I'm out here to find

out." Twisting into me, she opens a bag of Combos. "I've never loved the rat race of the tour. The exhaustion. I loved it because I was told I loved it. Because I felt like I owed Gavin."

Before I can ask what she means, she says, "I just want out. I don't want to go back."

Over my dead body.

I shake my head against the sudden fury.

"What would you do?"

"Anything but be locked up again."

My gut roils. When she talks…it's desperate. Caged. Christ, I hate it.

"Would you sing?"

"Only my songs. I'd do everything my way. I'd travel. Go to Paris. It's my favorite spot in the world." Gathering her hair over her shoulder, she begins to braid the long strands. "Either way, I'll be out of here by summer's end."

A pit opens in my stomach. I shake off the emotion. Of course she has to leave. This girl can't stay on the ranch forever.

She cocks her head. "What about you? Do you like it here?"

I think of the job offer hanging over my head like a noose. There have been two more texts from Savannah and a phone call from Jim. Screened them both.

"I do. It's the greatest gig in the sky. But sometimes I feel like it's not mine."

"What do you mean?"

Feeling like I've said too much, I rub my jaw. "It's not my ranch. I'm just here."

"Where would you be if you weren't?"

Good question.

"I got a job offer," I admit. Talking to Reese is easy. "It's in New York. I'd be working as a commentator for the Renegades."

Her eyes go wide. "Would you take it?"

"It'd mean leaving my brothers. This life."

"Well, if you like it here, you should stay," she says simply. "Do something you want, Ford. Put a baseball diamond in the pasture."

I chuckle. "Ain't a bad idea."

"When do you have to decide?"

"End of summer."

She gives me a sad smile. "Looks like we both have countdowns."

My teeth grind together.

Reese squeals as the fishing pole clatters to the ground. The line jerks tight, telling me we've got a fish.

"Shit." So damn involved in our conversation, I've barely paid attention.

We scramble up. I grab the pole and reel it in. Right before I can pull the fish ashore, it escapes the hook. Its colorful body splashes into the water.

"Get it, get it," Reese says, half-laughing, half-dancing beside me.

On instinct, I stick a hand into the water.

"Holy fuck," I blast. In my hand, is the wriggling fish. "I didn't think it'd actually work."

Reese screams and breaks into a laugh, which pulls one from me. Big and bright. I blink at the noise. It feels like it's been so damn long since I've had someone to share a moment like this with. My brothers are alright—but a gorgeous girl can't be beat.

She leans down and inspects the fish, her eyes wide and curious. "What kind is it?"

"Rainbow trout."

"He's so pretty," she breathes. Her green eyes find me. "Can we let him go?"

I swallow the tight knot in my throat. "Yeah, we can." My brothers would give me hell, but I crouch and release the fish into the water. In seconds, it's gone.

When I straighten, Reese is bending over to check the second line.

I grin. Fuck self-control. I never said I had any.

I slip my hand up her dress. "Oil check."

Reese gasps and spins around, her eyes widening. Then she smiles. "Better pay attention to the fish."

"Nah, baby." I tug at the end of her braid. Prowl for her. "I like you better."

A smile lights up her face. "You do, huh?"

I grab her up in my arms. She whimpers as my mouth meets hers. Walking her backward, I press her back against a tree and absolutely inhale her.

This girl is better than adrenaline, a rock climb, a day at the lake. She is pure bliss. Wild, fun, and fiercely sexy. She's the best damn time I've ever had, and I don't want to let her go.

I let loose a low moan into her mouth as her nails rake through my hair. My cock throbs. I feel like a goddamn teenage kid trying to rein in his hormones. Can't stay away from her—won't.

My hands quickly slip her lace panties down her thighs.

"Your body, Reese," I murmur, "is an absolute goddamn stunner. Has me absolutely fucking feral."

She clings to me, spreads her legs.

"Lord have mercy," I growl as I slip my cock into her warmth.

Over and over, I thrust. Reese's gasps sound in my ears. Sweat drips down my spine. Her body moves and bends with mine. The back arch, the hip roll, I'm out of my goddamn mind.

"That's how you ride a cowboy, baby. Just like that."

Voices sound from the forest. Glancing around the tree trunk, I spot guests led by a guide, traipsing for the falls.

Reese squeaks.

I grin.

"Oh my God, Steve, look at that spotted thrush."

"Ford," Reese hisses. Her cheeks are bright pink. "There's a group right there."

"So stop talking." I kiss her, shutting her up. Drinking in all that sweetness. "Before I spank that ass and give everyone a real show."

The hungry look in her eyes tells me she wants the sting of my hand.

Yanking her away from the tree so I have the best angle, I bring my palm up.

The sharp slap echoes through the silence.

The tour moves on into the forest.

Reese releases a sigh, the breathy sound shooting straight to my aching dick. She tilts her head back, blonde hair tangling in the tree bark. I run my hand up her throat and squeeze lightly.

She bucks wildly. "Faster, *faster*, Ford."

"Birdie girl," I whisper, gritting my teeth. "I'm going to fuck you so goddamn hard you'll feel me for days."

She whimpers, runs her nails through my hair, bites my shoulder. "So deep. I can feel you so deep."

I pump harder, drawing her into me. Our hearts thunder.

Mine.

Mine for the summer.

I don't get close. I don't do commitments. I don't know what the fuck I'm doing.

All I know is that the moment my lips meet hers, I know I want to keep doing it with Reese.

⁓

We get back to the lodge at dinnertime. Guests file around a corner and enter the cantina. After Reese and I return the poles to reception, she gives me a kiss, then turns to go.

I snag her hand. "Hey, where are you goin'?"

"I don't know." She gives me a teasing grin. "Nowhere?"

"Very fucking funny." I band my arms around her slender waist. "Want to keep the day goin'? Come back to my place?"

"And?" Green eyes glittering, she lifts a brow. "Ford Montgomery, are you trying to get me into bed? Again?"

Funny how weeks ago that'd be my MO. But for once, I'm not thinking about how to get this girl into bed. I'm thinking about how I can get her to stick around a little longer. I like talking to her. And if talking means we find our way into bed, I can deal with that, too.

"Could cook you dinner." I give her a smirk. "God knows you need a home-cooked meal."

She punches a finger in my chest. Scoffs. "Combos are a king's meal, and don't you forget it."

"Whatever you say, Birdie Girl." Then, because I'm an absolute sucker, I drop my mouth to hers and inhale this girl who's shaken up my entire world.

A throat clears from behind us.

We pull back from each other. Dakota stands nearby, a white pastry box in her hands.

"Playing hooky?" she asks.

"Don't tell the boss," I say.

She holds a finger to her lips. "Wouldn't dream of it." Dakota's dark eyes land on Reese.

"There's someone here to see you." Dakota hesitates. "He said he'd wait, but I'm not sure if he's supposed to be here."

Reese stiffens. Her eyes fly to the leather couch near the great windows. "Oh my God. It's Gavin."

My eyes lock onto the bastard. A man in his late forties adjusts his tie and scans the lodge with an expression of disdain. Suddenly, all I want to do is fasten him to my truck's hitch and do several hundred donuts in the parking lot.

"What the fuck is he doing here?" I take a step forward.

"No." Reese shoves me back. "Stay here. Let me handle it."

Before I can say anything, she rushes away.

Dakota comes up beside me. Her touch is cool as she slips a hand around my bicep. "She's scared of him."

My hand balls into a fist. "Yeah. She sure as fuck is."

17

Reese

THE SIGHT OF GAVIN SUCKS EVERY OUNCE OF JOY out of me. All afternoon my heart has been up in the sky with Ford but now this perfect day has plummeted into the ground like a landmine.

"Gavin, what are you doing here?" After our phone call, he probably thought I'd come crawling back because of my money problems. That I'd give in to his demands. That's why he's here. Because I've survived too long without him.

"Hello to you too, Reese." Gavin adjusts the cuffs on his Brioni suit. Always tailored. Always in control. That's Gavin.

"How did you find me?"

He arches a brow. "I have a tracker in your phone."

I stand there, rocked. "What?"

My conversation with Bosko made me think he was overreacting, but now I wonder if I haven't been paranoid enough. He *tracked* me. What else has he done without my permission?

"I have to take care of you, Reese," he clips. "Because God knows you can't do it yourself."

I close my eyes and pretend for one second he believes in me. Loves me. Cares about me.

But the lie doesn't land. Not anymore.

Gavin's eyes narrow. "You look different."

"I cut my hair. And I gained five pounds." Saying it out loud feels like I have power.

Annoyance creeps into his expression as he extends a hand to the buttery leather couch. "Sit."

Gritting my teeth, I obey. He settles across from me. Those cold blue eyes used to intimidate stylists, publicists stare me down.

"It's been a month. It's time to come home."

"You said the summer." I feel like a petulant child arguing with my father.

"We have contracts that still need to be ironed out." He squints, inspecting me. "Are you off your meds?"

"I ran out," I lie, hating myself.

"I thought so." Sighing, he pulls a pill bottle out of his suit pocket and sets it on the wagon wheel coffee table. "What would you do without me, Reese? You'd never survive."

But I have. And I can.

Time spent here has given me clarity. I don't feel as foggy or as numb as I typically do.

I've never let myself dream about anything other than being famous. It was already set in stone for me. But on Runaway Ranch, the possibilities seem endless. My life seems up for grabs. A life I wasn't sure I wanted at one time.

If I sing, I want to sing with my whole body. No more drugs, no more drink, no more strange men in my bed, or dark holes in my head.

"If we wait too long between albums, they'll forget about you. Right now, we can spin your absence to RCA as a resurgence. But that means there are contracts to sign and songs to sing."

I hold his gaze. "I don't want to do that album, Gavin. It's shit, and I sound like a robot. I want to do *my* songs."

"You disappoint me."

I flinch. It still stings.

Gavin leans in, his hands gripped so tightly around his knees I can see the white of his knuckles. "You'd give up everything we worked for…" His head swivels around the lodge. "For this? Some fucking summer vacation?"

"It's not a vacation, it's…"

Clarity.

Calm.

Hope.

"It's *my* life," I say, covering my bangles with one hand. "You're not allowed to control it."

He snorts. "Your life. Let me tell you about *your life*. Your parents didn't want you. They abandoned you, and now you're pushing me away. The one person who's been there for you. I've loved you like a father."

For the first time in forever, anger sparks inside of me. I don't trust Gavin.

Maybe I never have.

Memories crash into my head.

Gavin putting that pen in my hand. *Let me help you, Reese.*

Gavin tying my wrists to the saddle. *Let me help you, Reese.*

He didn't help me at all, did he? He hurt me.

He purses his lips. "Do you honestly expect me to let you go after I created you? After everything I've given you?"

A chill rolls through my spine.

"I'm done here, Gavin." I stand, but he's on my heels.

He clasps my elbow and pulls me close. "Don't make me get Muirwood involved. I will if you keep throwing these petty fucking tantrums."

The blood drains from my face. I stand so still my entire body is a heartbeat.

"That night you tried to take your own life, who stayed with you?" He leans in, a growl in his voice. "Who got you better?"

"You did." Tears well in my eyes. "You."

"That's right. So you think real fucking good about whether you want to bite the hand that feeds you." I flinch when he reaches out to stroke my hair. "Who will take care of you, my shiny little shooting star?" he asks in a softer tone. "Who will want you? Who will help you? What will you do? Because remember, you failed at that, too."

A tear slips down my cheek. I squeeze my eyes shut.

"There a problem here?" Boots thud and I open my eyes to see Ford at my side.

Gavin drops his hand.

"No," I whisper. I turn into Ford, trying to wipe my face covertly, but his eyes narrow. Damn him. The man doesn't miss a thing.

Gavin runs a hand down his tie. "Who's this? The help?"

A dark shadow crosses Ford's face, and he aims a glare so icy at Gavin that a chill runs down my spine. "Ford Montgomery," he says.

"I'm here to take Reese home."

Ford crosses his arms. "That wasn't the deal I heard was arranged."

"She spent the summer."

"Summer lasts until the end of August around here," Ford says easily, but the muscle jerking in his cheek tells me he's angry. "Not sure how you do it in the city, but that ain't it, son."

Gavin's nostrils flare at the barb.

I smother a smile.

"Reese." Gavin's face reddens, a telltale sign he's at his boiling point. "We need to speak. In private."

Bosko's words drop into my head like a whisper of help. *Whatever you do, don't go back with him. Lie. Put him off to buy yourself time.*

"We've said all we needed to." I take a deep breath and lift my chin. "If I go back, I want you to open up my accounts. I want to see everything. Contracts, lawyers, accounts."

The briefest flash of worry crosses Gavin's plastic face. I hide a smile. Gavin can make ripples, but I can make waves.

He laughs dryly. "It'll take time. But if that's what you need to come home…"

"I do." I smooth a hand across my dress. "I need that. And then I'll go to the studio. I'll do the album." I give him my sweetest smile. Whatever I have to do to protect myself, to buy me time. "I promise."

Gavin's gaze is dark, but he says, "I'll hold you to that, Reese."

Then, without another word, he stalks to the door, whipping it open and storming into the bright July sunshine.

Ford pulls me into him. "You okay?"

"I'm so sorry," I sniffle, fighting back tears. "I had no idea he was coming."

"How'd he find you?"

I flinch. I already know he won't like it. "He said he has a tracker in my phone."

Ford swears.

I stare at the door Gavin exited. The urge to give in like I've always done resurfaces. It all feels hopeless. Like I'll never escape.

"Maybe I should go with him." My voice is hollow. "Make it easier."

No matter how much anger and distrust I feel towards Gavin, there's still the fear he's right. What if I can't do it? Will the summer really make a difference?

I wait for my mother's voice. *Be brave.* Instead, I hear Ford's.

"Don't go."

I look up at him. "What?"

Ford's handsome face is creased with something I don't recognize. "I don't want you to go."

"You don't?" I breathe.

"No, Birdie. I don't."

"Why?" I bite my lip. "Because of Grady?"

"No." His throat works. "Because of me. I like you here."

"Yeah? You like me, Country Boy?"

"You're a pain in my ass, but yeah." His voice softens. "I like you."

My heart riots in my chest. I can't think of a time in my life when someone has truly wanted me around. It makes me feel more than wanted. It makes me feel everything. Especially happy.

Ford cups my cheek. "Stay, okay?"

And then he leans down and kisses me, on the ranch, in front of everyone.

The black hole, the past—I may never get over them.

But Ford makes me feel like I can. If only for a little while.

18

Ford

I T'S SEVEN A.M. WHEN I BURST INTO CHARLIE'S
cabin. I groan when I spot Ruby and Charlie in the
kitchen. So much for not getting hassled about why
I'm here. Charlie sits at the counter, paper in hand. There
are about half a dozen flower varieties scattered across the
kitchen table. Ruby stands over them, brown kraft paper
in her arms.

Making sure to school my expression into a scowl, I
start checking the cupboards. "Y'all got any honey?"

Charlie glances up from the paper. "Honey?"

"For Reese's coffee."

Ruby perks up. "Reese?"

Charlie looks doubtful. "Honey in coffee?"

Their interrogation grates on my nerves, but I keep my
mouth closed. The sooner I'm out of here, the better. I have
a naked girl in my bed, sleeping the day away like she damn
well should. I want to get back to my place, brew a pot
of coffee, and make Reese breakfast before she wakes up.

Christ. The things I'm doing these days. Cursing as I
trip over her high heels. Mouse preferring her more than
me.

For some reason, it brings a smile to my lips.

Charlie arches a brow. "Friends sleep over?"

Flower arranging forgotten, Ruby stares with rapt
attention.

"None of your business," I remind him. Spying the honey bear in the spice cabinet, I grab it up and make a mental note to pick up three or four of them on my next grocery run.

"My ranch, my business," Charlie grunts.

He has a point. Everyone knows about us now. Especially after kissing Reese in the lodge last week. The grapevine works fast.

"Heard you had words with Reese's manager," Charlie says.

I lean back against the counter, cross my arms. "I hate that guy."

He was worse than I expected. And I expected a lot based on what she had told me. Warning signs went off in my head the second I saw him. How can I let her go back now that I know what she's up against? It's clear there's no one in her corner who cares. Well, I fucking care.

I wanted to hit the guy. So damn bad.

He made her cry, and he put his fucking hands on her. He's lucky he walked away in one piece. Reese was good though, lying through her teeth to give herself time. Until then, I want to keep her close. And if close means she stays at my place every night, so be it.

"You want some flowers?" Ruby asks, pulling me from my thoughts. "For Reese?"

"If you got time," I say, trying to keep my voice casual.

"Friends get flowers?"

I round on my mouthy brother. "Is there an echo in here?"

"Hush," Ruby scolds Charlie. To me, she says, "What are her favorites?"

I scratch my head. I don't have the slightest idea.

Helping me out, Ruby says, "I'll give you one of each. For research purposes." She giggles.

I wag a finger at her. "None of fucking that."

"You swearing at my wife, asshole?" Charlie growls before slugging down his coffee and pushing back from the counter.

"She started it."

Hustling around the kitchen, Charlie sets his cup in the sink. "We're closing off the chalets."

"What, when?"

"End of summer. One of them has snakes. The other bad pipes. We'll either refinish or demolish."

"Reese is in a chalet," I growl.

"She'll be gone by then." Charlie grins. His eyes dare me to say otherwise. "Won't she?"

She will be, and a fire burns deep in my gut at the thought. But there's no other option. We're friends with benefits. That's how it stays.

Before I can rebut, my eyes snag on two overnight bags sitting by the front door.

"Y'all goin' someplace?" I ask.

"Bozeman," Charlie calls out, stomping down the hall. "Overnighter."

I drift toward Ruby. Her small hands arrange stems.

"Those." I point to a stem of small blue bulbs. My throat bobs. "She'll like those."

"Bluebells," Ruby says, giving the stem a delicate sniff. *Bluebells for my Bluebird.*

"They're fairy flowers. They mean strength." Her blue eyes flick to me. "Love."

I shake my head. "That's your forte, not mine."

As Ruby works, I glance down at the table. Beneath the

wrapping papers, my gaze snags on paperwork. Medical paperwork. Before I can get a good look, a large hand slams down, blocking my view.

"Nosy bastard," Charlie mutters.

"I'm your big brother," I tell him, punching a finger in his chest. "It's my job."

Charlie rolls his eyes, snatching up the papers. Then he kisses his wife, grabs his Stetson, and heads out the door.

Worry rising inside me, I glance at Ruby. "You okay, honey? Say the word and I drop him in a lake."

Ruby sets down the bouquet, a bright kaleidoscope of color. She tilts her blonde head, staring at me with serious blue eyes. "I am. Are you?"

"Yeah, actually, I am."

Never been better. I'm happy. Reese, with her big green eyes and sweet kisses, has unraveled me.

Ruby beams. "It's nice, Ford. You're not the relationship grinch."

I pinch my brow. "Fairy Tale, you're killing me."

She bats her eyes at me. "You learn why she's here yet?"

I give in. Fuck it. "No," I tell her. "She won't talk to me. Nothing deep at least."

Ruby hands me the bouquet. "Maybe you give her a truth to get hers?"

Considering it, I rub a hand over my jaw. "Give a truth, huh?"

One truth. Maybe that's all it would take to get Reese's.

19

Reese

HE TWO-WAY RADIO CRACKLES AT ONE A.M. *"Mayday, mayday, you fuckers."* Ford's snarl floats through the receiver. *"I'm in the barn if anyone wants to take a midnight stroll."*

Worry curdles my gut and I slip out of bed. I find a flannel shirt Ford left behind and put it on, the hem grazing the apex of my thighs.

Dead of night, I race across the farm. There's a light on in the barn and a dark shadow crossing the pasture at a slow lope. My heartbeat picks up.

With a deep breath, I step inside. The hay floor crunches under the soles of my slippers. "Ford?" I say softly. When there is no response, I keep searching. Finally, I find him in the last stall with the pregnant mare, Sassafras.

His head snaps up at my approach. "What're you doing here?" The worried drawl of his voice sends shivers down my spine.

"You were on my channel," I offer. "What's happening?" I glance at the mare lying in a bed of hay in the stall.

He sits back on his haunches, sighs. "She's foaling." His hand tears through his hair. "Normally, we let them do their thing, but she's having twins." Frustration stains his voice.

"Is that bad?"

"It's rare. Davis is trying to get a vet out here. But… typically, the second foal never makes it."

My heart hitches. "Well, we can't give up."

Ford blows out a breath. "All we can do is wait. Let nature take its course." He runs a broad hand down her nose. "I'm planning to stay. Sit with her."

"I'll stay, too. Keep you company," I say. He looks more distressed than normal. I hate the look on his handsome face. More than anything, I just want to be here for him. And the mare.

"It might not be pretty, Birdie."

I slip inside the stall, holding my bangles to keep them quiet. "That's okay."

"Then get warm." He passes me a blanket. Watches as I cover my bare legs.

Sassafras flops over onto her side.

Ford strokes his hand down her rump, then we settle in opposite corners of the stall. I stare at his handsome face, trying hard not to let the fire burn me up inside. Maybe it's reckless. I've never been in a true relationship. One I've chosen for myself. It was always for PR. For Gavin. For something. But the ache I have for Ford is different.

It's also something that can never be. He is a temptation I can't afford long-term. All we are is a train wreck going off the rails.

If I had better judgment, I'd leave. Stop sleeping with him. But the truth is, I need him.

Ever since the visit with Gavin, our conversation has been a heavy weight on my shoulders. Nothing has helped. Not swimming at night. Not ranch work. Not visiting with Ruby on her front porch. The black hole has grown. I was so hopeful here on Runaway Ranch. Hopeful it would all go away. But it hasn't. I'm still Old Reese. Sad Reese.

The darkness presses down, hollow and stifling.

"You wanna tell me why you dislike horses, Birdie Girl?" Ford's low drawl takes my attention.

I stare at my bangles, unable to look him in the eye. "They're just a bad memory."

"And you don't like talkin' about those?"

It's the silence that pulls it out of me. That great gaping need to reach for a light in the dark.

I lift my head. "Have you ever you been sad, Ford?"

A crease forms between his eyebrows. "Sure."

"Like really sad? Like a concrete body in water?"

He's silent, but his gaze stays on mine to show me he's listening

"You don't have to tell me," I say. "You don't owe me anything."

Ford looks to the mare, sitting motionless. Only that muscle jerking in his jaw tells me he's thinking. After a long silence, he says, "When I played for the Renegades, I was dating a woman. Savannah. We were together for three damn years if you can believe it."

I sit straighter and curl my legs to my chest. I always assumed Ford was a playboy, a new woman in his bed every night.

"I had this grand idea to propose on the field." He snorts. "Bought a ring, asked her daddy, the whole damn thing. I got down on one knee and popped the question. In front of everyone." He swallows. "She said no."

I gasp. "Ford. Why?"

"She made it clear I wasn't the one. Too country, too white trash, you pick one."

My heart aches for him. The nerve of her to break his heart in front of everyone, then tell him he didn't matter.

"Heartbreak makes you do fucked-up shit. I could sit here and tell you I wasn't sad, but at the time, she ruined my fucking life." Ford flinches. "It made me an angry person. I wrote the book on being an asshole. I made mistakes. Big ones. Fucked up in the worst way a man can."

I wait for more, but he stops there.

His throat bobs. "That's why I'm here. Because it hurt so goddamn bad, I had to run halfway across the world to escape it."

Hand threading through his lionlike hair, he says, "I haven't talked about her in a long time. I learned my heart was a whole lot happier when she stayed the hell away from it."

He sighs. "But sometimes that's just the way life plays. There's no use in looking back."

"I hate her for doing that to you." I lean forward, wanting to take away his pain. "You're not trash. You're the best person I have ever known. And I haven't known you for very long, but I already know this, so that's saying a lot."

He smiles, his eyes unreadable.

"Do you get sad, Reese?" Ford asks, voice pitched low. "Is that why you don't talk about your past?"

Tears fill my eyes. "Yes," I whisper.

My mind freezes on what to say. Here, in the protective quiet of the dark, I could tell him everything about my past. About Muirwood. But if he knew...he wouldn't want me. Even if we are temporary, the rejection would still hurt.

Before I can say anything, the acrid smell of blood floods the stall. The mare lies on the hay, staring at her already-standing baby. But there's one more on the ground. Unmoving.

I gasp, cover my mouth.

"Fuck," Ford grits. He hovers over the horse and blasts an order into the two-way radio before whipping to me and holding out a hand to keep me back. "I don't want you to see this, Birdie."

But I can't turn away. My chest swells. Heavy tears roll down my cheeks.

I hold my breath as Ford inspects the foal.

"Fuck. She ain't gonna make it." His shoulders drop.

"No," I say. "We can't give up." Eyes flooding, I crawl across the floor to the foal and rest a palm on its slowly rising belly. I just sit there and stare at her, trying real hard not to cry. "You'll know," I whisper. "You'll know when it's time to go or stay, okay? So you just be brave and make your choice and we'll still love you anyway."

Ford makes a kind of strangled noise in his throat. "Reese…"

I don't respond to Ford. All I do is remember—everything.

Putting on a paper dress and walking the halls of Muirwood. Saying everything but no. Gavin handing me a contract and telling me no one would ever find out.

Be brave, be brave, be brave.

My daddy singing me his songs, the Labrador that ran off, the food we didn't have. My mama picking mold off bread so we could still eat it. That's why I listened to Gavin. So I could be a star. So my past didn't matter. So I could be someone inside of me I never knew existed.

We stay where we are until the foal's chest stops rising. Until Ford takes my hand and helps me stand.

Ford touches my chin. But he doesn't kiss me. A cloud of worry darkens his face as he stares down at me.

He wipes a tear from my cheek with a calloused thumb. "You're trembling."

"I'm okay."

When we leave the barn, he doesn't let me look back.

20

Ford

SETTLING ON A BAR STOOL, I ORDER TWO BEERS AND watch through the window as Davis crosses Main Street. The auctioneer's frenetic bleat from the county livestock market follows him into the bar.

Age-old tradition: after the horse auction, Davis and I hit the Alehouse, a dive bar in the small town of Angel River. Four hours north of Resurrection, Angel River's annual horse auction is a hub for rodeo enthusiasts and ranch owners around the world.

We bid on two horses we wanted—a Quarter Horse and an American Paint. Now, we wait for the stable hands to prepare them for the ride back to town.

"How's it feel?" I ask when my brother settles beside me. "Break from the wife and kid?"

He chuckles. Twists the gold band on his ring finger. "Losin' my damn mind." He thumbs through his phone and angles toward me to flash a photo of Dakota and Squish in the bathtub. "Missing out on too much."

I chuckle. "Sucker."

Even for Davis, his smile is cheesy. "Wouldn't have it any other way."

Head down, I thumb through my own phone. Reese hasn't replied to my text from this morning.

Fuck it. I send another. Just in case she needs anything.

I'd never voice it, but I get what Davis means. My mind

has strayed to Reese more often than I'd like, clearly because I'm a needy bastard when it comes to her.

Three damn days I've been away from her.

I hate it.

Truth is, my mind hasn't eased since the night we spent in the barn.

I've spent my entire life on a ranch. I have a diamond-hard heart when it comes to death, but that night unsettled the hell out of me.

Thoughts of Reese and that dying foal flood my mind. Her saying, *We can't give up.*

Is that how she feels? That everyone's given up on her?

I think about what Grady said. *She's sad. She's not okay.*

That night in the barn, I told her about Savannah, thinking maybe my own secret would drag one or two from her. But she's locked tighter than Fort Knox.

I want to help her. I want more of her. Those big green eyes. Pouty pink lips. The way she laughs with her entire body and teases me incessantly. Her presence is a rush I can't get anywhere else.

"You give anymore thought to Donovan's job offer?" Davis eyes me over the rim of his beer. "Summer is halfway over." His tone is casual, but the question feels the opposite.

"Not sure yet."

There's a hesitation in my gut when it comes to taking the job, because it doesn't feel right. It doesn't feel like *me.* What Reese said about putting a baseball diamond in the pasture…now that makes sense. Makes me excited. I have to figure out what I can do with that. One thing's for certain, my girl's got answers.

"Got another idea?" Davis's brow is a deep furrow.

I grin.

My twin has always had my back. He's the only one who knows the truth about what happened after Savannah. The only one who's seen me struggle with depression after what I did to that kid. Somehow, he reads my mind when I can't seem to get out what I need to.

I sip my beer. "I'm thinking something up. I'll let you know when I know."

Davis lifts his palm. "Well, we'd miss you. *I'd* miss you."

"How about we talk about other matters? Other brothers." The faster I change the subject, the quicker I can get Davis off my back.

"Wyatt?"

"Charlie."

"What about Charlie?"

"Ruby and Charlie are acting fishy. Taking long-ass trips to God knows where. Every weekend they've been going up to Bozeman."

Davis laughs. "What? You think Ruby's a drug mule?" He shakes his head. "They're buying a flower shop. They're busy."

"C'mon, D. He's the same little shit who ratted you out when you got drunk and threw up in the barn in eighth grade. You don't buy his bullshit. I know you got a kid, but you got eyes on the ranch, too."

"Excuse me," a soft voice says. I look over as a redhead stretches herself over the bar, over me, to grab a napkin. The hem of her shirt slips up, and she gives me a bright smile, then heads to a spot at the end of the bar.

"Buying her a drink?" Davis asks, nodding in the direction of the redhead. "I'll wait."

"No." I shrug. "Not feeling it."

He raises an eyebrow in question. "That's a first. You sure?"

I eye my brother. This is Davis's dickhead way of testing me. Our usual routine was him going back to the motel, and me picking up a girl. Now that's the last thing on my mind. Why? My jaw clenches at the reason—because of Reese.

Slowly, she's taken me apart piece by piece this summer. I don't know how it happened. Just that it has. Reese wearing my shirts night after night. Smelling like me. Messing up my apartment. Feeding my cat. We say we're just friends, but there's a fucking string in my gut that connects me to her.

But these are not things cowboys say out loud. Feelings only go as far as trucks and beer.

"I knew it." Davis's voice breaks my reverie. "You only smile like that when you're getting laid."

Irritated, I swing my head in his direction. "You want to say what you fucking want to say?"

"Reese. You're getting in too deep with her."

"You're one to talk. You moved Dakota onto the ranch when she was—"

Davis swings a finger in my direction. "Don't say it."

I snap my mouth shut. It would be a low blow. But he knows I'm right. She was pregnant with another man's baby and Davis still claimed that kid. I would have done the same thing too, but he doesn't need to know that.

A tense silence falls over the bar top as we glare at each other.

"Look, I didn't see you tryin' to rein in Charlie when he was head over boots with Ruby."

"Is that what you are? Head over boots?"

Fuck.

"No," I grit out, tugging a hand through my hair. "I'm not."

Head over boots is for men who are ready to settle down. I'm not that type. Not anymore.

"And Charlie's different. He needed Ruby. I'm not so sure you need Reese. You've seen those articles," Davis says stubbornly. "She's a mess. Combustible. Y'all got nothing in common. She tours all over the world and you're a fucking rock. You drive a truck and she—"

"That's what we're talkin' about?" I laugh darkly, arching a brow. "Trucks?"

"You know what I'm getting at."

Yeah, I do. We're opposites. He thinks I'm making the same mistakes all over again.

I scrape a hand down my face. Anger bubbles under my skin. It takes every last therapy session in me not to put a fist in my twin's face. "You need to lay off," I snap.

Davis is a bossy bastard, but he's taking it to a new low.

On the surface, Reese looks a mess, but it couldn't be further from the truth. It takes a strong person to give up everything to find what they want and I'm learning that's Reese. Even if she doesn't believe that about herself.

"Hell, D, I've got articles out there. I fucked up, and your grumpy ass stuck behind me the entire way." I finish my beer, gesture for the tab. "She's in trouble. Her manager's a sleazy piece of shit. Reese needs someone in her corner. And that's me."

He's silent for a long beat then says, "Then you're what? A thing?"

I snort. "C'mon, man. That girl is wildfire. She'll burn

it on up, then tear it outta here end of summer." Even as I say it, the words sink heavily into my gut.

I tell myself I don't care if she goes back. I tell myself it's for the summer. I'm a cowboy. I'm helping her out. Picking me is the last thing she'd ever do. She's going places. I'm just a stop on her tour. And she's just a notch on my bed post.

But I don't know if I believe the lie anymore.

"She's destructive," Davis insists.

"Not destructive. She's broken."

"Ford. If she's toxic—"

"I got hazmat gear," I shoot back.

"Fuck," Davis mutters in exasperation.

Sick of the inquisition, I slam my beer down. "Fuck, why are you so invested in this, man? Why do you care?"

Davis looks conflicted. "Because I don't want to see you go to that dark place again, brother. When you fall, you fall fast and hard. This girl leaves, you're gonna get your stupid heart broken and I'm gonna be the one to scrape your sorry ass up and put it back together."

I face him, needing to own up. Because I get it. I've been doing the same thing with Wyatt this summer, trying to look out for him. "Reese isn't bad for me. And I don't plan on going to that dark place again." I give him a look. "I'm on drugs, man."

Davis tenses.

Grinning, I arch a brow. "Good drugs."

Davis relaxes. "Since when?"

"Last year. I got my shit together. Got back on antidepressants. Saw a therapist. Mood has evened out."

"What was the diagnosis?" Davis asks, seeming mildly interested. "Asshole?"

"Hardy fucking har."

We share a chuckle, then Davis claps my shoulder. Squeezes. "I'm glad, brother. Real damn glad." He exhales. "I'll back off about Reese."

We order one last round of beers and pay the tab. I thumb through my phone, on the hunt for a text from Reese. Still nothing.

The prickle of unease turns to worry.

After helping Davis unload the horses, I go in search of Reese. By now, her schedule's ingrained in my mind—four in the afternoon, she should be finishing up her day. A good thing, too. The sky is full of dark clouds and thick humidity clogs the air.

As the chicken coop comes into view, my eyes go to the door. Tim, a hired hand, is exiting, carrying a basket of eggs.

She's late. She's never late.

I frown at Tim. "This is R—Jane's job." She loves the damn chickens.

Tim grunts, then spits. "No one's seen her."

The bad feeling's back. "How long?" I bark.

He shrugs. "Three days."

My stomach flips.

I don't think. I run.

I don't bother slowing down, just barrel up to the front door of her chalet and grab the knob. It's locked. Now she fucking listens.

Fear drives through me like a knife, and I slam a fist against the door. "Reese!"

I don't wait for her to answer. I head straight for the

window. Grim thoughts take up space in my head. What if she's gone? What if her manager convinced her to leave?

Heart in my throat, I rush around to the side of the chalet and peer into one of the windows. Inside, it's dark—still. And then I see the bed. A small lump burrowed under the blankets. Blonde hair.

My insides twist.

Fuck it.

I run back to the front door, and when I reach it, slam my shoulder into the wood, fucking desperate as hell to get to her. Fucking out of my mind.

"Reese!"

Two more quick rams and it swings open.

I slip inside, and the smell of stale air and body odor hit me. I flip on the kitchen light, bathing the room in a soft golden glow.

My breath lodges in my throat as I approach the bed. "Reese?"

The mound of blankets moves. Barely. "Ford?"

I exhale, relief flooding me at the startled sound of her soft voice. A good thing too because I'm damn near ready to have a heart attack.

"You scared the hell out of me," I say roughly.

"I'm sorry," she whispers, lifting her head. She shivers, her arms clinging around her pillow, squeezing it tight. She looks helpless and fragile lying there, and damn if I don't feel the same way.

"Don't be sorry."

"I missed work."

"It's okay," I tell her, sitting beside her on the bed. "No one cares about work."

Her free hand rises to land on mine. The moment

she makes physical contact my entire body unclenches. She's here.

"I let the chickens down."

I chuckle. "The chickens will be just fine." I stroke her back. "What are you doin', Birdie Girl?"

"Being sad." The words are spoken in a small, shaky rasp. She nuzzles her face in the pillow. Sniffs. "Sometimes I get sad."

Her words tear a hole in me. One I'm not sure I can repair.

I've seen her lie, laugh, smile, tease, and argue. I've seen her on her knees in front of me. I've never seen her dark like this. It scares the shit out of me.

But it's nothing I can't handle.

I inhale a deep breath, searching for the words to comfort her.

"Okay," I say slowly. "Can I be sad with you?"

She lifts her head slightly. Those big green eyes focus warily on me. "What?"

I'm already pulling off my boots. "Is it okay if I lie here with you?"

"Yes." She rests her head back on the pillow. "It's okay."

Standing, I fill a glass of water and place it on the nightstand. I'm worried she hasn't eaten or drank anything in three days, but now's not the time to push.

I slip beneath the blankets and wrap my arms around her. I kiss her shoulder. Pull her close. Reese sags against me.

"Why didn't you call me?"

"I didn't want to bother you," she says, barely audible.

"Oh, baby," I whisper, her words ripping my heart out.

It all makes sense now. *She* makes sense. But I don't say it out loud.

She's on the ledge like I was. After Savannah, after I hurt that kid, for weeks, I could barely get out of bed. Life felt so heavy and significant. Christ. Why didn't I see it?

That's why she's here. She's taking a break from whatever burdens she's been carrying, to heal and recharge. And damn if I'm not going to give it to her.

She tips her head back, her eyes full of tears. "I thought I'd be okay here."

A crack tears through my chest. "You are okay here," I say gently. "You might not be okay now, but you will be."

No one's ever taken care of this girl, and I intend to be the first.

"I will?" she asks, peering up at me.

I hold her tight against me, breathing into her neck. "You will be. Don't forget that even though today may suck, you can always try again tomorrow. And the next day. And the next. Just keep trying until you hit a good day."

"A good day." She smiles. "I like that."

I slide my fingers through her sweaty hair, stroking softly through the snarls.

"Rest now. You're safe. I got you. There's no place for me to be, except here with you."

Her small hand strokes my stubbled jaw. "Thank you."

I close my eyes, but I don't go to sleep for a long time.

21

Reese

I OPEN MY EYES AT THE RUMBLE OF THUNDER. EARLY morning sunlight nudges against the windowpanes. I'm lying with my head on Ford's chest and his arms wrapped around me. I look up at him. He's so beautiful. The angles of his face. His lush lips. That head of dark golden hair.

I've been given everything I have ever wanted in my life. Diamonds. Drugs. Designer clothing. But nothing I needed. Last night, Ford telling me I was safe, that I wasn't alone, that he had me, was everything.

I wish we could stay like this forever, but we can't. I've been in this bed long enough.

Slowly, I wiggle myself out of the safe cocoon of his body and sit up. My bare feet on the cool hardwood floor is a delicious sensation.

The bed shifts.

"Hey." Ford sits up. His hand goes to my cheek, turning my gaze to his. "You okay?" I've never seen someone look at me the way he is now. Like I'm fragile. Like he's just now deciphering the code.

"I'm okay."

He's in jeans, no shirt. We've had sex numerous times over, and yet, him seeing me this way feels more intimate. I can't decide if I'm embarrassed or happy. I'm too exhausted to care. I'm relieved that it was him. That I had someone.

For so long, I felt like if I told anyone, I'd just infect them with my own sadness.

That's when I get a whiff of body odor. I wrinkle my nose. "I smell bad."

"I work in a barn," he says, grinning. "You wouldn't believe the smells I've smelled."

I smile softly, grateful he doesn't mention my greasy hair or baggy sweatsuit. He's just here.

It feels like some kind of magic.

"Let's get you cleaned up."

When I stand, a wave of dizziness hits me. No surprise, really. I haven't eaten in three days. I always feel so weak after the black hole gets me. I tuned out the world and now I have to fight my way back.

But Ford is already out of bed and picking me up in his arms. He carries me to the bathroom and sets me on my feet.

While I pee, I hear the sound of running water. When I return, Ford has the bathtub going. "What are you doing?"

"Running you a bath." His voice drops an octave. "I don't want you standing in the shower. Not until you eat something."

He helps me undress, tossing my dirty clothes into a pile in the corner. His eyes briefly graze my naked body before testing the water and shutting off the faucet.

I step forward, waving off the hand he offers me. "I can do it—" A fresh wave of dizziness hits me, and I press my palm against his hard chest to steady myself.

He looks down at me with amusement, but also with patience. "I think you need to shut that pretty little mouth of yours and let me take care of you."

I'm too shocked to argue when Ford strips off his jeans and climbs into the tub. All I do is stare at him.

He gives me a grin, holding out his hand. "Get in the tub, Reese."

This time, I take his hand. He helps me in and settles me in his lap, both of us submerged beneath the water. I feel his hardness pressing against me, but it's par for the course. "Turned on, Country Boy?"

He kisses my brow. "Still a brat," he murmurs, and we both laugh.

Ford dips a washcloth in the water. Runs it over my throat, the curve of my shoulder.

"Lie back."

"What?"

There's a smile in his voice. "I'm going to wash your hair, Birdie."

My eyes widen and then I comply. Once my hair is wet, I rest my head on his chest, reveling in the connection.

I hear the crack of the shampoo lid. Then, gently, Ford lathers the shampoo over my scalp. His hands are warm and soft and strong. I whimper at the sensation. It feels so damned good.

He runs his thumbs down my spine. "Feel good?"

I tip my head back. "Mm-hmm."

It's overwhelming. How incredibly cared for I feel right now. Ford doesn't have to do this, but he stayed all night. For me.

His lips touch my temple. I relax even further, absorbing his touch, our connection.

The string arches between us, tugging in my stomach. A funny feeling I ache to forget. Wish it to disappear. Because it means too much. And it can't mean a damn thing.

I stare at the bangles on my wrists, glittering gold beneath the water. At times, they feel like shackles. But not now. Not today.

In this bath with Ford, I'm free. I'm not Reese Austin, country superstar sensation who shakes her ass on stage. I'm Reese, a girl from Georgia who used to live on a peach farm. The real me. Even if it's raw and ugly.

Maybe that's why I ran. To show myself to someone who sees me.

Someone who is safe.

His breath hitches as his hands weave in and out of my hair. Taking his time, he massages my scalp, and I close my eyes, reveling in the intimate way his fingers explore. The sensation is wondrous. Better than sex.

Ford shifts me against him. His heartbeat matches mine. A steady beat of happiness.

When he's finished with the shampoo, he rinses my hair, then adds conditioner.

His palm pressing me up, I curl forward. Cool air hardens my nipples. Water cascades down my back as Ford rinses my hair. Just when I think we're done, he pulls me back down against his solid chest.

When I realize what he's doing, my breath hitches.

He's braiding my hair.

Those big, calloused fingers skillfully twist my damp hair into two thick braids.

"Who taught you how to braid?" I ask, delighted. I twist around to watch him, curling tighter in his arms.

"I did." His look is bashful, then hesitant as he says, "When I was ten, I was diagnosed with dyslexia. Words and letters were like soup in my brain. Every test I took, I failed. The only thing I was good at was sports. I didn't beat myself up, but I damn sure wasn't going to fail."

Guilt burns in my throat. Ford's shared so much with me, and I'm still holding back.

His face pinches with pain, with memory.

"Every afternoon I took my books and went to the barn. It was a quiet space to learn and let me get away from my asshole little brothers. I was fucking determined to beat it. I sat there and studied, and I braided the horse's hair." A deep chuckle vibrates both our bodies. "Every damn one of them. They all came out looking like they were in a beauty salon."

I laugh.

He exhales a ragged breath. "That's why I love baseball. It built up my confidence when I thought I had lost it. I may have been shit at everything else in life, but baseball was mine."

"It still is." I twist into him. My hands glide up his slippery chest. "You talk like you don't deserve it. Why?"

He leans forward, nipping at my collarbone. His big hand finds my thigh under the water, and he squeezes. "Let's get you out. You're cold."

He scoops me up and steps out of the tub. A fresh, fluffy towel is wrapped around me.

While I find clean clothes, Ford heads to the kitchen. I pull on a long slip dress and when I head to the main room, Ford's setting a peanut butter and jelly sandwich on a plate next to a bag of Combos.

"You're spoiling me."

He grunts. "You eat like shit, but you gotta eat what you like."

Dropping into a chair, I reach for the Combos, suddenly ravenous. With clear eyes, I evaluate the chalet. Every window and door is thrown open, allowing the morning breeze to chase away the stagnant air. The sunrise is a bloom of colors.

I inhale, exhale.

A new day. A new slate. Peace.

Across from me, Ford leans forward, rubbing his long fingers over his jaw. "So, what happened, Birdie?" His worried eyes search mine. My heart melts.

I swallow a bite of sandwich. Ford's showing me I can trust him. But do I want to? Trust means feelings and feelings mean complications. If I tell him the truth and this goes south, and I lose his friendship...it's too important. I can't do that.

"I don't know." I stick my hands between my knees. Try for honesty the best I can. "After Gavin and the horse, it all felt heavy."

He nods like he understands. "Like cement?"

"Yeah. Like cement." I hesitate. I already know he won't like it. "And then...I got a text from Gavin."

He goes still, eyes hard. "Show me," he orders.

"Ford—"

"Baby, if this asshole is fucking with you, I need to know."

Sighing, I hand him my phone.

A muscle works in his jaw as he reads. "What is this shit?"

"Plans for when I go back." I rub my eyes. It was the over-the-edge demand of a new tour the second I return to LA. The Reese Austin Comeback Tour. *Just like Elvis*, he said.

I'm already exhausted. I feel like I'll never escape this endless life Gavin's created for me.

Ford sits back in his chair. "This doesn't make you happy, does it?"

"No. It doesn't." Finally, I'm honest.

"When's the last time you were happy?"

The memory comes automatically. "Playing my guitar like no one was watching."

Ford stands and retreats to the corner of the room.

He lifts my guitar off the bench and returns to me. "Play it, baby."

I blink. I haven't touched the guitar since I arrived.

Stunned, I take it from him and nod gratefully. Then, like magic, my hands move over the strings. I tune, I pluck. The rhythm invades my bones and stays there. Electricity hums in my body. My soul.

As I begin to sing an old Johnny Cash song, Ford settles onto a chair, boot kicked up on his knee. His shoulders relax and his expression appears somewhat dazed as he listens. He keeps those amber eyes on me the entire time.

He makes me want to sing again.

Live again.

The thought is so pure, so sweet, a tear slips down my cheek.

My voice trembles as I switch over to Patsy Cline's, "Sweet Dreams." I sing higher and louder. The black hole shrinks. My heart lifts—free.

Ford's jaw works. "Reese."

He's looking at me like I'm a dream. Like I exist and he's the only one who has me.

Trying to ignore my heart pounding in my chest, I stop playing, reach out my hand. He does the same, braiding our fingers together.

Home.

This is what home feels like.

22

Ford

"**W**OULD YOU LOOK AT THAT, COUNTRY BOY?" With her face a bright beam, Reese points a finger at the laptop screen. At her own checking account and the small sum that sits there. "Two paychecks."

"Two paychecks." It's not enough. Not for her.

"I'm rollin' in money now," she jokes. "Might even buy some Louboutins."

"You're doin' it, baby," I say, proud of her. She contacted one of Bosko's lawyers. Ammunition on her side for when she needs it. "Every day you're closer."

"I am." She squints at the screen. "How do you do this again?"

She leans in and I catch a whiff of her peaches-and-cream scent. Fuck, I want to kiss her again. I want to hear that little whimper that pops off her lips every time I spank her ass.

Focus, asshole.

Clearing my throat, I tear my eyes from her face and show her how to track her checking account.

I stay still, watching her face, and loving the way she's so happy. Loving the way she's taken control of her life to get it all back.

It's been three days since I found Reese in her chalet. Three days of keeping a close watch on her. She seems happy, back to her life on the ranch. She gave me bits and pieces, but I'm annoyed I still don't have the full story. Girl's locked tighter than a fucking safe.

Hell, I'm the one doing the talking, baring my soul. It feels damn good. I've told her everything. Well…almost.

"Ford," Reese squeaks. "He's here."

The two of us watch Bosko stride toward us, wearing his usual look of murderous indifference paired with a suit and tie.

He slides into the seat across from us. "I come bearing updates," Bosko says. He drums the table. "I have good news and bad news." His gold tooth flashes as he grins. "Which one do you want first?"

Reese sits straight. "The bad."

"Good choice." From out of his shabby briefcase, he pulls a shit ton of documents. Charts, banking statements, and colorful graphs. "Gavin's stealing from you."

"Christ, man," I grumble, unhappy with his blunt tactics. If he upsets Reese he's going to have to deal with me.

"Are you sure?" Reese's voice trembles.

He pushes the papers toward her. "Take a look."

Reese bows her head, reading over the documents.

"You can see he's moving money back and forth between several accounts. The money always starts in yours and ends up in his. We went back ten years. You made six million on *Hell or High Water* and records show you only received three hundred thousand. Even after you paid out your crew, you should have had at least a million left."

Her bangles rattle as she shuffles through the papers.

"How is this legal?" I snap. Fury pulses through me. This girl's been used her entire life.

It's a nightmare.

Bosko looks to Reese, who nods. It makes me respect

the guy more that he honors her privacy. I just fucking wish she'd tell me.

"As her guardian, he controls finances. Which was fine when she was ten years old. As her beneficiary, if anything happens to her, he gets it all."

My stomach churns.

"Beneficiary?" Reese asks.

Bosko wiggles his brows. "The good news. I found your real contract."

Reese gasps. "How?"

"I have access to shady people a nice girl like you doesn't need to know about."

I don't even want to know what kind of creepy shadow-network Bosko has in his back pocket. As long as it helps Reese, I'll keep my mouth shut.

A contract's slid across to us. I pull it closer. I want to see this damn thing.

Bosko's finger lands on the contract like X marks the spot.

"Here. Clause 8 of your contact," he says. "*In the event of my death, I, Reese Austin, give all my tangible personal property and monetary income to my manager, Gavin Cross.* Yada, yada, yada, you get the point."

Reese swears. "Bastard."

I drag a hand through my hair. Every cell in my body screams at me that this is wrong. Dangerous.

Reese lifts her head. She's pale, but there's fight in her eyes. "How do I get my money back?"

"I like you, Reese. You ask the good questions." Bosko pauses, then says, "I can steal it."

I sigh, casting a glare in Bosko's direction. The last

thing I want is Reese mixed up in this. "Birdie, maybe we should—"

She elbows me and looks at Bosko. "Don't listen to him. Tell me. Steal it?"

"He stole it first." Bosko shrugs. "How's he going to argue that in court?"

"Okay." Reese grins. "Let's do it."

"If you're privy to a password he would use, that would speed up the process."

"I don't know. I don't think…" Her nose scrunches, then her eyes light up. "Wait. Try 'shiny little shooting star.' It's what he calls me."

Making a note in his notepad, Bosko nods, then places a hand over the contract. "You signed this when you were sixteen. Under duress. We can fight that in court, but that's court, and it takes time. But luckily, you don't need time."

Reese swallows. "What do you mean?"

"You're twenty-six now?"

Reese tilts her head in confusion. "I'll be twenty-seven on August 30th."

"That's the key. This contract is for ten years. It expires on your twenty-seventh birthday."

"Really?"

"Abso-fucking-lutely."

Reese sits shell-shocked. "That's why he's trying to get me back," she whispers. "Because he wants me to sign it again."

I try to avoid thinking about what I'd do to Gavin if I saw him again, because it would only end in a jail cell and an orange jumpsuit.

"It's also why he hasn't sued your ass for breach of contract," Bosko says. "Because he'd open *himself* up to scrutiny.

He doesn't want you to know time's almost up." Bosko nods. "Once it expires, he'll no longer be your guardian. He'll no longer control any aspect of your money, your career, your—"

A shuddering gasp escapes her lips. "My life."

"You'll be free," Bosko says.

A tear slips down her face. "Free."

"My advice is stay here. Do anything you can to put him off. Whatever commitments he's made for you, can be ironed out after your birthday." To me, Bosko says, "Is the ranch secure?"

The grim worry in his eyes pinches hard in my gut.

"What aren't you telling us?" I ask.

"I've dealt with men like this my entire life. When you take things away that they want, they get it back. Whatever way possible."

Declan Valiante. The mental image of Aiden King with his arm around Dakota, a knife to her belly. I picture it happening to Reese. Gone. Hurt. Scared. I squeeze my eyes shut, willing it away.

"Ford?" Reese's worried voice cuts through the fog in my head.

When I open my eyes, they land on Reese. "He won't get near you," I tell her. "Not with me around."

With those words, we stand and shake hands with Bosko.

She turns to me and sighs. "I don't believe it. I'll be free."

I wrap her in my arms. "You deserve it."

Tears fill her eyes, and her small hand lands on my cheek. "I've never had anyone do anything like this for me.

Thank you. Grady knew what he was doing sending me your way."

What he did for me. Sending me a goddamn angel.

My throat swells tight. "Nothing to thank me for. Just a cowboy helping a…"

She hikes up an eyebrow. "A friend?"

"Yeah." I tuck a lock of hair behind her ear. "A friend."

But do I believe those words anymore? Do I even want to?

She touches a finger to my mouth and smiles. "Well, Country Boy, come get your benefit."

As she presses up on tiptoes, I twist my baseball cap to the side. Then I angle my lips to hers and breathe in her sweetness and light.

Smiling as she pulls away, she says, "All I have to do is wait him out. And then I can do anything."

A pang slices through me.

I still feel like I don't know a goddamn thing about her.

⁓

Emptiness. Cool sheets. I lift my head and blink. Reese isn't beside me where she normally sleeps. My stomach roils.

"Reese?"

Silence.

I wait.

One minute.

Two minutes.

She's not here.

I draw in a breath and tear out of bed. Worry has me in a chokehold as I shove on jeans, boots. I hurry across the room, grab my wallet and my keys. Wherever the fuck she is, whenever I find her, she's getting a fucking talking to.

Just as I'm reaching for the doorknob, it opens.

My heart skips a beat when I see Reese in the doorway, soaked from head to toe. Water sluices from her damp hair, running over her silk sleep shirt. At her feet, Mouse meows, her slinky body weaving between Reese's legs.

"Where the hell have you been?"

She laughs nervously. "Keeping tabs on me?"

I rip a hand through my hair. "Yeah, I am. Especially when you're sleeping in my bed."

Edging around me, she shrugs a slender shoulder. "I went out."

"Out?" I exhale my frustration. Mouse meows, dropping a furry ball near my feet. I ignore it. "Reese, it's two in the morning," I snap. The fact that Reese is out on the ranch in the dead of night has fear creeping into my gut.

Towel in hand, she runs it over her damp skin. "Ford… I'm tired, okay?"

I grit my jaw. I don't want to do this. Fight with her. What I want to do is peel those wet clothes from her body and fuck her senseless. Only worry, anger rise up in me. A determination, a desperate need to understand this girl.

"C'mon," she says, taking my hand. "Let's go back to bed." She stands on tiptoes. Kisses my throat.

I grit my teeth. Those big green eyes, those heaven-sent kisses—I know what she's doing. And it won't work. Not anymore.

I step away. "What are you doing in the woods, Reese?"

"Chicken check," she jokes. But I'm not going to let her do this. Not anymore.

"Are you going to the lake?" I push. "Are you swimming? Is that what you're doing?"

She freezes. "No strings, remember?" Her eyes plead with me to let it go, but I can't. Not anymore.

Staying detached is a fool's errand. I'm getting soft. In over my head. But if I had the chance to go back, I wouldn't.

I want this girl's life story. Unabridged.

"Baby, you don't have to hide from me."

Laughing lightly, she turns her pale face to the window. "Hiding is what I'm doing here, Ford. You have to respect that."

I do, but it also pisses me off. Because she doesn't trust me. I don't blame her after what she's been through, but I want her to come to me when she's sad. Or mad. She doesn't have to fake it or lie, especially in the middle of the night.

"The last thing my mom said to me before she gave me away was, 'Be brave, Reese.' I'm not brave enough to do this. Not tonight."

"Then when?"

She flinches. "Please, Ford, just let me—"

"Lie?"

Her eyes widen. "I'm not doing that," she says in the softest tone. "It hurts that you'd think that."

I shake my head, not knowing what to think. All I know is she's pushing me away. She's doing what Savannah did those last few weeks—hiding from me.

The burn in my chest clenches.

It's too close. This feeling of having everything, right before losing it. My hands ball to a fist, and I feel like punching that goddamn jukebox all over again.

"You are. You're not telling me the truth and you're pushing me away."

Our gazes burn. Fire on fire.

"If you think that's what I'm doing, then you're an idiot." Nostrils flaring, she glares at me.

"Maybe I am." I clear my throat. "Maybe we should call it. Take a break."

She swallows. "You're serious?"

"Yeah." I shove my hands in my pockets, hating myself. "I am."

I don't know if I can do this again. I don't know if I can give my heart to someone and have them take it from me.

Fuck. I don't know if I'm strong enough for that.

Her lower lip wobbles. Her face softens momentarily before going hard again. "Fine. I get it. You got your rocks off with the famous country singer and now you're done."

I close my eyes against the sting. It would hurt less if she slapped me. "That's a bullshit thing to say and you know it."

I watch as Reese grabs the small bag she's been keeping here and furiously stuffs clothes and belongings inside. "What are you doing?"

Long, damp hair obscuring her face, she doesn't look up. "Going. That's what you want, isn't it?"

No.

I shake my head. "Reese..."

Tears in her eyes, she glances up. "I've played games all my life with Gavin. I won't do it with you." She inhales a shuddery breath. "You're right. We'll take a break. We're just friends, after all."

And then she's out the door, slamming it so hard I jump.

Mouse glares at me as if it's all my fault.

I tear a hand through my hair. "Fuck."

23

Reese

I FOLLOW RUBY THROUGH THE GLASS DOOR AND blink at the bright lights inside Main Street Drugstore. I feel like I've been in a cloudy fog for the last week. Angry, sad, and stupid. But that's what I get for getting too close. For letting Ford Montgomery in.

He charmed me. With his broody good looks and aw-shucks grin and we're-just-friends promises. I trusted him.

And it was a mistake. Because I lost him.

But did I ever really have him?

He wants to know, and I don't blame him. But how do I talk about it? All these years, it's been my dirty little secret. I've never told anyone. It's not like ripping a band-aid off. It's like peeling the skin off my skeleton. All the gory parts will show. What if he's disgusted by what he sees? What if one day he decides I'm not enough anymore?

It's better this way. The closer I get to being free of Gavin, the closer Ford comes to learning the truth.

"Reese?"

I shake myself out of my daze and take in Ruby's smiling face. I hitched a ride into town with her, because I refused to borrow Ford's truck. After our fight, I don't want anything from him.

Except him.

I miss him. It's been a week since he called it quits. A week since I've been in his bed. Since those calloused fingertips have run up my body with the gentle ease I'm used to. My body aches for him. But he's right. It's better this way.

No strings. Just friends. Without any of the benefits.

"C'mon," Ruby says. "You haven't had a Resurrection shopping experience until you've bought cow dewormer and a bolo tie."

We shop the aisles, and I add a box of hair color, nail polish, a few bags of gummy bears to my basket. Then I make my way toward the pharmacy. I want to show Gavin I'm still filling my prescription. But I've stopped taking the pills.

The spectacled pharmacist looks up from her screen. Snaps a bubble. "You're sure this is your prescription?"

"Yes, I'm pretty sure it's mine." I watch as she slowly moves the orange bottle and a clipboard to the counter.

I sign my name as the pharmacist snaps another bubble. "I don't know. What did you say your name was again? Are you—"

I grab up the pills and turn on my heel before she can ask any more questions.

"Are people always this nosy here?" I ask Ruby as we check out.

Ruby giggles. "Small town. Your business is their business."

I laugh. "Should put that on the town crest."

Linking arms, Ruby attaches herself to my side as we push out the front door and exit onto Main Street. The hem of her floral sundress flares as she bounces us down the street. "Let's go see Dakota's bakery."

We turn the corner when I feel eyes on me. I freeze. My heart pounds in my chest. A black SUV is parked two blocks away. *Gavin? Paparazzi?* I squint, trying to get a better look. Before I can, it slowly drives off, turning down a side street.

"Reese?"

I shake off the chill that's settled in my bones.

"Let's go."

A purple paradise awaits us in Dakota's bakery. Every shade under the sun decorates the shop. Though it's still under construction—paper screens obscuring the windows, and the countertops unfinished—the décor is above and beyond. Marble and lilac accents, floral garland, penny tile, and a flashing neon pinball machine complete the space.

"Oh, Dakota," Ruby gasps, hands clasped to her heart. She spins, taking it all in.

"It's beautiful," I tell Dakota. "It reminds me of Paris."

"Best compliment ever," Dakota says. Her long black hair is curled in loose waves around her face. There's a dusting of flour on her cheek. "Thank you."

"When do you open?" I ask.

"Two weeks." Dakota takes off her apron, revealing tight-fitting jeans and a silk blouse, and drapes it over the counter. "The night of the rodeo. It's our unofficial official opening. We'll have a booth there. Then the next day, we're officially open." She slides a platter of pastries our way. "Eat."

"Right on Main Street," Ruby says, picking at a pumpkin scone. "Nobody can miss it. It's the perfect place."

"It's a dream," Dakota agrees. "I never thought I'd have this." Her eyes take on a faraway sheen. "Any of this."

Dreams.

It hits me like a lightning strike.

I want *my* dreams.

"If ranch work isn't your thing," Dakota says to me, wiggling her dark brows, "I could always use help at the bakery."

I smile. I'm learning I might not be able to trust Gavin, but I can trust these women. I like them. Dakota always has a fresh pastry for me, and Ruby brings flowers to brighten up my chalet. It feels like I've been let into a glimmery circle of light.

The door swings open. Fallon walks in, duffel bag hooked over her shoulders. She's in torn jeans, boots and a tank top tied at the midriff. Her sharp hazel eyes scour the space before landing on her sister. "You ready?"

Dakota laughs. "If you say so."

Fallon pounds on the wall. The reverberation causes a photo to hang crooked on the wall. "Time to drink."

⌒

Sunday afternoon and Nowhere is busier than church. Scuffed wooden floors. Dirt-cheap whiskey. Grizzled men huddled on corner barstools. If the walls and floors in Nowhere could talk, they'd have serious stories to tell.

Beef, the bartender from my dance-on-the-bar escapade, groans when he sees us. He runs a massive hand over his bald head. "You're back."

"I am back." I bat my eyes at him. "I'll behave this time."

"I'll vouch for her," Ruby says.

"Shots?" Beef asks, his face softening slightly in Ruby's presence.

"Shots," Dakota instructs, bellying up to the bar. "I've been working all week. Keep them coming."

"I'll look at the menu, but I already know I'm getting the fries," Fallon says, dropping onto a bar stool.

"Comin' up." Beef gives me a conspiratorial look. "Try not to dance on anymore bar tops."

I lift my hand. "Scout's honor."

"This is it," Dakota says as we take seats at the bar. Dakota and I are sandwiched between Ruby and Fallon. "The cure for idiot men is Nowhere."

I arch a brow. "Why Nowhere?"

Ruby looks thrilled. "Because they realize what they have when you're here."

"Is that why we're here?" I ask. "To bait Ford?"

"How *is* your broody cat daddy?" Fallon asks me.

"I wouldn't know," I say. "I haven't talked to him."

"That explains it," Dakota says.

"Explains what?" I ask.

Dakota smirks. "Why he's moping all over the ranch."

I feel a tiny sliver of satisfaction I've managed to get under Ford Montgomery's skin.

"I've never seen him so grumpy," Dakota says.

Fallon shakes her head. "He's always grumpy."

"Do you like him?" Ruby looks hopeful.

Beef returns with the shots, crystal clear tequila and a deep honey-colored whiskey. The color reminds me of Ford's eyes.

My cheeks heat. "I mean, we're friends," I say, trying to act like I don't care. To kill the sting of the lie, I could take the shot. But I don't need a stiff drink to deal with this.

Fallon scoffs. "Men and women can't be friends." She slugs down a shot, then drinks mine. "They're either trying to kiss you or trying to kill you. Trust me, I know."

Beside me, Dakota's gone pale.

I bite my lip, look at Fallon. "I hope it's okay, but Ford told me what happened to you last year. I'm sorry."

Fallon lifts a hand like she's waving away my apology. "Whole town knows. You might as well join the club." Another shot.

Dakota eyes her sister, a worried expression on her face. "Are you sure you should be drinking with your medication?"

"No, I'm not sure, but YOLO, right?"

Dakota and Ruby share a wide-eyed look of concern.

"Fuck Danny or Aiden or whatever the hell his name was," Fallon says, raising her empty shot glass. Dakota winces. "Rot in hell, asshole."

"Yeah, fuck that guy," Beef says, setting down fresh drinks and a water for me. With a flick of the wrist, he sails a fancy pink drink down to Ruby who promptly attaches it to her lips.

"Okay, so at this bar, we do this thing," Ruby says when she comes up for air. Big blue eyes wide, she leans in. "We tell the truth, we don't bullshit."

"Honesty for honesty?" I ask.

"A-fucking-men," Fallon enunciates.

"What happened between you and Ford?" Dakota asks. "And I only ask because for one perfectly pleasant month he wasn't broody and bitching and I'd like to solve the mystery for my own sanity."

"We're on a break. Or something." I laugh, then sigh. "I think he got scared. I hurt him when I wouldn't open up."

"People who are scared push," Dakota remarks. "I know he's been through a lot in the past."

Damn it. It makes sense. Ford told me about his ex and her betrayal, and I probably just tore open the wound with my silence. That night, his gaze held a weight I hadn't seen before. Like he was trying to get himself under control. Like he was worried. Like he cared too much and hated himself for it.

A ghost of a smile plays on Ruby's lips. "Maybe he's scared because of what you mean to him."

I pick up my water. "We don't mean anything." The harsh statement goes straight to my heart. It feels like it's boiling.

Fallon leans an elbow on the bar. "What about you? How's your love life, Beef?"

Beef runs a hand down his scraggly beard. "I'll let you know when she moves in."

Ruby and Dakota hoot as Fallon pounds the bar top. "Now I have to know. A name."

"Nope. Bad luck." More shots appear in front of us. "This one is special. She's got a mouth like a razor blade." Goofy grin on his face, he moves down the bar.

Fallon wrinkles her nose. "Ugh, god, delete that image from my brain."

Dakota's thoughtful expression returns to me. "The ranch is for secrets, but they always come out."

Ruby breathes through her shot. "I lied to Charlie about my heart condition."

"And what happened?" I ask.

Pink stains her cheeks. "He loved me anyway."

My chest is heavy. Even if I told Ford about Muirwood, there's no love between us.

"We all have painful pasts but that's why you find your people," Dakota says. Her dark eyes linger on me. "The right people can handle it—hold it—but you have to tell them when you're ready."

"I don't feel like I have any people," I admit, cradling my bangles to my chest. "Sometimes I feel like a square peg trying to fit in a round hole."

"That's the best way to feel." Fallon grins at me. "Then you show 'em how the fuck it's done."

I smile at her.

"You're not a square peg," Ruby croons. Her voice is strong, firm. "You're our circle. And you have us."

Happiness washes gently over me.

Turns out, this is exactly what I needed.

In the music industry, true friends are a rarity. Other singers, songwriters acted like they were your best friends, when really all they were waiting to do was screw you over.

Here, in this dirty dive bar, with these women, I feel like I belong. Like it's one more inch toward New Reese. Toward a life of normality.

A cowboy in a bolo tie approaches. A Sharpie in his hand, gaze lasered on me. Hard glares on their face, Ruby and Dakota swivel on their barstools, blocking me in.

But it's Fallon who stands.

"You don't know her," she growls with a mean smile. "And if you think you do, no you fucking do not, understand me?"

I smother a grin, touched by her protection. It's clear Fallon lives and breathes to bully men at the bar.

The man looks at me. "I just wanted a—"

"Out." Fallon snaps her fingers. "*Beef.*"

Floorboards rattle, and with a sigh, Beef appears. He flexes a fist. "Let's go, man. You bother the women, you bother me."

"Do you miss that?" Dakota asks, wagging a finger at the man who's being escorted out of the bar by Beef.

"No way. I miss nothing about that life." I prop my chin in my palm, my stomach warm from the whiskey. "I don't want to be a superstar—"

"I do," Fallon interjects with a grin.

"I just want to be Reese. It probably sounds weird giving it all up, but…"

"Not weird at all," Dakota muses with a smile. "I thought I wanted a big fancy bakery in Paris or New York, but this life I made beats everything."

I glance at her—listening as she explains her past with Aiden King.

"Whoa." I sit back in my bar stool, awed by her story. "You survived, Koty."

Her eyes glisten. "I did."

"I didn't know what I wanted," Ruby says. "Or even what I could have with my condition. And I found it here."

A stab of hope rattles inside of me. I'm inspired by Dakota and Ruby. Both of them made something good out of shitty circumstances.

It's like a whole world of possibilities expands in front of my eyes. What if I went to school? What if I started my own label? And then—What if I stayed here? What if Ford and I worked it out?

For the summer. There's still so much time. It seems like a shame to waste it.

"We can change our life at any time," Dakota says sagely. "Sometimes you just need a boost."

"And more tequila," Fallon says.

My boost was Ford. All summer he's had my back. He's been my rock.

"Ugh," I groan. "I miss him."

All eyes turn to me.

"Who?" Dakota asks.

"Don't say it," Fallon warns me. "Then you're in it."

I wince. "Ford."

Ruby squeals.

I bury my face in my hands. "I disgust myself."

"But the question is…" Ruby bounces in her chair like she's my own personal shrink. "Why do you disgust yourself?"

"Because I'm hiding from him. Because I reacted on the defensive. Because I've never known what a normal life has looked like until I got here and met Ford. He's showed me things no one ever has."

At Fallon's raised eyebrow, I laugh. "Not like that. Boring things like balancing a checkbook and opening my own bank account. But he's also the best damn kisser." I finger the gold horseshoe necklace around my neck, my heart a wild thrum inside my chest. "And I've kissed a lot of guys. But…"

Ruby claps her hands together. "But?"

"But not like Ford," I say softly. "He's a man."

"A cowboy," Ruby whispers. She looks swoony.

"Yeah." A hot flush creeps up my cheeks. I've already said more than I should have. Surprisingly, it feels nice. Honesty.

"Is it hot in here?" Ruby exhales. She fans her face. "Or is it just me?"

Fallon grins. "It's because you're a ho for a cowboy, Ruby, and that's okay to admit."

Dakota mainlines a shot. "One thing about grumpy cowboys with impeccable face cards—they're gonna put you through the mattress."

"Ugh," Fallon says, slapping a hand to her face. "Why are you so domestic and gross?"

Ruby bites her lower lip. "Which reminds me…did anyone tell our cowboys where we are?"

"Do they care?" I ask.

Dakota laughs. "Blue-collar men gossip worse than any female in Hollywood. I guarantee you they're sitting around right now talking and worrying and wondering where we are." Her smile is wicked. "Trust me. It's good to make them sweat every once in a while."

"You'll find the right time to talk to Ford," Ruby says sympathetically.

"Or the wrong," Fallon quips. She slugs down a shot and tries to stand but falls into her sister.

Dakota steadies Fallon. Hiccups. "We need to call someone."

24

Ford

I slam into the Bullshit Box to find Wyatt flinging darts while Davis and Charlie shuffle through paperwork on their desks.

Davis arches a brow. "Lookin' for Reese?"

I glower. "No." Yes. All damn day. She's been MIA and I've been losing my mind.

I lower myself into the chair at my desk and pretend to be interested in the guest log. I scan the list of names booked into the chalets.

Austin, Reese, West

Ingalls, Charles, East

Ketchum, Brian, East

O'Brien, Ashley, East

"Reese and Ruby went into town," Charlie offers.

"Fuckin' fabulous," I mutter, frustration bleeding into my tone. I'm not her keeper, but I don't like not knowing where she is. Despite the fact that we argued, I want her to know she can come to me for anything.

Wyatt snorts. "She's got your ass stressed."

Davis twists in his chair. "What did you do?"

"What makes you think it's my fault?" When my brothers stare at me silently, I sigh and give up the fight. "I asked her what her deal was with her secrets, and when she wouldn't tell me, I told her we should take a break."

Wyatt's whistle sounds like a bomb dropping.

Davis arches a brow. "A break sounds like y'all were together."

"We ain't," I argue. "We're friends."

"Ruby was ready to run when she thought I was gettin' too close," Charlie says.

I think of Ruby and Dakota. Women with secrets, yet they were the best things to happen to my brothers.

I pop a cinnamon candy in my mouth. "Y'all relationship experts, now?"

Davis and Charlie share smug glances. "We're married."

I don't want to be married. I should say it, but the thought doesn't ring true. Not anymore.

Hell, I've been looking for my dream girl for a while. Tried to tell myself it wasn't meant for me. Tried to pretend I didn't want what my brothers had. But I do. I always have.

"If you're not serious about her, then why do you care?" Wyatt flings a dart, then plops onto the couch. "Just keep shit to the bedroom."

It matters because I miss her. I miss her like crazy. I miss cooking her breakfast and coming home to her after a long day on the ranch. I miss her turning up wherever I am. The sound of her bangles that's now damn Pavlovian to me because it means she's near. I miss her pouty kisses, the feel of her, all soft and sweet and sleepy in my arms.

There's no getting over this girl.

Fuck but I like her. More than friends. I let my fear push her away. When she called my bluff and walked out, I knew I had made a mistake calling things off. I'm the asshole who blew it because I was selfish.

Regret eats at me. I should have been patient. Whatever her story is, it's hers. Not mine.

"It's too late for that." I scrub a hand through my hair,

hating myself for what I'm about to admit. "I do care about her."

Davis groans.

"I let all my shit with Savannah wind me up and I pushed her away. I was an idiot."

Charlie and Davis stare at me with sympathy.

Wyatt shrugs. "No arguments here."

I open my mouth ready to remind him about the time he pissed his pants in third grade, but the vibration of Davis's phone fills the room.

He takes the call. From the soft, low tone he uses, I can tell it's Dakota.

Hanging up, he says, "Girls are at Nowhere."

Charlie scowls.

The thought of Reese being out at a bar without me has my hands pulling to fists.

The corner of Davis's mouth kicks up. "Need someone to pick them up. Drunk as skunks."

I shove out of my chair before anyone can beat me to it. "I'll go."

"Damn, man," Wyatt says, looking embarrassed for me. "Show a little restraint."

Fuck restraint.

When it comes to Reese, I'm a man on my knees.

⁓

The women are tightrope walking on parking blocks when I pull up to Nowhere. Wobbly and giggly, they're adorably drunk.

"Get in the truck," I call out, taking inventory of them. No one looks manhandled, near tears, or drunk enough to puke.

"We called Davis," Fallon argues.

"Yeah, well, you got me. You wanna walk, there's the road."

"Ford!" Ruby cheers, throwing her arms around my neck. Her blue eyes are bright, her smile a beam. "You're here."

I chuckle. "Hey, Fairy Tale."

"A rider to our rescue," she announces drunkenly.

"Charlie's gonna love you," I tell her, grabbing her elbow before she can face-plant.

I glance over to where Dakota and Reese stand. Dakota hops off a parking block with a gymnast's flourish. Reese, looking hotter than she has any right to, avoids eye contact and steps around me. The scorch of her cold shoulder, the sight of those high heels and short little skirt, sends a shock of need through my veins.

I deserve it, but damn, her distance pisses me off. I want to drag her against me and tell her to drop the fucking attitude.

But that'll have to wait.

"Okay, focus," I blast and all eyes whip to me "We have two objectives tonight. One is get in the truck."

"What's the second?" Fallon asks.

"Two is shut the hell up."

I yank open the passenger side door, watching as Reese, Ruby, and Fallon take the backseat. Dakota climbs up front. I join them and accelerate out of the parking lot. The sooner I get back to the ranch, the sooner I can get Reese speaking to me again.

Radio up, windows down, I take the windy county road back to the ranch. "Seatbelts on?" I ask.

Fallon salutes. Snickers. "Yes, Dad."

Ruby giggles. "Cat daddy."

"Been talkin'?" I ask Dakota dryly.

She keeps her pretty face neutral. "Your name may or may not have been mentioned."

Unable to help it, I glance at the rearview mirror. Reese's eyes meet mine. Heat sparks. Then, just as quickly, her gaze darts away.

Fuck it.

She can have her secrets; I just want her. I don't care anymore. If I push her away and she avoids me the rest of the summer…I can't handle that. Her on my ranch and not in my bed?

Absolutely fucking not.

My thoughts are diverted when I see Fallon with her head out the window. Her lonesome howl sounds throughout the cab.

"Christ," I mutter. Twisting around, I try to grab her pant leg. "Fallon, get your ass back in here. Stop acting like an idiot."

With a glare, Fallon slumps back down in her seat. "I've already been kidnapped and stabbed. What else can happen?"

"You wanna ease up on the death-defying stunts?" I grump at Fallon. "My brother's trying to look out for you and all you're doin' is giving him high blood pressure."

"Wyatt doesn't take me seriously," Fallon hisses. Her eyes are wild. "He doesn't think I can ride."

Dakota's head slowly swivels to me, a look of shock on her face. An awkward tension fills the cab.

"Hey, Fallon, shut the fuck up," I say. "That's not true."

When Wyatt came to the ranch, twelve years ago, at twenty-two, he was the cocky bad boy of rodeo. Fallon was still a sophomore in high school. I wasn't around to witness any of their early interactions. But apparently Fallon still holds a grudge.

I give her a long steady look in the rearview mirror. "I'll tell you right now, on the whole wide world of Wyatt, if he said that he didn't mean it. And if he did, he doesn't believe it now."

Fallon's face softens momentarily before turning to a scowl. "Whatever." With a flap of her hand, she says, "Koty, put some music on so I don't have to hear this cowboy's teeth gnash together."

Before I can stop her, Dakota hits CD on the player. *Fuck.*

Instantly, Reese's sweet husky voice fills the cab.

My knuckles tighten on the wheel.

A giggle comes from the backseat. Once again, my eyes flash to the rearview. Reese has a hand over her mouth to hide a smile.

"Number One Fan Club?" Dakota asks as Reese and Ruby belt lines from the backseat with invisible microphones.

I blow out a bad-tempered breath as the truck turns into one big karaoke session.

Three songs later, we roll up to the lodge. My brothers are out front.

"Everyone's back in one piece," I say as the women pile out of the truck. I look to Fallon. "Attitudes and all."

She flips me off and storms for the Edens, with Wyatt on her heels.

"You girls have fun?" Davis asks, wrapping Dakota in his arms.

"I did. How's Squish?"

"Sleepin' like a baby." He kisses Dakota. "Which is what we should be doing."

"C'mon, Sunflower. Let's get you to bed." The way Ruby giggles, and the way Charlie looks at her makes me think sleep's the last thing on their mind.

With that, the party breaks up as everyone heads to their respective homes.

Which leaves me and Reese.

"Excuse me," she says, doing her best to step around me.

Not fucking happening.

I step around her, blocking her path before she can go. I can't handle her being mad at me. Not for another damn minute.

"What do you want, Ford?" Nostrils flaring, she props her hands on her waist in a challenge, her bratty attitude a pretty little poison in my bloodstream.

"I want to talk to you." It feels like she's got my heart attached to a yo-yo.

I fucking love it.

"Well, I don't want to talk to you." She looks toward the barn. Crosses her arms. Does that haughty little chin tilt that pushes me right over the edge. "I'm mad at you."

My cock twitches. That pink pout of hers. Those beautiful emerald eyes flash fire. I can tell she's faking it, because I know her. Every goddamn inch of her.

Either way I have no intention of letting her walk away this time.

"I miss you," I rasp, stepping closer.

All my cards are on the table. Undeniable power over me. It's what this girl has.

She sniffs. "I don't miss you."

My hand shoots out, snagging her bangle-clad wrist. Her breath catches in her throat.

With a few gentle steps, I move her back toward my truck, pinning her there. "I don't believe you."

After what feels like an eternity of silence, her pretty face softens. "Fine. I guess I missed you, too."

Damn music to my ears. I blow out a breath. Smile. "You did?" It sounds too goddamn desperate but her missing me does something warm to my soul.

"I did." She touches the stubble on my cheek, then yanks her hand back. "But it doesn't matter. We're friends. That's all."

Friends.

The term makes me want to punch a wall, but I don't want to ruin it. Not when I just got her back.

"I was wrong," I admit, causing her eyes to widen. "I pushed you away, Birdie. I shouldn't have."

Her haughty chin lifts. "You did."

"I'm sorry." Truth pushes me to be honest. "I kept thinking about Savannah and what she did and—" I exhale roughly. "You're not her. I know that."

She gives me a small smile, understanding in her eyes. "Good. Maybe you're not an idiot after all."

I chuckle. "Maybe we're still friends?"

"Yeah. Still friends."

I lift a brow, tug on her arm. "Friends talk to each other."

Her lips thin. "I can't give you my secrets until I'm ready, Ford."

"I know. That's what I realized when you were at the bar tonight. I don't want your secrets." I lean in and her eyes widen. "I want you, Reese."

"That'll change once you know."

"Not happening." I catch her by the hips and pull her into me, instantly feeling calmer. "Whatever you tell me doesn't matter, so keep your pretty lips closed or don't. Either way, rest of the summer, I want you sleeping in my bed."

Her smile is happy. Beautiful. "Pretty big demands, Country Boy."

"We lost a week together, baby. Which means…" Grinning, I pick her up and she squeals. My heart wants to punch through my chest to hers. "We better get started. Fast."

I kiss her. Like it's the most primal need in the world.

Fuck Reese's secrets.

I just want her.

As long as I can have her.

25

Reese

THE HOT SUMMER JULY SUN BURNS. ONE HUNDRED degrees.

But what's even hotter?

Me and Ford.

Adjusting my skirt, I exit the Warrior Heart Home, quickly followed by Ford. One last kiss and we part ways. Buttoning up the pearl-snaps on his collared shirt, he glances over his shoulder and gives me a wink.

I blush. There's no escaping his charm.

As he hustles to the garage, my eyes linger on him. So damn handsome. My hardworking, blue-collared man. With that hat turned back, and those forearms of steel, keeping my cool has never been so hard.

Look at what we keep doing. All because I wasn't strong enough to walk away.

I decided to give in. To the madness. To his kisses. We may be friends with benefits, but it feels like more. He won't push me, and I'm grateful for that, but I have to tell him. Soon.

The ranch is abuzz with activity. Ruby is hosting a flower arranging class in the pasture, while Charlie leads a group into the lodge.

I wrap up my chores for the day—checking the chicken coop and pulling weeds alongside the cowboy cabins.

When I'm finished, as I make my way back to the lodge, my phone rings.

Slipping it out of my back pocket, I stare down at it. UNKNOWN NUMBER.

I swallow and think of the black SUV I saw on Main Street. I should have told Ford, but why borrow trouble if it's nothing? I chew a nail and examine my phone.

I wouldn't put it past Gavin to be calling from a blocked number. Except for a few texts exchanged, I've successfully avoided him since he showed up at the ranch. I hate that he still has the power to control me. The only thing that gives me slight satisfaction is knowing I'll be free in a little over a month.

I answer it.

"Hello?"

"Reese? Reese Austin?" A breezy female voice sounds on the other end of the line.

"This is she."

"Oh, wow. Let me just say I am ecstatic to speak with you right now."

I frown. "Who is this?"

"Of course. I'm sorry. This is Geneva Ritchie."

My eyes go wide. "Holy shit. It's an honor." Geneva Ritchie is one of the biggest names in indie music—a two-time Grammy award winner. She writes her own music, chooses her own clothes. No asshole manager screaming at her, no one cutting off her bank account. Dream career, right there.

"No way. The honor is all mine. Look, Reese, I'm not sure if you've gotten my message. I've been trying to get in touch with you for the last six months."

Damn Gavin.

"I know the offer isn't much, but right now the idea is still in its incubation period, which means I've had to get creative with funding."

Gripping the phone tightly to my ear, I move to stand in the shade of an oak tree. "I'm sorry, but I need to stop you there. I haven't heard anything about an offer." I shake my head. "If you've tried to go through someone else, there's a good chance I didn't get it. So it's best to tell me."

Geneva inhales like she's gearing up for a spiel.

"I'm looking to start up an indie record label run by women and that only represents women—a safe space for female artists. A space where we control our art and public image, not someone else defining us. But to do this, I need backing. I know calling you up for money is awkward. But it's also an opportunity."

It sounds beautiful.

"I'm searching for a few partners, co-founders. Right now, it's me, Alabama Forrester, and Daisy Boots." Her voice perks up. "And, hopefully, you."

"Why me?"

"I love your music."

I laugh slightly, surprised by how my heart warms. "You do?" Between Geneva and Ford, that's all the fan club I need.

She laughs. "Hell yeah, Reese. It's sappy pop-country, but sometimes that's what I need on the night I have a bottle of white wine and want to dance around in my underwear."

I smile. "I'm flattered."

"Obviously, this is all new and you don't have to agree over the phone. I can send you a contract and our business plan to review. Take your time."

I bite my lip. It feels like the sound in my brain is cranked up to full-throttle. "Do backers get a say in what the label does?"

"Of course." Curious, she asks, "Do tell, Reese."

"What if…what if we offered courses. Like music production and business classes for young girls looking to get into the industry?"

A long silence stretches between us, then she says, "I fucking love that."

I smile.

Soon, I'll have enough money to do what I want. And if I can save one girl from making the same mistakes I did, it will be worth it.

"Put everything together," I tell her. "I'll send it to my lawyer to review."

"Absolutely."

After we hang up, I stand there, breath held, phone clutched to my heart. Did that really happen? I look up at the sky. The black hole is smaller than it's ever been.

Ford.

I have to tell him.

Everything.

High on my conversation with Geneva, I rush across the ranch, searching for Ford. I spot Ruby heft a saddle and trek toward the pasture. Two horses are tied to the fence.

"How was your class?" I ask.

"Fantastic," she says, gesturing to the baby's breath in her hair. "We made flower crowns and cowboy bouquets."

"Sounds fun." I tilt my head. She's pale and breathing heavily. "Are you okay?"

"I'm fine," she chirps. "This is my horse, Winslow," she says, approaching the massive buttercream horse.

I hang back. "He's beautiful."

She smiles kindly, dropping the saddle to the ground. "You can pet him."

"I don't want to get too close," I say, touching my wrists. All summer I've been careful. "My bracelets."

"He's a kitten. Really."

I edge closer, but not because of the horse. "Ruby, are you sure you're okay?"

Flinching, she rubs her chest. A motion I've seen before.

Oh no.

Her eyes flutter and she grabs for something to catch herself on, but there's only air.

Frantic, my gaze scans her surroundings. She could hit the fence. Fall beneath the horses. Hurt herself.

I rush toward her, fast. My bangles jingle.

Winslow rears up.

And I scream.

26

Ford

S CREAMS ECHO ACROSS THE PASTURE.

The ranch goes as silent as a funeral home.

From my place in the garage, I watch in horror as Winslow's hooves come up. Flailing, sharp, deadly.

Watch as both Ruby and Reese hit the ground.

Ruby doesn't move.

Blood howls in my ears as I sprint across the pasture. From every direction, someone's coming. Charlie from the barn. Davis, the lodge.

Then, chaos.

"Ruby!" Charlie roars, his voice full of fear. He shoots in front of his wife, pulling her off the ground and into his arms.

Her eyes flutter and she comes to.

"I'm okay," she whispers, confined against his broad chest.

I grab Reese, struggling to get my breathing under control. "Birdie, are you okay?"

She nods, her mossy green eyes full of tears. "I'm sorry," she says, hands gripping my shirt. "I'm so sorry."

Holding the reins, Davis steadies Winslow.

Charlie whips to Reese. His eyes are frigid. "Those fucking bracelets," he growls.

Reese pales.

Fury pulses through me. "Leave her alone," I order,

putting my body between Reese and my brother. "You're acting like a maniac." He's worked up in a way I've never seen from my brother.

"She's a liability," Charlie growls. "I want her off the ranch."

"Say one more word about her," I snarl, "And I will bust your fucking head little brother."

Charlie's hard stare burns into mine. He's afraid because it was Ruby. I understand. But he has to back the fuck off Reese or else.

Wide-eyed, Ruby touches Charlie's broad chest. "Charlie—"

"Charlie's right," Davis says, his gaze hard, unflinching. "Ruby could have been hurt."

Ruby squirms out of Charlie's tight cradle. "Charlie, I'm—"

"Back the fuck off." I glare at them. Too far. They're both going too far.

"Listen to me." Ruby stamps her foot and goes to Reese's side. "It's not her fault. She was trying to—"

"It's okay." Reese shakes her head. Tears stream down her face. "I understand. I'll go." Lower lip trembling, she turns on her heel and races for her chalet.

I take a step toward her, my heart pitching in my throat. Then I whip my glare to my brothers.

"You both are assholes."

But it's not me who says it.

It's Ruby.

"I can't believe you, Charlie Montgomery." Drawing herself up, she gives her husband a frosty glare. I've never seen her this angry. Even Charlie blinks. "This is our ranch. We help people. And Reese was trying to help me. I almost fainted right there." She points at Winslow's hooves. "And you go and yell at her?"

Even as angry as I am, a grin tips my lips.

Fairy Tale activated is a sight to see.

Ruby balls her small hand into a fist. "Reese is trying. And Ford is happy. What more do you want?"

Happy.

Christ. I am happy. Happier than I've ever fucking been.

Taking deep breaths, Charlie blinks like he's just now realizing what he's said and done. "Sunflower," he says, his voice breaking.

"No," Ruby snaps, holding out a hand. "Don't follow me."

The look on my brother's face is like someone carved out his heart.

Ruby's gaze finds mine. "Go, Ford."

My eyes soften in thanks as Ruby spins on her heel and storms away from her husband.

I don't even hesitate.

I turn and do something my gut tells me I'll do for the rest of my goddamn life.

I chase after Reese.

⌒⌒

When I get to the chalet, the front door is open. Reese looks fragile, standing in the middle of her bedroom. Her suitcase is open on the bed.

"I thought I was doing good. I really did." Her voice is mournful, dejected.

"You are." I rip a hand through my hair, standing in the doorway. "My brothers...they're—"

"Right. They're right." A shudder shakes her slender frame. "I don't belong here. I thought I did, but I was wrong. I don't belong anywhere."

Her words break my fucking heart.

All I want to do is get her in my arms.

"You do. You belong—" *With me.*

The thought pops into my head like a plea, but before I can give voice to it, she turns sad eyes my way. "Ever since I got here, I've been messing things up and pissing people off. I didn't mean to cause more problems."

Slowly, so slowly, she strips the bangles she's worn all summer from her wrists. One by one, they slip free. White-knuckled, she sets the bracelets on her nightstand, the metal making a clanging tinny sound.

When my gaze drops to her wrists, I stop breathing.

Long, raised scars mar the inside of the delicate flesh.

The sight almost jolts me backward.

"Christ, Reese," I choke out. "What—"

She whimpers and wipes her face, running her hands over those high, beautiful cheekbones.

I ball my fists at my side. "Who did that to you?"

"I did." Her voice is soft but not weak. She lets out a long breath and finally meets my eyes. "Are you happy? Isn't that what you wanted?"

My heart clenches. "No, Birdie. It's not what I wanted."

"Now you know the big bad secret."

My mouth works but nothing comes out. I don't know what to say. I never imagined this. Fucking *this*.

I reach for her, inching closer, needing to hold her. "Birdie, I—"

"You don't have to say anything." Her shoulders rotate

back, her tone flat and emotionless. She's closing up again, cutting me off at the pass. "Just go, okay?"

"Reese."

"You can't save me, Country Boy. It's sweet of you to try."

"Fuck," I rasp. "Baby, I—"

"Go." Reese shoves me roughly toward the door. I stumble backward onto the porch. "Go, Ford."

She slams the door in my face.

$\sim$

"I can't believe I'm doing this shit," I mutter to Mouse. I'm in my truck, parked near the road, staking out Reese's chalet. Every cell in my body screams at me to go kick that goddamn door down. But she wants space, so I can't push. Even though I want to.

One thing's for certain—I'm not leaving her alone.

I won't let her fall.

Because that's what she's been trying to avoid this entire summer.

I haven't been able to unknot the ball of pain in my chest since she kicked my ass out.

How did I miss it? Sure, I sensed a sadness about her, but I didn't want to believe it. I waited for her to talk to me about it, when maybe it was bigger than me. Bigger than her.

But I understand it now.

She's not some aimless, confused girl. She's in pain. She has her secrets and her sadness but goddamn if I'm walking away now. Letting her handle it on her own isn't happening.

Never again.

I sigh, give a glance to Davis's place in the distance. I know my brothers are getting an earful from their wives. Best punishment that ever existed.

Running a hand over her soft fur, I ask Mouse, "What do you think? Go back and get my ass kicked?"

Mouse perks up, whiskers flicking. I follow her glittery green gaze.

Reese.

She's on the front porch of the chalet under the gingerbread eaves.

I straighten up, fully expecting her to head straight for my truck and rip me a new one with that fiery mouth of hers, but she doesn't even look my direction. Instead, she heads into the woods, moving like she's trying to outrun a bullet.

"Fucking A," I swear. I hop out of my truck and follow. Mouse on my heels.

Second time today I'm chasing this woman down. I'm so angry with myself. I shouldn't have left her alone for a minute.

My blood roars through my ears as I stalk after her. The worst feeling in my gut. A woo-woo feeling. Something bad.

Other than my twin, I've never had a connection to someone like this. A soul-deep burn that exists only with Reese.

I start to sprint, crashing through the forest, knocking away branches and brambles. Where is she? I never should have left her alone. Not when she looked like that. Not after what happened.

Panting, I emerge from the trees and find Reese standing on the bank of the lake. She wades into the water.

Deeper now. Her shoulders sink beneath the water, her wavy blonde hair trailing the surface. She tilts her face to the starless sky.

I go still, pulse catching in my throat.

She wouldn't.

But she does.

She goes under.

27

Reese

JUST BE BRAVE, REESE. BE BRAVE.

Sinking down, down, down, I hold breath in my lungs. Let my arms lift in the water. Let the gentle current carry me for a few seconds. Silence. Absolute silence.

And then it's like a bomb explodes in the water. My eyes fly open.

Big hands on my waist.

Then, I'm forcibly dragged to the surface.

I cough, sputtering on water. "Ford," I gasp. He's in the lake with me, fully clothed, his shaggy hair matted to his face.

"What the fuck, Reese?" Hand on my bicep, he shakes me. Anger darkens his handsome features. Tenses all those sinewy muscles. "What the hell are you doing?"

I meet his intense gaze with one of my own. "Midnight swim."

But his ever-tightening grip tells me I haven't convinced him. "Bullshit."

"Don't worry about me."

"Worry about you?" he shouts, hot fury in his eyes. "It's all I've done since you fucking got here."

"I'll go then." My heart hammers. Wrenching my arm from his grasp, I swim awkwardly for the shore, tripping over my feet.

From behind me, comes the sharp blast of his swear. "Like hell you're leaving."

He catches my wrist, and I flinch. Without my bangles, I feel exposed—vulnerable. He's touching my scars. Scars I've tried to hide for the last month.

I fight against his grip. "Let me go."

Ford turns me toward him, bringing the scarred part of my arm to his heart. "You can run away from your entire world, Birdie Girl, but you can't run away from me."

"Don't, Ford." He's being too sweet. I hate it. I can't have it.

"You're sad," he states.

"We're all sad, Ford. Some of us just want to do something about it more than others."

Alarm widens his eyes. "Is that why you're here? To do something?" When I stay stubbornly silent, he growls, "Tell me, Reese."

I loosen his grasp and start to move forward. "Why do you care?"

Water ripples as he follows me. "You might have gone your whole life without people in your corner but not anymore."

I spin around. "And why is that?"

Standing in knee-deep water, we glare at each other.

"Because you have me," he says gruffly. "Do you hear me, Reese? You have me."

"I don't have you." My eyes well with tears. "You don't have to pretend just because you're fucking me."

Ford stalks toward me, his expression fiercer than I've ever seen. "Never say that again. I don't need to fuck you to care about you. I know what it feels like to be lost." His voice sounds tortured. "I see you, Bluebird. Every version of you. Broken. Whole. Angry. Sad. I see you."

A sob escapes my mouth. All I've ever wanted is for someone to see me. Someone to get it.

He gently takes my wrist in his hand again. "Tell me what happened." His voice breaks. "Baby, just tell me before I lose my shit."

His pleading gaze makes my chest ache.

Steadying myself, I lick my lips and say, "I don't like my past." My voice wobbles out in a whisper. "I hate it. I feel ashamed. I don't want you to think the worst of me. I didn't want you to know."

He keeps me in his grasp, his gaze still locked on mine. "Know what?"

"When I was sixteen, I…I tried to kill myself." I swallow down the bile threatening to rise in my throat.

Ford's eyes close.

My heartbeat skips. "It's because of the horses." Memory assails me. "It was on the set of my movie. On the shoot, I couldn't stay on the horse. I had no training. We trained day after day after day, and I was so tired. I couldn't finish the scene. I needed a break. But Gavin… he…" I'm shivering so hard it feels like it's the dead of winter. "He wouldn't let me take a break. He duct-taped my hands to the saddle."

A shocked breath hisses out of Ford's mouth. "Motherfucker." He fights for control of his emotions, The only telltale sign of anger, the pulsing muscle in his jaw.

"He made me stay up there until I finished the scene." I swallow again. "Twelve hours. I couldn't walk when I got off."

"Reese. *Reese.*" He pulls me closer, deeper into his body. "I'm so fucking sorry."

I close my eyes, powering through the pain.

"That was the day I realized it wouldn't get easier. That my life would never be mine. It would always be Gavin's. So I…I wrote goodbye on the bathroom mirror in red lipstick. And then I got into a bathtub and…"

I exhale, unable to finish.

Ford's eyes search mine, his expression filled with raw emotion.

I take a breath and continue. Might as well get the worst out now. "Gavin found me. He put me in Muirwood, a mental health facility. He told the papers it was rehab to cover it all up. For weeks, I was out of it and didn't know what I was doing." A brittle laugh pops out of me. "I was sick and confused but I signed that fucking contract, because he saved my life. So, I owed him, right?"

"That's not a fucking manager," Ford says, looking like he's going to be sick. "That's a fucking monster. Christ, baby."

"Ever since Muirwood, I've felt like I have a dark hole. It's not always there, but it hovers—and it hurts." I'm breathing so hard it feels like my heart will fly away from my chest. "That's why I came out here. Where I was…it was bad for me. I could feel it coming back again."

"And now?" He swallows. "Do you feel it here?" His breath holds, and I see his worry, his fear.

That I'll do it again.

A shudder wracks my frame. "No. I don't." Tears slide down my cheeks in a salty stream. "I don't feel it here. I still get sad sometimes, but I haven't…I haven't wanted to end things since that day. But that's why I want *my* life. *Mine.*"

A strangled sob leaves my mouth.

"I didn't tell you because I didn't want anyone to feel sorry for me," I whisper, my breath hitching. "I worked through it, and it was so hard, but I did it. I didn't want you to think less of me."

Suddenly, years of shame and feeling unwanted swoop in. Embarrassment has me ripping my hand from Fords. Has me moving to the shore. I have to get out. Get away. From my panic, away from my shame.

I stumble when I reach the bank. But I can't hold myself up any longer. I sink to my knees and weep, digging my fingers in the sandy red earth.

Strong arms surround me. Ford cradles me to his chest.

I bury my face in his neck, trembling as I cry. "Am I broken, Ford? Am I a wreck?"

"No, baby." His deep voice soothes my soul. "Absolutely not."

I grip his shirt, like I can burrow into his body. "I try so hard to be good."

He strokes my hair, makes rough sounds of comfort. "Nah, baby. You try so hard to be bad. I see you, Reese. I see your sadness and your beauty. I don't want to break it. I want to hang onto it. I'll sit with you in it. As long as it takes."

Lifting my head, I meet his gaze. "You will?" I whisper.

"I will, Bluebird," he whispers back. "I promise."

～

Back in the chalet, Ford towers over me as he strips me down. His big hands remove my dress, until I'm shivering and naked, and only one thing remains.

Us.

I step into him. Chill bumps cover my clammy skin and yet, I burn.

He drinks in my body, his hands gripping my hips. "I want you warm, Birdie."

I nuzzle my nose against his warm chest. Inhale his scent of lake water, pine, and man. "Then make me warm, Country Boy."

His breathing hitches its rhythm. "Baby."

"Ford." My hands go to his wet shirt. "I need you."

If he rejects me…I couldn't bear it.

"Never," he growls as if hearing my thoughts. His strong, steady drawl eclipses my worry. His eyes have a wild primal look to them. "Never. You're mine, you hear me?"

Mine.

His words decimate me.

He looks as stunned as I do, but then like a rein's snapped, he hauls me against his muscled body and kisses me.

The world stops. Inside, I burn. Feverish and warm.

A guttural groan rises in Ford's chest, and he presses me against him, kissing me so frantically our mouths almost lose contact.

He's rock-hard.

Heat thrums through the bedroom, engulfing my senses.

My hands tangle in his hair. Tearing at his shirt, I cling to him like I'll die if he lets me go. I need him. Inside of me. All over me. Closer.

Ford chuckles. "Easy, baby, easy. We got all night. I want to show you something."

He spins me to face the mirror on my vanity. Makes me see myself, see my body. I whimper as Ford spreads my legs. His calloused fingertips hold my jaw, forcing my gaze to the mirror.

"Look at you," he murmurs, commanding. "Look at *you*. So fucking beautiful."

I shake my head, emotions drowning me like a flood. All I see is my wild hair and my tear-filled eyes. My scarred wrists.

"Baby, you think you're not worth it, but you are." His shallow breath warms my temple. "Say it."

My lips tremble as I squirm. "I can't."

"You're worth it, Reese." Eyes locked on me, his chest heaves rhythmically up and down. "You're worth me. You're worth yourself."

"Stop," I whisper. I feel more vulnerable than I've ever allowed myself to be.

"Say it," he demands.

"I'm broken," I choke out.

"Never." His long fingers dip into an open palette of gold eye shadow. He lifts my wrists and streaks the gold across my scars.

"See yourself," he says, his voice hoarse. His eyes travel down my wrists, mesmerized. "As beautiful as I see you."

Tears in my eyes, I watch as he paints my body. Streaking my scars, my skin, my breasts with slashes of gold.

"You're like the wild, baby. You're always gonna burn, but you come back better than ever."

His fingers slip inside of me.

Oh, God.

My head lolls against his chest. I'm already wet, slick against his hand.

Gaze heated, he says, "Drip for me, baby. That's right."

Something eager and brave opens inside of me and warms my stomach. Someone else knows about my past. It's not a secret anymore. I did that. I feel purged and strong.

"I'm worth it," I gasp out.

"Good girl."

Ford's relentless. Looking me in the eye through the mirror, his fingers pump inside of me, fucking me like a cock. I can feel myself clenching around him.

"Ford," I cry out, bucking.

His voice strangles. "You're gold, Reese. You're beautiful. You're mine."

A feverish warmth fills me. My breath comes in sharp bursts. Close. So close.

"Do it," Ford growls against my neck. "Come for me."

"Yes, yes," I gasp.

I'm exactly where I'm supposed to be. Where I want to be.

Here with Ford.

This ranch.

This life.

Mine.

My hips twist and I scream. Warmth drips down the inside of my thighs. Ford holds me against him, forearm bracketed across my chest as I buck in his arms. When I'm exhausted, limp and flush, I collapse against him.

Ford gathers me into his arms and we melt onto the mattress. Burning, bare bodies.

Slowly, he sinks inside of me. His amber eyes hold mine, steady and strong.

Our breaths grow shallow, desire deepening in my stomach. All summer we've snuck around and fucked, but this is different. I can see his face. The way his eyes darken. The hard bob of his Adam's apple.

It means more. Means everything.

The ache in my stomach deepens, connecting us. Ford slides his hands under my ass, lifting me slightly as he thrusts deeper into me.

"It's never been like this with anyone but you," he rasps against my neck.

"Yes," I say, sex clenching. I scrape my nails down his back, nip at his shoulder. "Never."

He captures my mouth on a strangled moan. His kisses turn possessive, frantic. I can barely get air, but I relish it.

"So fucking tight," he murmurs, pressing my knees closer to my shoulders. "Bluebird, you're a goddamn dream."

I moan, lost in him. We move against each other like tides. He pumps in and out slowly, torturing me.

"Ford." I arch my back off the bed. "It's perfect."

"Fuck," he grits out. "You're perfect."

I throw my head back and whimper.

"Need those eyes open, Birdie. On me." His stern command draws me back.

"Yes," I gasp. "Yes."

Our gazes lock. Ravenous desire explodes between us.

Ford's languid rhythm changes. He pumps harder. Faster. Fucks me like he's starving. His hips roll against mine as I writhe beneath him. His animalistic hunger, his primal eyes, they take me over. Possess me. I want nothing else. No one else.

His eyes never leave my face as he melds me to his body. He doesn't just make me feel like gold, he makes me believe I am.

I slide my hands over his muscled back and grip the curve of his ass.

"*Reese.*" He rasps my name like a prayer, pushing me over the edge.

We climax together, hips rolling, breaths panting. I wrap myself around him, burrowing into his tall body. We shake together, our heartbeats syncing.

When our bodies calm, he rolls off me and cleans me up. Dresses me. I don't fight him. I let him take care of me.

Back in bed, I curl up on his chest. Our breaths pulse. Our hearts beat as one. We lay there and talk into the night. We talk about Georgia, our hometowns, the struggles of fame. He tells me about climbing his mountain, the rush he gets. Vintage cars are his weakness, mine is jewelry and high heels.

I tell him about my phone call with Geneva.

"What do you think?" I ask, lifting myself up to look at him.

"I think it sounds like a damn good opportunity."

"I think so, too." I trace my fingers over his bronze skin. "It's hard to know if I'm making another mistake."

"It's not a mistake," he says. "Whatever happened in the past shouldn't stop you from making plans in the future."

"Pretty wise for a cowboy."

He wiggles his brows. "Learn from your elders, baby."

"I'm so glad I found you," I murmur, lying back down in his arms. "If only for a summer."

His entire body tenses.

"Thank you." His voice is rough. "For telling me."

"I thought hiding it would have been easier."

"You don't have to hide yourself, Reese." His fingertips stroke through my hair. "Not from me."

"For so many years, I thought I owed Gavin—"

"You don't owe anyone anything. That's your money, baby. Your body, your voice."

"I know." My voice shakes. "He took advantage of me."

"He did." Ford hugs me to him. "You're not leaving the ranch. You're safe here."

"Are you sure that I shouldn't go?" I bite my lip, remembering the awful scene in the pasture. "What about your brothers?"

He shoots me a look infused with regret, anger. "I'll handle them. They never should have talked to you like that."

"What if…" I swallow before voicing my unsaid fear. "What if Gavin tells the world what I did? Everyone thinks it was rehab." Another fear pops into my head. "He threatened to put me back in Muirwood. What if he really forces me to go back?"

Ford's face is dark, dangerous. "Another man touches you, Reese, and you're going to see how fast I can bury a body."

"Ford—"

"Don't worry. We'll figure it out."

I smile at *we*. All summer he's been by my side. The man I needed. A hero.

A cowboy.

A diabolical grin tips his lips. "Besides, we have better things to do."

I shiver as he flips onto his hands, sliding down my body.

We fuck again, an exploration of hunger we never knew we had. Then we sleep until dark turns to day and the sun comes up over the horizon.

28

Ford

MIDDLE OF JULY AND HALF OF RUNAWAY RANCH is taking a day trip down to the river to float the rapids. Everyone but me. I've got plans with Reese. She just doesn't know it yet.

Reese tried to kill herself.

It's the phrase running through my head ever since I left her sleeping this morning. Just the reminder has white-hot rage sweeping my skin. Amping my pulse.

I grip the wrench in my hand and take my fury out on the Chevy's carburetor, twisting the screws so tight I strip them.

She was a fucking kid. Her monster of a manager, someone who was supposed to protect her, strapped her to that fucking horse. Stole her innocence. Pushed her to that dark place and then took advantage of her in her most fragile state.

I want to fucking throttle every person that taught her she doesn't deserve to be anyone's first choice, that she doesn't deserve to have freedom. Protection. Love.

It was abuse plain and simple.

Every molecule in my body aches to gut the bastard.

Now that I know her entire story, her past, her pain, there's no chance in hell I'm letting that asshole get close to her again.

I'll keep her safe, if it's the last thing I fucking do.

My only consolation is that she's almost out of her contract.

And then what? And then she's gone?

It's how it has to be.

Shaking the thought from my head, I blow out a breath. Toss the wrench in the toolbox.

An image of Reese's distraught face, begging, asking, *Am I broken, Ford? Am I a wreck?* shreds my heart.

Absolutely the fuck not. Reese is strong.

Never broken.

She's lived her entire life at eighty-five miles per hour. I want to show her that she can slow down. That she can put herself first. That she deserves love and peace and protection. Ever since she got here, that girl has been a scream in progress. I blame myself for taking this long to hear her.

She warned me about her past. Her dark hole. Last night, I saw fear in her face. She thought I'd leave once I saw every side of her, including the dark, but she doesn't know that she's my light.

I said she was mine. And I meant it. It wasn't a slip of the tongue because of what she's been through or a way to make her feel better. It's the cold hard truth.

I don't know what it means for us.

All I know is I'm fucking prepared to bulldoze every single wall she's put up.

"You look like shit," comes Wyatt's amused voice.

I glance up, forcing my brain away from obsessing about Reese.

"Yeah, well, you ever have to track down a runaway country singer in the woods at midnight?"

Wyatt runs a hand down his scruffy jaw. "Heard about the dustup with you and Charlie."

I slam the hood on the Chevy. "Me and Charlie will work it out."

Wyatt grins. "Fists out in the cornfield?"

"Fuckin' right." Though I'm pissed at my brother, he's the least of my worries. I clean my hands with a rag. "Let me ask you something. Fallon ever talk to you about what happened with Aiden King?"

"No." His gaze shifts, past me to the ranch. "She can barely look at me."

"She ever see a therapist or…"

"Like a shrink?" He makes a face. We're cowboys. The only ones we tell our feelings to are the cows.

I hit him with the rag. "Yeah, like a shrink, asshole."

"No, she's too busy trying to kill herself on a bull these days."

My mind returns to Fallon's drunken outburst the other day. "She's drinking too much. Acting up."

He swallows. "I know," he finally says.

"Might be a good idea," I hedge. "I know it was for me."

He shoots me a look infused with curiosity. "You saw someone?"

"Hell, yeah. Do you think I'm just naturally sane?"

He laughs. I settle onto a stool.

"After Savannah…" Wyatt's face grows serious. "I didn't come to the ranch to help Charlie, man." I run a hand through my hair and squeeze the back of my neck. "I came to help myself. And I think that's what Reese is trying to do."

"Well, good luck wrangling Fallon." Wyatt shrugs, but his eyes are worried. "She ain't into all that mushy shit. She thinks if she sticks it out, she can get through anything."

Dangerous thinking. For anyone.

A shuffling sound has both of us looking over.

Reese stands in the doorway of the garage with Mouse in her arms. The sight of her has warmth spreading across my chest.

"Hi," she says, scanning us. "I hope I'm not interrupting."

I slap Wyatt on the shoulder. "Get the fuck outta here."

"See ya." Wyatt flips me a wave and flashes Reese a smile as he strides past her for the double doors.

Reese stands there, seeming uncertain. Shy.

Not wanting her to feel awkward, I toss her a lazy grin and say, "Hey, Birdie Girl."

She grins back and comes to me, releasing Mouse into my arms. Mouse butts her head against my chin. Her purr is like the low vibration of a jet engine.

I rough her fur. "What's up, you little fur missile?"

"You know, a big strong cowboy with his very small affectionate cat is one of my favorite combos," Reese says.

I laugh and kiss her, then kiss Mouse before letting her roam.

I slide off the stool, tugging Reese's fingers from her side to hold on to them. Small, soft, and warm.

Her pretty face is bare of makeup, and wild waves of blonde hair hang down to her tiny waist. The bangles are back. She looks ethereal and fragile. So goddamn beautiful.

"Sleep okay?"

She nods. "About last night..." She worries her lip between her teeth, then says, "I don't want anyone to know."

"They won't," I promise her. It's her story to tell when she's ready.

Threading my fingers through hers, I bring her closer. "Listen," I say thickly. "There's one thing you have to do for me after last night—if you need to go to the water, you tell me."

Every time she slipped out of my bed, she went to the lake. A midnight trek across the ranch that, even now, stops my heart.

Her gaze focuses on a spot over my shoulder. She hates the idea. Well, tough shit. She can run to that water all she wants, but not without me.

"I mean it, Reese." I grip her chin and force her to look at me. "I wake and you're gone—I will lose my mind. Don't do that to me."

"You can't worry about me, Ford." She scans my face, gives her head a slight shake. "I told you about my past, but you can't use it against me."

"I will never use it against you." I drop a kiss to her lips. "I'll take your worst day and give you my best. But I will always worry about you."

As long as she's in my life, I'll worry about her.

A soft sheen fills her green eyes. She blinks quickly, then says, "We should get to work."

I tuck a lock of golden hair behind her ear. "Nope. Not today."

"What are we doing?"

"I'll tell you on the way."

I'm terrified she'll hate the idea, but I have to try. She needs help. It's not enough to talk to me, or be on the ranch.

"You know, I had a black hole, too."

With a surprised expression, she says, "You did?"

My chin dips. "I did."

Her inquisitive gaze scans mine. "Will you tell me why?"

"I will." I hold her beautiful face in my hands. Peer into those grass-green eyes and wonder how I got so damn lucky. "Right now, though, we're gonna make that head of yours a nice place to be, okay?"

29

Reese

I'M STUNNED, TOO STUNNED TO EVEN VOICE WHAT
Ford's done for me. Hours ago, we left the ranch, and
he drove us to Bozeman. Now, I'm in a plush leather
chair, in a therapist's office. I stare out the window at Ford,
who's pacing near the tailgate of his truck. His presence
soothes me.

"Reese?" Dr. DiFeo's voice pulls me back. "Where
would you like to begin?"

"Do you have a time machine?"

Dr. DiFeo makes a soft, amused sound. She's an older
woman with a stylish auburn bob and a low voice. Sitting
across from me, she holds a notepad in her lap.

"Have you done this before?"

"A few times. My manager found someone to see me.
We didn't vibe."

"I see." She makes a note. "Are you on medication?"

"I was." I pull the bottle out of my purse and hand
it to her. "I stopped taking them when I got here. They
made me tired."

As she examines the bottle, an expression I can't place
crosses her face. Then she smiles. "I'll check on the meds
you were taking and prescribe you something if you need
it."

An awkward silence. My eyes dart around the

room—sheer curtains, warm beige walls, rustic décor—
glad to have something else to focus on.

"Why don't you tell me about your life the last few
months, and why you're here."

I flinch. A clammy, tense feeling overtakes me. "Just
talk?"

"Just talk."

I do. It all comes out. Well, as much truth as fifty min-
utes allows. I talk about everything from my parents to
Gavin and his contract, to my suicide attempt and the way
I left everything behind to run.

"I feel stupid. Like an idiot."

"Tell me why."

"Because I waited so long to leave." My voice trembles.
"Because I didn't see."

"People stay because they want to be loved, even when
it hurts." Dr. DiFeo puts down her pen. "It doesn't matter
if you left after the first time or the twelfth. It takes a lot
of strength to break a tie, Reese. It takes a lot of self-love
to choose yourself."

Tears well in my eyes.

"Why do you think it's your fault?" DiFeo asks, pulling
my attention. "Why do you think you are in the wrong?"

I shrug. "I don't know. I just do. Sometimes I feel so
crazy."

"Crazy. Who taught you that word?"

It comes automatically. "Gavin."

I was crazy when I wanted medication. Crazy for wanting to write my own songs. Crazy when I needed a break.

She purses her lips. "Have you ever tried to leave him
before?"

"Once." Memory wells. I close my eyes and see Gavin.

"The day of the shoot. I told him I was done, and then he…" I clasp my bangles.

"I see." She makes a note. "There's a lot to unpack here. You're in the high stages of trauma, Reese."

"No shit." I cover my mouth. "Sorry."

She smiles. "How do you feel where you are now versus where you were?"

My heartbeat skips. "I feel happy. I feel scared. I feel silly. I left everything behind. Who does that?"

"I think the fact that you're scared and feel a bit silly is a great sign." DiFeo nods. "Use this time to write. To know it's not your fault."

Warmth spreads through my chest. Maybe I knew that, maybe I didn't, but it's nice for someone to take my side.

DiFeo's eyebrow lifts. "Write songs that you'd be proud to give the world, Reese. And be free."

⌒

Dust spewing in the air, tires squealing, Ford shifts the old Chevy in gear. Arm draped over the steering wheel, he steers us out of the parking lot, onto the freeway.

"How was it?"

"Good, actually," I tell him. "It's just *feels* good."

I feel good. Happy. Lighthearted. Like the first step in a series of steps to get me somewhere else.

"We made some telehealth appointments. Twice a week for the next month." I blow out a breath, stare out the window at the gray skies and acres of land. "And she gave me a low-dose prescription for an antidepressant."

One of his hands, large and tan, settles on my thigh. Squeezes. "I'm proud of you, Birdie."

I smile at him. "I'm proud of myself, too."

He nods. "Look in the glovebox."

I do.

Speechless, I stare. "What is this?"

"A present." A crooked grin pulls at his mouth, all boyish and embarrassed. "For you."

Awed, I lift it up the gold necklace. This time, a little cowboy boot hangs in the center of it.

"You went shopping," I say, affixing it around my neck next to the other necklace. I pretend not to notice the way it hangs low. Close to my heart.

His throat bobs. "Positive reinforcement. Make you a cowgirl, after all."

My heart is a throbbing warm ache. I sniffle.

"Birdie, don't cry." His gaze lands on my face, a sweet kind of panic in his eyes. "I can't fucking stand it."

Ford's phone rings.

CHARLIE.

"Aren't you going to take that?"

"Later," he grits out, his eyes on the road.

"Ford, you can't be mad at your brother forever."

"Watch me. Longest grudge held is me and Wyatt. Lasted from Christmas Day to Easter. It's a family record." He scoffs at the memory. "You don't touch another man's razor."

I roll my eyes.

Releasing my seat belt, I scoot closer to him. "Well, you may be a stubborn cowboy, but I love the necklace. Thank you, Ford." I press a kiss to his cheek. His neck. The corner of his lips.

Ford's hand comes up to catch my chin. "Reese, you

want me to crash this fucking truck?" His voice is low, hungry.

My eyes latch onto his. "Live dangerously, right?"

With a hint of a smile pulling on my lips, I lean in and unzip his jeans. Ford's breath hitches as I take him in my hand, stroking his hard, warm length.

Between the therapy appointment and the necklace, I can barely keep my hands off him. I've never been more turned on. I always thought men like this were a country song soundtrack. Fictional. Too good to be true. But Ford's heaven-sent. He's funny, sweet, and patient. And he communicates.

Old Reese doesn't know how she feels about it all. Only that I'm really happy.

Something's changed between us after last night. We belong to each other. At least for the summer.

I drop my head, sliding my mouth down his shaft. I go deep, drawing him in.

"Fuck," he groans, looping an arm around the back of my seat. "Baby, I'm pulling over."

I feel the rattle of the truck as it slows and takes a trail or a side road. He throws it in park and cuts the engine.

"Reese. *Fuck*." His voice is ragged as his hands fall to my hair to help me with the rhythm. My pussy clenches. "I'm so damn close, baby. So close."

I hold him there, impaled in my mouth as I go deeper, sucking him hard. Ford tenses, and a guttural groan fills the truck as he releases into my mouth. I smile against him, feeling the throb of his cock as he empties himself.

His head falls back against the seat, the taut cords in his neck pulsing with adrenaline. When he lifts his head, he stares at me with heavy eyes for a beat, then he grins wickedly. "Now it's your turn."

Before I can argue, he grabs me up and settles me on his lap, so I'm straddling his thighs. I shift my hips to give him better access, and then he's hard again. And inside me.

My head falls back at the intense, solid feel of him, like steel. So much man I can hardly stand it.

The horn honks, and we ignore it.

"I need you, Ford." My heart pounds. I squirm on top of him, digging my nails in his broad shoulders.

He holds my arms, pulling me closer to him. His eyes firmly locked on mine. A look I've never seen from anyone else. Worship. Adoration. It steals my breath. "Baby, you got me," he says, voice strangling. "You got me, Reese."

Here. It's where I'm supposed to be.

Just me and Ford and broken hearts and broken pasts.

"Good girl," Ford groans, thrusting slowly. Heat, fire spirals between us. That hook in my stomach jerks, cementing me to him. "Good fucking girl."

I grip the back of the headrest, roll my hips and ride his cock. Through it all, Ford keeps me in his gaze. We fuck hard and fast until we detonate. Until I collapse on top of him, both of us gasping for air. Ford gathers me close against his iron chest, kisses my temple. We stay wrapped up in each other, sweaty and disheveled, like teenage kids parked at lover's lane. And for a second, this is all that matters.

Dusk falls, and I stare out over the Montana wild. The sky is dark. Big, ominous clouds loom on the horizon. My mind goes back to our conversation this morning in the garage.

I run my hand over his scruffy cheek. "Will you tell me why you saw a therapist?"

Ford, strokes a hand through his hair, and says in a pained tone, "It's not pretty."

"I'm not pretty."

"Birdie, you're beautiful."

His baseball cap casts a shadow over his eyes. Wanting to see him better, I take it off and run my fingers through his hair. "Talk to me, Country Boy. It can't be worse than what I told you."

He nods slowly. "After Savannah, I wasn't the best kind of person. Put shit up my nose, in my veins. I was off the fucking deep end." His lips quirk. "Pretty much an idiot twenty-four-seven."

He takes a shaky breath, his body lifting mine with his. "It was night two of the World Series. We were playing against the Dodgers. I was pitching, and I shouldn't have been." A ragged sound tears up his throat. "I was fucked up on God knows what so my aim was off. I couldn't stay on the plate, and I threw a pitch and—" His throat works. "I hit a kid. A little boy."

I let out a gasp.

He gives a bitter laugh. "Everyone said it was an accident, that shit happens, but it wasn't." He closes his eyes, agony on his expression. A war he's been fighting for so many years. "I fucking hurt that kid because I was an idiot asshole."

His guilt, his pain is palpable. A crack rips through my chest. "I'm so sorry, Ford."

"I don't know who he was or what happened to him. The owner refused to let me reach out to him—said it would be bad PR to admit fault." His face screws up with disgust. "He didn't die. That's all I know."

My heart aches for him.

Ford's eyes briefly flutter shut, like he can't bear the memory. "I got off easy. My coach pulled my ass and told me to go see someone. Which I did. I got on meds and talked until I couldn't talk anymore." His eyes flick to mine. "That's the real reason I left baseball and went to the ranch. Because I'm a fuck-up."

"You're not a fuck-up." I stare at him, hating that he feels that way about himself. When I look at him, I see a man worth everything. A man who's made mistakes and owns it. A man who's done more for me than anyone.

A tear drips down his cheek. He presses those long fingers to his eyes. "Christ. I hit that kid, Reese. I *hurt* him."

I sweep my nails through his hair, kiss his crown. He wraps his arms around me, holding me tight. "You're worth it, too," I whisper against his neck. "You're a good man, Ford. A good person." A hot tear slides down my face. "I would never think less of you for your past. You are a man worth everything. Forgive yourself. I do."

He crushes me to him. "Birdie Girl." An exhale rattles out of his lungs, like he's letting it all out. Like he believes my words. Like he's finally okay. "My Bluebird."

30

Ford

A BRIGHT YELLOW STICKY NOTE PEEKS OUT FROM the window on my Chevy. I pull it off and read:

You're as handsome as the sunset, Country Boy.

Grinning, I tuck it under the brim of my cowboy hat with the rest of the notes I've collected.

Love notes. Love songs. All from Reese.

Ever since her session with the therapist last week, she's been writing lyrics on sticky notes and scattering them across the ranch. Wyatt found one on his boot. Dakota on her front door.

It's like she's come alive in front of my eyes.

And I feel the same damn way.

You're a good man, Ford.

Reese's words echo in my head. It feels like the gears have shifted. It feels like I'm forgiving myself—something I haven't done since I left baseball.

How long have I been living in slow motion, never caring for anything but my brothers or myself?

Telling her made me feel raw, vulnerable. But hell, if that wasn't what I needed. I wasn't talking to a therapist. I was telling Reese.

My girl.

I could have lied, but I told her the truth.

Reese listening and understanding was like the calm after a storm.

The way her pretty face was filled with sweetness, not pity.

She's a damn good woman.

And for the first time in a long time, I want to keep a woman. I want Reese.

We've shared everything. I can't remember the last time I trusted a person aside from my brothers. She is a home I've never had. Not down in Georgia, not with Savannah. Not even with my brothers. Reese breathed her own kind of life into me with her first high-heeled stomp onto the ranch. Strutted her way into my fucking heart.

Suddenly temporary feels like bullshit. Feels like the biggest bullshit lie I've told myself.

The two-way radio crackles on my hip.

"Ford, we got a cow in distress out on Old Mill's Farm. Need you to go check it out. Make sure it's not a calf."

"Fuck." I sigh. "Always the goddamn cows." Into the receiver, I say, "Roger that. I'll load up Eephus."

I head for the barn and outfit Eephus for the twenty-minute ride there and back. As I settle a saddle on his back, I lift my eyes to the early morning sky. A summer storm advisory has been in effect all week. The air is thick and humid as dark storm clouds muscle their way over the horizon.

I don't like it.

"You wanna get roped, Country Boy?"

I laugh as Reese tugs me back by my belt loops. When I spin around, my eyes slide over her toned legs and cowboy boots. In her milkmaid sundress, she's the prettiest country girl I've ever seen.

She lifts her radio. "Heard you got a cow call."

"Headin' out. Should be back in twenty minutes."

Before I realize her intention, she nods at Eephus. "I want to go with you."

I frown. "Reese."

"What if you need help?"

"With what, my patience?"

She moves closer, smiling that little siren's smile. I feel my willpower die a slow death.

"Please, Ford, I want go." Standing on tiptoes, she nuzzles my cheek. Her breath is warm against my neck. "Please."

My blood roars to life. I crush my mouth to hers, not giving a shit who sees. Everything I want is Reese. I inhale the sexy little gasp that pops out of her mouth.

"I can't be without you," she whispers against my lips.

I manage to tear my mouth from hers for a split second. Grip her fingers at my fly. "That your plan to win every argument?"

She bats her lashes. "So you're telling me I won?"

"Fine." It's fucking ridiculous how fast I cave. How hard my cock is.

"Good," she says smugly.

I slap Eephus on the rump. "We can take the UTV."

"No." Her hesitant eyes move to Eephus. "I want to be brave, Ford."

"Baby, you don't have to do this." Now that I know her story, forcing Reese to get on a horse is the last thing I want to do. I'm proud of her, though. She's down to one bangle on each wrist. She's taking her meds daily. She's got this. And when she doesn't, I'll be there.

Her eyes soften. "I can if I'm with you."

I swallow. A bloom of pride fills my chest. Each day she trusts me more and more. It scares me shitless.

I give her a grin. "Let's do it then."

We finish loading up, and as I'm securing a canteen to the saddlebags, Charlie appears. A yellow sticky note pokes out of his shirt pocket. Between his out-of-town trips and ranch work, it's been easy to avoid my brother for the last week.

"Storm's coming," Charlie says.

"You got a radio," I say. "Could've said that there."

Thinning her lips, Reese throws a sharp elbow in my side.

"Came to talk to Reese." Charlie grunts, clears his throat. "Reese, I'm sorry for last week. There's no excuse for the way I talked to you."

A smile teases Reese lips. "Thank you, Charlie. I appreciate it."

Scrubbing a hand down his beard, Charlie turns to me, his face contrite. "Ford."

"Gotta get." I swing myself up on Eephus and hold out a hand to Reese. My brother can sweat for another week. "C'mon, Birdie."

Fear crosses her face, but then she steadies her breath and sticks out a hand.

Our palms meet, and the jolt of connection is so damn electric it ripples through my veins.

My girl.

With a grin, I swing her up into my lap. Prettiest

passenger I've ever had. With a sharp *hyah* I nudge Eephus into a trot and we head toward Old Mill's Farm.

⌒

From its hiding spot in the brush, the trapped calf bellows at me. Two babies and their mother watch me from afar.

I dismount Eephus and help Reese down. "I gave that calf a shot last week, and she's still pissed at me."

"She's got it out for you, Ford," Reese says solemnly.

"Yeah, well, feeling's mutual. May calves—bastards, all of them."

We're ten miles from Runaway Ranch, prairie in all directions. Meadow Mountain looms in the distance, dark and imposing. The lowing of cattle drifts across the plains as I eye the ominous black cloud creeping closer. Worry curdles my gut. I have to work fast.

When I near the calf, I see she's tangled in twine or string. It's snarled around her feet and winds through tangled in the brush and around trees, making it hard for her to move. I pull my knife from my hip pocket but every time I attempt to cut the twine, she bleats and writhes, pulling the knots even tighter.

"Get over here, Birdie." I move around the cow.

"See?" Reese says triumphantly. "You do need my help."

"Take this." I hand her a bag of apple slices, a cow's kryptonite. "Distract her while I cut."

"Here, pretty girl," Reese croons, distracting the calf. She giggles as the calf strains at the rope, trying to follow her.

I make quick work, slicing at each knot until the calf is free.

Then, like it's been yanked, the calf lurches at Reese.

The abrupt motion sends Reese backward onto her butt. She sits there in the snarl of weeds and laughs as the calf noses her shoulder.

"Greedy, aren't we?" She passes the calf the rest of the apple.

Awestruck, I stare at her. She's a filthy mess, her boots muddy and her dress torn, but goddamn, she's insanely beautiful.

"Get outta here, you little bastard." I slap the calf's rump, sending her out of the brush and onto the prairie to join her mother. I go to Reese, helping her stand. "You okay?"

She wobbles and flashes a smile so bright my heart skips. "Never better." Gaze drifting, she scours the prairie. "Is this land yours?"

"It's for sale," I say, nodding at a crooked metal sign ten yards from us. "Thirty acres that back up to Runaway Ranch."

Cattle mill around us. Thunder rumbles in the distance.

Reese closes her eyes, extends her arms and inhales. "It feels like a dream out here. Like the perfect country song."

I stare at Reese. Her long strands of blonde hair dance in the wind. In this moment, it all seems so simple.

"What if I bought it?" I ask.

Her eyes flash open. "What?" she asks, and then she screams it to the sky. "What!"

"The land." My heart hammers hard and heavy. Emotions well up inside of me. "I can see it. A baseball field. A Georgia mansion. Land like I always wanted."

With Reese, I don't want to avoid the world. She's reintroducing it to me one day at a time. I feel like I can fucking do anything, be anything. I ache to pick up a baseball. To do something better with my life. And maybe this is it.

"Yes." She grasps my hands and squeezes. "Yes, Ford."

I pull her into my arms, laughing. "It's a fucking dream."

But saying it out loud doesn't feel like it. Not anymore.

Reese's grin falters. She's stares at something over my shoulder.

I glance behind me, my eyes widening in panic.

"Fuck." The storm cloud now has a tail. The sky is an ugly, almost evil, green color.

Reese's hand flies to her mouth. "Is that bad?"

"Yeah, it's real fuckin' bad."

She stares as if entranced. My stomach tightens as she takes a step toward the dark tail.

It scares me how fearless she is.

"Reese, baby, we gotta ride." I snag her hand and run toward Eephus, moving faster than any pitch I could ever whip out.

The minute we remount, the sky unleashes. An unholy roar fills the air. A monster rising from the earth to devour us.

Reese screams.

"Hold on to me," I order, whipping the reins.

She twists around so she's facing me and burrows into my arms.

All I can do is ride like hell. We're on the prairie. There's no shelter and making it back to the ranch is impossible.

We have to outrun it.

31

Ford

WE'RE LOST. WE'RE DRENCHED. BUT WE'RE ALIVE. We've ridden straight into the afternoon. The worst of the storm is behind us, but rain still falls. Thunder still rolls. Through it all, Reese rests in my arms. She faces me, head on my chest, blonde curls blowing in the wind. Never had anything more beautiful. More precious.

My gut knots with every thunderclap. I never should have taken her with me. She's in a dress as thin as cellophane, and we're miles from the ranch. The rain cuts my vision, making it hard to see in each direction. I have no idea where the hell we are.

I should stop. But I have to keep going. Keep Reese safe.

"We'll be okay." I kiss the top of her head and ride on. "You'll be okay."

It's one thing I'm certain of.

Another—I want more time. More time on the ranch. More time with her. How the fuck is summer halfway over already?

I look down at her gorgeous face.

For her, I'm a cowboy. That man she needs. White horse. Sunset. All of it. Anything she asks for, I'll give it.

This lying like a dog has got me dog tired. Tired of lying about what we are. I'm getting older, and I want kids, a family, a damn Georgia mansion. Now, when I picture my life, it's not a nameless, faceless dream girl standing beside me.

It's Reese.

She's the girl in my dreams.

Indescribable. Infuriating. And all fucking mine.

I love her.

For some time now, but I've been a damn idiot for refusing to admit it.

I don't want memories of Reese to follow me around for the rest of my life.

I want her with me. Forever.

But how do I tell her that? That shadow of doubt hovers, whispering that I don't deserve her. That she's too good for me. That she'll leave the ranch and forget all about me. And why wouldn't she? I haven't told her what I feel. What she means to me.

My hand shifts on her back, pressing her closer.

I have two options: stay a stubborn coward and let her leave at the end of the summer, or man up and tell her how I feel.

I blow out a breath. Resolve fills me.

My heart hammers like I've just pitched a strikeout.

I won't let her go. I can't.

⌒

I exhale a sigh of relief when I spot a marker designating the outskirts of the ranch. The storm has chased us off course, but I have my bearings now. What should have been a twenty-minute ride has turned into five hours gone.

No doubt the ranch is on high alert. That is, if it's still in one piece. There's no service on the two-way radio, and the prairie is strewn with debris. To the west, the afternoon sky is still pitch-black. Otherwise, it's blue sky everywhere else.

Reese stirs from her sleep. Yawning, she lifts her head. "What time is it?"

"Four," I tell her.

She touches my chest. Her green eyes widen. "Ford. You rode all this time?"

I grin down at her. "Nothing I can't handle." Blowing out a breath, I tell her, "We're about twenty miles off course, but we should make it back to the ranch by evening." I need to see if my family's okay.

I stop Eephus near a riverbank. Reese and I dismount. As he drinks, I give him a quick once-over. Earlier, I let him rest for a few hours. I hate running him into the ground, but the dark clouds overhead didn't give me much choice.

Passing Reese the canteen, I watch her while she drinks. Beautiful and rain soaked. There are pieces of straw pressed against her cheek, a scratch on her neck. Her face is tired, but strong.

I step forward, rubbing her arms to warm her. "You do okay on a ranch, Birdie Girl."

She bats her eyes at me, smiling. "Just like a cowgirl?"

My heart does a slow roll in my chest. "Just like a cowgirl."

I mean it. She's done things this summer, put up with shit, and never once complained.

Backs to the dark, we stare into the blue sky, the wind buffeting across my face.

"It's beautiful," Reese says simply.

The bright July sun stretches across the horizon in a brilliant blast of gold.

It's like peace across the prairie. The same peace reflected in my chest.

As I look around, I realize Eephus has drifted into the tall prairie grass in search of food.

I whistle.

When he ignores me in favor of his meal, I shake my head and stomp through the tall grass. "Let's go, you stubborn bastard."

I barely get the words out when excruciating pain lances up my leg.

Hissing a breath, I double over. "Fuck."

As I pat the leg of my blue jeans, I look down in time to spot a dark shadow slithering away, tail vibrating with the familiar rattle of danger.

My stomach drops.

Oh shit.

"Ford, what happened?" I can hear the worry in Reese's voice.

"Back up, baby." Grabbing her arm, I give her a clumsy shove, desperate to get her out of harm's way.

I lose my grip on Reese.

Blackness crashes in and knocks me to the ground.

32

Reese

I SHRIEK WHEN FORD COLLAPSES ONTO HIS SIDE.

"Fuck," he groans. "Fucking snake got me. Dirty bastard."

My mind does a cartwheel of realization.

Ford. Snakebite. Hurt.

Oh no.

Falling to my knees, I hover over him. My heartbeat is so loud I can hear it in my ears, feel it in my palms. "What do I do?"

The color drains from Ford's face. "Take off my boots."

I yank them off. Gasp.

The snake's fangs pierced through the leather. His leg is already swelling, and a trickle of blood seeps from each of the small puncture wounds on his right calf.

My hand flies to my mouth to hold in a sob. "You got bit, Ford."

"No shit, baby." Ford grinds his teeth together, trying his best at a smile. Even now, he's fighting against falling apart in front of me. "Come on. Let's get the fuck outta here."

I help him sit up. He loops an arm around my neck. I try to help him stand, but he's too heavy. He collapses on his back, breathing heavily.

"It's okay, it's okay."

I move like I know what to do. I find the canteen and

put a blanket beneath his head. Quickly, I slip off Ford's outer shirt and drench it in water before placing the wet fabric over the wounds.

"Good girl," he says.

Suddenly, he looks very, very tired. His amber eyes close.

I grab the two-way radio. Tears spring to my eyes at the NO SERVICE signal. Even so, I keep hammering its SOS button.

He lifts himself on his forearms. "You have to go."

Panic rises, and I frantically shake my head. "No." I tug on his arm, trying to lift him up. "I'm not leaving you."

"You can't lift me." His voice cracks. "I'll never stay on Eephus, anyway."

I scrape tendrils of hair from my face. Shock paralyzes my limbs. "I can't leave you, Ford. I can't."

"You have to." His voice is steady, but I see it in his face. That spark of fear. "You have to…get to the ranch." His chest heaves as a tremor runs through him. "Get help. We have…an antivenom kit there."

My gaze latches onto Eephus and my stomach roils.

I rode with Ford, but me in the driver's seat? I clench my eyes shut. Fight the flashbacks.

Gavin and the duct tape. The day turning to night. Being left out there all alone.

Ford looks like he hates himself. "I know, baby. I know." Glassy-eyed, Ford clutches my hand, his voice breaking as his calm fractures. "Birdie, you gotta ride."

I blow out a breath, staring at his pale face. "Okay."

Groaning, he rests his head back on the blanket. "Tell my brothers we're near the ravine on the Pancake Flats."

I nod.

"It's a straight shot back," he rasps. I have to lean closer to hear him better. Another tremor rocks his body. "Ride straight and you'll hit it in an hour. Maybe less."

Leaning down, I smooth his unruly hair back. "Kiss me or I won't come back for you."

His chuckle is pained. "Brat." Trembling hand finding mine, he brings it to his lips. "Baby, ride easy." He gives Eephus a nod. "Take care of her, you bastard."

I wobble to my feet.

Eephus looks at me. I look at him.

Chuffing, he backs up.

"C'mon, you asshole," I hiss, taking a step toward him. "Don't make me turn you into cat food."

Slowly, I strip off my bangles. His black eyes follow me as I drop them on the ground. "There. That better?"

I grab his reins and he shakes me off.

He backs up. I follow.

"Please," I beg. "Please."

Our stare down lasts another second, and then he slowly lowers himself so I can climb on. Ford tilts his face to the sky. Relief there.

As I mount the saddle, memories assail me, making my heart race.

Only this time, I block out the bad. I focus on the good. Ford.

I know how to ride. I remember.

I snap the reins. With a squeeze of my legs and a wild cry from my lungs, I kick Eephus into a gallop. To a desperate push north to Runaway Ranch.

I don't look back. I just ride.

No time to spare.

Ford needs me.

As we speed across sun-drenched prairie, I sing to calm my mind. Waylon Jennings, Hank Williams. My songs. My parents' songs. I'm not helpless or crazy like Gavin has so often told me.

I'm free.

And I'm riding like the fucking wind.

Farmland turns to forest. The miles pass by in a frantic blur. My legs are numb, but I push on. I can't ride fast enough. Can't stop hammering my thumb on the radio's SOS button like it's a prayer heaven sent.

Finally, Eephus breaks through a bend on the dirt road, and I see the ranch.

A scream fills my lungs, but there's no need.

They're already looking for us. Dozens of cowboys. One on a black horse. Another is on an ATV heading straight for me. My chest swells with relief.

A sob erupts in my throat and my defenses crumble.

I did it.

I fucking did it.

As the ATV roars closer, I see it's Davis.

Help.

"Reese, thank God, you're okay." Brown eyes wild, he searches the horizon behind me. "Where's Ford? Where's my brother?"

"He's hurt," I gasp. "He got bit by a rattlesnake."

"Fuck," Davis rasps, paling. His hardened features crumble, like the news has aged him twenty years. "Where is he?"

"Near the ravine on the Pancake Flats."

"Christ." A look of astonishment crosses his stern expression. "You rode here. Straight?"

I nod.

The severe line of his mouth moves as he speaks into the two-way radio. "I need Curtis and an antivenom kit. Now."

An immediate response crackles back. "*On our way.*"

Davis twists toward the ranch, every muscle in his body strung taught. "I'll get you back to the house—"

I shake my head, already moving Eephus into position to ride again. "No. I'm going with you." The muscles in my legs spasm but I refuse to stay behind, refuse to leave Ford. He would never stay behind if it was me. "I can show you where he is."

A millisecond of uncertainty swings his gaze from me to the vast farmland. Then, decided, Davis lifts the radio once more to his mouth. "Reese and I are headed to get Ford." His rough voice is stern, commanding. "Meet us at the ravine on the Pancake Flats. If you're not there fast, you're all fucking dead."

⌒

Waiting for word on Ford is sheer torture.

Less than two hours after my arrival, we brought Ford back to the ranch. Now, the staff medic, Curtis, tends to him in a back bedroom. Davis and the rest of Ford's brothers are pacing a hole in the hallway. Everyone assured me he'll be okay, but I won't believe it until I see him again.

Touch him.

For now, I sit on the couch in Dakota and Davis's living room. Ruby brought me a change of clothes—a buttery soft flannel and leggings. Dakota hot chocolate to warm me up. Thunder rumbles. The ranch is in one piece, but I'm not.

My heart is a heavy, clenched ache.

I just want him to be okay. Please be okay.

If he isn't…

I think about Ford, keeping me safe all through the storm, holding on to me tight.

His amber eyes.

His amazing heart.

I blow out a breath. Needing a distraction, I pull out my phone.

I freeze.

I have twenty texts. All from Gavin.

A chill skitters over my spine.

> **You're playing games, Reese.**
>
> **I will bring you home. One way or another.**
>
> **Time's almost up.**

Something clicks inside of me, like a lock turning a key. Gavin doesn't matter.

All that matters is Ford.

All that matters is me.

What I did today.

I survived. I found a piece of the old Reese. Which means…maybe I can start over. Maybe being brave is easier than I thought. Maybe Doctor DiFeo is right. I haven't given myself enough credit.

"How are you holding up?"

The husky sound of Dakota's voice has me looking up. She enters the living room with Duke in her arms.

I leap to my feet. "How is Ford? Is he okay?"

"He'll be just fine," Dakota says softly. Brown eyes shining with tears, she reaches out to squeeze my arm. "You got him help in time, Reese. You saved him."

Tears threaten, but I clear my throat, pushing them away.

Dakota hugs me and I lean into her touch.

We pull back, and I smile at Duke, tickling his chin. He coos, reaching for my hair with fat little fists.

Dakota adjusts her son on her hip and says, "Don't worry. He'll be back to his grouchy self in no time."

I laugh.

Davis steps into the room. Keena bounds at his boots, wagging her tail heartily.

"He wants to see you," Davis rumbles. He rubs the back of his neck.

I hesitate, feeling awkward under Davis's cool stare. "Oh, I—I don't know."

Dakota peers at me. A smile tips her full lips. "You should go up."

"He's pumped full of drugs," Davis says. "So he's acting like a damn idiot, but he, uh, also needs to see you. He won't shut up about it." Despite the gruff tone of his voice, there's relief on his chiseled features.

I nod. "Okay. I have to do one thing first."

Half an hour later, I'm back at Davis and Dakota's house, heading down the hall with a bundle of black fur in my arms. Charlie and Wyatt, standing guard outside the bedroom door like a pair of cowboy sentries, each give a nod when they see me. Gratefulness shines in their eyes.

I chew my lip. "Davis said it was okay—"

"Go ahead," Charlie commands somberly.

Then I'm stepping into the room.

Ford's in bed, propped up by pillows. Shirtless, he's hooked up to an IV. His eyes are glassy with drugs, but when he sees me, he gives me a big, lopsided smile.

"Birdie Girl," he exclaims joyfully.

At the sight of him, my knees go weak.

"Hi," I say. "I brought you someone."

I place Mouse on the bed. She heads for Ford, and his hand comes out to clumsily stroke her fur. She arches under his touch, butts her head under his palm. *More, please.*

And then Ford's free hand, large and warm, wraps around my wrist. Pulling gently, but firmly, he sits me on the edge of the bed.

I stare down at my wrist, blinking. I forgot I didn't have my bangles.

"How are you?" I ask, fighting hot tears in my eyes.

"Better than ever, baby."

I laugh. "Somehow I doubt that." I sweep a lock of hair off his brow. My touch seems to comfort him, so I do it again. Eyes heavy, he settles back against the pillows.

"My dream girl," he murmurs, kissing my palm with exquisite care. "You and me, meant to be."

His words sink into me like sunlight.

"Hush. You're talking foolish, Ford."

"But I'm not, baby," he says in his deep, drugged voice. "I dreamed about you, and you came true."

"Sleep, Country Boy."

"Don't wanna," he slurs, fighting to keep his eyes open.

But I have the trick to make it happen. I scratch my nails through his hair. A soft, satisfied noise rises in the back of his throat. Smiling, I watch as his eyelids get lower and lower until he's asleep, his broad chest slowly rising and falling.

The most beautiful sight I've ever seen.

He's alive and okay.

Hot tears fill my eyes.

What would I do without him?

I want to exist—not because of him, but *for* him. All because I—

I gasp.

So loud in the silence. So loud that Mouse lifts her head to scrutinize me. *About damn time.*

I cover my mouth with a trembling hand.

No. Impossible. I cannot love this man. This—this cowboy.

I look at his large hand wrapped around mine, his calloused fingertips gently covering the scars on the inside of my wrist.

I do.

I love him.

Dual waves of panic and joy crash over me.

Would he love me back? Could he? With my past, my chaos, am I more a burden than he needs? What if he considers us friends and nothing more? Still, despite my what-ifs, my heart is a wild tremble. A lick of flame igniting hopes and dreams long buried.

Maybe this is why I'm here. Maybe everything has led me to Ford.

Standing, I untangle our hands and lean down to press a kiss to his brow. I breathe in his scent, feel the ache in my gut snap tight.

When I open the door and step outside, I run into a solid wall of muscle.

Davis.

His hands fist at his side. "You don't have to go," he says.

I palm my hands to my heart. "No. I should." My gaze locks with his. "Take care of him, okay?"

I'm halfway down the hall when Davis booms, "Reese."

Breath held, I turn.

"I'm sorry." The smile he gives me is soft. "I was wrong about you."

I smile back at him.

"Yeah," I breathe. "I think I was wrong about me, too."

33

Ford

VOICES. LAUGHTER. FROM INSIDE THE ROOM OR far away—I can't tell.

All I know—with a singular fucking focus—is that the sun needs to die.

A few muttered curses, then, "Looks like sleeping beauty's coming around."

"Fuck off," I mutter. Even slightly delirious and in pain, I know an asshole little brother when I hear one.

With that, I push through exhaustion and open my eyes, hissing a breath as the sun sears my retinas.

"Put me out of my fucking misery," I rasp.

Chuckling, Charlie pulls the blinds closed.

"How you feelin'?" Davis asks.

"Glad to be alive, that's for damn sure."

I shove a hand through my hair, sit up, and scan the room. The clock on the wall says four in the afternoon. My brothers sit in various positions around the bed. Their expressions border on amused and worried.

"How long was I out?"

Hands on his thighs, Davis pushes to standing. "Two days."

"Jesus."

"Only pissed the bed twice," Wyatt adds.

"Fuck you."

Wyatt and Charlie snicker.

That's when the last few days hit me like a freight train.

"Reese." I thrash in the sheet, jerk upright. "Where is she? Is she okay?"

"You're back here, aren't you?" Davis says. "She's okay."

Pride flares in my chest. Good girl. Good fucking girl.

I relax against the bed, only vaguely aware of Mouse nudging her head beneath my hand, where I give her an absentminded pet. "Where is she?" I ask, too relieved about Reese to be annoyed that she's not the first one I see.

"Dakota has her helping out at the bakery," Davis offers.

"What about the chickens?" Impatiently, I shake my head. "I gotta find her." Davis and Charlie exchange looks of amusement.

Wyatt shoves a hand against my shoulder when I make a move to stand. "You got bit by a goddamn snake, man. Sit your ass down."

I pull back the covers to look at my leg. White gauze wraps around my calf. A searing pain makes its way up my ankle and through my bloodstream.

"Doctor said it would be like that for a couple of weeks," Charlie says when I hiss a breath. "Gotta move slow. Take it easy."

I groan.

Davis nods gravely. "Came too goddamn close to putting *Rest in Peace, Asshole* on your tombstone."

A serious silence falls.

Charlie's jaw works. "I'm sorry, man."

I hold his eyes. Give him a nod. "I know."

And just like that, we're good.

"About Reese," Davis says. I stiffen. "I was wrong about her. She's—"

"Fierce," I finish. I look at my brothers. "If y'all see me, you're gonna see Reese. So get right with it."

Davis's eyes widen. The corner of his mouth kicks up. "Holy shit. You love her."

"Yeah," I say, emotion clogging my throat. "I do."

Wyatt scoffs. "Took you that long to figure it out?"

Charlie's dark gaze lands on me. "No arguments from me."

My heart burns inside my chest. "That girl might turn around and set my whole life on fire."

Davis looks amused. "Is that good or bad?"

"I'll let you know." I grin, glad we're finally on the same fucking page. "Now help me change."

They all sigh but do what I say.

Twenty minutes later, Charlie drops me on the opposite side of the ranch.

My blood roars between my ears as I limp my way up to her chalet. I need Reese.

I need her *now*.

Something inside me feels changed. Wrecked. Like it'll never be the same. I'm alive because of Reese. Through it all, I never doubted her. I trusted her. A level of trust I've only had with my brothers.

The tight ball of tension in my gut unknots when I see her on the front porch of her chalet, key in hand. Flour dusts her cheekbones, and she's in tight jeans and a Huckleberry T-shirt tied at the waist.

"Goin' somewhere?'

At the sound of my voice, she jumps and drops the key. Surprise and relief flash in her emerald eyes. Instead of coming to me like I ache for her to do, she props her hand on her hip.

"Finally out and about, Country Boy?" She smiles lightheartedly, but I sense an edge. Her guard's up.

Suddenly I'm pissed. She saved my life, and now she wants to give me a cold shoulder of the highest order. I don't fucking think so.

"Where've you been?" I rasp, hating that she's keeping her distance. Not now. Not when I fucking know what this is.

"They put me to work in the bakery," she says with a little smile. "Odd-job queen over here. Looks like you might have some competition on the ranch."

"That so?"

"Oh, it's very so." Her eyes flare with heat, and she crosses her arms like she's actively stopping herself from reaching out.

I stare at her, heart hammering. "You still got your chickens?"

"Yeah," she breathes. "I love those stupid chickens."

I take a step closer. "Reese…" My voice cracks.

And so does she.

Suddenly, she flings herself into my arms. Our breaths catch together, shaking us both. *Thank god. Thank fucking god.*

I squeeze my eyes shut, stroking her wild hair. "'Bout time you dropped the fucking attitude."

"Tough," she whispers. "It's all yours."

Yeah, it is.

She wraps her arms tighter around my neck, doing her damndest to cut off my air supply. "Thank God you're okay."

"Sounds like you were worried about me, Birdie Girl."

She laughs, her breath a warm pulse against my throat. "You're hard on the heart, Country Boy."

Our heartbeats slow in our chests, mapping each other.

When we pull back, Reese runs her small hands up my shoulders to clutch at my face. She bites at her lower lip, then asks, "Are you sure you're okay? Shouldn't you be in bed?"

"I'll be moving slow for a few days, but nothing I can't handle." I glance down, checking her over. "What about you? Are you okay? You've been takin' care of yourself?"

She gives me an exasperated look. "Ford. I'm fine."

Reese stiffens when her phone vibrates. Her hand flies to the back pocket of her jeans, and I don't miss the flash of fear on her face.

"What is it?"

"It's Gavin."

My hand curls around her phone.

Last chance to come home, Reese.

I need you back, Reese.

You're mine, Reese, and don't you forget it.

"Motherfucker." I seethe.

Her eyes flick to mine. "They're just texts."

"They're not texts. They're threats." My vision goes red. "Piece of fucking shit."

Rage gnaws at me. I hate that I was out of commission and she was going through this alone. Gavin's fucked in the head. All the signs point to him being controlling, but this…it's something else entirely.

"He's scaring me, Ford. He's never acted like this before." Her hands are firm, but lightly trembling as she takes the phone.

I step into her, gripping her tight. "I won't let anything happen to you."

"I know." She smiles and kisses my lips. Her trust messes with my head. My heartbeat. "All I have to do is hold out four more weeks."

My heart thunders. Four weeks until Reese is free of her asshole manager. Four weeks until I can figure out how I keep this girl.

I slip a hand into her hair, hold her eyes with mine. "Reese, I—"

I stop short of telling her that I love her. That I want her on the ranch. Because am I a selfish bastard for wanting her to stay? Everyone's always kept this girl. She's never had a choice. I don't want to cage her. Hell, I won't.

But I can be honest.

So I take two steps back and go about it the old-fashioned way. The cowboy way.

"I want to take you on a date."

There's something hesitant in her emerald eyes. "A date?"

"Yeah. A date."

She laughs. "Ford. Friends, don't—"

I gently grip her jaw, cutting her short. "We're not friends, baby. Say that word again and I'll put you over my knee and spank that ass pink until you forget it."

Her pouty pink mouth forms an O of surprise. She stares at me with dazed eyes, then, as if snapping herself out of it, she shakes her head. "Why are you telling me this, Ford? Why does it matter?"

I give her a look, effectively ending her protest. "Don't you dare act like you don't want this as much as I do." My hand curls around her neck and I pull her closer. "I won't play games about what this is and what you are to me."

She tilts her chin. The fire in her eyes scorches. "What am I?"

"Birdie Girl, you're pretty much my goddamn everything."

She's out of my league, but I'm not worried about keeping up. Because I'm keeping her.

The brightest smile tugs at her lips. "I am?"

My heart skips a beat. "Yeah. You are."

Joy. It's all over her face. And it's all I want to see for the rest of my damn life.

I kiss her then. Hard. Hungry.

The ride, the rush, Reese—I'm all in.

34

Reese

"THERE, THERE!" DAKOTA CRIES.

I rush around and drop napkins onto a picnic table.

She thins her lips, gives me an abashed look. "I feel bad bossing you around."

Charlie, crouched behind the food stand, snorts. "You learned it from your husband."

I bat my eyes. "Stars are just like us." She laughs and I touch her arm. "This is fun. Really."

The Rough Rider Rodeo—an annual tradition in Resurrection—is a sight to see. Small-town charm at its finest. The mouth-watering scent of elephant ears and hotdogs lingers in the air. News crews roam with video cameras, while a local band belts out country music on stage.

The Montgomery's are a full-throttle force. It's all hands on deck for Dakota. As a food vendor, she's selling hand pies before the rodeo begins. Her unofficial official opening of The Huckleberry.

Everyone's here. Ruby's in the booth with Dakota assembling desserts. Charlie's hammering on the busted side of the booth. Davis keeps running into town whenever supplies get low, and Stede's taken Duke to the calf-roping exhibit.

And I'm manning the coffee station while Ford wipes down picnic tables.

The only ones missing are Wyatt and Fallon, who've gone to get ready for the rodeo.

Belonging—that's what this feeling is in my heart.

Something's shifted in the last week. Ford's brothers treat me like we've been friends for years. And right here, at this rodeo, with this family, I feel more at home than I ever did on stage or with Gavin.

Ford, in ranch jeans and a gray T-shirt, hustles food to guests. As he passes by, he flashes me a sexy smirk. My heart flips as I stare at his handsome profile. His chiseled jaw and day-old scruff is quintessential heartbreaker. And damn the audacity of that backward baseball cap.

Something's shifted between us, too.

Ever since he dropped the no-friends bomb, we've been moving fast. Every night I stay over at his place, it feels like I'm sealing my fate. To stay. To trust. To love—so deeply I almost don't know what to do.

Except tell him the truth. Tell him I love him. But can I trust him not to leave me? Do I trust him to love me back? That feels like asking for the world.

Besides, he has a job offer waiting for him. Whatever's between us, I'm terrified of ruining it. So, I busy myself with all things rodeo.

By the time late afternoon falls, I'm a sweaty, sticky mess.

Ford pulls me from the booth and hands me a bottled water. "Here, take a break."

I glance over at Dakota, making sure she has it under control before I sink onto the picnic table bench.

His phone chimes. He glances at it quickly, then me. "Your pill."

I blink. "You set an alarm?"

"Yeah," he gruffs. "I did."

I smother a smile at the pink flush on his cheeks. He can act like a bulldog all he wants, but he's really a golden retriever in disguise.

I take my medication, covertly popping the pill into my mouth.

"How's it going with DiFeo?" Ford asks.

I finger the newest necklace around my throat, tracing the small gold cowboy hat. "I like her. She's no-bullshit."

After six therapy sessions with Dr. DiFeo, I feel strong. Happy. I wonder why I didn't do it earlier and that's when I remember Gavin wouldn't let me. Well, fuck him.

I'm learning from Dr. DiFeo that I am worthy. And Ford's been showing me too, in the way he looks at me, the way he treats me. I am his obsession, and he doesn't hide it.

He's stocked his kitchen with honey bears just because I love them, stays up late with me to talk about our days, and after every therapy session, he buys me a new necklace as a reward. Most people assume who I am, but Ford understands who I am. And he doesn't try to change me. He treats me in ways I've never been treated. Plain and simple, I love being with him.

"So, is this our date?" I ask.

"Hell no." He looks offended by my question. "An actual date off the ranch, Birdie Girl. No ranch shit."

"But I like ranch shit."

"Yeah, but I want to know what you like." He takes my hand, braiding his fingers through mine. "It's important."

Heart hammering hard, my eyes scan the picnic tables, the Montgomery's. *How do I leave him? How do I leave all this?*

But I remind myself, there's been no promise of the

future. No three little words exchanged. We're more than friends, yet there's no real commitment.

Soon, the crowd dwindles, and the booth is closed. An announcement goes up over the loudspeakers.

"If you can believe it," I tell Ford. "This *is* my first rodeo."

"We're done," Dakota announces, collapsing beside me.

Davis hands her a bottled water while Ruby sets a platter of hand pies in the middle of the picnic table.

"Got a blueberry for me?" Wyatt asks, rocking the table as he drapes himself between me and Ford. With clumsy hands, he hunts through the stacked pastries.

"Right on time," Dakota quips.

Ford elbows his brother. "Move your ass."

"Hey, man, I gotta eat."

Charlie sighs.

"Soothing your self-destructive tendencies with sugar?" Fallon's husky voice settles over us. Eyes on Wyatt, she slips through the crowd to join us. "You did it, Koty." A rare smile graces her pretty face. "Hand pies."

Standing, Dakota pulls her sister into a hug. "Hand pies at the rodeo. Although, I seem to remember you sticking around to serve them."

Fallon laughs.

Dakota tugs the fringe on her sister's vest. "Did you take your medication?"

Wyatt looks like he's about to burn right through Fallon with his stare.

She sighs, levels her sister with a stern glare. "Dakota."

Stede appears, walking Duke on the tops of his boots. "Pumped him full of sugar just for you."

Dakota shakes her head. "Thanks, Dad."

Davis chuckles and lifts his son into the air. "Kid's gotta live."

Stede turns to Fallon. Pride shines in his eyes as he takes her hands. "You got this, Fallon. You ride hard and you ride fast."

Fallon gives him a curt nod. "Yes, Daddy."

"My girl, my girl, my girl," booms an unfamiliar, male voice.

Fallon snaps her muscled body into place. Her smile is feline as she turns toward the source of the noise.

A rotund man—looking every bit the part of a wealthy Texas cattleman in his three-piece suit—confers with Fallon. To her left stands a lanky, golden-haired guy, his face shadowed beneath the brim of a cowboy hat. He carries water bottles and Fallon's gear.

"Who's that?" I ask, leaning into Ford. The way everyone's face has gone stormy makes me think they hate the guy.

"Fallon's entourage. Fat guy is Pappy Starr, her agent."

I watch, fascinated but worried. Already, he reminds me of Gavin. Power hungry. He'll shape her, make her, then break her.

"What about the skinny kid?"

"Tripp Hendrix." We look over at Dakota. She's smiling. "He's been in love with her since high school."

"He's her water boy," Wyatt adds, looking none too happy. "Follows her around like a goddamn puppy."

Davis rolls his eyes, puts a broad hand on his brother's shoulder. "Easy."

"Pappy wants Fallon to go big time," Charlie explains, dark head dipping close. "If she wins today, she could get a sponsorship. She's the first female who's ever been this close."

Turning to Pappy, Dakota crosses her arms, her stance protective. "Is my sister ready?"

Pappy snaps his suspenders. "As ready as ever. I should know. I trained her."

Dakota's pretty face darkens. Davis lays a hand on his wife's shoulder like he's holding her back.

"Training a woman, Pappy. Never thought I'd see the day."

Every single eye snaps up at the deep voice. Boots crunch on the dust and dirt. I hear someone whisper, "Hey, that's him."

Gasping in surprise, Ruby stands on top of the picnic table bench to see better.

Ford swears. Charlie bristles.

But my jaw drops.

The man looks like a storm sweeping the horizon. Every inch of him screams *bull rider*. Broad chest. A sharp square jaw. Large, calloused hands. A large man only made larger by the vest, spurs, chaps and brace. He's closely followed by his entourage, men who look nowhere near as scrappy as Fallon's team does.

Ruby grabs my hand. "That's Cole Weston. He's Fallon's competitor." Charlie gives his wife a proud smile, like she's a pro at the sport. "He's the reason for the cameras."

Fallon opens her mouth, but she's cut off with a lift of Pappy's hand.

"Fallon McGraw plans to be your fiercest competitor yet, Weston. Mark my words."

Nostrils flaring, Fallon grips her vest like she needs to give her fists someplace to still.

Amusement lines Cole's rugged features. "I highly doubt that."

I arch a brow at his arrogance.

This time, Fallon moves. Striding closer, she jabs her finger in Cole's chest. "You're gonna get your ass stomped, Weston."

Davis groans and closes his eyes.

"I don't argue with little girls," Cole snaps at her.

"Oh fuck," Charlie mutters.

Steam is practically coming out of Fallon's ears.

But it's Wyatt who's in Cole's face so fast I never saw him move. "You call this woman a cowgirl. You fucking hear me?"

Fallon's surprised eyes slice to Wyatt, but she says nothing.

Beside me, scenting the potential for a fight, Ford and Charlie are on their feet. The only thing keeping Davis in place is Duke in his arms.

Ruby, chewing her lip, sinks beside me on the stool.

"Oh lord," Dakota murmurs, looking like she wants to chuck the remaining hand pies at her brothers-in-law.

Pappy holds out a hand, chuckling. "A little healthy competition never hurt no one." His other hand, holding a cigar, gestures at a camera. "In fact, it's good for business."

But Fallon's once again sizing up Cole, that fiery glare returning.

"Don't let him rile you," Wyatt orders softly. He holds her arm, and I don't fail to notice the way Fallon leans into him. "It's what he wants. Save the angry for the bull."

Instead of a cutting, sarcastic remark, she gives a sharp, obedient nod.

Stetson low on his brow, Cole turns to leave. "I don't

care how bad you are, darlin', the fact that you think you can win this is fucking laughable," he tosses over his shoulder as he stomps away.

"Asshole," Ford mutters, wrapping an arm around me.

For one long second, Fallon stands there fuming.

Pappy gives her a look, and she immediately shrugs out of Wyatt's grip. Then she storms in the direction of the arena and does not look back.

～

We take seats on the bleachers. I listen intently as the brothers try to explain rodeo to me.

"If she reaches the threshold to score, she'll make history in Montana," Davis says.

My eyes bounce between them. "I thought she already rode professionally?"

"She does. But she wants the NFR," Charlie says. "She wants to win that jackpot."

Ford takes pity on me. "Eight seconds. That's all you gotta remember."

"Eight seconds," I echo, looking toward the ring. I'm not sure I'll ever understand those souls brave enough to get in a ring with a bull, ready to get their shit rocked.

"Fallon's the definition of insanity," Ford explains. "She keeps doing the same thing over and over and expecting a different result."

"Expecting not to die," Charlie mutters from his spot on the bench in front of us.

"Why does she do it?" I ask Ford.

Ford looks unhappy. "Death wish. Glory."

A hush falls over the crowd as Fallon claims her place atop her bull.

"Where's her helmet?" Davis blasts.

"What?" Dakota cranes through the crowd.

"Oh fuck." Ford groans. Fallon wears a cowboy hat.

"Is wearing a cowboy hat that bad?" I ask Ford.

He smears a hand down his face. "It ain't good."

We all lean forward, watching Fallon get into position in the chute.

In the thousand glittering lights of the outdoor arena, even though she's not here for beauty, Fallon stuns in simple cream and brown attire. Ribbons dangle from her vest. Her thick caramel braid tucked under her hat. Limbs tense, she's fierce and coltish in the twilight.

In her face I see the same restless search I once felt. Who am I? What do I want? One thing is clear: she craves the spotlight. Nothing wrong with that. I used to love it, too.

But not anymore.

And that's when I realize I know what I want. I might not be New Reese, but I'm good enough. Right here. Happy. Alive. And that's everything.

Ford's arm tightens around me. "You okay?"

I kiss him softly. "I'm perfect."

Then the announcer's voice echoes around the arena. "From our very own Resurrection, Montana, our hometown girl, our woman bull rider, Fallon McGraw!"

The horn sounds and the chute flies open. Bull and beast come roaring out. Fallon's poised, right arm raised, left hand gripping the braided rope handle. I know nothing about bull riding, but she looks wild and free.

Like she could do it every damn day for the rest of her life.

That's love.

That's lunacy.

It's exactly how I feel about Ford and this life of mine.

The bull thrashes Fallon, but she hangs on. Eight seconds feels like eight years.

I'm wincing, covering my eyes, while watching through my fingers.

The crowd lets out a deafening roar of excitement as the buzzer rings, signaling she made it the full eight seconds.

"Oh my god!" Dakota screams. She launches out of her seat. "She did it."

Fallon hits the ground—hard—and then pops up to standing, dusting herself off. If she's in any pain, she hides it like a pro.

"Holy hell!" the announcer screams. "Fallon McGraw has just made history in the fine state of Montana, folks!"

A beaming Fallon steps into the spotlight, tears off her Stetson, and tosses it into the air.

I've never seen her look this happy. The weight she's carried this summer is gone—if only for a second.

In the crowd, I spy Wyatt hanging on the rails, a Cheshire cat grin spreading across his face. Relief, pride in his eyes.

Media swarms Fallon as she exits the ring.

The tension eases, and we settle back to watch more bull riders. Cole Weston takes the lead, draws a massive bull. An hour drifts by, then it's time for Wyatt—bareback bronc riding to close the rodeo.

In the chute, Wyatt glances around the arena. Beside me, Ford's body stiffens. Around me, all the brothers have gone on alert.

I glance at Ruby, who shakes her head, just as confused as me.

I touch Ford's arm, noting the deep crease of worry on his face. "What's wrong?"

"Wyatt doesn't normally ride bareback." He shakes his head. "He's looking for Fallon. Goddamn idiot."

"His mind needs to be on that bronc," Charlie snaps, eyes locked on Wyatt.

Baseball hat gripped in his hands, Ford half-rises in his seat as the horn sounds and the chute opens. Wyatt and the bronc explode into the arena.

Grip firm, Wyatt's upper body bends in ways I had no idea a human body could bend. His back slams against the horse's back, keeping a perfect rhythm with the animal. He makes it look easy. Effortless.

As the eight second buzzer sounds, Wyatt tries to release his hand. But he can't. His riggin' has slipped, dragging his body sideways at an almost horizontal, eerie angle. For a brief second, panic flashes on his face as he tries to wrench himself free. A pick-up man on the side of the chute reaches for him, but it's useless. As the bucking horse comes in closer, we all watch in horror as Wyatt is slammed against the rail.

Gasps ripple through the crowd.

Free of the riggin', Wyatt hits the ground.

But he doesn't get back up.

"No." The word falls from Ford's mouth in one strangled syllable.

The beast of a horse continues to buck and run around the arena. Too close to Wyatt. Too deadly.

My heart races as Ford rockets to his feet. "Get my brother out of that fucking ring!" he screams, eyes wild.

The pick-up men scramble, but they're a beat too slow. Rodeo clowns try to corral the horse, but it's a monster— pissed off, frantic, unable to be caged. Vicious white hooves pound near Wyatt's head.

"Oh my god. Oh my god," Dakota chants.

We're all on our feet.

Movement in front of me. Charlie.

In two seconds flat, he vaults the fence and jumps into the ring. He races over to Wyatt and covers his brother's unconscious body with his own, shielding Wyatt from the bronco's hooves.

Ruby barely blinks, squeezing Dakota's hand.

"Stay here," Ford says to me before he races down the aisle.

"Goddamn it!" Davis whips Duke into Dakota's arms and takes off after Ford.

My panicked eyes watch as Ford enters the ring. He grabs the horse's reins, swings himself up, and rides him into the chute.

Ruby bursts into tears as Charlie and another cowboy quickly lift Wyatt and carry him out of the arena.

The crowd begins to file out. Ruby, Dakota and I go in search of our cowboys.

It's dusk, the sun beginning to creep low behind Meadow Mountain, in a deep amber glow. As we pass through the dusty parking lot, I look over at the entrance of the fairgrounds. A black SUV slowly cruises past the gate.

A shiver rolls over my spine, and I freeze.

Gavin?

But when I blink, the car's gone. Disappeared into thin air.

35

Ford

"Y'ALL ARE IDIOTS." DAVIS GLARES AND SLAMS THE door as the nurse exits.

"You're just jealous you weren't a hero." Charlie sits on the end of Wyatt's hospital bed, holding a foam coffee cup. They both wear shit-eating grins. After all the chaos at the fairground, we took Wyatt to the hospital to get checked out. He has a minor concussion and a sprained wrist. Now we wait for him to be discharged.

Wyatt wiggles his brows. "Hat stayed on at least."

"Like he said," I say, crossing the room to swat the back of Wyatt's head. "Idiots."

"Damn, man," Wyatt complains. "I'm already in the hospital."

Davis levels a dry look at me. "You didn't help, Ford."

I shrug, keeping it casual, even though I'm all kinds of shaken up inside. "Couldn't let them have all the fun."

There was no way to keep a cool head when both of my little brothers were in that ring. A stampede couldn't keep me away from them.

Davis sighs and shakes his head. "This is not how I wanted the summer to go. Both of you hurt within two weeks." His gaze drifts to me, then to Wyatt. "It was close, Wy. Too close."

Charlie's smile fades, and he says in a low voice, "If you

were paying attention, if your head was in it, you would have known that riggin' was looser than normal."

Wyatt swallows. "Charlie, man—"

"You know I'm right."

Guilt and shame engulf Wyatt's face.

I sigh, recognizing the come-to-Jesus chat we need to have with our little brother—the one we've tiptoed around all summer.

"End it," Davis orders. "Take the contract for the training job, Wyatt."

"It's time," Charlie agrees.

"Ford," Wyatt croaks, looking at me helplessly.

Because he knows I know when he's done. It's the same feeling I had when I was over baseball. You're so blocked you can't see anything else, not even a way out. I had to quit. And Wyatt has to do the same.

Because if he doesn't, he won't hurt someone else— he'll hurt himself.

I swear under my breath, hating to say it. But I have to.

"You'll kill yourself if you keep going this way," I say bluntly.

Charlie winces.

Davis settles a hand on Wyatt's shoulder. "We won't let you do that."

A muscle jerks in Wyatt's jaw as he stares down at the thin blanket draped over his legs.

I study my little brother, taking in the dark circles under his eyes, then I tell Charlie and Davis, "You two go ahead. I want to talk to Wy."

Charlie nods. Davis hesitates, like the thought of being left out of one conversation in his entire bossy ass existence will kill him, but after a second, he follows Charlie out.

"I don't need an intervention," Wyatt complains, his face stony.

"Tough. I'm your big brother. You sit in that bed and you fuckin' listen to me."

Wyatt grumbles, and I sigh. The limits of patience have never been tested until Wyatt was born.

Sitting on the edge of his bed, I say, "Did I ever tell you why I really left baseball?"

"Because Sav left?"

"Partly. But it was also that kid."

He blinks. "That bad pitch?"

"It wasn't a bad pitch, man." I tell him the story that Davis and Reese know. How much of a mess I was. How I fucked up and hurt that kid.

Finished, I run a hand over my jaw. "I don't want you in the same boat, Wy. Get out while you're clear headed. Get over Fallon."

Bullseye.

Wyatt's gaze snaps to mine and hardens. Fallon's like a grenade strapped to Wyatt's chest. When it detonates, he's done.

"I see what you're doin' little brother. You think that if you attach yourself to her side, you can protect her. But you can't. If she doesn't want you to take care of her, you have to move on."

"I wasn't there." His glassy blue eyes take on a faraway light. "I should have been there that night, and I wasn't."

I feel for my brother. "Punishing yourself for what you did and didn't do ain't a way to live, kid."

It's been my MO for the last seven years. With baseball. Staying at the ranch. Not moving on. It's easy to recognize yourself in someone else who's fucking up. I see myself in Wyatt and all the ways he's trying to hang onto the past.

Onto Fallon.

I lean in and level with him. "It's still going to hurt, you know. When she gets hurt, whether or not you're together, it's still gonna hurt."

Wyatt flinches.

Because it's not *if* anymore, it's *when*.

He's silent for a long beat, then says, "You don't know what fucking hurts."

I sit there, rocked by the bitterness in his tone, waiting for him to say more. Instead, he looks down at his hands.

"Y'all are right. I'll quit rodeoing. My heart isn't in it anymore."

I eye him warily, hoping we haven't made a fucking mistake. Hoping he doesn't brood around the ranch for the rest of his life instead of on the rodeo circuit.

"What about you?" He nods. "You gonna take that baseball job? Leave the ranch?"

It's not a hard choice. Not anymore.

"No," I tell him as Reese's gorgeous face fills my head. "I don't want the job. I want the girl."

I never expected her. *This*. How one moment I never knew she existed, and now I know an embarrassing number of things about her. I don't want to fuck anyone else. I don't want to leave the ranch. And I sure as hell don't want Reese to leave.

"Well, you should keep her," Wyatt says. "Sav treated you like you needed fixing, but that girl there…" Full blaze smile on his face, he nods at the door. "She doesn't."

Startled, I turn to see Reese standing at the window. She lifts her hand, giving us a little wave.

My heart flips over.

Wyatt shifts in bed, wincing. "Go, man. I'll be out of here in five minutes."

"Make sure you check out," I warn him. Memory montages. Fourteen-year-old Wyatt. A bad horseback riding accident that left our entire family shaken up. After treatment, he ditched his gown in the hospital stairwell and bailed before discharge. He left the nurses to panic and effectively scared the shit out of our parents.

"Yeah, yeah," he mutters, already tearing his hospital bracelet off.

I step out into the hallway.

The sight of Reese in her tiny shorts and knee-high boots nearly knocks me over. Trips my pulse.

This entire summer, everything about us has felt right. Tonight, on my arm, at the rodeo. Living in my small town. Sleeping in my bed. Since day one, it's clicked. Nothing hard or forced.

It's been a dream.

My dream girl.

I plant my hands on Reese's waist. "You're here."

"Of course I am." She touches my chest, and the weight of tonight, the worry over my family, falls away. That's the power of Reese. She calms me.

"It's late, baby," I tell her, fighting emotion in my throat. I tuck a lock of wavy blonde hair behind her ear. "You should have gone back to the ranch with Ruby and Koty."

She shakes her head, a stubborn glint in her green eyes. "I didn't want you to be alone."

My heart seizes at that. An obstruction the size of the Rockies forms in my throat.

This *fucking* woman. I never thought a woman could

hold my heart and break my soul, but here I am. Broken. In love. Whipped.

So damn natural. So damn easy. Like I wound up for a pitch, and by the time I let it whip, the game's already over.

But my world with her is just beginning.

"How's Wyatt?" she asks.

"An idiot, but he's still breathing." I tug on her hand, pulling her closer. "Has a minor concussion, but he'll live to annoy again."

A shaky laugh pops out of her. "Good." She pokes a finger in my chest, her pretty face stern. "You have to stop scaring me to death, Country Boy."

I chuckle. "Gotta keep you quick on those high heels, Birdie Girl."

Above us, the neon light flickers. Bootsteps sound down the hall and Reese stiffens, fear on her face.

She relaxes when Fallon slices down the hallway like a shark. When she sees us, she says nothing, only slips by to enter Wyatt's hospital room. The door clicks closed.

I look at Reese. "Birdie, what's wrong?" By now, I can read her.

She bites her lip, then says, "I saw a car."

"What kind of car?"

"A black SUV. I've noticed it around town a few times. And tonight, it was at the fairgrounds." She shivers. "Like it was watching me."

I exhale, frustrated she kept it from me. "You should have told me."

"I didn't want to worry you."

"Always worry me when it comes to you. You hear me?"

She nods.

"I'll handle it." I drop a kiss to her lips, wrapping my arms around her waist. "You wanna go home?"

Home. That's what she is.

"Yeah." She smiles, and without another word, holds out a hand to me.

I take it, and then I lead her back to the ranch.

36

Reese

S LEEP. FOOD. SEX. PEACE AND QUIET. RANCH WORK.
Sex. Sex.

Life has been scarily, blissfully perfect.

Ford and I are essentially living together, if living together constitutes me at his place twenty-four seven. Between therapy, Ford, and working with Geneva on our new venture, I feel like I'm blooming in slow motion. Bosko continues to dig into Gavin's finances. He has the password to get my money. All he's waiting for is for me to say go. But not yet. I want to play my cards just right.

Which I hope I am.

That's the inevitable thing about perfection. There's always room to fuck it up.

God, I hope it doesn't all fall apart because…this man…

This summer…

It's been nothing short of magical.

"I come bearing dinner," I say, slipping into the apartment.

"Pizza?" Still in his dusty ranch clothes, Ford's barefoot, standing at the open back door. He shakes a bowl of cat food.

"The answer is always pizza." I shrug off my bag, set the boxes on the counter. I've worked all day in town at Dakota's bakery. "And pastries. Your sister-in-law sees us as nothing more than pawns." I check the clock on the wall and smile, nerves welling up inside me. "But first a surprise."

Silence.

I turn. Ford stares outside, his handsome face creased in worry.

"What's wrong?" I ask.

"Mouse," he says, shifting his gaze to me. "She didn't come back last night."

"Oh no," I say, crossing to him. I look out the door at the wide expanse of ranch. The August sun is setting, getting lower and lower earlier and earlier. "Has she ever done this before?"

"No." Ford clears his throat, clears his withdrawn gaze and looks at me. "Probably out chasing mice. She'll be back." He chuckles, but it's strained. Amber eyes softening, he runs a hand over my shoulder. "Now, what's this about a surprise?"

Heart beating hard, I take his hand and lead him to the table. "Sit."

With his brow arched in amusement, he settles into a chair.

Last week, I hatched a plan and called Bo Bosko. Then, I used my star power to get an easy in. I mean, what's the point of being world famous if I can't cash in now and then?

I have to do this for Ford. Because he's done so much for me.

I wet my lips. "Okay, listen," I say, after I fire up the laptop and open Zoom. "I'm going to do something for you, and you might hate me, but…" I exhale. "Are you ready?"

With an easy nod, he sits back in his chair.

I click the number in the link and the call goes through.

A teenage boy fills the screen—thirteen, with shaggy brown hair peeking out from under a baseball cap. He's wearing a Phoenix Renegades jersey and an ecstatic grin.

Ford sucks in a shocked breath. Every muscle in his body has gone rigid.

He knows who it is.

His eyes flick to me, then back to the screen. He says nothing. I can't tell if he's angry or upset. If he was, I'd understand, But I had to take this chance.

I know what it feels like to not grant yourself forgiveness—to feel like you deserve to be stuck in the sad. He deserves this.

"Holy shit! I don't believe it," the boy says, and when he smiles, every muscle in Ford's body relaxes.

"Hey…uh, kid."

"Mark," I whisper.

"Mark," he says.

"I didn't believe that you wanted to talk to me, but here you are." He looks offscreen. "Mom! It's really him."

"I've thought about you a lot," Ford says. "About what I did." He drags a hand through his floppy gold hair. "I'm sorry for fucking up."

"You don't gotta be sorry," Mark says, genuinely puzzled.

A muscle jerks in Ford's jaw. "But I am, kid. I'm really sorry."

"Man, are you kidding me? I'm going to put that on my college application. *Beaned by Ford Montgomery*. I kept the ball." The camera swivels to show a baseball sitting on a dresser.

Ford laughs, a husky rumble that has my heart beating double time. "Come out to the ranch and I'll sign it."

He scans the kid's face. "So you good? In school and—and everything?"

"Yeah, man. I got straight As last month." His face wrinkles in disgust. "I hate math."

"Same." Interest lights Ford's expression. "You play any sports?"

"Of course." A beam tips Mark's mouth. "Baseball. Oh! And soccer. What about you? You ever going back to playing baseball?"

I tense. Sorrow clogs my throat.

Soon, the summer's over. I should be focused on what happens after. My freedom. The end of my contract with Gavin. But that's not what really matters to me.

Not anymore.

"Not sure yet," Ford drawls. "Got some things happening, but you'll probably know when I know."

A sly smirk crosses Mark's face. "Are you really dating Reese Austin?"

"Nosy as hell, ain't you, kid?" Ford says, but he's grinning.

Mark laughs. "That's what my dad says."

"Yeah," Ford says, reaching out to clasp my hand. "That's my girl."

I flush. *My girl.* Sweetest words I've ever heard in my life.

"Say hi, Reese."

Cheeks heating, I peer into the camera and flutter my fingers. "Hi."

Mark hoots. "I don't listen to country much anymore, but your first album was the best."

I smile. "I like that one, too."

"Holy shit!" Mark drums the desk in front of him. "You

two have the same numbers. Your jersey is ninety-eight, the same title as her first album."

Ford and I stare at each other in stunned silence, jaws slack.

Then he chuckles, rubs a hand over his jaw. "Damn, kid. Just spreadin' all kind of revelations over here, aren't you?"

They talk for a few more minutes, then with promises to keep in touch, end the call.

Grinning, Ford tugs me into his arms so I'm sitting on his lap. He lets out a watery breath. "Thank you."

"You're welcome."

His fingers stroke my cheek, and my heart beats faster. "I was broken, Birdie. Until I met you." His throat works.

I smile up at him. "You're not your past, Ford. And I'm not mine."

For the first time in my life, I believe it.

∽

In the blue moonlight of our bedroom, I stare at the text from Gavin.

> **Say goodbye to summer, Reese. Soon, you'll be home.**

It feels like a threat.

It is.

I screw my eyes shut. The black hole above me pulses as memories surface of Gavin pulling me from the tub. *You'll never leave me, Reese. Never.*

When I open my eyes, I glance at Ford sleeping beside me. His face boyish and sweet. One big arm under the pillow, the other possessively tossed over my waist.

Carefully, I slip from Ford's tight grasp and slip out of

bed. I change, then pad barefoot to the door. Hand on the knob, I look back over my shoulder at Ford.

I made a promise to tell him when I need the water. To trust him. And I do trust this man. I can't remember a time I trusted someone so fully. With my entire soul.

Thanks to him, I'm in therapy. I know how to balance a checkbook. I've reclaimed my life. Acknowledged my past.

He doesn't tell me to be less. He looks at me from across the room and tells me to do more. He accepts me for exactly who I am. He tells me I am enough. And if I can't be enough, he's enough for both of us.

I love him so damn much.

I tiptoe back to bed. "Ford," I whisper, shaking his shoulder. "Ford, wake up."

He blinks, lifts his head. "Birdie, what is it? You okay?"

My heart clenches at the sound of his raspy voice.

"I can't sleep. I need the water."

It's all I need to say.

Rousing, he pushes up on his shoulder. Eyes never shifting from mine, he scrubs a hand down his face, then grabs his jeans. "Let's go."

37

Ford

REESE GLANCES OVER HER SHOULDER AS SHE wades into the water. Her defiant gaze says, *Yes, see me.*

I stand on the sandy bank of the lake with worry churning in my stomach, but I let her go.

Reese held up her end of the deal and trusted me enough to tell me. Trusted me enough to let me see her sadness.

And I do.

Every beautiful part of her.

She melts into the water, her blonde hair spreading out behind her. Christ, she looks like a goddess, ethereal in the moonlight. The curves of her silhouette. Her long golden hair…

My heart clenches.

She swims to the center of the lake. With a laugh, she spins around to face me. Teasing smile on her face, she strips out of her slip. Blood rushes to my cock.

I see what she wants.

To go after her.

Like I always fucking will.

I strip off my jeans and swim toward her, hissing a breath at the icy water. Her green eyes meet mine, light and vibrant and beckoning.

When I reach her, I don't say anything.

I just kiss her.

A whimper tumbles from her mouth as I ease back from her lips. My pulse racing, I drink her in. My beautiful, lovely girl.

There are no words for what she's done for me.

I lift her in my arms, stroking my fingers over the curve of her spine. Her legs wrap around my waist. It's cold in the water, but it feels like she's burning against my body.

"Do you know why I love the water?" she asks.

A ragged breath draws from my lungs. "Reese—"

"Because it feels like starting over. Everything bad gets washed away. But I stay and get to try again. I can always keep trying."

I kiss her again, a greedy need hammering at my control. An ache building in my chest. "Tell me this is real," I rasp against her hair. It's as close as I can get to saying those three little words. "Tell me."

"It's as real as the stars," she whispers. Tentative green eyes flick to mine. "But stars go out."

"Nah, baby. Not us." She laughs as I haul her higher on my body. Her breasts draw my eye. Full and gorgeous and rosy. "We burn." My rough voice is heated and firm.

Her eyes fill with tears. "We do?"

"Fuck yes." A burn lights in my chest. "I care more about you than I do anyone else on this planet, Reese."

"Ford," she whispers.

I trail my nose along her jaw, kiss her cheek, her throat. Tangled blonde strands drip down her shoulders like honey. I try to rein in my hunger.

Our kisses turn frantic, heated. Her moans mingle with mine. I hold her tight, urgent, like I'm physically unable to let her go. Need more Reese. Need her closer.

Pressed to my heart, my bones. That bond I felt from the second we met. Incomparable. Insatiable.

We both laugh as Reese slips into the water. I grab her before she can go under and adjust her in my arms.

"Better hold on to me, County Boy," she teases. "If I die, Gavin gets everything."

I shake my head, half-laughing, half-horrified. "Jesus, Birdie, that's morbid as fuck."

She wiggles her brows. "It's the truth, but not for long. I am going to fly."

Fly away.

Fuck that.

I have to tell her I love her. That I don't remember what my world felt like without her.

I wet my lips. "Reese, I—"

"Ford," she whispers, tensing. She points over my shoulder. "Someone's in the forest."

I whip around, protectively placing myself in front of Reese. *What the fuck?*

That's when I see a shadowy figure moving in the woods, hear the snap of twigs beneath their feet.

"Stay here," I warn.

I snatch up my pants, dressing quickly before I race to the edge of the tree line. With only the moonlight, it's too dark to see properly. I wait a beat or two, scoping out the area, not breathing. Unnerved.

When I return to the lake, Reese is dressed and shivering, arms wrapped around her waist. I slip my dry flannel over her shoulders.

"See anyone?" she asks.

"No. Could be a guest, could be an animal," I tell her, wiping a drop of water from her lip. The thought of someone watching me—watching Reese—fills me with anger.

I pull her close, kiss her brow. "Let's get the hell outta here."

⌒⌒

The next morning, I wake before Reese. She's buried in blankets, one tan leg tossed over the comforter. I sweep a kiss over her bare shoulder before slipping out of bed. I want her to rest. Especially after last night.

I head straight for the lake. There are footprints on the red sand bank, leading to the woods, the chalets. Reese's or mine or someone else's—I can't tell.

An icy feeling settles in my gut.

I think of the black SUV Reese told me about.

The shadow in the woods last night.

Damn if it doesn't feel off. Everything feels off.

I head back to the garage and leave a bowl of kibble for Mouse. I haven't seen her in a week. She's a ranch cat, but hell, I'm worried.

Before I can head back upstairs, my eyes light on a yellow, sticky note on the window of my old Chevy. I must have missed it earlier.

I pick it up and smile.

You're the best serotonin boost I've ever had.

My heart thrums against my chest like a kick drum.

It hits me what I have to do.

I yank my phone out of my pocket, scroll through my contacts, and hit dial.

Jim Donovan picks up on the second ring. "About damn time, son."

"I'm afraid I got bad news for you," I tell him. "I'm not taking the job."

His exhale is long and loud. "That's disappointing. Better opportunities?"

"Something like that."

"Think I could change your mind?"

"You can try. But I'm locked in."

"You know I don't back down from a challenge."

I grin as Reese, sleepy-eyed and messy-haired, appears on the stairwell. She waves, giving me a bright smile.

"Neither do I."

Never backing down. Not from her.

For so long, Runaway Ranch felt like a tentative place to land until I figured it out. Watching out for my brothers, watching out for my heart. But with Reese, it feels like home. The three short months we've been together matter more than the three years I spent with Savannah.

When Charlie gave me the chance to walk away two years ago, I didn't take it, and I still wouldn't.

I love this life, and I don't have to change it to be happy. I have the ranch. I have baseball. All I need to do is add to it. And that's Reese. The biggest, brightest part of my life. A friend, a lover—a soulmate. I'm a goddamn sap for that girl.

She's mine. Now she just needs to know that.

38

Reese

SILVER SPRINGS, A QUAINT MOUNTAIN TOWN TWO hours north of Resurrection, is so adorable it puts every country song I've ever sung to shame. Main Street teems with old brick buildings that house museums, restaurants, boutiques, and western stores. Motorcycles line one side of the street, while a jagged mountain looms over the town square, giving a postcard-perfect backdrop.

I duck out of a boutique, scour the surroundings, then smile when I spot Ford coming down the opposite end of the street.

Ford slips something in his shirt pocket when he reaches me. "Good haul?"

I lift the bags. "You'll never break me of shopping." We've spent most of our Saturday running ranch errands, but I couldn't resist a detour into a cute shop.

"Never dream of it," he says, face solemn. Twisting, he drops the bags of feed into the bed of his truck.

"Should we get back?" I ask after we finish loading up the truck. The late afternoon sun hangs low in the sky.

"Nah, baby. We're not goin' back." His eyes soften as he says, "It's time for that date."

I hold his gaze. "Really?"

"Really." He pulls me close. "Been working you to the bone, Birdie Girl. Time to have some fun."

Over the last week, it's been chaotic bliss. I've spent my

days working in Dakota's bakery. Ringing up customers, taking out the trash, helping her with lines out the door. Evenings, I go back to the ranch and tend to the chickens. Then, it's me and Ford.

On the ranch, life doesn't feel overwhelming like it does on stage. It's easy. Freeing. I can't tell if it's meds or therapy. Either way, they're both working. I haven't worn my bangles in a week. That dark hole glimmers less and less.

After locking his truck, Ford places a protective hand on the small of my back. "Dinner?"

I bat my eyes at him. "All planned out, Country Boy?"

He wraps an arm around my shoulder, steering me in the direction he wants us to go.

No man has ever taken me on an actual date. Ford has been different ever since he told me we weren't friends. More serious, more intense. I like that he told me where we stand, but I still don't know what happens after the summer. Go back or stay? And who's saying Ford even wants me to stay? He has a job offer he's still considering. An actual life. Would I throw a wrench in everything if I said I love him?

First things first. I need to focus on getting my money and getting out of my contract.

Then I'm free.

Then I can do anything.

And if it means telling Ford I love him, well, maybe I'll do that, too.

I've been brave all summer. I can do a little thing like tell this broody mechanic I love him. Even if it feels like the scariest thing I've ever done.

"Here," Ford says, gesturing to a red brick building with a sign above the door that reads Butcher and Baker.

He opens the door for me and we step into a dimly lit, elegant restaurant. Ford checks in with the hostess and then we're led to a small table covered with a crisp white cloth. We're tucked by the window, where the evening glow adds a touch of warmth to the scene.

Ford pulls out my chair, pressing me into it with a hand on my shoulder.

My heart flutters. "You made reservations."

He sits across from me, touching his shirt pocket like he's reminding himself there's something in there. "Yeah, I did." His voice holds an edge I've never heard before.

After we order drinks, I watch as he picks up the large leather-encased menu. His face is boyish and awkward.

My stomach drops into my high heels.

I see what he's trying to do. Show me we can work. That he wants to do this. The glass of red wine by his hand when I know he'd rather have a beer. The stiff starched shirt when he looks so damn good in a baseball cap and torn up t-shirt. He thinks I want a fancy date.

A hard swell of love nearly knocks me over.

He doesn't belong here.

Hell, I don't belong here.

It's like the sun breaking through the clouds. That slow burn of realization. Everything clicks. My new life will cost me my old.

I don't care. Fame, fortune—they can have it.

I'd rather be with Ford than anywhere else.

I lean in. "Psst. Country Boy."

Brow furrowed, he glances up from the menu.

"This doesn't feel right." I reach across the table to take his calloused hand in mine. "Let's go."

"Where?"

I smile. "Somewhere more us."

Ford grins, then he tosses a large tip on the table and we all but run out of the restaurant.

Outside, Ford looks up and down the block. The sun sinks below the horizon. "Lead the way, Birdie."

I take a step toward a neon lit bar when my phone rings.

I groan. Ford stiffens.

Then I blink.

"It's Doctor DiFeo." I answer it. "Hello?"

"Reese?" Doctor DiFeo's voice sounds over the line. "I'm sorry to call after hours, but I had something that couldn't wait."

"Of course."

"Those pills you brought me on your first session, well, I wanted to confirm it before I said anything, but…they're not depression meds. They're sedatives."

It feels like I've been sucker punched. I gasp. "What?"

I'm vaguely aware of Ford. His hand going to my shoulder, his amber eyes worried and searching.

My head spins. "But—But I was taking those for such a long time."

"I suspect you were drugged, Reese. Without your consent." Over the line, the flip of papers. "It's a high dose prescription. I suspect your manager or therapist was slowly upping the dosage when you became resistant to its effects."

Rage heats me up. That's why I was always exhausted and never felt like I was getting better. Why, when I arrived here, I felt more awake than I ever did.

Grief and rage consume me.

All this time I wasn't crazy or broken and it could have been easier? Gavin could have helped me, and he didn't?

The lengths he's gone to control me. My IUD, what I wore, my money, my contracts…

At first, I thought it was business, but now it's terrifying. I ran because I felt that dark hole caving in on me, but what if it was saving me? My doubts and hesitations about Gavin have been right all along.

"I want you to be careful around this man, Reese," DiFeo instructs, pulling me from my thoughts. "You're my patient and your safety comes first."

Oh god. Dizziness swims around me. I brace a hand on the brick building to steady myself.

"I will," I tell her.

After thanking Dr. DiFeo, I hang up the phone and explain everything to Ford. His eyes widen in understanding, and I watch the realization—the rage—hit him.

"Motherfucker," he swears.

"I don't know why I didn't see it. I didn't…"

"Don't do that," he orders in his deep, stern voice. "Don't blame yourself. This isn't your fault."

My cheeks heat with anger. "I hate him. I hate that I have to play this game because it feels like he's still winning."

A muscle jerks in Ford's jaw as he covers his mouth with his large palm and thinks on it. His worried gesture. The intensity of his fury, his protectiveness, crackles in the space between us. "You're not going back, Reese. I won't let you."

He tucks me against him, his piercing amber eyes scouring the street like Gavin's out there, watching us.

What if he is?

"Let's go back to the ranch," Ford says.

"No." I blow out a breath. "This doesn't ruin our night."

I'm not letting Gavin interfere with my life ever again.

Last Chance Honky-Tonk is the diviest dive bar on the windiest back road. Sawdust-coated dance floor, flickering neon on the walls, and guitar picks hot-glued to the ceiling. Ford and I sit at a sticky table, ignoring the suspicious stares from beer-guzzling locals. We order food, shots, and a pitcher of beer.

After the phone call with Dr. DiFeo, Ford's handsome face still hasn't lost those tight lines of tension.

"Relax, Ford." I touch his arm. "You look like you want to commit a murder."

Ford stares at me like he's furious and amused at the same time. "I *do* want to commit a murder."

I laugh, then bite my lip. "He can't get to me, right?"

"No." His words are heated, angry. "He can't."

"So let's forget about it. I'm here and you're here and we're going to have fun." I swirl a finger around our drinks. "C'mon, Country Boy, show me some of that swagger."

Ford studies me, rolls out his shoulders, and takes his shot. I follow suit.

"This is what you had in mind, Birdie Girl? Slummin' it?"

"No," I tell him. "It's never slumming with you."

He scrapes a hand along his jaw, holds it in contemplation. "I've been thinking…"

"Dangerous business."

He gives me a grin and says, "I put an offer in on Old Mill's Farm." At the arch of my eyebrow, he goes on. "Hell, Birdie, you gave me the idea. I want to start a baseball camp for kids. Put a big fucking baseball diamond smack dab in the center of that field."

"And your Georgia mansion."

"Yeah," he husks. "My Georgia mansion." He refills my beer from the pitcher. "What do you think?" His voice holds a nervous edge.

The idea is so perfectly Ford. Outdoorsy and free and easygoing. It's what he wants. It makes him smile. I love it for him.

"I think it's fucking amazing." I tilt my head. Hope and worry duel inside me. "But what about the job offer in New York?"

"Yeah. About that," he says, his eyes never leaving my face. He wraps his broad hand around my wrist, holding it tenderly, like my scars are his as well. "Listen, baby, I—"

"Hey, man, you're Ford Montgomery." A guy, barely older than twenty-one, comes close to us with a Sharpie in his hand. "Can I get an autograph?"

"On a date," Ford grunts.

"Coward," I tease. Smothering a smile, I glance over at the fan. "He really loves autographs. Make sure he signs everything you own."

Ford laughs and snatches the Sharpie from the guy's hands. With a flourish, he signs the back of the guy's T-shirt. His sneakers. Ball cap. Even his beer glass. "Go to school, use protection, don't fear tomorrow," he drawls, before sending him on his way.

I can't help but laugh. "Wise words."

The strum of a guitar has me looking over at the stage.

Ford studies me curiously. "You miss singing?"

"I do. I really do. But not the crowds or the money. I miss…that." I nod at the person on stage. "Intimate audience. Small stage. Doing it for me."

"You should go play."

"What?" My eyes widen when he stands. "No. Ford—"

I try to grab the hem of his shirt, but he's too quick. I watch in horror as he strides over to the singer on stage. They duck their heads and confer, then Ford slaps a wad of cash into his hand. He heads back to me.

"You're up."

I blink at the people craning on their high tops. "I don't believe you."

His grin gets wider. "You scared, Birdie?"

"No, I'm—"

"If anyone recognizes you, they'll think you're staying here. Not in Resurrection."

I arch a brow. "Very sly of you."

He just grins. "My plan all along."

I roll my eyes.

Ford follows me and helps me onto the stage, which is a small platform covered in peanuts. As I settle on a rickety bar stool, Ford places the borrowed guitar in my hands.

He gives me a charming smile. "You got this. You do *you*."

I swallow and lean into the mic. "I'm just a simple Georgia girl telling a simple story," I say to the crowd. "But I hope you like it."

My heart pounds. Ford's right. It's me and the music. I can be myself now.

I think of those yellow sticky notes.

I think of this summer.

I think of Ford.

I close my eyes and sing the song I've been writing ever since I arrived in Resurrection. It's messy, but it has good bones.

Goose bumps skate across my arms. My voice lifts, and

I open my eyes, focusing on the twangy hum of the six-string. Ford leans in to watch me, his amber eyes bright and intense.

Gavin would call this burning my life down, but it's the opposite. It's clawing my way out of the darkness to find the light. To find a place—or a person—who is mine. Who makes me happy.

Ford is a gift. He's healed my damaged soul, my broken and wild heart. In three months, he gave me the life I've always dreamed up.

And I want to keep it.

I'm ready to choose him.

When I finish singing, the applause is loud and sharp. Whoops and surprised cheers come from the audience. I laugh, wave off the claps, and cover "Delta Dawn." I've been dying to perform it my entire life, and tonight, I sing better than I ever have. By the time the chorus rolls around, people are clapping and dancing on the sawdust-covered floor.

When I finish, the bar erupts.

My heart beats in a rapturous rhythm. I slip off the bar stool and hand the guitar back to its owner. Ford, now beside me, holds out his hands, gesturing for more applause. And it comes. So loud, so thunderous, it's the best standing ovation I've ever had.

"Baby, you were amazing," a woman says as Ford helps me off the stage. "You should be famous."

I smile. "Maybe one day."

Ford pulls me into a corner. "You're shaking," he murmurs against my hair.

Exhilarated, I tug on his shirt. "I'm just happy."

"You blew the doors off the place, Bluebird," he husks. "You were perfect." Pride shines in his eyes. My entire body heats. The way this man makes me feel special is incomparable.

"You're a star, baby."

"Yeah," I admit breathlessly. "But I don't want to be."

"What do you want to be, then?"

"With you."

A muscle works in his jaw. His eyes grow soft. "I want that, too."

"You do?"

"I do."

Our gazes lock, heat.

More. So much more to say.

It feels bigger than this bar. Bigger than tonight.

Like Ford agrees with me, he touches my cheek. "Let's get a motel. I need to talk to you. We aren't finished."

"Okay. One dance before we go?" This cloud-nine high is too good to get off. I want to stay on it as long as I can. With Ford.

He grins. "Can't say no to my girl."

My girl.

With a wild hoot, Ford swings me into a frisky two-step. Forget one dance. We dance until midnight. Eventually, the bar clears out in a horde of stomping boots and raucous conversation. As we head to the truck, people mill in the dusky parking lot. I feel eyes on us.

Beside me, Ford tenses. I don't miss the way his hand palms the small of my back.

"What's wrong?"

"Not sure yet. Stay close to me."

My heartbeat kicks up when I see it. I gasp and tug on Ford's arm. "That black SUV—it's here."

His eyes narrow. Before he can say anything, a man

from the bar ambles over to us. "Hey, you're that missing singer."

"Wrong girl, buddy," Ford grunts. He tries to grab my hand, but the cowboy steps between us.

Another voice. "Holy shit, it's Reese Austin."

An unfamiliar hand touches my arm. "Can I have an autograph?"

"Oh, uh…" My eyes flick to Ford. His jaw is tense as he scans the crowd.

I take the pen I'm offered. Quickly, I sign a cocktail napkin, then another.

A small circle has formed. Suddenly, I'm desperate to be away from here. To be alone with Ford. Adding to the madness, car doors slam. From out of the SUV, come paparazzi.

They've found me. They've been following me all this time.

"Reese, is this where you've been hiding?"

"You look beautiful, Reese. Give us a smile."

"Ford," I say, looking toward him like he's my home base. There's fear in my voice.

Someone flashes a camera. "Aren't you supposed to be in rehab?"

"Get the fuck away from her," Ford snarls.

Before I know what's happening, I'm mobbed. People and cameras head toward me like a stampede of cattle.

Fear races through my chest. The crowd's drunk. Who knows what they'll do?

"Ford!" I stand on tiptoes, trying to find him in the crowd.

"Move, fucking move," he roars.

My knees go weak at Ford's voice, and I move fast,

skimming under an arm, searching for a way out. Someone grabs the back of my shirt. I twist around, angry now. "Get off me, asshole!"

A strong hand comes out, catching my wrist.

Ford.

I catch a glimpse of his furious face before I'm yanked into his arms.

I cling to him, burying my face against his chest. Trusting him to get me out of here. This *man*. Fierce. Protective. *This* is why I've stayed—why he's the one. Because his arms are the safest place I've ever been.

When someone steps in front of him, blocking our escape to the truck, he doesn't even hesitate. He just swings with his right while holding onto me with his left.

Somehow, he gets us to the truck and throws open the door, depositing me safely inside.

And as he speeds out of the parking lot, white knuckling the wheel, I sit back against the seat and stare out into the dark. Maybe this won't work after all. Maybe Ford is just another dream I can't have.

39

Ford

I T'S ONE IN THE MORNING WHEN WE FINALLY DRAG our exhausted asses into the motel room. I toss the keys on the dresser with a clatter and stare at Reese. Fuck if I'm not rattled after the events of tonight. She's lucky she wasn't hurt.

Those fucking paparazzi. Vultures. Who knows how long they've been following her?

"Are you okay? Are you hurt?" I try to turn her toward me, so I can look her over, but she shakes me off.

"No. I'm not hurt." She perches on the edge of the mattress, staring at her scarred wrists. "I'm mad."

I sit beside her. I've been waiting for her to talk to me since the scene in the bar, but she's been silent. Every ounce of happiness sucked right out of her. "Talk to me, baby."

"The paparazzi. Gavin." She huffs out a breath, tears in her eyes. "They won't leave me alone." The pain and fear in her voice cuts me. "They won't let me have the life I want."

My stupid heart's about to explode, but I force the question out. "And what life is that?"

"A life with you," she admits. Every inch of my skin heats at her words. Then just as quickly, she shakes her head. "And that's silly and stupid of me, isn't it? I've known you for a summer. We've only been on one date. Nothing turned out the way I thought it would. And maybe that's perfect. But maybe I was wrong."

I swallow the lump in my throat. "About what?"

"Us." She stands and paces. "Me. I thought I could do this. What if I can't?"

My heart pounds like it will break free from my chest. *Fuck. I can't be too late.*

I shove up from the bed. I have to tell her before I lose my chance.

She thinks she's temporary when she's my forever.

Around her, I don't own any part of my heart anymore. I don't even own myself. She does.

"What if there's no point in staying?" Her voice is pitchy, breathless. "What if there's no point in *us*? My past will never let me be. I can't change it. It doesn't matter—"

"It matters." I cross the room, boots storming. "*We* matter. How can you say that?" I turn her toward me. "After this summer? After what we have?"

"We had a summer. That's it." She looks me in the face, defiance lacing her husky voice. "Don't worry, you'll have another one next year with someone else."

Her words tear a hole through me.

"Don't you fucking dare." If she wants to play this game, run that stubborn bratty mouth of hers hoping to push me away, she can. But I plan to win.

When it comes to my girl, I don't lose.

Because it takes a strong man to love Reese. Not because she's hard to love, or she's difficult, but because she's the most amazing woman that I've ever known. She forces me to be better.

And me—I'm her cowboy. I'm the man who loves her. And I will always do my damnedest to deserve her.

Starting now.

I hold her gaze, capturing her wrist. "If you're tryin' to start a fight right now, end it, it ain't gonna work."

"Let me go."

I don't. I keep hold, my touch steady.

"And go where, Reese?" I ask, testing her resolve. "Go back to Gavin?"

Nostrils flaring, she stomps her high heel. "No. I'll never go back to that man. Fuck him. And fuck you for suggesting it."

The fire in her eyes rages like a wildfire.

"That's right, baby, let that fire burn." I spear her with a cocky grin. "And get it through that pretty little head of yours. You ain't goin' back."

"And why's that, Ford?"

I swear violently, and then drag her against me. "Because I love you, Reese. Can't fucking live without you."

She freezes, going slack in my hold. Tears slip down her cheeks. "What?"

"I love you, Birdie." I give her a squeeze, needing that gorgeous body against mine. "The day you stomped your way onto the ranch and sassed me with that smart tongue of yours, I considered you mine. There hasn't been a day where I haven't thought of you."

"What if I'm not good enough for you?" she whispers.

I chuckle. Here I've been thinking I'm not good enough for her when she's been thinking the same damn thing.

One thing is for sure, we're both fucking idiots.

"You're perfect for me."

"I'm crazy."

"You're not, but I'm sane, so we'll be okay."

That haughty chin lifts. "I cost too much money."

"Good thing I have it."

"We fight too much."

"And it makes me hard as hell," I growl, causing her stunning green eyes to widen.

"Ford—"

I wrap my arms around her, lock my gaze with hers. "Run your mouth, woman, because it doesn't matter. I love you. Nothing you do or say will change my mind. You're it for me, Birdie. No more running. No more searching. It's you."

Reese stares.

I feel like I'm bleeding out, waiting for her response.

A shudder of a breath blasts out of me. "Christ, baby, would you say something?"

A stunning smile fills her face. "I love you, too."

My breath hitches. "You do?"

"Yes. I do. I love you, Ford."

Those three little words heal something deep inside me. Having someone to love like this only existed in my dreams. But not anymore. It's Reese. Etched into my heart, my fucking soul.

"Reese." My voice breaks. Hot tears cloud my vision.

She palms my face with warm hands. "You've been my angel, Ford Montgomery."

I clear my throat from emotion. "You've been mine, Birdie Girl."

I kiss her. Deep, heated. Our tongues wage a battle before we break away, breathless.

"I love you," I tell her again. "I'm so fucking in love with you, Reese. And I won't lose you now."

"What does this mean?" she half-laughs, half-sobs.

"It means…" I grasp her neck, pulling her forward until our brows touch. "If you leave, I'll never recover. Say the word and I go with you. If you want to sing, I'll be in the front row every goddamn night."

"You'd do that for me?"

"I would."

She bats those big, beautiful eyes. "Sorry to say it, Country Boy, but I kinda like the ranch."

Christ.

"Stay then. Stay with me."

"Yes, yes," she gasps. Cups my face and searches my eyes. "But what about your job?"

"I turned it down."

"What?" Her pretty face screws up. "Why would you—"

"There are other things in life. Things that are more important than baseball."

"Like what?"

"You."

Tears glisten in her eyes. "Ford."

Remembering what's been on my mind all damn day, I reach into my shirt pocket and pull out a small velvet pouch. "I got you this."

I slip the necklace out and lift it high. A special order I planned last month—my name in delicate gold script.

Her fingers come up to cover her mouth, eyes wide and shimmering. Then she reaches out to touch it, almost reverently. "Ford, it's beautiful."

I fasten it around her neck and say, "You wear this necklace on your throat, baby. Show the world you're mine."

With heavy-lidded eyes, she stares back at me. "I'm yours."

Her words crack like a whip.

"Do you see what you do to me?" I press her hand to

my cock. She whimpers, small gasps filling the air between us. I move her hand to my heart. "Do you see how much I love you? You brought me back to life, Bluebird."

A sob escapes her. "You are my joy, Ford Montgomery."

My breath hitches.

I interlace our fingers and lift her arms, backing her up to the wall, kissing my way up her scars. "My favorite part of you," I murmur. Tears stream down her face. "They remind me you exist. You're alive." Leaning close, I brush my lips over her mouth. "And you're not hard to love. You are mine to love. Never forget that."

Her eyes shutter. "I won't," she promises.

And then we're on each other. Ruthless and raging. I kiss her pouty lips, desperate to consume her. To reassure myself that what's just happened is real. She's here, she's mine, and nothing can change that.

Fucking nothing.

40

Reese

BAR M ON A FRIDAY AFTERNOON IS EXACTLY where I want to be. The lodge buzzes with life as guests order drinks and take them into the cantina or to their cabins. I sit at the back of the large living space, strumming my guitar.

This summer feels like I've been testing all the ways I can exist. Playing in the lodge, working in a bakery. Exploring every part of the future I want to build—my own label, my music. All of it feels possible. That night in Silver Springs unleashed something in me. I've been given the freedom to move, to choose, and it feels so easy.

I know in my bones that I will somehow make a beautiful life for myself, no matter what the world throws at me.

Especially with Ford. I showed him my truth, my scars, and in return, he loved me more.

I'm all in—heart first, fearless.

For the next thirty minutes, I play covers of familiar country songs. People stand around and listen before tossing dollar bills in my guitar case. They clap or sing along, their smiles showing they enjoy the music. But there's no mob. I'm just a nobody girl playing her guitar. And I love it.

The set ends and I pack up before heading toward

the bar. Fallon is perched on a stool while Ruby wipes down the bar.

"Thanks," I say when Ruby slides me a glass of ice water.

"The guests love the live music." Blue eyes bright, she looks at me hopefully. "Is it here to stay?"

I flush.

It's been a week since Ford's *I love you*, and we've been caught in a perpetual state of bliss. We've spent most of our time making plans or having sex or planning to have sex.

I feel delirious. Like I've won the lottery. Like nothing is real.

But it is real.

We're real.

I trust Ford with my life. My heart. But more importantly, my future.

Our future.

Before I can answer, Fallon swivels to face me. "It has to be. Did you see the paper?" She nudges a copy of the *Billings Gazette* my way.

> Country Music Star Reese Austin Spotted with Baseball Legend Ford Montgomery

I smile. The best headline I've ever seen.

"I don't know about the music," I say. "But I'm here to stay."

Ruby squeals.

Fallon's hazel eyes scan the photo of me and Ford, fingers laced, leaving the bar. He has a protective arm out, blocking me from the crowd, and I'm gazing up at him like he's every star in the sky.

"Fuck, they're too cute." Fallon slams back her beer. "I'm lighting my house on fire."

"You hear from the boys?" I ask, glancing out casting my eye to the window. Big, black clouds hover ominously. Storm of the Century, the papers are calling it. Ford and his brothers took a trip to Elk River to lay sandbags before the incoming storm.

Ruby shakes her strawberry blonde head and starts cleaning empty glasses, her pretty face tight with worry. "Charlie said we might have to close early for the season."

Fallon hops off her barstool. "Beer for the road?"

Ruby hesitates. "Don't you have practice?"

"Maybe you shouldn't drink and operate heavy machinery," I suggest gently.

Fallon's eyes get a sad, faraway look to them.

"Are you okay?" I ask.

"Fine." She jerks her chin toward the door. "Anyone want to tell me who the creeper is?"

I follow her shrewd gaze.

Then I see him.

Gavin.

My stomach plummets as he stalks toward me, an expression of fury on his face.

"Oh shit, oh shit, oh shit," I whisper, suddenly wishing Ford were here.

Ruby tosses a panicky glance at me. Her phone is in her hands. "Should we get help?"

"No." I swallow, taking a step toward Gavin. "I'll handle it."

I think about picking up my guitar and taking a swing at him, but I remember Bosko's words of warning. Play it cool. Lead him on. Lie.

Gavin meets me in the center of the lodge. For one long second, I don't know what to say. To think. Then I start with the obvious.

"What're you doing here?"

Gavin runs his eyes over me. "I'm here because you're avoiding my calls. Avoiding business that needs to be done."

I sigh. "I wasn't avoiding you, Gavin, I was…" I shake my head, too exhausted to get into it. "It's my break. I'm taking a break."

"Enough with the fucking act, Reese." He's so close I can feel his breath. "You're lying to me. You're not planning to come back."

I nearly take a step back. There's something different about him. The look on Gavin's face is cold, bordering on desperate. His dark gray suit is rumpled and red sand clings to the sides of his loafers. None of the polish I've come to expect from Gavin Cross.

Panic spirals in me, but I choke it down. Force a bright smile. "Of course, I am. What are you talking about?"

"You're not that good of an actress, Reese." He catches me by the arm, digging his fingertips into my biceps. "You think I'm going to let you go when I worked so hard to get you?"

I shake my head. "Get me? What do you mean?" He's not making sense.

"It's my job to watch you, Reese. To take care of you."

"No. All you want to do is control me."

"I control you because it's *my* job. I protect you."

"Bullshit," I hiss. Fuck this man's attempts to make

me feel guilty. "You've never protected me in your life. You need to leave, Gavin. Now."

He tightens his grip. "This is what you choose to do with your free time? Singing shit songs and dressing like a fucking whore?" His gaze darkens as it lands on Ford's necklace around my throat. He reaches for it, but a spray of water arcs across the room. Gavin swears and drops my arm as it drenches his face.

"Get your fucking hands off her," Fallon shouts, leaning over the bar, soda nozzle in her hand like a pistol. Ruby talks fast on her phone as Fallon turns the water on the guests who have filed out of the cantina, cell phones recording everything. "You too, assholes. Mind your fucking business."

Not wanting to cause more of a scene in front of the guests, I weave through the couches and push through the front door. The sight of the ranch calms me.

For a brief second.

And then Gavin's stepping into my space and boxing me against the wall of the lodge. Nausea swims in my belly as he gets close.

"You little bitch," he snarls, his voice hot with anger. "You think you can walk away from me?"

"Go home, Gavin," I say calmly. "Go back to LA, and if you're lucky, I'll come back. Maybe I'll make you some money."

I can't resist the dig. The gaslighting. Like he's done to me all these years.

"Fuck you, Reese." I gasp when he grabs both my wrists. Sweat beads his hairline. "Now stop talking. You're coming with me."

I shake my head. "I'm not going anywhere with you."

He squeezes my wrists, and it's like I can feel that blade all over again.

Images flash in my mind. Gavin shouting at me before a show. Forcing me to go on stage two weeks after my suicide attempt. Never letting me have my own life. Telling me I wasn't pretty or skinny enough. Using me for my money, my body, my voice.

"Why? Because you're in love?" His growl jerks me back to the present. "Because you sang 'Delta Dawn' once in a bar and now you don't need me?"

My mind spins. He saw me. He was here.

He releases my wrists, and his hands land on my throat, squeezing.

I twist away, trying to break his hold on me. "Gavin. You're hurting me—" The air around me becomes foggy. My breaths come faster and faster.

"Hurting you? What about *me*? Now it's the principle. The fucking gall. You leave me? When I made you?"

"Stop," I beg, gulping air. "Stop."

He moves closer. The grip on his control thinning. His eyes raging and wild. "You're not free until I say you're free, Reese."

"Take your fucking hands off her. Now."

I go weak at the sight of Ford.

He's here. Of course he's here.

Ford and his brothers are climbing out of their trucks. Fists clenched. Mutinous fury on their rugged faces.

Gavin's hands fall away from my neck, but he doesn't step away from me, still boxes me in against the side of the lodge. "This is a conversation between me and my client."

I almost laugh. Gavin has no idea what's coming.

Ruby and Fallon burst out of the lodge. There's a knife in Fallon's hand, and a wine bottle held like a base-ball bat in Ruby's.

Ford stalks our way, like a Gavin-destroying missile destined for destruction. "Doesn't look like a conversation," he snarls. "Not when you have hands on my girl."

Anger flashes in Gavin's eyes. "She's not yours. She's mine."

An icy shiver goes down my spine.

That muscle in Ford's jaw is working overtime. "Back the fuck up. Now."

Gavin's face turns bright red. "You don't know anything about this. Stay out of it."

Ford sneers. "I know you're a piece of shit who's taken advantage of her. I know you've made her feel like she doesn't deserve to be here. I know you've hurt her." His amber eyes flick to me, silently telling me it'll all be okay. "Last chance," he warns, striding forward. "Get away from her."

"Fuck you."

"Wrong answer," Ford drawls.

Charlie lets out a sharp whistle and tosses a set of keys to Fallon. She promptly locks the lodge's door, keeping the guests inside.

A big sigh from Davis. "Keep it quick." His voice is ominous, resigned.

Then, without warning, Ford hits Gavin in the face. I scream as his head snaps back.

Wyatt grabs my arm, pulling me away from the scene.

"You stupid fuck," Ford hisses. Grabbing Gavin by

the neck, he bounces his face into the side of the lodge. There's the sound of bone on bone as Ford hits him again. Blood spurts from Gavin's mouth. Lost in a haze of raw, animalistic rage, Ford hits him again, and again.

I should be horrified, but I'm not. No one has ever fought for me in my life. It only has me falling even deeper in love with him.

"Ford." Davis clasps his shoulder. Worry swims in his dark eyes. "You gotta stop, brother. Now."

One last punch, then Ford straightens up, wiping the blood from his knuckles on his jeans.

Gavin crumples to the ground and crawls away from Ford like the coward he is.

Thunder rumbles in the sky, but it's dwarfed by Ford, saying, "You come near her again, I'll kill you."

The next thing I know, Ford wraps me in his arms, pulling me to him. "He hurt you?"

I shake my head, clutching at his warm, steady presence. "No."

Gavin stumbles to his feet. Blood trickles down his chin. "You're crazy, Reese. You'll always be crazy."

"I'm not crazy," I seethe. Hard as I try, I can't keep it in anymore. Anger swirls inside me, the black hole suddenly a living, breathing thing. "I know what you did, Gavin. I know everything. All these years, you were drugging me. Taking my money."

Ford curls me closer in his arms, but his dark gaze stays glued to Gavin. A shudder rolls through my body. "I have the original contract." Gavin pales. "It expires on my birthday." I laugh dryly. "I am not going back with you. We're done."

The truth freezes him for only a moment. His face changes. So cold, so still, I shiver.

"I have leverage Reese, remember that." Teeth bared, he says, "Muirwood. Your suicide attempt."

Someone sucks in a breath. Who, I can't tell.

I blink back tears, embarrassed. But I shouldn't be. A hand lands on my shoulder. Ruby. Another one. Fallon. My eyes sting at the kindness, the understanding. It means so much. It means everything.

"You can't make me go back." My voice wobbles.

"I could put that tidbit about you in the papers. It would make a pretty story." He smiles, thinking he has me.

But he doesn't.

Be brave, Reese. Be brave. Only it's not my mother's voice anymore.

It's mine.

"So tell it then," I say, calling his bluff. "Tell my story, Gavin. And I'll tell yours." I stand tall. "You don't get a goddamn thing anymore. Not one more piece of me. Or my money. You won't see a single dime."

Gavin takes a step toward me.

Instantly, the brothers stand shoulder-to-shoulder, blocking me and Ford. Tears sting my eyes. These big angry cowboys willing to go to battle for me.

"You're going to regret this, Reese. I told you once, you don't leave me."

At his words, fear lodges itself in my throat. I turn my face into Ford's chest.

His voice is a powerful rumble as he says, "Breathe in her direction again, and I end you, you hear me?"

Gavin laughs, a manic sound that sends a chill up my spine. "Be careful, Reese. I will finish what you started."

"Stay off my ranch," Charlie orders, stepping forward. "You come back, we ain't talking."

After a last glance at me, Gavin turns on his heel and heads toward the road.

"You okay?" Ford asks, framing my face in his hands. "Birdie?"

"No," I say, trembling. "I'm not."

The gravity of what I've just done hits quick.

I told Gavin everything.

My hands fist in Ford's shirt. "We have to call Bosko and get my money," I growl. "Now."

41

Ford

I SLAM INTO THE BULLSHIT BOX TO FIND DAVIS combing through security footage from three days ago. The storm outside is nothing compared to the one in my head.

Davis arches a brow, his expression amused. "Hello to you, too."

"Fuck you." Beside me, Keena lifts her head and whines.

Charlie leans back in his chair and sighs. "I think I liked you better when you hated love."

"Fuck you, too." I flex my fist. My heart hammers a crazy, feral beat in my chest. Punching Gavin wasn't enough. I need him to be hit by a fucking bus.

Davis shakes his head, then asks, "Reese all set?"

I blow out a breath and drop into a chair. "Got her money yesterday."

Charlie grins. "Rich woman."

"Yeah." Despite everything, I can't help but grin. "She is."

Bosko worked quickly. True to his word, after Reese called and pulled the trigger, he had her money transferred over to the Montana State Bank in less than twenty-four hours. She's got it all.

It's hers.

And soon, she'll be away from her prick of a manager.

Easy. Too easy.

I don't trust it.

Everything feels too goddamn precious. Tentative.

I have a family I care for. A woman I need to keep safe. A ranch that in a few days' time could be ten feet underwater.

"She hear from Gavin yet?" Davis asks.

"Only every other goddamn day," I growl. "You should see the texts he's sending her."

The asshole's still harassing her via text. Vulgar and degrading threats that make me see red. The minute she took that money out, he snapped. It takes all my self-control not to smash her phone to pieces.

She's taking it better than I am. I'm furious he won't let her go. The last few days, she's been fielding calls and emails from reporters, battling the story Gavin leaked about her suicide attempt and time at Muirwood.

I'm so goddamn proud of her. I was worried the stress would break her, but not my bluebird. She's strong as hell.

Me, I'm the weak one when it comes to her. Reese has unlocked that protective primal side of me and good luck getting it back in the bottle.

"Got something else to show you that's gonna piss you off." The keyboard clicks as Davis pulls up the security footage. "Take a look at this."

Charlie and I slide our chairs his way and stare at the screen. The footage is of the day Gavin ambushed Reese. He walks into the frame of the main camera and into the lodge.

I exhale and flex my fist, wanting to hit him all over again. "He got on the ranch that easy?" Not even the paparazzi camped out have made it past our gates.

Davis clicks through the different cameras showing different angles of the ranch. "He's here." A new angle. "And here. But there's no car. Like he never arrived that day."

The fuck? It makes no sense.

Outside, thunder rumbles. The monitors go fuzzy. Scowling, Davis slams his fist against the side of the display.

Charlie roughs a hand down his dark beard. "All the guests get in and out with a key card through the access gate, or with our employees. We don't look too hard at them, only unannounced arrivals who don't use the com system."

"So, what? He was announced?" I run a hand along my jaw. I'm worried. Really fucking worried. The cameras don't catch everything. We have no clue what's behind the scenes.

As the video plays, my eyes are drawn to Gavin pinning Reese up against the wall of the lodge.

Red rises in my vision, and I breathe through the rage that holds me hostage. Crazy shit has happened on the ranch, and I've stayed composed. But touch one hair on my girl, and best believe I lose my shit.

That fucker putting his hands on Reese came within a heartbeat to hell.

Davis nods at the video. "That's cold-blooded rage. Personal." Shooting me an apologetic look, he exits the footage.

I arch a brow. "You know what we should have done…"

"Don't," Davis says, leveling a stern finger. "I know what you're thinking."

"Twin sense?" Charlie asks.

"Murderous sense," Davis says.

As twisted up as I am, I grin. "What's one more body on the ranch, man?"

Davis and Charlie exchange a quick glance. My eyes narrow.

For the last two years, there's been some kind of secret conspiratorial bullshit between them.

I pin them both with a glare. "All right, you fuckers, y'all keep doing this. Who else is buried on this ranch?"

Davis glances at our younger brother. Charlie's jaw is set.

A long silence. Outside, the wind rattles the tin roof of the Bullshit Box.

Then Davis sighs and clips, "Declan Valiante."

I gape at him. "That was you?"

"Afraid so, brother." Davis's mouth thins. "Not a word to Wyatt. This stays between us."

I drag a hand down my face. "Jesus Christ."

Charlie studies me for a moment. "You think he'll leave her alone when her contract ends?"

Reese gave me permission to share her story with my brothers. When they heard what Gavin had done to Reese, it took everything in them not to follow the bastard and beat the living shit out of him.

I look to the window, worry in my gut. "Not sure."

"Listen. You don't want to hear this, but I'm going to say it, anyway." Leaning forward, Davis hesitates, then says, "I wouldn't put it past him to come after her, Ford." My twin's eyes are pained, faraway, and I know he's thinking of Dakota.

He's right.

It's human nature to crave power.

And Gavin craves Reese.

The possibility that it's more dangerous than either of us considered hangs over me. The way he was talking to her, looking at her...it bordered on obsession.

I squeeze my eyes shut and grip the desk. If anything happens to her, I wouldn't survive it.

"Keep her close," Davis warns, pulling me away from my grim thoughts. "We'll be on the lookout, too."

Charlie dips his bearded chin. "We got your back. And hers."

I give them a nod of thanks, emotion clogging my throat. I love my brothers for sticking up for my girl. We fight, we bicker, but family having your back is everything. And Reese saw it. Saw they're her family. That she's meant to be here.

At this point, I'm not taking any chances that Gavin won't show his face again.

Reese is under lock and key until that contract expires.

Luckily, Runaway Ranch—and my bed—is the best place for her to be.

"Thinkin' we turn the guests loose tomorrow," Charlie says, shuffling papers on his desk.

"That necessary?" It's a week early.

"Hate to do it, but I don't want any guests on the ranch when shit hits the fan."

I follow his gaze to the dark clouds brewing on the horizon.

Hell. It's gonna be bad.

A tinny knock on the door has our heads snapping up.

"What?" Davis barks. His face softens when Dakota opens the door.

"Ford." Dakota's voice is hard. "You have a visitor."

⟶⟵

I follow Dakota down the walk to the garage. Parked in front of one of the doors is a red BMW. Standing beside it, Savannah. The wind whips her short shaggy platinum hair, and I really wish it would just blow her off the edge of the earth.

I have no idea what the fuck Savannah's doing on

Runaway Ranch. After all the shit she did, said, she's got some nerve.

Savannah uncrosses her arms. Her defiant gaze clashes with mine. "You don't look happy to see me, Ford."

I shrug. "It's been a long time."

"Not long enough," Dakota mutters, low enough for only me to hear.

Savannah looks at Dakota. "Do you mind? I'm here to discuss business."

Dakota snaps open her mouth, and I chuckle, laying a hand on her bristling shoulder. Pissing off the women on the ranch won't do her any favors.

Fire in her eyes, Dakota looks up at me. "Let me know if you need anything. Beer. Pastry." Her hard gaze lands on Savannah. "Arsenic."

"Easy, tiger." I give her an amused look. "Go take that aggression out on a pie."

She strides away, leaving me and Savannah alone.

"So…" Savannah's blue eyes scan the ranch, disdain all over her face. "This is what you turned down my daddy for?"

"I wasn't aware I didn't have a choice."

Before she can say another word, I enter my garage. She follows, each click-clack of her heels like needles in my brain. There's only one woman I want wearing heels in my garage, and it's not Savannah.

I watch as she inspects the space, silently, curiously.

Emotions roll through me, but not the ones I'd expect. There's no regret, no bitterness—just annoyance. Annoyance that she's here, that she thinks my life needs her, when it's the opposite. I already have everything I want.

Turning toward me, she runs a finger along the smooth lines of my Chevy. "I remember this."

"Don't do that," I warn. "Act like you still know me."

The fire dims in her eyes.

Crossing my arms, I lean back against the shop table. "Why are you here, Savannah?"

Her red lips turn up. "Right to the point. I like that." She nods like it's obvious. "I'm here for you, Ford."

I rub my jaw and glance around the shop. A pang goes through me when I see Mouse's empty cat bed. "What are you talkin' about?"

"When my father told me he was considering you for a job, I thought it was meant to be." She lifts a shoulder. "I thought if you took the job, maybe we could…reconnect. Have a second chance."

I laugh out loud. She legitimately believes she could get me back. Savannah and I are in the past. It's all just another life that doesn't matter because Reese wasn't in it.

Second chances are for Dakota and Davis. Not me and Sav.

Chuckling, I shake my head. "Honey, we're dead and buried."

She bites her lip. "I messed up, Ford." A long, heavy pause. "I shouldn't have said no."

I shrug. "Best thing that ever happened to me."

For a long second, she's speechless, then she scoffs. "You should take my daddy's job. Help you with your career." Her lip curls. "Or lack of one."

There it is—the same spoiled Savannah, lashing out when she doesn't get what she wants.

I shift, shaking my head. "Don't need your help."

"It's a good offer."

"I got good things here."

"Like?"

As if on cue, the apartment door opens. My gaze travels up the steps. To Reese.

I grin, my eyes eating up her beauty. She makes every other woman irrelevant. Forgettable and that includes Savannah.

Long wavy hair, cowboy boots, and those short shorts that drive me wild. A tiny tank top clings to her, and my name gleams in gold around her neck. She looks like a dream. My dream girl.

"Sorry." Reese's steps are hesitant as she makes her way down the stairs, holding a bowl of kibble in her hand. She sends me a curious look. "I didn't know anyone was here."

Shoulders rigid, Savannah's burning gaze travels from me to Reese.

Before Reese can head for Mouse's bowl, I pull her into my side. "Savannah and I are just talking business," I tell her, not wanting her to get the wrong impression. "She's going now."

Reese tenses. "You're Savannah?"

Savannah's jaw tightens, her teeth grinding together. "I am. And you?"

"Reese Austin. I'm sure you've heard of me." The haughty brow, the ice-cold chill in her voice have me smothering a smile. My girl is ruthless.

Fuck, but I love it.

Savannah's eyes go wide when she sees the necklace with my name.

"Whatever you're offering, it won't be enough." I tuck Reese closer, making sure I'm crystal clear. No confusion.

Not about what Reese means to me. "I've got everything I need right here."

"I see." Adjusting her purse on her shoulder, Savannah gives a quick nod. "I'll be on my way then."

At the garage door, Savannah turns back toward me. "Ford—"

But she doesn't get to voice whatever she planned to say.

"He's mine now," Reese says, laying a protective hand on my chest. My mouth goes dry at the simple action. The love this girl's shown me eclipses Savannah, any woman, by a country mile. "You had your chance."

No malice or bitterness in her voice. Just plain fact.

Goddamn truth.

With that, Savannah disappears out the door and into the whipping wind. I dip my head, drawing Reese closer.

Like I said, dream girl.

42

Reese

"**D**on't look," Ford orders.

I giggle as he guides me, eyes closed, up a step and through a door. All I hear is country music and familiar whispers.

"Wyatt, you drop that cake, and I will murder you."

A grumble. "Didn't realize I was here with the party police."

"Everyone shut up." Davis's voice rings with authority.

A giggle from Ruby.

"Okay," Ford says, stopping. "Open your eyes."

"Oh my God," I breathe. A smile stretches across my face.

It's Nowhere, but Nowhere transformed into something special. Streamers hang from the ceiling, and a high-top table in the corner has a reserved sign. Bags of Combos and gummy bears sit next to a beautiful cake on top of the bar. Behind it, Beef raises a pitcher of beer. Locals lift their glasses, then turn back to their own business.

Ruby squeaks and grips the table as a rowdy bunch of rednecks slam into it. "I'm not sure this is the best place for a party."

Ford scrubs the back of his head. "We couldn't rent it out, but—"

"No. It's the perfect place." Full circle.

I blink back the tears that threaten to fall. I've never

had an actual birthday party. But it's more than a birthday party. It's a Reese-is-almost-free party.

In two days, I'll be twenty-seven. Two days until I'm free of Gavin.

Not even his texts, his threats, can chase away this bright ray of hope. Of happy.

I grip Ford's shirt and kiss him hard. "Thank you. I love it."

"Happy birthday, baby." The apple of this throat works. "You deserve it."

I wrap my arms around his neck. "You ready to chase me around the bar again, Country Boy?"

His eyes darken. "I ain't gonna tell you what to do, Birdie. Just know that if you dance on a bar top, I'll get into a fight tonight."

I flush as his heated gaze drinks me up. I have my best dress on. Slinky and golden.

"He's kidding," Davis tells the group.

Ford gives his twin a look. "I'm not kidding."

"Fuck yeah, here we go," Wyatt drawls, rubbing his hands together in glee.

Davis rolls his eyes. "No fights."

Fallon scoffs and slinks around their massive frames. "These Neanderthals don't have a chance." She glances at Dakota. "Let's light this fucker."

Wyatt whips out a lighter.

I can't take my eyes off the glittering candles of the birthday cake.

"Make a wish, Reese," Ruby says, sitting on Charlie's lap.

I lean in but pause. If you would've told me last year

that this would be my life now, surrounded by friends and family, I would have laughed. Dreams do come true.

"No wishes," I tell the table. Slowly, I puff out each candle. "We should play a game."

Davis looks uneasy. "We don't do so well with games."

"It's your typical bloodshed sport," Charlie offers.

"A game?" I wonder.

Ford says, "Stick with us, you'll see it all."

"Here we go," Fallon mutters, then glares at Wyatt.

"Shut up and eat your cake," Dakota instructs. She hands out plates with fat slabs of red velvet. Then passes more around the bar for everyone to have.

I laugh. "Everyone tell me something happy and good. Something real." At that, Fallon gives me a proud nod. "That's what tonight is for."

Ford gives me a wink. "Good things, huh?"

I kiss the tip of his nose. "Good things."

"Let's start with that drink," Fallon says, smugly gazing at her sister. Dakota instantly avoids eye contact. Davis too. "You don't expect me to believe that's vodka soda."

"Fallon!" Koty squeals, but the pink tinge on her cheeks says everything.

Wyatt grins. "Holy shit."

Ford nods at his twin. "Congrats."

Davis grins and scruffs a hand over his dark hair. "We weren't really trying, but..."

A chuckle from Ford. "Next thing you knew..."

"Yeah." Grin fading, Davis scans the table. His and Dakota's eyes move apologetically to Ruby and Charlie. "We wanted to wait to say something..."

Charlie holds up a hand. "We're happy for you."

"We are. So happy." Ruby inhales a deep breath. For

a second, I think she's going to burst into tears, but then she smiles and her hands go to her heart. "We're going to have a baby, too."

Beside me, Ford hitches a breath.

Charlie laughs and strokes his wife's shoulder. "We're going to use a surrogate." A mischievous expression crosses his face. "That's why we've been going to Bozeman every weekend. We've been doin' all the tests and everything to get us there."

"It might be a while," Ruby says resolutely. Bravely. "But it'll happen." She's not crying, but there are tears in her voice. In Charlie's eyes.

"Damn right it will," Ford murmurs, his voice cracking.

Wyatt and Davis lift their beers. "Congrats," they say in louder than normal voices, as if to mask any emotion chipping away at their tough cowboy facades.

Dakota wipes her eyes while Fallon stares out the window with that stubborn strength of hers.

"And you? What about you?" I ask Ford.

He fights a smile. "What about me?"

"Don't you want to tell your brothers something?"

Davis eyes his twin with suspicion. "Tell me you didn't elope."

Ford barks a laugh. "Not yet."

His words go straight to my core. My heart hammers.

His face turns serious as he takes a fortifying breath and says, "That land at Old Mill's Farm...I bought it."

The table falls into stunned silence.

"I turned down the offer from Donovan. I'm going to put a baseball diamond on the land and start a camp for kids. A baseball youth training center." He grins at his

408   AVA HUNTER

brothers. "And if you assholes are lucky, maybe I'll let you use some of the land, too."

A laugh goes up around the table.

"Bastard. Stole it right out from under me," Charlie grumbles, but he's grinning. They're all grinning. They're happy Ford is staying, their rugged faces relieved and full of joy.

Ford reaches for my hand and settles it in his lap. "Maybe have a couple of babies—do that picket fence shit y'all seem to enjoy." Ford's gaze flickers to me and locks. My heart pounds. In a room of so many, it feels like there's only me and Ford. I stare at him, knowing he's everything I ever wanted. A protector, a hero, my backup. But most importantly, my freedom.

Anything I ask for, he'll give it.

But all I want is him.

"Grow old and happy?" Dakota says.

"Something like that."

"Aw, Ford," Ruby croons. "I always knew you were a romantic."

Ford grins. "You know, Fairy Tale, I think you might be right."

⌒

With the cake finished and the happy thoughts proclaimed, it's time to hit the dance floor. Davis and Dakota are the first ones on it, while Charlie heads to the bar for another pitcher of beer. I sign two autographs before slipping back to rejoin Ford and Ruby at our high-top.

"Having fun?" Ford murmurs.

"So much fun." I kiss him, then pull back. "I'm not sure about those two."

He follows my line of sight and sighs.

Across the room, in a darkened corner, Fallon and Wyatt are deep in conversation—or maybe it's an argument. Either way, it's like love, hate, and everything in between is exchanged during their heated looks.

Fallon storms for the exit, but Wyatt follows, catching her wrist. She whirls around and hits him with a look that would scare a fully grown man. But Wyatt doesn't back down. They stand inches apart, eyes blazing.

Ford leans in, flipping his baseball cap backward. "Fallon chooses violence, and Wyatt says, *Please, may I have another?*"

"Everyone, hush, my show is on," Ruby says, waving a hand, her eyes glued to Fallon and Wyatt.

Charlie settles beside us. "Ah, Christ, not this again."

"You're all very invested in this," I say, slurping a bright pink concoction Ruby recommended. The furnace in my stomach tells me it's working.

"We have to be," Ruby says solemnly. "They want to kiss each other."

"Or knuckle box," Charlie says wryly. Then he growls, running a hand down Ruby's ass. She squeaks and practically dives into his broad chest. "C'mon, Sunflower. Let's dance."

Ford holds out a hand to me. "Want to show 'em how it's done, Birdie Girl?"

"I do." I bite my lip, watching as Fallon slams out the front door. "One second, though."

"Don't go far," he says, always worried.

"I won't." I give him a smile. "Pick us a song."

His face softens. "I can do that."

Outside, I find Fallon kicking gravel in the parking lot.

A cigarette dangles from her lips. Wind tears at us, and a rumble comes from the sky.

"You know," she says as I approach, "I'd like to lightly pummel someone or destroy something or gnash my teeth until I feel like someone real and deserving again."

"Are you okay?"

She takes a drag on her cigarette. Looks toward the window where our group dances inside. "Everyone's too goddamn cute. Too goddamn happy."

"And what are you?"

"Me?" She considers the question. "I feel like I'm a constant, screaming panic attack."

"You don't care if you live or die, do you?" I ask, thinking of her on that bull and wondering if anyone else has put it together.

Fallon goes still. So still, I'm uncertain if she heard me. Then, in a low voice, she rasps, "No. I don't."

"Fallon—"

"I fucked my sister's abusive ex-boyfriend." Her face twists in disgust. "Who does that?" She spits the words. "That asshole took everything from me. My head hurts all the time. I lost a year riding bulls. I lost—" Her gaze flicks to the window where Wyatt scowls in a corner.

"It isn't your fault," I say quietly.

"I can't get him out of my head. It's like…like a spot." Fallon points at a place beneath her chest. "Right here. Sharp and painful and it doesn't go away. Even when I sleep. Riding reckless is the only way to get it out."

"Mine was there." I point above my head. "Like a hole."

Fallon inclines her head. "Is it still there?"

"Yes," I say softly. "But it's smaller now."

There's no cure for that black hole—not love, not the

ranch. Maybe my depression will be less here, or maybe it won't. But Ford will be there with me every step of the way, reminding me I can save myself, like I've done this entire summer.

"Have you talked to anyone?" I nod at the window where Dakota dances with Davis. "Your sister?"

Fallon shakes her head, her eyes glazed. "No. I don't want to bring her down with my bullshit."

"It's not bullshit. They're your family. They love you."

A hesitant smile curves her lips, as if believing it hurts too much.

She turns to look at me. In the inky darkness, her face is a shadow. "Did leaving your life behind work out for you?"

I recall her question from our first meeting. Now, I finally have an answer.

"Best thing I ever did."

She bites the inside of her cheek, considering me. "Leaving, huh?"

I inhale. Exhale. "It's okay to go. To move when you need to run." I smile. "It's okay to stay, too. Maybe talk to the people who love you a lot."

She lets out a small laugh, a little shakier than usual.

We both jump when there's a bang on the window.

Ford.

He gestures for me to come inside, a goofy smile on his face. Then he breathes on the window and draws a heart in the fog.

Fallon chuckles softly. "Another Montgomery man pathetically in love." She sounds both amused and disgusted. "Nice going, Reese."

We laugh.

Thunder rumbles overhead.

Fallon ashes her smoke and stamps it out beneath her boot. A wicked smile tilts her lips. "So do we get drunk and commit even more feral acts tonight?"

A sunrise lifting in my heart, I link my arm through hers. "Most definitely, yes."

43

Ford

"**N**EVER THOUGHT YOU HAD IT IN YOU," DAVIS says from his barstool.

"What? Party planning?"

He arches a brow. "Love."

I laugh, glance down at my boots where Reese's name is written in Sharpie on the outsole. "Man, you ain't seen the half of it."

Me and my brothers hover at the bar with cold beers in our hands. A few Resurrection locals stand over our table, eating the remains of the cake. Koty and Ruby dance in the center of the room. Beef returns with another round of drinks.

I lift my beer, tipping it to Reese, who walks inside with Fallon. "I look at that girl right there and you know what I see?"

"The love of your fucking life," Charlie says, his eyes on Ruby.

"Yeah," I husk. "The love of my fucking life."

I smile, watching the way all heads turn as she crosses the floor. Damn if she doesn't shine like gold in that dress.

Too goddamn beautiful.

Mine.

The stool rattles beside me as Wyatt plops down, signaling for a drink. He looks like he needs to blow off some steam.

"You okay?" Davis asks, clocking Wyatt.

"Fine," he says, his voice tight.

"By the way…" I shoot back my shot. "I need the name of the jeweler you used for Koty."

Wyatt groans, covering his face with his hands. "Y'all gotta stop makin' plans without me."

I slip off the stool. "C'mon. We ain't gonna get the girl sitting at the bar."

"Hey there, Country Boy," Reese says, meeting me in the middle of the bar. "Save me a dance?"

There's so much love in her eyes, it nearly knocks me over.

"Every dance tonight and every dance after." I pull her into my arms and onto the dance floor.

She shakes her head, smiling. "Smooth talker."

I spin her and return her to my arms. The jukebox plays George Strait's "I Cross My Heart."

She lays her head on my chest. "Think this just might be our song."

"It is," I husk.

The dance floor is crowded and hot, but we dance the night away.

"You could say excuse me!" The husky female voice floats over the bar, louder than the music. Angry.

Reese and I come to a halt on the dance floor.

Beside me, Davis and Koty freeze. "Where's Fallon?" Davis asks, craning his head.

"Oh no," Reese breathes, fingertips going to her mouth.

We all look over to see Fallon punching a finger in a cowboy's chest. A burly, sweaty, tobacco-chewing musta-chioed man with American Flag tattoos on his biceps. "You must be the cunt of the litter."

"Fuck," Charlie groans.

"We leave her alone for twenty minutes and she's already shit-talking," I mutter.

"What do we do?" Ruby whispers.

Dakota shakes her head. "We stay out of the way."

I tense as the guy grabs Fallon's arm. She flinches like she's been slapped. "You're dead," she growls, before wrenching her arm from his grip and balling her fist.

Before she can take a swing, Davis grabs Fallon around the waist and hefts her into the air. "Fuck's sake, Fallon, you can't go around punching anyone you want to."

She wiggles in his tight grip. "Who wants to live forever, anyway?"

Davis swings her to the side, and instantly, Wyatt's storming the floorboards. The immediate beeline, the manic look—he's all in for Fallon.

But, from my vantage point, he's in the wrong position. Before Wyatt can square up, the guy's fist catches Wyatt in the jaw. My brother staggers back, slamming into the wall. Charlie hisses a breath.

Davis and I exchange a look. That's civil fucking war right there. If someone touches our little brother, they die by our hand.

"Stay here," I tell Reese.

Together, we step forward.

"Hey, man," the guy bleats, lifting tobacco-stained hands. "That little bitch started it—"

Davis hauls back and hits the guy in the face. He wobbles once and lands on his ass in a puddle of beer.

I clap my twin on the back. "Still got it, brother."

The fight's over. The man's down.

But Nowhere isn't ready to quit.

The dance floor goes wild. Stomping boots. Flailing fists. Beer bottles break. Across the room, cake splatters the wall.

A hand grabs the front of my shirt. I just grin and deliver a one-two punch that has the guy sailing across the room.

Wyatt and Fallon are having some kind of stare down, and I make a note to tell them later to shit or get off the pot.

Davis ducks under someone's arm, Dakota's hand in his. "Outside. Now."

My attention's stolen by Ruby. She stands on a chair, dumping beer on the wild crowd. "Go get your woman," I tell Charlie. He appears beside me, easily landing a knockout punch to Lionel Wolfington.

He arches a brow and grins. "Get mine? What about yours?"

That's when I see her a bright flash of gold as Reese jumps on some guy's back. Her tiny fists pummel his shoulders and it'd be fucking hilarious if I wasn't worried about her getting seriously hurt.

"Shit." I fly across the goddamn bar and hook my hands under her arms, grabbing her off the guy's back. "Let's go."

"Where?" Reese's voice is an exhilarated scream.

Charlie passes beside us, Ruby slung over his shoulder. "Don't just grunt at me instead of using words, Cowboy," Ruby tells her husband, but she's laughing as he carries her out the front door.

I grab Reese's hand and weave our way through the crowd. We slam out the back door. "Up here," I say, grabbing the fire escape ladder that leads to the roof.

We climb and then we're three stories above Main

Street. Glittering lights. Jagged mountains. Lightning sparks in the sky.

I glance down, checking her for injuries. "You okay?"

"That was wild," she says. Her hair is disheveled and her eye makeup smeared, but she's never looked more beautiful. More free.

Exhaling, she looks out over Main Street. "I want this, Ford," she breathes, pressing herself against me. "I want all of this with you."

My fist throbs, my heart hammers, but I've never been so goddamn happy.

I take her in my arms. "You've got it, baby." I lean down and kiss her like the world's on fire. Then I pull back from the kiss. "Marry me."

Those stunning green eyes widen. "Getting kinda sentimental, aren't we?"

"I'll do it proper; I'll do it right." I cup her cheek. "Build you a Georgia mansion."

"I don't need a Georgia mansion."

"You're not living in a garage, Reese."

A stubborn tilt of her chin. "Maybe I want to live in a garage with all its wonderful smells."

I growl at her. "You gonna argue with me or tell me yes?"

She dances her fingers up my chest. "Maybe I like making you sweat."

"Now ain't the time for that," I tell her sternly. "It's time to let me love you. For the rest of your life." I slip my fingers into her hair, cupping the nape of her neck. "When I count my top five home runs, I count you, Reese. I thank fuck every day that I found you."

Her eyes soften, fill with tears. "Yes. I'll marry you."

She touches my cheek, smiling. "You're the greatest love song I've ever sung, Country Boy."

I pull her into me, crushing our mouths together.

A clap of thunder rumbles through the air, and Reese squeals.

And then the gray, growling sky opens up and unleashes.

44

Reese

DAVIS WINCES, BIG FINGERS ON HIS BROW AS HE leans back against the counter. "I'm dying."

"You're hungover," Dakota admonishes. Dark head dipping, she sticks a pie in the oven.

Outside, the storm roars. Fortunately, it's chased off any remaining paparazzi. Inside, we're toasty warm and crammed inside Dakota's kitchen for an all-day brunch. As if good food and more drink will take everyone's minds off the shadows settling over the ranch.

"Face it, brother," Ford says. "After we hit forty, it's all downhill from there." He holds me in his arms, stroking a hand over my own.

I laugh. "Speak for yourself, Country Boy."

Both Ford and Davis bark a laugh.

Keena stretches out on her dog bed. Wyatt, Fallon, Ruby, and Charlie are playing trucks with Duke on the living room rug.

I've never felt so content. So happy. Everyone has good things coming their way, me included. Ford and I—we're getting married. We have a future. This is the last day I'll ever be beholden to Gavin.

With a growl, Charlie drops into a chair. "Next year, we ain't drinkin.'"

Ruby laughs and kisses his temple. "Next year, we don't drink *so much.*"

"Or start fistfights," Davis adds.

Ford snorts.

"Food," Dakota announces, slamming a platter of cinnamon rolls down.

Everyone lunges like we've been starving for days. We eat standing around the breakfast bar like hungover heathens. Wind rattles the windows. It's chaos. Duke's crying, Keena is barking, and Wyatt and Fallon are arguing, but all I can do is smile.

"Oh my gosh," I breathe. "It's a madhouse." I look up at Ford. "I want one just like it."

He meets my gaze. "Way it's gonna be, Birdie." His voice is husky. "Can't fucking wait."

The crackle of the two-way radio cuts through the chatter.

"*Anyone alive up there?*"

"You got all of us, Tina," Davis says as he moves away from the breakfast bar to speak to the ranch's Guest Services manager. "What's goin' on?"

"*Did everyone check out of the chalets?*"

From his spot in the hallway, Davis looks at me. "Reese is in one of the West Chalets."

I laugh as I grab a muffin. "Time to kick me out."

Ford chuckles, gives my hand a squeeze. "You're not goin' far."

"*We had another guest in there this summer,*" Tina says. "*Before you started the reno. I show they're still active in the East Chalets.*"

Charlie groans.

The radio crackles. "*And not to add more bad news, but two horses got out of the barn.*"

Another groan. This time from Wyatt.

"Thanks, Tina," Davis says. "We'll handle it."

"Should you be out in the storm?" Dakota asks, worried.

"No," Davis says, holstering his radio. "But we can't leave the horses or a guest unprotected." He glances at Ford. "You and Wy take the chalets? Make sure they're clear."

Ford nods, and Wyatt takes a huge bite of a cinnamon roll in answer.

The brothers move away from the table, grabbing jackets, securing two-way radios, and everyone follows.

"I can help," Fallon says, reaching for her rain jacket.

"No, you can't," Wyatt grunts, and Dakota puts a hand on her sister's shoulder.

Davis roves his intense gaze around the group. "I want y'all staying indoors. That means you too, Fallon."

She rolls her eyes.

Charlie tugs the two-way radio off his hip and hands it to his wife. "Phones are down, Sunflower. Use this if you need anything."

Gripping Ford's arm, I pull him toward me. "Be careful."

"I will." He cups my cheek in his hand, his amber eyes burning. "Stay here."

"Don't be a hero," I tease. "I love you."

Eyes darkening, Ford lowers his mouth to mine for one hard kiss. "Love you, baby."

Hushed whispers float through the air as everyone says goodbye, then the floorboards rattle as the men storm for the front door. My heart thumps as they melt into the storm outside.

⌒

"Men are the worst," Fallon grumps. She sits cross-legged

on Dakota's rug with Duke in her arms. She kisses the top of Duke's dark head. "Except you."

"They want us safe, Fallon," Dakota says. She sets a tray of hot tea and coffee on the coffee table. Despite the storm, the large sliding glass doors are open to the deck. Rain comes down in a drizzle. Though it's only noon, it's nearly pitch-black outside. A heavy, eerie feeling lingers in the air.

The men have been away for only thirty minutes, but the storm outside is unnerving. Biblical. I hope Ford makes it back quickly.

"No. They want to corral us like cattle because we're the weaker sex."

Ruby, curled up in a blanket on the couch, chirps, "I guarantee none of them can ride a bull like you."

Fallon smiles, but it doesn't reach her eyes.

A rush of wind whips through the open doors, scattering napkins, and I jump off the couch, hurrying to close them. Before I do, something catches my attention and I gasp. "Oh my God."

"What?" Dakota asks.

"Do you hear that?" I listen closely. There, coming from outside, the faintest of meows. "It's Mouse." I look over my shoulder at the women. "I'm going to get her."

"Reese," Dakota says, lifting Duke in her arms. "I don't think—"

"I'll be fast. Promise." I grab a flashlight from a side table and slip out the door. I take the steps two at a time down to the grass, calling for Mouse.

I have to find her for Ford. Ever since she went missing, he's been a mess.

"Mouse? Here, kitty, kitty." Rain mists over my body,

soaking my sweatshirt, and I shiver. Thunder rumbles across the sky. Another lonesome mewl.

"Here, kitty, kitty. Please come here."

I keep close to the house, then move beneath the deck. Even with the bright beam of the flashlight, I have to squint to see.

That's when I feel it. Eyes on me. I straighten up, turning to face the darkness. It's the strange prickling sensation I've had all summer. Like I'm being watched.

Another meow.

I wave the flashlight over the grass.

Relief floods through me when I see Mouse and her little pink collar. She stands in the flashlight's glow blinking those big green eyes.

"Oh, thank God, you little—"

"Reese." Barely a hiss of a whisper, but I hear it.

Close. Too close.

Before I can run, I'm grabbed roughly from behind. I fall backward against a body. A hand clamps over my mouth, and a sharp stinging sensation pricks my elbow.

Looking around in confusion, I struggle, reaching behind me to claw at my attacker. But the surrounding air is heavy, darker than it was minutes ago.

My arms fall limply to my sides. I let out a desperate, muffled cry. "No, no, please…"

A whisper in my ear, "Just go to sleep. Go to sleep, my shiny little shooting star."

I can't even scream.

I'm just falling.

Into blackness.

45

Ford

WYATT AND I TREK THROUGH THE WIND AND
the howling rain. Trudging through the thick,
high grass is like wading in water. Flashlights
bob in our hands. The two-way radio hooked to the side
of my hip crackles.

"What are we gonna do if someone's there?" he asks.

"Kick their ass," I say. "Then move them closer to the
house. It's a liability for the ranch if they're out here alone."
Once a year, we always have a guest who gets ballsy and
tries to overstay their welcome on the property.

The search of the first three chalets turned up empty. If
this last one is clear, then it's just bad bookkeeping, which
is fine by me. Makes my life easier. All I want to do is get
back to Reese. Christ, the ache I have when I'm not near
that girl is almost embarrassing. But I'll take it. Every damn
day for the rest of my life.

Boots settling on the front porch, I pick through the
ring of keys and give a brief rap on the wooden door.
"Hello?" After a beat of silence, I say, "I'm coming in."

I unlock the door. It heaves open with a creak.

"Fuck," Wyatt swears as we enter the cabin.

And I know why. The unmistakable scent of dust, sour
alcohol, rotting food, and sex hits us. My eyes water at the
harsh odor.

In the dark, I feel around for a light switch. Chuckle. "Kid, I think you're too young to see this."

I flip the light on.

I blink, uncomprehending.

It's not what I expected. A trashed chalet. Bottles of alcohol, drugs.

It's worse.

Horrifying.

"Holy shit," Wyatt breathes.

Everything in me tenses. My ears ring as I step deeper into the chalet. What I see makes me retch.

It's Reese. She's everywhere.

Old and new photographs of her pinned to the wall. Sexy photos from her tour. Photos of her on the ranch. Newspaper articles. Clothing. Lipstick. A pair of her high heels sit in the sink. Condoms full of dried cum lay on the countertop. Maggots swarm over a bowl of cereal. On the floor, an axe and a hammer. Scrawled on the fridge in pink lipstick is the word *GOODBYE*.

It's a shrine. An actual fucking shrine.

Obsessed. It's the only way to describe it.

"What the fuck, Ford?" Wyatt whispers in his deep drawl. He moves beside me, his expression full of concern. "What the fuck is this?"

His voice has me jerking out of my daze, and then I'm moving around the chalet. I search the bathroom, the back porch, the upstairs loft. Empty. It's all fucking empty.

My gaze catches on the ranch's guest registration paperwork on the table. I grab it up, my eyes scouring it frantically.

Ingalls, Charles.

Fuck.

That name. Picture-perfect TV families. One of the aliases Gavin used for him and Reese. She mentioned it during her talks about her non-existent birthdays.

I clench my fist, bowing my head. "I'm going to fucking kill him."

That's when my gaze locks on the check-in date. Dread blooms in my stomach like a thundercloud.

Wyatt takes hold of my arm. "What is it?"

"He's here."

"Who's here?"

"Reese's manager. Gavin. He's been here since June." I rip a hand through my hair. "Fuck. *Fuck.*"

This was planned. Gavin biding his time, waiting to see what hand Reese would play. If she would come back willingly...

And if she wasn't going to...

That means...

The air around me seems to roar. Mind spinning out, I rasp, "The girls. We left them alone at the house."

Wyatt pales.

As I bolt for the door, the two-way radio on my hip crackles.

"*Ford.*" Dakota's teary voice sounds on the line. "*We can't find her. We can't find Reese.*"

46

Reese

A LOUD, HIGH-PITCHED LAUGH WAKES ME.
My eyelids flutter. A powerful wave of nausea sweeps over me, making my body tremble. Everything feels heavy, like a blanket covering my vision.

Finally, I manage to blink my eyes open. Images blur, then come together.

I'm in my chalet, on the bed, propped up by pillows. My wrists are tied in front of me, my feet bound with rope. There's a glass of whiskey on the table. One of my stage outfits, a short dress with fringe, hangs on the wall. At the foot of the bed, my contract.

Bile, panic surge in my stomach.

"No," I gasp when Gavin steps out of the bathroom with a knife in his hand.

"It's your selfishness that brought us to this moment, Reese," he says in a voice of disapproval. "Remember that. Your selfishness. Not mine."

"Why are you doing this?"

A sneer spreads across his lips. "You are *mine*, Reese. My money. My star. And you want to leave me?"

I strain against my binds. "I'm not yours, Gavin. And I never will be."

"Do you know the things I've done for you? I've turned down the bad roles. I made you a star. I've protected you from people who want to hurt you."

"*You* hurt me," I shoot back. "You drugged me. You controlled me."

He stops at the side of the bed. His eyes look like black rocks in a pale piggish face. "I had to. You were crazy. Uncontrollable."

"*No*," I scream in rage. "*You* made me think I was crazy. I'm not crazy. You're the fucking crazy one."

In a fury, his hand lashes out. I cry out as he grabs my hair, yanking my face to his. Violent pain shoots through my head. The world blurs.

Outside, the storm rages. The air in the chalet is humid and electric.

"You stupid bitch. Time's up."

"What do you mean?" I croak. I have to do something, say something, to keep him talking. To buy me time.

He releases me with a snap. "The world knows about Muirwood. They'll think the stress got to you. You ran. You couldn't handle it. You ended it all." A gesture toward the mirror. There, in red lipstick, the word *GOODBYE*.

My breath catches at his plan. Oh God. He's going to kill me and make it look like I did it. Terror overtakes my body, making me tremble.

"Which makes me your sole beneficiary. I get your money. Your inheritance." Gavin checks the clock on the nightstand. "Twelve hours until midnight."

"Please, Gavin. I want to go back to my family."

"You don't have a family. I'm your family. I took you from your parents." He giggles. "They wanted you back, Reese. Did you know that? They came begging for their little girl back. But you were mine."

"What?" I tug on my restraints, my thoughts spiraling. "What are you talking about?"

"It was supposed to be a favor. Take care of you while they were down and out. But I kept you. I kept you for myself."

My stomach roils. My parents wanted me back?

"They didn't fight because they couldn't. So poor, so stupid." He closes his eyes and slowly smiles. "I told them if they came after you, I'd kill them. And then you."

"You're a monster," I hiss.

"I am, Reese. I'm your monster. You made me love you, and then you took it all away." I flinch as he sits beside me. His eyes are manic in a way I've never seen them before. A way that makes me terrified.

That makes me want Ford.

Ford.

At the thought of him, I close my eyes. His handsome face. That lazy grin. How safe he makes me feel whenever I'm with him.

We made promises just the other night—our future, our hope. Only to be snuffed out by Gavin. He's ruined so much for me, and he won't ruin this.

Mustering all my strength, I look Gavin in the eyes. "Ford will come for me."

"He doesn't love you," he taunts.

Never. I'm never going back to that place where Gavin breaks my will. Takes my freedom. My hope. My joy.

My voice tremors. "He does. He loves me."

At my words, Gavin explodes off the bed, the knife raised in his hand. I flinch, waiting for it to rip through me. Instead, he stabs the papers at the end of the bed in a froth of anger, desperation. Over and over, he shreds my contract. "I love you, I love you, *I love you*, you little bitch!"

I stare at him in horror as he screams. He's going crazy now.

Gavin's head jerks up. "He doesn't deserve you. So that means I take you away from him."

Breathing heavily, he drops the knife and crosses to the kitchenette. He mutters as he unzips a duffel bag, his back to me.

Nausea swirls as my eyes race around the cabin. My heart jumps when I spy the two-way radio on the nightstand. Ford's words float through my memory.

Glitchy wiring.

Sweat drips down my spine. Keeping one eye on Gavin, I wiggle the best I can toward the edge of the bed. To the two-way radio.

If I can just knock it over...somehow turn it on...

I wiggle my toes. No longer numb. Whatever drug Gavin's injected me with, it's wearing off.

Hope flickers.

With all my remaining strength, I lift my arms to the edge of the nightstand and knock the corner. The radio wobbles once. Steadies.

I choke on a sob.

Fuck. Please work. Please glitch.

"One last song, Reese." Gavin's voice jerks me from my task.

He stalks toward me, a syringe in one hand.

I recoil and scream for Ford, for someone, but he's too fast. The needle slips into the crook of my elbow, and I yelp in pain. Sudden dizziness surrounds me. My fluttering eyes look up at him in horror as I slump back against the pillows.

"No," I slur. "N'more. Please...please..."

"That's right, Reese. No more. After this, no more."

My head swims. Darkness drifts over me like a wave.

"But first, before you go, you have to look the part, Reese," Gavin's voice croons. Sitting beside me, he smooths my hair back. His hot, putrid breath washes over my face. "My star. My shiny little shooting star."

He unties my hands, my feet. I try to move, but my entire body feels like it's made from cement. A hollow ringing fills my ears.

My stomach roils as he slips my cut-offs down my legs. My damp sweatshirt and boots follow. Tears stream down my face. I'm powerless in my own skin. Just what he wants.

As I lie in my underwear, waiting for the worst, Gavin lifts me in his arms.

My body, my mind lose all sense of where I am as he caresses and brushes my hair. "You have to be pretty, don't you? My pretty, pretty girl." He dabs perfume on my neck and kisses my cheek.

I whimper. The world fades out. I'm floating.

Through a haze of pain, I realize he's tugging the fringed stage dress down over my head. Slipping tights on my legs. Black high heels on my feet.

I'm laid back down.

My head lolls across the pillow. The world spins, warps.

Hope slips away as Gavin looms over me at a strange angle and says, "You made a mistake, Reese. The last one you'll ever make."

Something cold presses against my wrist. For one long second, it's numb, but then I feel a sharp, searing pain spread through my skin.

Warm, slick heat courses down my arm. Blood.

He's stabbing me, slicing my arms over and over again with the knife. Lines of fire roll across my skin.

I scream until I pass out.

Minutes, seconds, God knows how long.

When I blink my eyes open next, everything's still.

My arms are stiff and sticky. The sheets, the comforter are soaked with blood.

My blood.

I feel so weak. So exhausted.

In my periphery, I can see Gavin pacing in the kitchen. Muttering to himself. Over and over again in a frantic murmur. "Do it. Just do it. But I love her. I can help her."

In his hand, the knife jerks wildly, the tip of it cutting into his pants, his leg. Blood spreads.

He's furious. Insane.

Be brave, Reese.

His shoes stomp across the tile. Fear spikes. He's coming back for me.

I reach deep inside myself. One last chance.

When Gavin is close, I kick with all my remaining strength. I miss connecting with solid bone, but something else happens. I knock him off balance. He mutters and falls back, rocking the nightstand.

The two-way radio topples to its side. I hear the crackle as it glitches on.

I lick my dry lips, turn my face toward the mouthpiece. "Ford, please. Please, I need you."

Gavin cackles and leans in close. His fingers wrap around my wrist possessively. "You think he can help you? You're mine, and it's over now. It's time to take a swim."

The last thing I hear before I fade out is the crackle of the two-way radio.

47

Ford

Davis, Charlie, and the girls meet us on the porch.

I stalk toward them. "Where is Reese?"

The look of fear on Dakota's face stops me in my tracks. "She went out."

"Alone?"

Ruby looks near tears.

Fallon swears violently. "We should have gone with her."

Charlie squeezes my arm. "Easy, brother."

"How long has it been?" Davis asks.

"At least thirty minutes. She thought she heard Mouse," Dakota says. "She went down the deck to the—"

I shake off Charlie and rush around to the side of the house. The rain whips my face, the sky still dim but casting enough light that I can see. I yell her name. Nothing.

Pure panic swarms me. I'm on the brink of a fucking heart attack. My girl snatched out of thin air. Gone. She's just fucking gone.

That coward took her.

My brothers are right behind me, fanning out across the lawn. I duck beneath the deck. Rainwater has soaked everything. My gaze catches on something gold glinting in the shadows.

I kneel and nudge away the long grass with my fingers.

I nearly stop breathing.

Reese's necklace. It lies on the ground, torn from her throat.

"No," I choke out, curling my fingers around the thin gold chain.

I squeeze my eyes shut. *Be wrong*, I beg the universe. *Please be wrong.*

Davis is by my side in a flash. He crouches down, evaluating the scene. "Brother, I need you to stay calm."

Calm. Calm is a word for a sane man. Because that's sure as fuck what I'm not right now.

Davis hauls me to my feet, jerking me out of my daze, and then my boots hit the ground. I'm running across the ranch, splashing through mud and rain.

"Reese!"

Hard boot stomps behind me. The quick breaths of my brothers.

"Ford. Ford."

But I don't stop. I don't listen. I'm off the deep end and nothing or no one can call me back until I find her.

All I see is Reese. Her beautiful face pulses in my mind like a heartbeat.

Those big emerald eyes. That fierce mouth. Her loyal heart. Her telling me I mattered, that she loved me.

I didn't promise I would keep her safe only to fail her now.

I haul open the door to the chicken coop. She's not in there. She's not in my apartment or the garage either.

I race to the Bullshit Box, nearly ripping the door off its hinges. My brothers file in behind me, their faces hard and alert. They snap into action. Davis is on the HAM radio to Chief Richter, while Charlie pulls up the security cameras. Wyatt slams the two-way radios onto the charger.

"Cameras are down," Charlie announces, hitting the screen over and over.

Face grim, Davis hangs up the phone. "Richter can't get anyone out here until morning. The road going in and out of town is flooded."

A tortured roar erupts from deep within my chest. "*Fuck.*"

My brothers eye me like I'm one second away from going on a murder spree and that's what I feel like. Fucking insane.

Crossing the room, Davis grips my arm. "We'll look, Ford. We'll cover the ranch, no matter how long it takes."

"It's Gavin," I grit out. "He's here. He's been checked in as a guest for two goddamn months."

Charlie and Davis gape at me. Wyatt and I tell them about the scene at the chalet.

Davis swears.

"How did he get past us?" Charlie rumbles.

"He never tried. That day he surprised Reese, he never left. He checked in under an alias. We didn't look at the registry because we didn't know." I seethe. "We didn't fucking know."

I check the clock on the wall. Minutes feel like they're crawling by. It's been an hour since Reese went missing. What is that motherfucker doing to her right now? What if she's hurt and I can't help her?

My throat grows tight. The possibilities scare me shitless.

I tear a hand through my hair. "What if he took her off the ranch? We don't know a goddamn thing."

The thought makes me want to put a fist through the wall.

A screw tightens in my chest. "He's been here, watching her, waiting the entire time."

"Waiting?" Wyatt asks. "Waiting for what?"

Reese's voice sounds in my mind. The faintest memory from our swim at the lake. Reese laughing in my arms and saying, *"If I die, Gavin gets everything."*

My head snaps up. "To kill her." Icy terror settles in my bones. "He's going to kill her. For her money." I bend at the waist, hands on my thighs, trying to breathe. It feels like my world's falling all around me.

A big hand clasps my back. "Ford, you have to be strong," Davis says. "For Reese."

I straighten up, breathing shakily. "I failed her. I promised she'd be safe here."

"You didn't fail her."

"I did." My voice breaks. I rest my brow against the wall, fighting tears. "Fuck."

"We're gonna get her back, brother." Davis squeezes the back of my neck. "You feel her, right? That woo-woo shit?"

"Yeah," I say quietly. "I do."

With every bone in my body, I feel her. Her heart. Her laugh. Her black hole when it hangs too low, and she fights something bigger than herself. She fought so fucking hard to be on this earth. This bastard won't take it away from her now.

He won't take her away from me.

She's still breathing. She's fighting.

And I'm going to find her.

"Hold on to that," Davis orders. "We're gonna find your

girl. We have to." He grins. "She's the best thing that ever happened to your grumpy ass."

I nod curtly. "Damn straight."

"Davis." Charlie launches himself out of his chair. "What about Keena?"

Davis tenses, looking upset he didn't think of it himself. "We can try." He whips his head to me. "I'll get her."

They disappear out the door, leaving me and Wyatt alone in the Bullshit Box. But I can't wait. Can't sit around doing nothing.

I open Davis's desk drawer and grab his gun.

Wyatt snags a half-charged radio.

"Let's go," I clip, moving instantly for the door.

"Ford, please."

Reese's breathless whisper stops me in my tracks.

I snatch the radio from Wyatt's hands and hold it close to my ear.

"Please, I need you."

Shock and panic rip through me.

"She's here." I holster the radio and race for the door. "She's still on the fucking ranch."

48

Reese

I DRIFT IN AND OUT OF A DRUGGED SEA. I CAN'T fight. I can't move. The pain, the exhaustion, is too much, like that black hole above is beckoning now. Waiting.

Blood drips down my arm, my fingertips as Gavin carries me. I hear the crunch of his shoes over rock and dirt.

Icy terror slips over me when I see the green leaves of the forest overhead.

We're going to the lake.

Oh God.

He's going to drown me in the lake. The beautiful lake I've loved this summer. Where I swam with Ford. Burned away my demons.

Tears leak from my eyes.

Ford will never find me. It'll be too late.

"Please, don't do this," I beg, but my words fall into the ether.

His smile drips with malice. "When you die, I'll be the one to carry on your legacy. I'll be the one who loved you the most. The one who only wanted the best for you."

"Fuck you," I whisper.

I hear splashing. Gavin moves into the water at a lumbering pace. I gasp as I'm lowered into the lake. A dark, depthless grave.

"Goodbye, Reese."

My eyes flutter as my gaze tilts to the sky. I can feel him. In my bones. Coming for me.

I just hope he's not too late.

Ford. I love you.

Gavin releases me into the water, and everything fades away.

49

Ford

WE RIDE.

For Reese.

"Her chalet?" Wyatt shouts from beside me, racing Pepita like hell.

"No. The lake."

I know where she is. Unexplainable. Inevitable. That tug in my gut that will always lead me to my girl.

I eye my little brother. "Head on a fuckin' swivel, kid." He's helping me out, but if anything happens to him…

Wyatt nods.

The pistol on my side slaps. Rain pelts us, harsh and disorienting. Sunlight struggles to slip through the clouds. Either way, the light is dim, but we have enough to get us there.

I shut my brain off, so I can't think about what that motherfucker is doing to Reese. I focus on speed. On the pump of my heart, on that ache in my gut that tells me she's near. She's still alive.

We wind our way through the trees, parallel to the chalets. Even with the mud and broken tree branches hindering our path, Eephus is fast. Almost like he knows everything is at stake.

Goddamn everything.

When we round the bend to the lake, I stop and jump

from Eephus. I don't wait for Wyatt. I take off, crashing through the brush and the high grass.

Don't be too late, please don't be too fucking late, I beg the universe.

I sprint toward the lake, my breath coming in harsh gasps of air.

And yet, I don't stop.

I break out of the forest and spot Gavin. He stands chest-deep in the lake, cackling at the sky like a maniac. But there's no sign of Reese.

My heart drops.

No.

Rage blooms inside of me. Everything I see is red.

I sprint, splashing into the water. "Where is she?" I scream.

Surprised, Gavin turns. Then he laughs maniacally.

I grab the collar of his shirt, shaking him. "Where the fuck is she?"

Murderous rage spreads through my body. Fuck the gun. I want bone on bone. Blood on blood. I wind up my arm like it's the best pitch of my life and let it fucking rip. Right into the asshole's face. His left cheek collapses. My knuckles bust. The blood, the pain, feels good. I could keep going. Kill him without batting an eye. Tear his throat out. Torture him for everything he's done to Reese.

But I have to find her.

"Tell me where the fuck she is," I yell, shaking him.

"She's mine!" he howls. "If I can't have her, no one can."

Panic creeps up the back of my neck.

I follow his eyeline.

Beneath the water.

God no.

"Get her." Wyatt's bellow rings out beside me. "I got him."

I release Gavin and dive into the water.

Sound disappears, replaced by silence. I swim hard toward the bottom, searching.

There she is.

Reese floats limply in the murky water, her wavy hair mushrooming, hiding her face completely.

I grab her wrist and shoot us for the surface. I swim to the shore, sheltering her face against my chest so she doesn't inhale more water.

When my feet touch solid ground, I curl my arms beneath her, lifting her from the water and rushing to the muddy bank.

I drop to my knees, turning her onto her side. Water pours from her mouth.

She's still. So goddamn still.

"Reese," I choke out, putting my fingers to her neck to check for a pulse. It's thin and thready, but it's there. I hear Reese's lungs bubbling and struggling, but air still fills them.

Panic rises in my chest. "Breathe. Fucking breathe."

Reese's mouth parts slightly, her eyes fluttering as violent coughs erupt from her throat. Her chest rises, each breath a shaky shudder.

I curl her into my body, cradling her close. "That's it," I say, pushing tangled hair out of her face as she gulps air. "That's my girl. That's my good fucking girl."

I nearly lose it when she lays those emerald eyes on me.

"You found me." Her voice is a soft breath of sound. Sweet and sad, it slips over me.

I cup her cheek. "Never losing you. I told you that, didn't I?"

"Mouse," she gasps. "She's okay." Her smile is weak.

A shaky laugh tears out of me. "Goddamn, baby. We're gonna have a talk about that later."

At the sounds of a struggle, I glance back over my shoulder.

"Wyatt," I shout as he goes under.

But I shouldn't have worried. He pops quickly to the surface with Gavin's collar clenched in his hands. Wyatt knocks him out cold with an uppercut to the jaw, and he sinks beneath the water.

Wyatt hesitates.

"Leave him," I order.

That's where he stays—rotting at the bottom of the lake. He took Reese from me. He doesn't get another chance.

I turn my attention back to Reese.

My stomach plummets.

Blood. It streams down her arms, her fingertips. Seeps from violent, jagged wounds, staining the mud beneath us. There's so much of it. Too much.

"Christ," I rasp. My heart feels like it's being ripped in half. "Christ, Birdie."

"Sorry," she slurs, pale and trembling. "I didn't do it. I didn't do it…"

My vision blurs as hot tears stream down my face. I rock her in my arms, trying to warm her body. "I know, I know, baby."

"Fuck," Wyatt whispers, collapsing to his knees.

"Don't go to sleep," I order when her eyes flutter shut.

Panic rises in me. "You hear me? Stay with me. I won't lose you."

Wyatt shucks off his overshirt. Using his knife, he cuts the fabric into thin strips of makeshift bandages. With shaky hands, he ties the fabric around Reese's wrists and the jagged cuts on her arms.

"Thanks," Reese whispers.

Wyatt swallows, the muscles in his jaw working as he forces a smile. "You got it." My brother meets my gaze. "Ford," he says low and serious.

The pity, the fear in his eyes, scares me shitless.

My hold tightens around Reese. "Let's get you up, Birdie. Get you better."

Wyatt and I move as one. I gather Reese up, carrying her to the trailhead. Her head hangs limply over my arms. Her face is pale, her lips blue. Each breath she takes is less full than the last. Our boots pound down the trail.

"Reese," I bark, and slowly, with fight, she opens her eyes. "You fucking hang on, you hear me? No sleeping. Not now."

She whimpers. "Ford...I—"

"Don't," I warn, seeing what she's about to do. I squeeze Reese to my chest. Like I can give her all the blood in my veins. "Don't you fucking dare say it."

"I'm gonna say it," she whispers.

"You're a brat," I growl.

"I—"

"No."

I grit my teeth and push faster, running now. Lights flicker in the distance. Headlights.

"Country Boy." Her voice is so quiet, so damn soft. "I love you."

"Fuck." Tears stream down my cheeks. My heart breaks. Everything that matters is here in my arms. There's no me without her.

"I love you," I husk. "I fuckin' love you, Birdie Girl."

But she doesn't open her eyes.

"Reese?" I shake her, frantic. Her face lolls against my chest.

Then, out of the forest, a roar of an engine.

Davis's truck crashes through the trees. I almost scream out to the sky.

We're going to make it in time. We have to.

50

Reese

VOICES. FROM FAR AWAY. LIGHT YEARS.

Burning on my arm. Fire licking up my veins.

I feel like I'm in a trance, walking a tightrope between light and darkness. But I never get too close to that black hole, because Ford always pulls me back.

"Don't give up, baby. Not when you're so close. We're so close. Wake up."

I hear his lazy drawl, but there's a strange desperation in his voice. Full of gut-wrenching pain and anger. I've never heard him sound like this.

I ache to reach out, to comfort him, to tell him *I'm okay, I'm here*, but I'm so tired. My limbs have never been so heavy.

Ford's voice fades and blissful oblivion sweeps me up.

～

"Ford, you need to be prepared."

"Don't."

A long pause.

"If she doesn't—"

"*Don't.*"

～

"Reese."

A growl.

"You want to die, you do it on your own time. You hear me, Birdie? You ain't doing it here. Not while you got me. You got me, baby. Whether you like it or not, you got me."

Lips sweep across my palm. My brow.

"Where's my Bluebird? Where are you?"

The world tilts as I sit up in bed, weak and confused. My blurry vision clears as I look around the room. I'm not in a hospital or a black hole. I'm in a bedroom with pastel walls. On the nightstand, coffee cups and a stethoscope. Above me, an IV pole with a bag and tubing.

Outside the window, bluebird skies and the rugged terrain of Runaway Ranch. The storm is over. Like it never happened.

Joy sparks when I spy the small black cat curled beside me. Mouse yawns, flexes her sharp claws. Smiling, I reach out and pull her into my arms.

That's when I see white bandages wrapped around my arms from wrist to elbow. Marveling, I trace fingertips over the length of them.

My heart skips a beat and then resets itself in my chest.

I survived.

Gavin, the storm, the lake—I survived it all.

I pull back the covers and place both feet on the cool hardwood. I'm dressed in an oversized Runaway Ranch T-shirt and the silk underwear I only wear for Ford.

Ford.

Pushing through exhaustion, I stand, swaying ever so slightly. After steadying myself, I pad across the floor and open the bedroom door.

I gasp.

Ford stands there, hand outstretched for the knob. His body tenses when he sees me.

I brace a hand on the doorframe, drinking in his handsome face. The dark shadows beneath his eyes, the scruff he's let grow in. And that mussed lionlike mane he's clearly been running his hand through—his telltale sign of worry.

"Ford," I whisper, raspy.

His broody amber eyes are unreadable as he scans my face. "Reese."

He says my name like a prayer. Like I'm everything.

Tears build in my eyes. My heart hammers.

And then—

One big stomp and he's in my space.

"Reese," he breathes again. I gasp as his hands cup my face and his lips devour mine. His heat is scorching. His big hands move in a velvet caress as they touch every inch of me. Then I'm crying and laughing at the same time.

"You should be in bed," he husks, kissing my cheek, my throat. Then he picks me up and carries me back to the plush white bed.

He pours me a glass of water and perches on the edge of the bed, near my waist.

But I don't want water. I want Ford. I wipe my face, drying my tears, then I reach out, my fingers skimming his scruffy cheek. "Come here. I need you."

His face almost breaks. "You have me," he says, pulling me into his arms and resting his forehead against mine.

"How long have I been asleep?" I ask.

"Long enough for me to be out of my damn mind," he says gravely. Sighing heavily, he lifts his head and locks his gaze to mine. "Three days."

"What happened?" I look around the room. "Where am I?"

"Ruby and Charlie's." His Adam's apple bobs. "The road into town was out because of the storm. We had to set up a hospital room on the ranch with our on-site medic."

I shut my eyes and take a shuddery breath. "How close was it?"

His face darkens. "Gavin shot you up with so much fucking sedative it's a wonder you woke up." I watch the way his muscles tense at the memory.

I look down at my bandages, my eyes like saucers. "My arms…"

"He missed," Ford says bitterly. His face clouds with pain. "You were lucky. Any deeper and—" He breaks off, unable to finish.

"What happened to Gavin?"

Ford's face tightens. "He drowned."

My eyes widen in understanding, in disbelief, as his words settle over me.

I'm truly free. I don't know how something so horrifying feels like a relief.

Tears blur my vision, and I ask what I already know. "Ford, did you…"

Ford's vigilant gaze stays on my face. "He hurt you," he says, the primal protection in his voice catching my breath. "He took you from me. No regrets."

I sit there, stunned. Overwhelmed by what he did. This man rode in on a white horse and crushed my demons.

All the pain that Gavin inflicted, all the hurt I survived, it's over.

I cover my eyes and cry. Ford holds me.

"Just breathe, Birdie." His big hand strokes over my hair. "It's over. He can't hurt you anymore."

"I'm glad he's dead," I whisper. "I'm sorry, but I am."

"Don't apologize. Not for him." He brings me tighter

against his chest. "I hope he burns in hell." His voice bites with murder.

I cup his scruffy cheek. "Ford."

Guilt and agony war on Ford's handsome face. He dips his head, sweeping his lips across my palm. "I told you I'd protect you."

"And you did," I say sternly, refusing to let him blame himself. "You came for me. You saved me."

"It was too close." The tone of his voice is rough and low. "I was almost too late."

"Don't." I wrap my arms around him and pull him close. My body molds to the man I'm meant to love. I inhale deep, smelling coffee and soap on his skin. Ford buries his face into my neck, his entire body trembling. A burning flame crackles between us.

"Here." His voice vibrates through my body. "You were missin' this."

From his pocket, he lifts the gold necklace with his name. My heart flutters as he fastens it around my neck. I cover his name with a trembling hand, feeling the beat of my heart.

Love too strong rushes through me.

Ford places a stern finger under my chin and directs my mouth to his. "I love you," he murmurs against my lips. His trembling hands tangle in my curls. "My beautiful, Birdie Girl."

That string in my stomach unravels, tightens.

Knotted—the two of us.

Forever.

51

Reese

"**Y**OU SURE YOU WANT TO DO THIS?" FORD ASKS AS we leave the bright sunshine behind and step into the lodge.

I squeeze his hand. "I'm sure."

He sighs. "Reese."

I press a hand to his chest. "And then a nap. I promise."

"Deal," he grunts. He hasn't stopped scowling since I woke up. The last two weeks, he's been a tense muscle, always by my side as I give interviews to podcasts and newspapers. If I didn't already have a new publicist who's an absolute bulldog, I'd hire Ford.

Slowly, he guides me across the wood-planked floor. The pain medication I'm on makes me drowsy, but it's only for one more week until I get my stitches removed. Ford has hardly stopped fussing over me since I woke up. Bullying me to nap, to rest. I can only love him for it.

Now closed for the season, the lodge is a strange sight to behold. It's been cleaned recently, and the air smells like fresh lemons. Drop cloths cover the furniture, with only the leather couches left exposed. And there, waiting for me, is Bo Bosko.

He stands, stretches out a massive paw. "And so she lives."

Ford scowls.

"So I do," I say with a smile.

When I lift my arm to shake his hand, I wince and try to reset my face into a neutral position, but Ford's fast.

"Sit down, Birdie," he says, placing a protective hand on my back.

Bosko lifts a brow. "New bodyguard?"

I eye Ford with amusement as he settles on the couch beside me. "Something like that."

"Thank you for coming," I say. "I wanted to thank you for all your help."

Bosko grins at me, that gold tooth flashing. "You're the one who did everything. All I did was get you the evidence."

Evidence I used.

I finally put my voice out there. For the fans, for the world to hear. It's everywhere—on the television, on the radio, on the internet—and it's getting support. I'm getting support.

I gave interviews about my suicide attempt, and the documents I provided showed Gavin's misconduct and mismanagement of my career. His entire team—doctors, publicists, lawyers—threw him under the bus the first chance they got.

Exposing his truth, and mine, was like a weight released. For so long, Gavin used Muirwood and my suicide attempt as power over me, to keep me silent, to strip me of my autonomy. I never trusted my own thoughts or feelings, and speaking about what happened feels somewhat healing.

It will still take time—but I'll get there.

Bosko looks at Ford. "The papers are asking where Gavin is."

"He took a trip," Ford says.

Bosko grins. "Long trip."

I bite my lip. Ford and his brothers took care of Gavin. What they did, they won't say. All I know is that it's over.

I hate what Ford did, because he did it for me. But I love him so damn much for doing it, too.

Ford clenches his jaw. "Can we wrap this up? I want Reese to rest."

"Ford." I lay a hand on his leg, and he settles. Somewhat.

"There's just one last thing." Bosko's dark gaze lands on me. "Your parents."

My breath catches. Ford pulls me tighter against him.

"I got in contact with them like you asked."

I clear my throat. "And?"

"They want to see you, Reese. If it's what you want."

A gasp escapes me. I close my eyes.

After years of thinking my parents didn't want me, the truth has come to light. They were trying to do their best, and he took advantage of them, just like he did me. After watching me night after night in dark bars, after noting our struggles, Gavin presented himself as an agent. He told them he could make me a star and offered to help them in their difficult time.

But when they were back on their feet, he refused to give me back. They couldn't fight him, and they've spent the last eighteen years watching me from afar. I can't imagine how awful and painful it was for them.

A tear drips down my cheek. "Yes," I whisper.

Ford runs a hand down the back of my hair. His vigilant gaze stays on my face. "We can go whenever you want. You just say the word."

Every damn thing I need to happen, Ford makes it come true. I'm the luckiest woman in the world.

"I'll pass along their information." Bosko gives a curt nod. "Now, if you'll excuse me, I have a plane to catch."

Ford stands first to shake his hand, then I throw my arms around him in a hug.

We say goodbye to Bosko and watch him stride silently out of the lodge to wreak havoc on his next poor, unsuspecting victim.

I let out a long breath.

"You okay?" Ford asks, taking my hand to lead me through the lodge.

"I am. I'm happy."

"You're exhausted."

I arch a brow. "You're hovering.

He frowns. "I'm not hovering."

"Prowling," I snap back.

"You like it when I prowl," he jokes, but the smile doesn't reach his eyes.

I stop him near Bar M. "Ford, you have to believe I'm okay."

"I do." He swallows, his Adam's apple bobbing. "I'm the one who's not okay. But I will be."

The pain in his eyes wrenches my heart. The kidnapping and its aftermath will always live in my mind, and I know it will haunt Ford. But I never doubted him. I knew he'd come for me.

"We'll both be okay," I tell him.

"Yeah," he says softly, running a thumb over my bandages. Ford's seen it all. The ugly aftermath. My scars. They'll be faint, but I'll always have them.

"No arguments," he says, his expression stern. "Nap time."

"Beck and call, huh?"

"Until you're better, Birdie." The look he gives me scorches. "And every day after."

I step into his arms and give his neck a nuzzle. "This is where we met."

Glancing over his shoulder at the bar, he chuckles. "Still want to throw a glass of water in my face?"

I grip his shirt and tug him closer. I'm so damn ready for him to kiss me. "I can think of better things to do with you now."

He leans in and kisses my lips. "Prove it."

52

Ford

"**F**ORD, PLEASE," REESE POUTS OVER THE SOUND OF the game coming from the TV. "I can't watch anymore baseball."

I hover behind the back of the couch, beer in hand, eyes on the screen. "But it's the World Series," I answer cheerfully.

She tilts her head back to look at me. "The Yankees win. The Yankees always win."

"Then a nap," I say smugly, leaning down to scoop her off the couch.

Her face pulls into suspicion. "You're trying to distract me."

Damn right I am, but she doesn't need to know that.

"Takin' care of you, baby." I tuck her into bed, kissing away her protest. "I want you to rest, okay?"

She nods, all sweet and sleepy-eyed. Fuck, she's beautiful.

"Don't go." My chest aches as she stretches a slender arm out.

I touch her fingertips. "I'll be right back."

"Hurry." She cuddles the pillow and shuts her eyes.

I stand there a long second, drinking her in, fighting emotion. My beautiful, brave girl. The best thing that's ever happened to me is safe and warm in my bed. I'm well aware I've been acting like some overprotective fool for the last month, but I can't fucking help it. I almost lost her.

A stab of pain goes through me when I see her scarred arms. When I think about what could have happened— how close I came…

It'll haunt me for the rest of my life. But when I reach over at night, feeling for her, she's there. Never leaving my side again.

She's still healing, still haunted by what happened, and I'll be protective every step of the way.

One last look and then I force my pathetic ass out of the bedroom and through the apartment. My heart beats a nervous rhythm in my chest as I get busy around the kitchen. I fumble with my phone and put on a playlist I know Reese likes.

Reese was right when she said I was trying to distract her.

I am.

Next week, we fly to Georgia to meet her parents. And then mine.

There's no damn way she's not wearing my ring on her finger.

I'm not wasting any more time. No question, I'm ready for this life with Reese.

A scratching at the front door has me hustling over.

"Hey, you little bastard," I say when I open it.

Mouse meows, winding her way through my legs. I crouch down, running a hand over her silky fur. A new pink collar, complete with a GPS tracker hangs around her neck.

"Can't escape now, can you?" I tell her, scratching under her chin.

With that, I look out over the ranch. A lilac sunset paints the sky. The brisk October air tells me that winter's close. The ranch is quiet, but not for long.

Engines cut. Doors open. Someone shouts.

I needle my brow. A day of peace, I'd like just one god-damn day of peace.

More trucks. Charlie, Wyatt, Stede.

"What now?" I mutter.

I don't want to be more than a foot or two away from Reese, but it looks like I don't have a choice.

Groaning, I stand and move my boots down the stairs and across the ranch to the lodge parking lot where my family has gathered. "Could y'all shut the fuck up? Reese is sleeping upstairs and if you wake…"

I trail off. *Fuck.*

Dakota's crying. She wears a purple apron, streaked with flour. In her right hand, a clenched piece of paper. Davis tries to turn her toward him, but she shakes her head and moves away.

"Let me see it, Cupcake."

Worry lines his expression, but in a different way than I've come to expect from my twin.

I meet Davis's gaze. "What's goin' on? Y'all okay?"

Charlie, Ruby, and Wyatt hurry forward.

Dakota blows out a deep breath mixed with a sob. "Fallon left."

A gasp from Ruby.

I drag a hand over my face. "You're serious?"

Dakota's lip quivers. "Her cottage is all packed up. Her horses are gone. This was in the bakery." Sniffling, she holds out the letter to me. I take it, blinking a few times as I read.

A hand grips my bicep. "What's wrong?"

I twist, tucking Reese under my arm. "Fallon's gone. She ran."

Charlie and I look toward Wyatt. Our little brother looks like someone punched him in the face.

"Oh no," Reese breathes. "It's my fault."

I shake my head. "Birdie, no."

Tears fill her eyes as she looks up at me. "I told her—"

"I told her to go."

All eyes fly to Stede.

"Daddy," Dakota says, palm pressed against her stomach.

Stetson in hand, he hobbles toward us. "It's not your fault," he tells Reese kindly. "I let that girl loose."

Face solemn, he looks at Dakota. "Fallon was dying in this town, daydreamer. She was stuck here, helping me with my treatment. And after what happened last year…" His voice clogs with emotion, and he turns to face the group. "That girl is the wind," Stede says. "She's going to ride the sky, and no one can stop her."

"Where is she?" Charlie asks.

Wyatt's blue eyes blaze.

"I'm not sure." Stede strokes a finger down his mustache. "She didn't want to share. I didn't ask. Whether or not she comes home—that's for her to decide."

Dakota's face crumples. A sob rocks her, and we all watch as Davis pulls her into his chest.

A door slams.

Wyatt's truck spins out in the gravel drive and tears down the road to the highway.

Silence. There's nothing more to say. Davis takes Dakota's hand and pulls her toward the truck. Ruby and

Charlie follow. Stede takes the note from me and returns to his truck.

"Damn." I scrub a hand through my hair. "Didn't expect that today."

Reese grips my arm. "I'm sorry, Ford."

I look down at her. "You were right about Fallon."

"I wish I wasn't," she says, dark lashes lowering.

I exhale, regret filling me. "I think we all missed a lot of shit."

Everyone's going to have their guilt. Especially Dakota and Wyatt. I feel for my family. My brother. Fallon needs space and time, something she wasn't getting in Resurrection. After this summer, I got the impression that this town was her shadow. A weight she couldn't shake. A weight Reese recognized.

Taking her hand, I walk us closer to the lodge, where we sit on a fern-covered log.

"I saw myself in her," she murmurs. "All that dark." Her pretty face creases. "Wherever she is, I hope she's okay."

"That girl will find her way." I wrap an arm around her. "And so will we."

Sighing, Reese rests her head on my shoulder. The sunset is a burst of color. The evening air crisp. The beauty of Runaway Ranch stuns, but it's nothing compared to my girl next to me.

I point in the direction of Old Mill's Farm. "That's where we'll build our house. We'll have a gate with our name."

A happy sigh pops out of her. "Yes."

"Raise our babies. Take them fishin'. Chase some chickens."

Reese giggles. "Yes. All the chickens. All the babies."

I think of the ring in my pocket. It's not what I had planned, but Reese wasn't planned. Best surprise of my life.

I swallow, twisting my body to turn into her. "And this is where I ask you to marry me."

Her eyes widen.

Heart hammering, I slip off the log and kneel at her feet. From my pocket, I pull out the ring. The five-carat emerald cut diamond solitaire glitters in the sunset. My throat's too tight, but I get the words out.

"You and me, we got good bones, Bluebird. We're never breaking. Swaying in the wind, maybe, sputtering through the snow, for sure. But busted and broken, never." I swallow. "I don't want to waste any more time. You have my heart, even on rainy days. And we're gonna fight, because it's in our fucking blood, but you're the love of my damn life. Will you marry me, Reese? Will you let me give you everything you've ever wanted?"

Sniffling, she stares at me. Says nothing.

Now, I'm nervous. "For fuck's sake, woman. You gonna answer me or make me sweat the rest of my life?"

She arches her brow and breaks into a laugh. She slips off the log, dropping to her knees beside me. "Yes," she says, cupping my face. Tears shine in her beautiful emerald eyes. "Yes, I'll marry you."

I sweep her up, capturing her mouth against mine, drinking in her sweet kiss. Already planning our future, all the years to come on Runaway Ranch.

Epilogue

Reese

"**W**E HAVE FIVE MINUTES UNTIL WE HAVE TO cut the cake, or Koty will hunt us down and snap our necks."

"Fuck that," Ford murmurs, kissing his way across my mouth, causing my knees to go weak. "I'm takin' my damn time with my wife."

I smile against his lips. *Wife*. It's a dream.

Our wedding was a dream, too. Earlier today, we had a family-only ceremony on the cliffs overlooking Runaway Ranch. Waylon Jennings played as I glided toward Ford with bluebells in my hair.

Now, our brand-new Georgia farmhouse plays host to our wedding reception.

But the reception is the last thing on my mind.

I can only think about Ford and his broad hands running over my arms. His amber eyes glassy as he kisses me breathless.

I moan, tearing my hands through his lionlike hair. I'm ready. So damn ready.

Roughly, Ford shoves my short dress—my beautiful designer dress that I spent a fortune on—up over my hips. He pins me to the wall in the first-floor guest bathroom. So damn hot. So damn illicit, fucking in the bathroom when a few dozen people are outside waiting for us.

"Fuck me, ruin me," I gasp as my husband's mouth plunders mine. My frantic hands dip lower, unbuckling his pants and freeing his cock.

Gaze dipping to mine, he grins. His eyes are dark, drugged, hungry for me. "Turn around." With that order, he spins me to face the bathroom wall. A pleased groan tears from his lips. "Christ, baby."

I smile. He's spotted my lacy pink panties with his name embroidered on the cheek.

"You're all mine, Birdie Girl," he growls, kissing his way down my neck. "Just keep your eyes on me and take it. I'll handle the rest."

"Yes, yes," I breathe.

His hand lands a short, hard slap on my ass.

A rumble shakes out of him.

"Watching this luscious ass turn pink is what I dream of, baby."

I moan, and he moves closer.

Arms and legs entwined.

Hearts in sync.

And then he's inside of me. Hard. Hot.

I gasp, clenching around him, lost in the rhythm of his warm, heavy body.

A rap on the door. "Ford. You in there?"

I squeeze my eyes shut, arching against him. "Faster."

Ford grits his teeth, pumps away. "You're dead, Wyatt."

A chuckle as bootsteps fade.

"Birdie, I'm the luckiest man in the world," Ford groans deeply as he buries himself to the hilt. I whimper as he slams into me. Healing me. Loving me. "I love you so fucking much. I'll give you anything you want. Anything."

I close my eyes, tears streaming down my cheek.

He already has.

From traveling with me to Nashville to set up the indie record label with Geneva Scott to building the home we dreamed of together, complete with my own studio, Ford's given me it all.

His voice breaks. "Promise me, I have you. Promise me you're mine."

I grip the gold necklace around my throat. "This is us, Ford. Forever."

I belong to him—heart, body, and soul.

It overtakes us at the same time. That clench in our gut, that full-body electric ripple. We come together, me half-gasping, half-weeping as he roars his release into my neck.

We burn wild and free.

Minutes later, we head down the hallway. I wiggle across the room to cut the cake, doing my best to hold back laughter. I can still feel Ford's handprint on my ass.

Soon, the cake is cut, and the toasts are made. Our new house hums with life—great music, loud conversation, and so many friends and family that my heart wants to burst. Everything is perfect. Above us, the angled wooden beams are strung with glittering lights, and blush garden roses fill the house. The antique dining table is covered in various desserts, courtesy of The Huckleberry.

Amidst the chaos, I spy my parents.

"Hi," I say, sneaking up behind my mom to give her a side hug. "Are you surviving the madness?"

"Reese, honey," she breathes, hugging me back. "We are. How about you? Are you eating enough? Do you need anything? Did you manage to pee in that dress?"

I chuckle at her motherly fussiness. Ever since we made

contact, Bonnie Austin has sent me texts every morning and every night just to make sure I'm doing okay.

My father grunts. "I'm sure she's just fine, Bonnie. It's her wedding day." Morgan Austin stands stoically, arms crossed. I can barely make out the grin beneath his thick blond beard, but it's there. Green eyes softening, he flashes me a grin before reaching out to squeeze my shoulder. "Still not too late to run."

I laugh, smiling up at them. It's been the greatest gift in the world to have my parents back in my life. Though we've taken our time getting to know each other, we're in a good place. Being away from my parents was like a missing puzzle piece, and now I feel whole. They're still the same parents who kissed my skinned knees and showed me every chord on a guitar. I love them. They tried to do something selfless to help me, but it ended up backfiring because of Gavin. But we have many more years to get it right.

"I'm having a blast," I tell them both. "I hope you are, too."

"We are." My mother's lower lip trembles as she drops her hand to mine. She squeezes, sniffling. "We're so honored that we're here. That we…" She looks at my father, whose eyes are surprisingly shiny with tears. "Get to see this."

I shake my head, feeling my own eyes heating. "Don't, Mom. Please."

My father takes a sip of his beer and clears his throat, trying to sound gruffer than he looks. "Bonnie, honey, you already had your tears today."

"No more crying," I order with a smile. "It's party time." Stepping between them, I give them each a kiss on the cheek, and then I'm off.

After making a lap around the house to greet our guests, I wander into the kitchen. Dakota sits on a barstool at the island with her newborn, Lainie, in her arms. Her peony pink bridesmaid dress is a mess of rumpled silk.

"How's she holding up?" I ask, peeking over her shoulder. The newborn has Dakota's raven hair and Davis's stern expression.

Dakota smiles. "I think she's as tired as me."

I move around the island and face her. "How are *you* holding up?"

Her smile falls. "I'm okay. Fallon should be here," she says, her voice quivering. She looks down at her daughter. "She's missed so much."

"I know," I say, my heart aching for her.

The rest of the Montgomery brothers crash into the kitchen with plates of cakes in their hands. Ruby bounces in behind them, delicate flowers in her hair.

"What are you all doing?" Dakota asks, covertly wiping her face.

Wyatt shoves a hunk of cake into his mouth. "Hiding out from the adults."

"Hate to break it to you, Wy, but we are the adults," Davis says dryly, feeding Dakota cake while she juggles their squirming newborn.

Mouse, wearing a tiny tuxedo suit, saunters across the hardwood floor.

"Now I've seen everything," a deep voice drawls.

"Grady!" Spinning around, I throw myself into Grady's arms. "You made it."

"Hell, three planes later, and I'm finally here." He squeezes me tight as he's rocked by hearty backslaps from his big brothers. "Wouldn't miss it for the world."

The world—he gave it all to me the night he sent me to Runaway Ranch.

A frazzled world, but a happy, beautiful world, nonetheless.

I have everything.

A man who loves me more and more every day. My new album, *bluebird*, debuted at the top of the charts last week. Ford's school opens in a month. Ford and I—we're moving at ninety-five miles per hour, but unlike my life a year ago, it's my choice.

Emmy Lou, Ford's sister, rushes through the kitchen. "Three down, two to go," she chirps triumphantly before racing after one of her twin daughters.

Grady laughs and swoops up Duke. Wyatt settles onto a bar stool and stares into an empty beer glass.

My cheeks heat at the sight of Ford in the open door, taking us all in. He's so damn handsome. Long and lean, my golden-haired broody country boy is a sight to see.

His gaze lands on me. "Checking me out?" Looking deliriously happy, he flashes the gold band on his finger. "Sorry to say, I'm a married man."

My lips quirk and I bat my eyes. "Lucky girl."

Ford whistles, getting the attention of his brothers. "On the field, assholes," he drawls, rolling up his cuffs.

"You ain't serious," Charlie groans, tucking Ruby under his arm.

"As a heart attack." He flashes me a grin and pumps his arm. "We got to break this baby in. Get ready to feel that 100 mph heat."

"Cocky bastard," Charlie grumbles.

With that, Ford takes my hand, and we herd our family and friends onto the rustic wooden deck. My breath hitches at the otherworldly view. While Charlie and Ruby have a pasture, we have a baseball field. Green and lush, lit up by the glow of stadium lights, it's beautiful.

Ford still plans to work at the ranch this summer, but his baseball camp opens in July. He's also signed up to coach Resurrection's Little League team in the fall, before going on tour with me later this year. Like I said, our plates are full. I wouldn't have it any other way.

We all assemble on the field. Ford gives directions, splitting us into two teams. Bride versus Groom. Ruby sits in a director's chair, keeping score.

I slam a fist into my mitt and dance around Ford. My wedding ring glints in the sunset. The massive diamond could put an eye out, but the band with a small bluebird etched on the side is simple and perfect. "You're goin' down, Country Boy."

"Later, baby," he rasps, running his broad hands down the tight bodice of my dress. He wiggles his brows. "Save that for later."

We take our positions. Ford pitches. The game is chaos and commotion. No one knows what they're doing. Keena chases the ball as Lainie screams her adorable heart out. Charlie and Wyatt argue over a stolen base.

It's everything I've ever wanted.

For the fifth time today, tears fill my eyes.

It's been nearly a year since Gavin tried to destroy everything.

But he didn't win.

I did.

Therapy, medicine, love, the ranch—it brought me back. Sometimes life is still hard, and some days I fight a silent battle with that black hole, but Ford is always there.

He chases my dreams like they are his own. Treats my wounds like they're his own. He's not my cure, but he is a help. Because he understands. He stays. And that's all I need.

He's my rock and I'm his peace.

And together, whatever life throws our way, we take it together.

The sound of a whistle signals *game over*.

My husband spins around on the pitcher's mound and gives me the biggest grin.

I fly at Ford and he catches me in his arms like he always has. He picks me up, lifting me into the air and twirls me around.

"You look like you love me, Country Boy," I drawl, cupping his cheek.

"Rest of my life," Ford says, his voice low and choked. "Rest of my life, Birdie Girl."

Bonus Epilogue

Ford

" **I** HATE YOU," REESE FLINGS.

Smothering a smile, I stroke her sweaty hair and try to remember the steps to stay calm. After all, it's not my first rodeo. Even if it is *my* first baby.

I lean closer. "I love you, Reese, but you say what you need to say."

"This is all your fault," she accuses, her voice laced with pain and rage. "You did this to me."

I bite my lip as my eyes drink her in. Those wild curls. Those pouty lips and sparkling green eyes. Even snarling at me while in labor, Reese is goddamn beautiful.

I can't get enough of this woman. Nearly seven years of marriage and she still turns me on like she's that stubborn, bickering girl who stormed the ranch and flipped my entire world upside down. Every day I wake up is another day that I'm filled with gratitude she's mine. My strong, beautiful Bluebird.

I splay a hand over her tight belly. "If I remember correctly, you were there that night, too."

The exact night is etched into my mind. The ACM Awards After Party. Reese had just won Entertainer of the Year. We were high on life and had a jukebox on blast and a full bottle of whiskey, which we quickly emptied. Then there was Reese scratching her nails down my back and whispering, *"Fill me up, Ford. All of you, forever."*

Fuck if I didn't do just that.

Her eyes narrow, and she pants. "I regret that night. And I regret—" She breaks off as a contraction has her gritting her teeth and groaning.

"C'mon out, kid," I tell her belly. "Your mama's sick of you."

"Don't tell him that," she scolds, her eyes wide. "He'll think I'm awful."

I plant a kiss on her sweaty forehead. "You got this, baby."

"Don't touch me," she growls, glowering at me.

The nurse chuckles, shooing me away, which immediately prompts Reese to burst into tears. "No, don't go."

Grinning, I lope back to her and take her hand. The overhead lights dance over the faint, silvery scars on her arms.

"I can't do this," she huffs, her eyes full of fear.

I tuck a lock of hair behind her ear. "You can. You got this, Reese."

She did it once. She can do it again.

If I thought it wasn't possible to love my wife anymore, I found out I could the day she came to me and suggested being a surrogate for Ruby and Charlie when they were out of options. It was an easy decision. We put our plans for a family on hold until my brother and his wife had their own. I'm still in awe of Reese's strength, her selflessness.

"Let's talk baby names," I say, hoping to distract her. Hell, distract me.

I bawled at Meadow's birth; I can only imagine how much of a mess I'll be when I see my son.

"Okay," she agrees, her green eyes sparkling with tears.

"Kit?"

She shakes her head. "No."

"Hayes?"

"No-*ooo*." She breathes through a contraction and squeezes my hand so tight I almost fall off the stool.

I give her a look. "Shootin' all my baby names down."

"Because they're bad, Ford." Her nose scrunches up. "They sound like cars. Or cows."

I chuckle. The battle of baby names. In all honesty, Reese can have any name she wants, but I like it when she argues with me. That bratty mouth of hers still makes my blood burn.

I'm distracted when the two nurses in the corner of the room step forward. I spy the Sharpie in their hand. I'm prepared for it.

"No," I growl at them, and they freeze. "One more step and I throw both your damn asses out of this hospital."

At the monitor, Dr. Weir lifts her head. "Ladies," she snaps. Instantly, they jump back to their work.

I roll my eyes, settle my attention back on Reese. Where it belongs.

Sometimes I forget Reese is a superstar. At the ranch, she's my wife, my Birdie Girl. Chicken wrangler, junk food eater. And now…Mom.

Though it's been seven years since her kidnapping, I'm still an overprotective bastard. When she tours or fans are around, it's a constant reminder that she was almost taken away from me. But I fight those dark thoughts every damn day.

Hell, if I thought I was protective over Reese before, her being pregnant amped it up into overdrive. After the chaos that was Meadow's birth, I'm not taking any chances. Her entire pregnancy, I've been following her around with a fucking padded pillow.

Doctor Weir settles between Reese's legs. "Reese, it's time to push."

Her terrified eyes flash to mine. "Ford."

I lace her fingers through mine. "You got this, Reese. I'm right here. I'm right fucking here." Emotion clogs my throat. "I love you so fucking much for giving me everything. My entire world. My reason for breathing."

"I love you, Ford. So damn much." Reese chokes on a sob, then those brave green eyes flick to me, and she grins. "Now let's get this baby out of me."

⌒

I run a finger down my son's downy cheek, tuck him in tighter into his swaddle. "Look at him," I marvel. "He's perfect." I lie next to Reese in the bed. I'm never moving from this spot.

Reese rolls her head across the pillow, tears in her beautiful green eyes. So damn beautiful she steals my gaze. "He's so small," she whispers.

I fight emotion, using a free hand to stroke her hair. "You did good, baby. So damn good."

Forever a warrior, my wife. Reese slams it out of the park with each new movie, each new album she releases. Plays her guitar at Nowhere on Friday nights. She's an advocate for survivors. Her Bluebird Foundation, founded two years ago, helps female musicians find their paths and avoid predatory agents.

Words aren't enough for what this woman means to me. She's given me peace. Loves me for who I am. Stands beside me as my best friend. Now, she's given me our beautiful son.

My dream girl.

Every day, I live in awe of her resilience and strength.

I stare down at my son, curled in my arms. Tiny and perfect and dark-eyed. He cocks his head and looks at us, a small, adorable yawn scrunching his face and button nose. "He's so beautiful," I marvel.

"Takes after his daddy."

I chuckle, kiss her temple. "Nah, baby, that's all you."

"Ford," Reese murmurs. She sounds dazed as she stares up at the two of us. "You should probably let in the cavalry."

"Two more minutes," I grumble.

Our entire family is camped out in the waiting room waiting for word on the new Montgomery. But hell, I'm a selfish bastard, wanting to keep my wife and my baby all to myself. A few more seconds of *just us*.

Finally, carefully, I place our son in Reese's arms and whip open the door. "All right, get in here."

Excited squeals and hushed whispers surround me as our family crowds inside the room, enclosing the bed in a loose semi-circle.

"He's so precious," Dakota breathes, one hand on her very pregnant belly. "How do you feel?"

Reese smiles. "Like a horse ripped me in half."

Davis jostles both Duke and Lainie in his arms, always an excuse to show off his muscles. "Hands full, brother," Davis says, somehow slapping me on the back.

I nod, tickling Lainie in the side. "Damn straight."

"Well, don't keep us in suspense," Charlie growls. "What's his name?"

I look at my wife.

"His name is Ellis," Reese breathes. "Ellis James Montgomery."

"The most perfect name," Ruby says, her voice quivering. She steps forward to place a bouquet of wild bluebells on the dresser. She looks down at us, then throws her arms around me. "I'm so happy for you."

I squeeze her tight. "Thanks, Fairy Tale."

Wyatt chuckles, grinning down at Ellis, wrapped tight in a blue bandana-print swaddle. "Kid already looks like an outlaw."

Fallon, a dusty cowboy hat shading her eyes, lifts a bottle of whiskey and a box of cigars. Her limp is barely noticeable as she shuffles forward. "For when Mom and Dad need to party."

Reese laughs. "Try me in about five years."

"Excuse me."

We all look down at the bright chirp of sound. Releasing her father's hand, Meadow squeezes through Charlie's legs. My three-year-old niece is all sass and sunlight. Thank fuck, she takes after her mother and not my grumpy-ass brother.

"Miss Merry Meadow," I drawl, flashing a grin. "Fancy meetin' you here." The bond I have with my niece is forged in fucking steel. Anything that little girl wants, she only needs to ask.

With unabashed bravery, Meadow climbs up on the bed beside Reese. Smiling, Reese curls her in her free arm. With wide blue eyes, Meadow pokes Ellis's blanket and asks, "Is this my brother?"

I chuckle.

Ruby and Charlie share an amused look. Meadow

knows the story that Reese was a safe place for her to grow before she was born.

"Not your brother," I tell her. "But you two are gonna be pretty close."

"Then he's my best buddy," she announces, decided.

I press a hand to my heart, pretending to be offended. "What about me? I thought you and I were cool, kid."

She giggles.

Charlie peers close at the bundle in my arms, his rugged face softening. "Looks like a Montgomery."

Pride swells in my chest. There's a burning sensation at the back of my eyes, and I don't bother to chase it away. "He is."

"Three more," Davis says, evaluating our family. "And we'll have a full baseball team."

Wyatt's eyes flick to Fallon as she scoffs. "Don't hold your breath."

After our family finally disperses, I climb back on the bed next to Reese. Our son's asleep, swaddled tight in her arms. Everything I've ever wanted, right here. My purpose. My two reasons for living.

Reese sighs. "Do you hear that?" she murmurs, resting her blonde head on my shoulder. "Just us."

I lean down and brush my lips over hers, then sweep them over my son's fuzzy blond hair. "No idea how I got to be so lucky, but fuck, what a life."

She smiles. "It's a good one."

I swallow the lump in my throat. "Damn good."

Sniffling, she looks down at Ellis. "It's ridiculous how much I already love him."

"I know." I look into those bright green eyes and say, "I love you, Reese."

She cups my cheek. "I love you."

The rest of my life plays in front of my eyes. Trips to the lake. Fishing. Baseball games at Fenway. Teaching Ellis to throw the best pitch, ride the wildest horse, climb the fiercest mountain. Loving my wife so damn hard, making sure she always feels safe and protected and happy. And when she gets sad, when she's the fire of the sunset and the rage of the river, all I will do is love her every damn day for the rest of my life.

Sliding my palm over my wife's cheek, I pull her close. "Thanks for burning my entire world down, Birdie Girl."

She smiles before kissing me, soft and sweet. "Anytime, Country Boy."

Thank you for reading!

If you enjoyed the book, please consider leaving a review on Goodreads and the site you bought it from. Every review means the world to indie authors.

Don't miss out on Ava Hunter's upcoming books! Sign up at www.authoravahunter.com to be the first to get the latest book news and bonus content.

Acknowledgments

Thank you to Echo Grayce at Wildheart Graphics for another perfect discrete cover, and Paula at Lilypad Lit for working magic on my words.

Thank you to my amazing beta readers—Anna P., Tabitha, Mary, Yolanda, and Rachel—for your endless support and feedback. You always give me the confidence to make the book better and then go forth and publish.

Thank you to my family for letting me be obsessive and dream about cowboys in my spare time. I promise that I love you more.

Thank you to the bloggers and influencers who have taken a chance on my words. You can change lives, and you've changed mine.

Lastly, thank you to my readers. I am eternally grateful for the way you have loved these cowboys! You have made all my author dreams come true and I cannot wait to do this for as long as you love my books. Thank you, thank you, thank you.

About the Author

Ava Hunter is an Amazon top 50 bestselling author. She writes romance with heart, humor, and heat. Her bestselling books include Babymoon or Bust, an accidental pregnancy rom-com, and Tame the Heart, a grumpy/ sunshine cowboy romance with Yellowstone-vibes. When she's not at her computer with a hot cup of coffee, you'll either find her reading the latest true crime book or traveling with her family. Otherwise, she'll be behind her desk, plotting out or typing up her next dreamy love story.

CONNECT WITH AVA:

WEBSITE: www.authoravahunter.com

NEWSLETTER: www.authoravahunter.com

FACEBOOK: facebook.com/authoravahunter

INSTAGRAM: instagram.com/authoravahunter

TIKTOK: tiktok.com/@authoravahunter

Printed in Dunstable, United Kingdom